Mix Tape

www.penguin.co.uk

Ali and Dan's
MIX TAPE

'PUMP IT UP' ELVIS COSTELLO & THE ATTRACTIONS

'PICTURE THIS' BLONDIE

'WAITING FOR A MIRACLE' THE COMSAT ANGELS

'I DIDN'T SEE IT COMING' BELLE AND SEBASTIAN

'THINKIN BOUT YOU' FRANK OCEAN

'SO FAR AWAY' CAROLE KING

'LET'S DANCE' M. WARD

'WILD IS THE WIND' DAVID BOWIE

'NORTHERN SKY' NICK DRAKE

'FROM THE MORNING' NICK DRAKE

'ROAD' NICK DRAKE

'I FALL APART' RORY GALLAGHER

'I'M NOT SURPRISED' RORY GALLAGHER

'DO I WANNA KNOW?' ARCTIC MONKEYS

'OPEN UP YOUR DOOR' RICHARD HAWLEY

'I GO TO SLEEP' THE PRETENDERS

'GO DOWN EASY' JOHN MARTYN

'YOU'RE THE BEST THING' THE STYLE COUNCIL

'SOMEONE LIKE YOU' VAN MORRISON

'A CASE OF YOU' JONI MITCHELL

'SUNSHINE SUPERMAN' DONOVAN

'I WANT YOU' ELVIS COSTELLO & THE ATTRACTIONS

'I CLOSE MY EYES AND COUNT TO TEN' DUSTY SPRINGFIELD

You can listen to *Ali and Dan's* MIX TAPE
on Spotify here: bit.ly/MixTapePlaylist and on iTunes here: bit.ly/MixTapeSongs

Mix Tape

Jane Sanderson

BANTAM PRESS

TRANSWORLD PUBLISHERS
61–63 Uxbridge Road, London W5 5SA
www.penguin.co.uk

Transworld is part of the Penguin Random House group of companies
whose addresses can be found at global.penguinrandomhouse.com

Penguin
Random House
UK

First published in Great Britain in 2020 by Bantam Press
an imprint of Transworld Publishers

A CIP catalogue record for this book
is available from the British Library.

ISBNs 9781787631922 (hb)
9781787631939 (tpb)

Typeset in 11.25/15.25pt Sabon MT Std by Jouve (UK), Milton Keynes.
Printed and bound in Great Britain by Clays Ltd, Elcograf S.p.A.

Penguin Random House is committed to a sustainable
future for our business, our readers and our planet. This book
is made from Forest Stewardship Council® certified paper.

1 3 5 7 9 10 8 6 4 2

For Melanie

I

There they go, at the beginning of it all, their younger selves, walking through the dark, winter streets of Sheffield: Daniel Lawrence and Alison Connor. He's eighteen, she's sixteen, it's Saturday night and they're heading together to Kev Carter's Christmas party, and nothing much has been said since he met her from the bus, but each is achingly conscious of the other. Her hand in his feels too good to be only a hand, and his presence, by her side, makes her mouth feel dry, and her heart beat too quickly, too close to the skin. They walk in step with each other along the pavement, and there isn't far to go from the bus stop to Kev's house, so it's not long before a throb of music fills the silence between them, and he glances down, just as she looks up, and they smile, and he feels that pulse of pure longing he gets when Alison's eyes alight upon him, and she . . . well, she can't think when she's ever felt this happy.

Kev's front door was wide open to the night, and light and music spilled out on to the weeds and cracked flags of the garden path. Kev was Daniel's friend, not Alison's – they were at different schools – and she hung back a little as he walked in, so that Daniel seemed to be pulling her into the room after him. She enjoyed that feeling, of being led into the room by this boy, so that everyone could see she was his, he was hers. There was Blondie on the tape deck, 'Picture This', playing too loud so that the bass distorted, vibrated. Alison liked this one, wanted to shed her coat, get a drink, have a dance. But then almost at once Daniel let go of her hand to hail Kev across the room, shouting over the music, laughing at something that Kev shouted back. He nodded and said, 'All right?' to Rob Marsden, and nodded and smiled at Tracey Clarke, who grinned back knowingly. She was leaning on the wall, on her own, by the kitchen door, as if she was waiting for a bus. Fag in one hand, a can of Strongbow in the other, dirty blonde hair with Farrah Fawcett flicks, plum lipstick, and kohl-lined eyes that cut a cool, considering gaze at Alison. Tracey took a long drag on her cigarette and sent the smoke out sideways.

'You going out wi' him?' she said, tossing her head in Daniel's direction. Tracey, older and wiser, no longer a virgin schoolgirl, money in her purse and a boyfriend with a car. Alison didn't know this girl and she blushed – couldn't help herself – and said yes, she was. Daniel was just out of reach now, so Alison just stared hard at the back of his dark head and willed him to turn around. Tracey raised one eyebrow and smirked. Smoke hung in the air between them. Alison's shoes were killing her.

'You want to watch him,' Tracey said. 'He's in demand.' There was a beat of silence when Alison didn't reply, then Tracey shrugged and said, 'Drinks in there.'

She meant the kitchen behind her, and through the open door ahead Alison saw a great crush of people around a green Formica table, and a mess of bottles and crisps and plastic cups. She slid away from the vaguely malevolent attentions of Tracey and pushed her way in, thinking Daniel could've got her a drink. *Should've* got her a drink. But, look, he'd been commandeered by all these people that he knew, and she didn't. Now Jilted John was on the mix tape, so suddenly people were singing but nobody was dancing, and behind Alison there were even more people pressing into the tiny room. She didn't recognise a soul, although there must be somebody she knew here, because the place was packed out. She edged through to the table of booze, aware of a strong smell of cigarettes and cider, and, suddenly, Old Spice.

'All right, Alison?'

She looked round and saw Stu Watson, all cockiness and swagger in his denim jacket with an upturned collar and Joe Strummer's scowling face on his T-shirt. Pound to a penny he couldn't name a single song by The Clash, but anyway she was glad to see a familiar face. Stu's quick, narrow eyes swept over her with bold appreciation.

'You look all right, anyway,' he said.

'Right, well, you look pissed, Stu.'

'Just got here?'

'Obviously,' she said, pointing at her coat. 'But you've been here a while by the look of you.'

'Early bird, me,' Stu said. 'What you drinking?'

'Nothing yet. Martini, I suppose.'

Stu grimaced. 'How can you drink that shit? It tastes like fucking medicine.'

Alison ignored him. She was too hot but she didn't know what to do with her coat in this unfamiliar house, so she let it drop a little way down her back and Stu's eyes wandered down to the newly exposed skin of her neck and throat. Alison looked behind her for Daniel and she could see him, still in the living room, not looking for her, but talking to another girl. Mandy Phillips. Alison knew her from the school bus. Tiny like a child, henna curls, pixie nose, tipping her face up towards Daniel's and all bathed in light by his attention. His arms were folded and there was a space between him and Mandy, but from what Alison could see, his eyes were all over her. As Alison watched them, Mandy reached up and pulled Daniel by the shoulder towards her, cupped her sweet hand, said something into his ear. Daniel gave her his trademark smile: hesitant, a half-smile really. His hair was dark and longish, falling into his eyes, and Alison wanted to touch it.

Stu was looking in the same direction. 'I'm Mandy, fly me,' he said. 'Fuck me, more like.'

'Oh, piss off, Stu,' Alison said. She spun away from him and lifted a bottle of Martini Rosso from the table, sloshed a generous measure into a cup and took a deep drink. He was right, it *was* kind of disgusting, bitter, but also very familiar, so she took another swig, then wiped her mouth with the back of her hand, ditched the cup on the table and took her coat off, slinging it on to a chair. She was wearing Wranglers that she'd worn in a hot bath to shrink them down to a second skin, and a new shirt that looked good, looked bloody great; she should know, she'd spent long enough staring at herself in the bedroom mirror. It was white, looked and felt like slippery satin, and she'd opened one more button since leaving home. Stu couldn't take his eyes off her but she didn't even glance at him as she took back the Martini, had another swig and edged her way through the bodies, out of the kitchen.

Alison was talking to Stu Watson, a fucking wily ferret, a creep with hungry eyes, arms like wandering tentacles. Daniel could see them both in the kitchen, and he was stuck here with Mandy Phillips, whose own manipulative eyes were filling with tears as she told him Kev Carter had finished with her, tonight, at his own party, the bastard. This was what happened to Daniel.

Girls cleaved to him and spilled their souls. He didn't have to encourage them; they just sensed something about him, even he didn't know what it was, and they talked and talked. Only . . . Alison Connor didn't. He'd asked her to go out with him and she'd said yes, but in the day or two since then she'd hardly spoken to him in the brief times they'd been together, and yet he wanted her by his side, knew it was right, knew there was something about her. But she'd already said more in the kitchen to Stu sodding Watson than she ever had to him. Meanwhile Mandy was on the second telling of the same sad story and he knew it was all leading to a come-on, a why-not, a kiss and a promise. Kev was busy clowning around, catching his eye, giving him the thumbs up, as if Daniel might need his cast-offs. Life was just a big game to Kev Carter; of course he'd dumped Mandy tonight – he liked a bit of drama, and where was the fun in knowing whose knickers you'd be getting into later?

Now 'Night Fever' was blasting out through the speakers and Mandy was starting to move her shoulders in time to the music. There was a line of girls in the middle of the room working their Travolta moves, a line of boys watching them and arsing around, trying to copy. Mandy tugged on Daniel's shoulder and he leaned into her so she could cup a small hand round his ear.

'Do you wanna dance?' she whispered, her breath warm.

He didn't hear, pulled back and smiled at her. 'What?' he said.

'Do you wanna . . . ?' She paused and smiled. 'Y'know . . . dance?' She cocked her head and said 'dance' in a way that suggested much, much more. No tears now. Kev was ancient history.

'No,' Daniel said, and stepped back. He looked towards the

kitchen for Alison, but he couldn't see her now, or Stu. He should've stayed with her, taken her coat, fetched her a drink, and he cursed himself for being drawn into Mandy's crisis.

'What?' Mandy said, loud enough now to be heard over the music without breathing in his ear.

Daniel was distracted by Alison's absence and he cast his eyes round the room, but at the same time he said, 'No, Mandy, course I don't want to bloody dance with you.' He was panicking, wondering if Alison was even still here, at the party. She might have bolted. He wished he knew her better, knew how her mind worked.

'You're a bastard, Daniel Lawrence,' Mandy shouted, and she slapped him across the cheek, ineffectually because she was drunk, but still, her nails grazed his skin.

'Fuck's sake, Mandy,' he said, looking down at her in disbelief.

She burst into easy, meaningless tears and turned away, looking for another shoulder, and Daniel touched his cheek where it stung. Christ Almighty. And he hadn't even had a beer yet. Some fucking party. He moved towards the kitchen and, as he did, the Bee Gees came to a brutal halt because Kev ripped the tape out of the deck and put another one in, so suddenly the room filled with the insistent drum and bass opening of 'Pump It Up', and Daniel was rooted to the floor, waiting reverentially for Elvis Costello's voice to weave its way into his head.

And oh God, Alison, there she was. She was dancing, alone, in the crowd. She'd kicked off her shoes so she was barefoot, and she was dancing with her eyes closed, and she didn't move her feet at all, although the rest of her body was caught up in the music, and her arms made wild, wonderful shapes above her head. She danced like nobody else. She danced in a way that the others tried to copy, but each time they almost got it she changed, shifted, did something different, but her feet didn't leave the floor. Daniel watched her, completely transfixed. He'd never seen anything so beautiful, so uninhibited, so fucking sexy, in all his life.

2

You could always spot a journalist at a gig. Standing at the back, no drink, an air of having seen and heard it all before, and straight off out of it the moment the set ended. Dan Lawrence was one of them, and there he was again, at the Queen's Hall, watching Bonnie 'Prince' Billy singing spry and catchy songs about the death of love. Dan never sat if he could stand. You should never sit at a gig; it wasn't sodding theatre, it wasn't cinema, it was music. Once, when he first came to Edinburgh, he'd come to the Queen's Hall on a free ticket to see Prefab Sprout and found he was marooned up on the balcony in a numbered seat, but he'd stood up anyway, looking straight down at the heads of the band, trying to read their set list, which was directly below him, taped to the stage. Tonight, though, he was in his favourite spot, leaning against the wall, as close to the exit as possible. Dan liked Billy – a grizzled alt-country geezer from Louisville – but you wouldn't know it from his expressionless face; he wasn't even taking notes, just absorbing precisely those elements of the set that would make good copy, and thinking about what else he could do with the material, what else he could turn it into, in exchange for money.

Afterwards, he walked out of the venue into Clerk Street, without looking for familiar faces or a sniff of a pint, and set off for home. Katelin would be in bed already, sleeping with deep and wild abandon, flat on her back, her arms flung over her head like a child. They often kept different hours, and when he slid into bed alongside her, her steady breathing sent him to sleep like a gentle metronome, and she rarely even stirred: she slept the sleep of the righteous.

He was entirely the wrong side of Edinburgh here, and it was already half past eleven, but there was something about this city that compelled him to walk through it, not take a bus or flag down a cab. He considered it the great architectural love of his life, austere and stately, but increasingly hip. It felt ancient and modern at one and the same time. Compared to Sheffield – the Sheffield he'd left behind in the early eighties, anyway – it was fucking Xanadu. Admittedly, Katelin had been the lure at the time, and without her the city might have seemed considerably less appealing, but still . . . Dan had recognised home when he saw it, and home it had remained.

He was crossing George IV Bridge now, head down, hands thrust deep into the pockets of his leather jacket, earphones in, iPod on shuffle, so he nearly died of shock when Duncan Lomax grabbed him by the shoulder, forcefully, like a policeman with an arrest warrant.

'Jesus, Duncan!' Dan said. He pulled the buds out of his ears. 'Are you trying to bloody kill me?'

Duncan laughed and punched Dan between the shoulder blades. 'Been following you for half a mile, man, catching you up. You running away from somebody?'

'Getting home sharpish, that's my only goal.'

'You been at Bonny Billy?'

'Yeah, you too?'

'Aye, last-minute freebie. Jesus, he can be a miserable bastard, can't he?'

'Can't we all?'

'Aye, right enough. Look . . .' Duncan shucked his army-issue rucksack off his shoulder and delved inside, pulling out a CD, no cover, no image, just a plastic case and a handwritten track list. Dan smiled.

'What you got there?' he said. 'The next big thing? Again?'

'Willie Dundas, an East Neuk fisherman, for Christ's sake, plays the guitar like Rory Gallagher, sings like John Martyn.'

'C'mon!'

'Not a word of a lie. Have a listen.'

He handed Dan the CD. Duncan had a finely tuned ear for quirky, original, mind-expanding talent, and he encountered a lot of it in his failing record shop in Jeffrey Street: music nerds, too introverted to sing their own praises, writing lyrics and scores in their bedrooms at home, destined never to be heard were it not for Duncan. He was forever buttonholing Dan like this, not that Dan minded, because what was life if not a search for the one perfect album that was missing from their collections, recorded by the one genius nobody else had discovered? They dropped into step, Dan adopting Duncan's more leisurely pace, walking alongside each other through the pleasant, mid-week, late-night quiet of Edinburgh's Old Town.

'Fancy a single malt?' Duncan said.

'You seen the time?'

'Ah, don't be like that, you know fine well there's no such thing as after hours when you're with Duncan Lomax.' Dan laughed. Duncan nudged him. 'A wee dram,' he said, hamming up his solid-gold Edinburgh burr. 'Och, where's the harm?'

There was no harm, Dan decided, no harm at all, and they

changed course for Niddry Street where they ducked into the twilight zone of Whistle Binkies, open till 3 a.m., live music every night, and properly bouncing at just gone midnight when they walked through the door.

He'd got home at half past two in the morning and let himself into the still, silent front hall with the exaggerated caution of the mildly drunk, but he'd still woken up McCulloch, the doughty little Jack Russell, who'd then left his basket with the resigned air of an elderly retainer and followed Dan all the way to his office in the eaves, at the top of the house. It was an awkward room really, with sloping ceilings and only one small window, but it faced west, so on a cloudless evening it poured a gentle stream of sunshine on to the dark wooden floorboards. The room contained a chipped and scarred industrial desk and an old brass anglepoise lamp from the offices of an Edinburgh mill; an original Eames chair, black leather, metal frame; a turntable, a CD player and an iPod dock; three specially built steel cabinets for LPs and singles, and a fourth for CDs. He'd kept his cassette tapes too, hundreds of them, but they were in plastic crates in the basement. One wall was given over to books, another to a vast world map, and a third was plastered with memories, every one of which had a hold on Dan's heart. A signed black and white shot of himself with Siouxsie Sioux after a gig in Manchester in 1984. An official framed photograph of the Sheffield Wednesday League Cup winning team of 1991. A publicity poster for Echo and the Bunnymen's *Evergreen* album tour of the States – the tour he'd been on with them, like, *really* with them, researching and writing their authorised story. Photos of Alex, felt-tip and crayon pictures by Alex, and a densely illustrated poem by Alex, aged eight, for Father's Day:

> *He plays guitar and drives our car and makes me*
> *chips for tea.*
> *He plays football, he's good in goal and his favourite*
> *person's ME!*

Photos of Katelin, holding Alex, pushing him on a swing, holding his feet while he stood on his head. A photo of the three of them wide-eyed with happiness the night Alex got his stellar Highers results. And there in the centre of them all, a snap of Dan and Katelin, looking like children, standing against a backdrop of bougainvillea in a shady alley in Cartagena, smiling not at the camera but at each other, like two people with a secret joke. They'd hardly known each other then. Dan couldn't remember who took it.

From behind his desk, he let his eyes roam over his past. It told the story of his life, that wall; it kept him steady in this house in Stockbridge, with its long back garden, its shed for the bikes, its front door painted Sheffield Wednesday blue. He and Katelin had been itinerants at first: moved five times in as many years. Then he'd written a brilliantly precocious and obsessive history of the *NME* and got a half-decent advance, the like of which didn't happen any more in music publishing, and suddenly gone were the days of dossing, the mattresses on the floor, the mildew on the ceiling, the naked light bulbs, the kilims nailed to their bedroom windows creating a permanent, seedy gloaming. God, though, those days were something else. She was studying Spanish at the university, and Dan spent his nights at gigs and his days writing unsolicited music reviews for the *Scotsman*. They'd lived on Katelin's grant and the occasional tenner that Dan made for his writing. They'd met in Colombia, a bar in Bogotá. Katelin was plucky, an intrepid, red-haired, sturdy girl from Coleraine, with skin as pale as milk, even after two months travelling in South America. She spoke fluent Spanish, drank like a navvy, and sang raunchy Irish ballads – folk filth, she called it – when she was hammered. For the first time since arriving in the country, Dan had started having a good time.

They stuck together. She'd gone back to university to finish her degree in the September, and Dan had called on his folks in Sheffield to fill them in on his future, then hitched and walked, with a rucksack and his guitar, all the long way to Edinburgh. By the time he knocked on the door of Katelin's Marchmont Road flat, he had holes in his trainers, blisters on the soles of his feet, and he hadn't eaten for a day and a half. He waited on the doorstep, light-headed, half-starved, and for the few minutes it took her to answer, he considered the possibility that she'd be horrified to see him, or – worse – that she didn't really exist. But then the door opened and Katelin was there, all the flesh and blood of her, assembled exactly as Dan remembered. She'd smiled and said, 'You took your feckin' time,' and that was that.

Long time ago now: long, long time. Dan sat at his desk, up in the eyrie, just a few minutes before 3 a.m., and allowed whisky-fuelled thoughts to cascade through his mind about the passing of time and its heedless, terrible speed. It was a shortcut to melancholy, but in the nick of time he remembered Willie Dundas, and he pulled the disc out of his jacket pocket and slid it into the CD player so that immediately his office was flooded with a guitar intro that made Dan smile: first, a single chord that hung in the air like a promise, then a quick-fingered bluesy riff and then Willie's voice, low, mellow, impressionistic, laying down his lyrics with careless flair, as if he might be drunk, or barely had the energy to articulate them. It was a kind of genius, but Dan had been here before with Duncan's finds; so full of artistic integrity that you couldn't winkle them out of their fishing smacks, or their bedrooms, or their garden sheds. Dan let the music roll while he booted up the Mac for a quick, dutiful surf across Twitter, and he thought about Willie Dundas, singing on his herring boat in the North Sea, and wondered if he could be persuaded to sing in front of a room full of strangers at a place like Whistle Binkies.

Twitter bloomed bright blue on the screen in front of him, and a stream of tweets appeared in the feed, in all their self-referential glory. Twenty-eight notifications from people to whom Dan was barely connected. Seven direct messages from people he actually knew, but nothing that had to be dealt with at 3 a.m. You had to be careful not to appear unhinged, leaving replies in the small hours, under the influence of Laphroaig. He scrolled idly through the morass, with that glazed disengagement that Twitter always induced in him, and he was about to shut down and go to bed, when a new notification pulsed on to the screen. Kev Carter. Always worth reading Kev's messages, whatever the time of day or night. Dan leaned in closer to the screen, then immediately retreated, as if he'd been slapped.

Ey up @DanLawrenceMusic remember Alison Connor?
Look what's she's up to . . . only bloody famous!
@CarterK9
    @AliConnorWriter

Alison Connor. Jesus. Dan stared at her image.
Alison Connor.
Alison Connor.
@AliConnorWriter.
It was the first time he'd laid eyes on her for, what, thirty

years? God Almighty. She looked the same: older, obviously, but the same. He clicked on her name, and the screen changed to her page, then he clicked on her picture, and it filled the screen. His mouth went dry, and this astonished him, because he'd made himself get over Alison Connor three decades ago. But she looked so lovely still, so intelligent, so vulnerable somehow. God Almighty. He studied her face. Yeah; she looked fucking incredible. He clicked back to her profile page:

Ali Connor
@AliConnorWriter

Tweets	Following	Followers
165	**180**	**67.2K**

Writing my books, playing my songs, counting my blessings.

♀ Adelaide, SA
▦ Joined November 2011

Dan sat back in his chair, folded his arms, and contemplated the world he lived in: the same world as Alison Connor, who unbeknown to him had moved to South Australia and forged a career as a novelist. A bestselling novelist, if those stats were anything to go by.

'Sweet Jesus, Dan, what do you need to do on your laptop at this hour?'

Katelin had left their bed, walked upstairs, opened the door and was now leaning on the frame watching him, evidently disgruntled, and he hadn't heard a thing. He felt obscurely guilty, then immediately defensive.

'All sorts,' he said. 'You might be sleeping but half the world's awake.'

'I'm not sleeping, Dan. Your music filtered into my dreams.'

'Ah, sorry, did it wake you?'

She shrugged, relenting slightly. 'Well, no, I needed the loo, but then once I was awake, I could hear it through the floor.' She ran a hand through her hair and it stuck out at all angles, so that she looked comical standing there, slightly grumpy, in tartan pyjamas.

'Right,' he said. 'Sorry. Willie Dundas, fisherman from the East Neuk.'

'Great. Well, can you switch him off and come to bed?'

'You got it.' He looked at her and smiled, but he didn't switch off his Mac. 'Just doing some notes on Billy.' Jesus, he thought. Why am I lying?

She rolled her eyes. 'Now? Really? Can it not wait?'

'I promise I'll be with you in five.'

'God, McCulloch's up here too.'

'He followed me. I'll put him back when I come down.'

'In five.'

'Yep.'

She looked at him as though he was a lost cause, and turned away, padding barefoot back downstairs. He really must go; there were no notes to be written on Billy. There was nothing to keep him up here, and he was dead beat. But he hung back anyway, considered @AliConnorWriter for a while, for just one more minute – two minutes – three minutes. She was hard to leave, so soon after finding her. For almost ten minutes, in the end, he looked at her face, scrolled through her tweets, then googled her name and saw a whole world of information on the rise and rise of Ali Connor. Then he thought: Fuck it. He went back to her Twitter profile, clicked on the 'Follow' icon, snapped the lid of his laptop shut, silenced Willie Dundas, and went downstairs with McCulloch.

3

Alison Connor's mum's friend was a Ten Pound Pom called Sheila; with that name, she used to say, she'd fitted right in in Australia. She'd sailed to Adelaide from Southampton in 1967 on one of those dirt-cheap assisted passages, following the promise of a new life in Elizabeth and a job at the Holden car plant, and there, she'd met and married Kalvin Schumer, an engineer, a real Australian, born and bred in Adelaide to German parents and as fine and strapping a man as Sheila had ever laid eyes on. At weekends, he'd wooed her on long trips north out of town to the desert, shooting big red roos to feed to his dogs, and snatching up snakes from the red earth, cracking them to death on a rock, like a whip.

All this was in her letters, which for a while after she emigrated came about once a month, a conscientious and lyrical correspondence that really got on Catherine's wick. She'd known Sheila Baillie when they were girls in the same street, but then the Baillie family moved to Liverpool, and Catherine only saw Sheila once more, at her own wedding to Geoff Connor, but Sheila hung on to the friendship, never quite grasping either the extent of Catherine's indifference, or her relationship with the bottle, so she didn't know that her letters from South Australia, chock full of verve and immigrant zeal, only shovelled further misery and bitterness into Catherine's soul by flaunting a vivid picture of the world, so different to her own drab orbit.

There was nothing drab about Sheila's letters, oh no. She detailed her adventures in a looping, gregarious hand and peppered the words and phrases with exclamation marks, as if the tropical climate and lethal spiders and vast horizons weren't exotic and surprising enough; as if she had to flag them up for her audience in case they missed the best bits. Her traveller's tales were read aloud to little Alison when the pale-blue, tissue-thin airmail letters arrived addressed to Catherine. If Catherine had ever written back to Sheila, doubtless the tales of life down under would've continued, but Alison's mum was a drinker, not a reader or a writer. She'd only paid any attention to the first letter, and it had made her very cross; Alison didn't know why. After that, she'd pick them up from the mat and flap them disparagingly, like used Kleenex, and say sour things such as, 'Heat and dust and bloody spiders. Does she think we're interested?' Then she'd drop the unopened envelope in the kitchen bin and later, when the coast was clear, Alison's brother Peter – older than her by six years – would fish it out from among the tea leaves and peelings, slice a knife though the seal with a piratical flourish, and hold 'story time' in his bedroom, reading the letter aloud to his sister, both cross-legged on his bed.

Sheila's letters filled Alison with a kind of courage and resolve. She kept them as totems, slipping each new one between the base of her bed and the mattress, and when the letters stopped coming, when Sheila stopped writing to Catherine, Alison felt bereft. It never occurred to her that she could have written back herself; well, she was so young, she didn't have the know-how or the confidence or the money for a stamp, and she was growing up with Catherine for a mother. But she treasured the letters, read and reread them until all the best parts were memorised, so that even when Catherine found the stash one day and put them on the fire to punish her for treachery and deceit, Alison still had them in her mind and could recite whole paragraphs, reverentially, as if they were sonnets or psalms.

There are cockatoos in the trees here, white with yellow crests, and noisy devils! They eat the plums from our garden and stare at us with bold, black eyes. Koalas, sweet as pie, curl up in the boughs of giant gums, endlessly sleeping, like old men after Sunday dinner. The spiders are as big as a man's hand, spread out flat. Imagine that! But they're not the ones to worry about – the killers are the redbacks, much, much smaller, but lethal when rattled. Kalvin says always look in the mailbox before putting your hand in!

As for the heat! The grass in our back yard steams in the mornings as the sun comes up and sometimes the road starts to melt! We grow flowers, though. Poinciana do well, but so do petunias and humble pansies, if they get plenty to drink. But the dust puffs up round my feet when I'm gardening and even though the desert's a long drive away, somehow it looms, hot and red, and I never forget it's there.

This is a wonderful country, Catherine, a lucky country, and you'll know what I mean when you come to visit. Do come!

Those words lived with Alison, once she'd heard Peter read them. *And you'll know what I mean when you come to visit.* Did this person, Sheila, expect them? Might Alison and Peter be given the chance to grow up in a faraway place called Elizabeth, instead of Attercliffe? Peter didn't know, and their mother couldn't be asked: not this, nor anything else. Catherine Connor had no patience for questions. They reminded her of her responsibilities.

So these memories, all of them, the pleasure and the pain, bloomed in Ali Connor's mind every time a journalist, interviewing her about her new success, asked what had brought her to Adelaide. The climate, she'd say. The Adelaide Hills, the gracious city, the infinite ocean, the food, the rainbow-coloured parrots, the luminous sun-flooded early mornings, the inky nights, the space to write. And all these things were reasons she'd stayed, but none of them were why she'd come. She'd always kept those to herself, hadn't told her husband, hadn't even told Cass Delaney, who thought she knew every secret skeleton in Ali's closet. They were sitting together in a café in North Adelaide, reunited after Cass's working week in Sydney, and she'd heard Ali three times today already, twice on the telly on *News Breakfast* and *Sunrise*, and once on the radio, and soon Ali'd be back at the ABC studios for a pre-record with the BBC. Cass was buzzing from it all, getting a huge vicarious kick from her friend's moment under the media gaze – but why, she wanted to know, did Ali always sound so bloody cagey?

'All those platitudes!' Cass said now. 'Just quit the crap about the scenery, it makes you sound pretentious.'

'Don't listen then,' Ali said. 'I'd prefer it if you didn't anyway, to be honest. It makes me anxious.'

'You sound all uptight, like you don't wanna be there. You're an Aussie, girl! Behave like one, hang loose, spill the beans. Tell 'em about how you picked up Michael in Spain, and he followed you for weeks, like a sad puppy, before you caved in and crossed the globe with him.'

Ali laughed, then sipped her coffee. 'Honestly, Cass, I'm just being myself, and if it was up to me, I'd say no to all this publicity. I'm only doing it for that nice girl Jade at the publishers. She's making all this effort, I feel I have to turn up.'

'Oh, c'mon, you gotta bask in the spotlight while it's still on you.'

'I wish you could do it for me instead. You'd be so much better at it.'

'I've never been known to shrink from attention, this is true.'

'I just like sitting alone at a desk, making up stories and not having to get dressed or wash my hair if I don't feel like it.'

'You gotta wise up,' Cass said. 'You're famous now, whether you like it or not, and if you don't start coming over as a warm human being with a story to tell, people might take against you. You don't want the tide to turn.'

'Rubbish. I'm not famous at all,' Ali said. She looked about her, at all the oblivious people around them, eating and talking and ordering food. 'See? Nobody cares. My *book's* quite well known, but I bet half the people who've read it couldn't name the author, and thank God for that.' She leaned forwards, elbows on the table, resting her chin in two cupped hands. 'So, how was your week?' she asked.

'Yeah, so-so,' Cass said. 'Mad busy, as usual. Wrote a big piece for the magazine, "Greed as the new economic orthodoxy", if you're interested.'

Ali shook her head. 'Nah, not really.'

Cass laughed, and winked at her. 'Hey, are you coming to Sydney any time soon? I've got a new squeeze, Chinese-Australian guy, a bit short for me, but they're all tall enough when they're lying down.'

'Oooh, what's his name?'

Cass pretended to think for a while. 'No,' she said. 'It escapes me.'

Ali laughed and said, 'Good-looking, though?'

'Well, he wouldn't set Sydney Harbour on fire, but he's quite cute. Come and see for yourself, but come soon before he gets the flick.'

'Well, I might just do that. My editor's on at me for a date, she wants me to meet her boss and talk next book.'

'And *is* there a next book yet?'

'Nope.'

'Still no ideas?'

'Plenty, but none that relate to *Tell the Story, Sing the Song*.'

'Ah, gotcha, they want more of the same?'

'Precisely. I haven't yet decided whether I'm willing to bend enough to keep them happy.'

'You've written the new *Thorn Birds*, babe, you can do what you like. You not eating your cake?'

She shook her head. 'I told you I didn't want one. Coffee's all I wanted.'

'C'mon! We don't want to hear your belly rumbling on the radio.'

Ali shook her head, then checked the time on her phone. 'Look, I'm going to dash home before that interview,' she said.

'What? Why?' Cass was supposed to be driving her up there. That was the plan.

'I just want to, not sure why.' Ali stood up and drained her coffee. 'I have time: I'm not due at Collinswood for another forty-five minutes. I'll drive myself there from home, don't worry.'

'You'll be late.'

'I won't!'

'Seriously, Ali, don't be late for the BBC. They're your people, after all.'

Ali laughed. 'Cass, you talk such bullshit. Not five minutes ago you told me I was an Aussie.' She slung a small black leather rucksack over her shoulder and pushed her hair away from her eyes, tucking a few strands behind her ears. Her lovely face was pale, Cass thought, eyes a little strained, and perhaps she was a little too thin.

'Thank God it's radio,' Ali said, as if she could read her mind. 'At least it doesn't matter what I look like.'

'Well, you look ravishing as usual,' Cass said. 'But a bit of lippy wouldn't hurt, in case there are autograph hunters?'

'Very funny,' Ali said, and she blew a kiss and swung away.

Cass watched her go. In a desert island situation, if it came down to a choice between Ali Connor or a young Paul Newman, she'd have to regretfully push Paul back into the sea, because she couldn't do without Ali, no way. Cass had heaps of friends in Sydney, women and men, and she loved the buzz of the city's nightlife, but very often by Thursday or Friday she would fly home to her Adelaide roots, and Ali was top of the list of reasons why. She saw her friend thread her way through the busy café, open the door on to the street, step outside into the sunshine where she paused to put on her sunnies, then she was off.

'I'm right behind you, sweetheart,' Cass said, watching her go.

It was only just over a kilometre from Jeffcott Street to her house, but still, Ali walked briskly, knowing she was probably pushing her luck to get home and then across to Collinswood in time for the interview. She could have – should have – stayed put with Cass, had a second coffee, then be driven in her smooth, silent, air-conditioned company Merc up to the ABC studios, to arrive serenely on time. But she'd faced three presenters today already, and a whole battery of personal questions, and she had an overpowering desire to shut the door on the world for a while, shut it even on Cass. She half walked, half ran, head down, full of purpose, through the streets of North Adelaide, and by the time she reached the house, her face and throat, and her bare arms, were covered in a fine layer of sweat, and she experienced a swell of pure relief as she put her key in the front door and opened it. Once inside, she closed it again and stood for a few moments on the burnished parquet floor of the hall-way, breathing in and out, in and out, letting the house calm her, absorb and dissipate her tensions, hold her steady between its solid colonial walls.

This house was very fine: a stately bluestone mansion, Michael's inheritance. They were already husband and wife when he first brought her here to meet his family, but even so she had been promptly – and somewhat coldly – billeted by his mother in one of the spare bedrooms, and only after a full twelve months of married life did she permit them to openly share a room, and a double bed. Margaret McCormack had been a force of nature, an impossible, indomitable, high-handed martinet of a woman who believed her son had been hood-winked by Ali, because after all, what did the girl have to offer? Margaret saw no cachet in the English accent, was unmoved by Ali's obvious beauty, and was maddened almost beyond endur-ance that the young woman quickly found herself a job behind a bar in a pub on Hutt Street. But the young couple toughed it out, and Michael told Ali that his mother would love her in the end, if they just played by her rules when they were in the house. Anyway, he said, this house was a treasure: why pay rent some-where inferior, when they had no money as it was? So, for a year, Michael – an adult, a medic, a married man – crept across the expansive Turkish rug on the first-floor landing to find Ali, awake in her chastely single bed, waiting for him. Hard to imagine, if you'd never met Margaret, that such a situation could go unchallenged, but they perfected the art of silent sex, and Margaret – who must have known what was going on, because only a fool could *not* have known, and she was no fool – seemed satisfied that her supremacy remained undiminished. A year after she arrived, to the very day, Ali had gone upstairs to find the single bed stripped of linen, and her belongings – clothes, toiletries, cosmetics – gone. Margaret, behind her on the landing, had said, 'Your things are in Michael's room. I had Beatriz move them while you were out. No need to thank her, she's more than adequately paid. You may, however, thank me.'

Now, of course, Margaret was long gone, but Beatriz was still here and she was sitting at the counter shelling peas when Ali walked into the kitchen. The old lady had her long grey hair piled into its habitual turban, and she wore a quaint, outdated housecoat, bright florals, gold buttons, to keep her clothes clean. Her fingers worked expertly at the pods and her broad, open face creased into an affectionate smile when she saw Ali.

'Ali, my girl,' she said. She held out an unpodded shell, and Ali took it, cracked it open, and tipped the row of peas into her mouth. Beatriz looked at her with love.

'I'm not here for long,' Ali said through the peas. 'I have to go up to Collinswood, to the studios.'

Beatriz shook her head sadly. She had such expressive eyes, thought Ali; they could communicate every emotion: joy, desire, sorrow, disdain, anger, amusement. Right now, they showed only pity.

'Busy, busy, busy,' she said. 'Always busy, always running somewhere, never time to sit with me and shell the peas.' Her Portuguese accent was undiminished even after nearly sixty years in Adelaide, but it was always only a question of tuning in, like learning to love a different kind of music.

She bent her head, getting back to the task in hand, and Ali watched her for a few moments, then said, 'How's your hip today, Beatriz?'

Beatriz looked up again and said, 'No better, no worse.'

'Don't sit for too long,' Ali said. 'Have a walk, keep it moving. Have a dip, be a devil.'

Beatriz threw back her head and laughed, and said, 'You know how I hate getting myself wet.'

'It's very therapeutic,' Ali said. 'And there's a pool out there that nobody seems to use any more.' She took a glass tumbler from the cupboard and poured water into it from the bottle they kept in the fridge. It was shockingly cold, and Ali felt a stab of pain at her temples, and in her teeth. Beatriz was involved with the peas again, and Ali wandered out of the open back door into the garden, where the irrigation system had turned on and was sprinkling the lawn. A small flock of rainbow lorikeets were dancing in the fine arc of drops, and when Ali kicked off her sandals and joined them on the damp grass, they eyed her beadily, and stood their ground. She walked across the lawn to the swimming pool – a narrowish rectangle of aquamarine, startling against the old stone pathway that surrounded it – hitched up her skirt, and sat down on the very edge, so that her feet and calves were submerged, almost up to the knees. Then she lay down, and let the warmth of the stone and the damp cool of the grass support her, while the water lapped, barely perceptibly, around her legs. She closed her eyes against the too-blue sky, and listened to the squawking chatter of the birds and the thrum of water from the sprinkler, and allowed her thoughts to float loose and free; then a shadow fell across her face and she heard Stella's voice.

'Mum, your skirt's soaked.'

Ali opened her eyes. Stella, impassively beautiful, stared down at her. She was seventeen, and she had Ali's dark brown hair, Ali's hazel eyes, Ali's nose and mouth and chin: but her attitude was all her own.

'What the hell are you doing anyway? You look so weird.'

Ali closed her eyes again. 'Cooling down, chilling out,' she said, and then, after a pause, 'Don't pass remarks, Stella.'

The girl dropped down next to her and crossed her legs, and Ali opened one eye to take a sideways look at her younger daughter. She was chewing the nail of her left thumb and staring at the pool water.

'You good?' Ali said.

Stella shrugged.

'What?' Ali pushed herself back up into a sitting position and noticed as she did so that Stella was right, her skirt *was* soaked. 'Stell, what's up?'

From the house, Beatriz called, 'Ali, Cass's here with her car, says she's driving you to Collinswood,' and Stella looked at Ali, and tutted and rolled her eyes.

'Cass can wait,' Ali said to Stella. 'She wasn't supposed to come here anyway.'

'Whatever,' Stella said. She turned away with a sort of gloomy fatalism. 'Just go.'

'Stella,' Ali said. 'What's wrong, darling?'

Then Cass's voice came, loud and clear, through the open back doors. 'Ali Connor, your time is now,' she shouted, completely misjudging the mood out there in the blissful perfection of the McCormack garden.

'Zip it, Cass,' Ali shouted.

'Don't try to be cool, Mum,' Stella said with that flat, teenaged disdain.

'I'm not trying to be cool. I'm just pissed off with Cass. What's going on, Stella?'

'Coo-ee, Stella babe,' Cass called, waving wildly from across the garden, but Stella barely glanced at her.

'Seriously, Mum, just go.'

'Look, OK, I better had, but I'll catch you, right? Later, or in the morning? I have to get to the studios again, it's—'

'—your book, I know, I know, off you go.' Stella spoke with that toneless, disillusioned voice she used to communicate infinite ennui, and Ali knew there was no talking to her anyway now this mood had descended, so she left her by the pool, staring malevolently at the ripples in the water.

'Uh-oh, trouble?' Cass said as they left the house.

'It'll pass,' said Ali.

The book. The book. A great big readable tome, 150,000 words, straight into paperback, and as far as Ali was concerned no better and no worse than her previous three novels, which had been modestly well received in Australia but were unheard of anywhere else. But *Tell the Story, Sing the Song* was officially a phenomenon. A quiet start after publication, then a speedy, influential burst of online reviews, a flood of sales, book club fever, and a scramble by the publisher to get the next print run out, then a phone call to her agent in early October from Baz Luhrmann's office: name the price for the rights, they said; Baz wants this, Nicole's on board, so's Hugh. Thousands of books were selling each week around the world, and Ali's paltry advance had earned out in record time. For the first time in her life she was making money from her writing, and Jenni Murray, in an interview for *Woman's Hour* on BBC Radio 4, was asking her how this felt.

'Unreal,' Ali said, headphones on, alone at the green baize desk in an ABC recording suite. Through the glass wall she was looking directly at Cass who'd come into the studios with her and was sitting at the panel, reapplying her make-up and listening in. A young studio manager chewed gum and looked thoroughly disengaged, but she kept a weather eye on the levels, and the mics.

'Unreal, and slightly obscene,' Ali added.

'Obscene?' Jenni Murray said. 'That's an unusual choice of word.'

'Well, I find myself in an unusual situation,' Ali said. She could feel it happening again; feel the drawbridge coming up. And the sound of her own voice in this situation stunned her. Her accent was considered very English, comically so, among her family and friends in Adelaide, but now she heard the broadcaster's rich, modulated, faintly plummy tones and her own voice bore no comparison. It lacked substance, she thought: a thin, hybrid drawl. On her side of the window, Cass made sweeping gestures with her hands, urging her to expand. Ali nodded. *Yeah, yeah, hang loose.*

'Does the money make you feel uncomfortable?'

'It makes me think,' Ali said, 'about the arbitrary nature of success.'

'So you didn't know, when you had the idea for *Tell the Story*, that it might strike gold?'

'Well, no, of course I didn't,' Ali said. 'My three other books had done nothing of the sort, and to be honest I think they have no less merit than this new one. Sometimes a book just captures the public imagination, I suppose.'

'So why do you think it succeeded in the way it has?'

'Not sure,' Ali said. 'If I knew that I guess I would've written it sooner.' This was meant to be funny, but as soon as the words came out she knew it only sounded rude. 'No, seriously,' she went on, trying to redeem herself, 'I suppose it tells some truths about Australian life, about our collective past. And it's accessible, but also thought-provoking; at least that's what I was aiming for. It reflects a lot of the preoccupations of right-thinking Australians.'

'The plight of the indigenous people, you mean?'

'Among other things, yes, and I've plenty to say about that, but it's poverty that my story addresses, and although that's predominantly and historically a black issue, it can cripple white people too, especially in rural parts of South Australia, and I don't know how much you know about the state, but the rural parts are vast-beyond-vast. We have a cattle station here that's bigger than Wales, if that helps paint the picture.'

'It does indeed, the mind boggles. And how much research did you have to do? It's such a multi-layered book, perhaps that's why it appeals to such a diverse readership.'

'Thanks, yes, I hope it does. I did heaps of research for some aspects of it, not much at all for others. The music, for example, the young Aboriginal singer, I had her in my head and ready to go.'

'She's a wonderful character. Is she real?'

'Yes, and no,' Ali said. 'Like most aspects of the book.'

'Well, I couldn't put it down,' Jenni Murray said. 'You've written a fascinating novel, and as I travelled into London by train this week, I saw so many people reading it.'

'I guess the rest of the world must be more interested in Oz than we realised,' Ali said. 'Also, it's set in Adelaide, and people don't hear so much about this city. I think that maybe makes the book different, and appealing.'

'Because Adelaide is different and appealing?'

'Yes, I think so. We get a lot of stick from Sydney and Melbourne for being boring, but I reckon that's sour grapes. To me, it's always seemed a kind of paradise,' Ali said.

'Gosh, praise indeed!' But because this wasn't a question, Ali said nothing, so Jenni Murray filled the silence. 'You've lived in Adelaide for thirty years or so, but of course, you're a Sheffield lass by birth?'

'Yes,' Ali said. 'Correct.'

'And how have the people back home reacted to your success?'

'Home?' Ali said.

'I beg your pardon – I mean, in Sheffield, in Attercliffe?'

'Oh,' Ali said flatly. She hesitated, then said, 'I don't know. I mean, I'm not in touch with anyone there, not any more.'

'Family?'

'Nope.'

'So Adelaide really is home, in every sense?'

'Yep, one hundred per cent.'

Afterwards, in Cass's car, she dug out her phone and switched it on to scroll through the myriad messages and notifications waiting for her on the screen. She'd refused her publicist's suggestion that she join Facebook, but had begrudgingly agreed to be a presence on Twitter, and it still amazed her how something so essentially trivial and self-referential could be held in such fawning esteem by so many. However, each day she garnered new followers, and whenever she posted something it was immediately 'liked' and retweeted again and again, and if she didn't have a solid core of humility and good sense running through her, she might have begun to believe she was loved and adored by thousands. It was all cobblers, she thought, but needs must.

'I'm going to please Jade and tweet about the wonders of *Woman's Hour*,' she said to Cass.

'Good girl, that's the spirit. You did well back there, darling, you sounded *très* switched on.' She reached out and turned on the radio, and the car was suddenly filled with Motormouth Maybelle singing 'Big, Blonde And Beautiful'. Cass whooped and joined in; Ali groaned.

'Really?' she said. '*Hairspray?*'

'All hail, Queen Latifah,' Cass said, turning it up.

Ali laughed and said, 'You really should do musical theatre,' then she looked back at her phone, running her eyes down the list of notifications.

'Oh,' she said suddenly, and her voice was strange.

'What?' said Cass, immediately alert. 'Trolls?'

'No, no,' Ali said. 'No. No.'

'That's a lot of "no"s.'

Ali was silent. *Dan Lawrence followed you.*

'Ali?'

She was looking at Dan's face now – a straightforward photo, no gimmicks, just him in a white T-shirt, looking directly at her – and after all this time, after all these years, he was utterly familiar. Daniel Lawrence. Oh, heavens, she thought. She forced herself to take a long, deep breath, but it shook on the exhale and gave her away.

'Ali? What's wrong?'

She stirred herself and managed a smile. 'Oh, nothing, nothing, a name from way back, that's all. Took me by surprise.'

She tapped on Dan's name to open his profile, and then stared at the screen of her phone.

Dan Lawrence
@DanLawrenceMusic   Follows you

Following **825**   Followers **28.3K**

I know, it's only rock 'n' roll,
but I like it. WTID.

♀ Edinburgh, Scotland
🗓 Joined July 2009

'I'm at a severe disadvantage here, babe,' Cass said. 'I can't see what's grabbed you.'

Dan Lawrence.

Daniel Lawrence.

Daniel. That lovely boy, a man now, and there he was, smiling at her again.

'Ali?' Cass said, worried now, because her friend was staring at her phone in a most uncharacteristic manner, and she didn't answer, but was gone, temporarily: lost, somehow.

'C'mon, talk to me,' Cass said, and switched off Maybelle. 'What you looking at?'

Ali still didn't speak, but because they'd stopped at a red light, she tilted the screen so that Cass could see.

'Mmm, nice,' she said. 'Right up my alley. Great stubble. Who is he?'

'He *was* Daniel,' Ali said.

'Dan now, evidently. What's that?' She pointed. 'WTID? Is that some kind of code? Does it mean anything?'

'Yes,' Ali said. 'It means Wednesday Till I Die.'

'Wednesday? Why Wednesday, why not any other day of the week?'

'Football team,' Ali said. 'Soccer.'

'English guy?'

'Yeah.'

'Right on,' Cass said, leaning over for a better look. 'Oh yes, keep on stirring, baby, till it hits the spot.'

4

The music throbbed through the floor from the room below, and a muffled hubbub of raucous voices – singing, shouting, laughter – rolled about the house like a secondary soundtrack, pressing itself up the stairs and through the cracks around closed doors. Alison and Daniel were in a small bedroom at the back of Kev's house: a box room really, a place where useless things were stored and immediately forgotten. There were ragged stacks of newspapers and magazines on the floor, an obsolete Bush television set, a hamster's cage, a suitcase with a rusted, busted lock, a cardboard box filled with ruined paintbrushes, a roll of pebble-print lino and a roughly folded heap of thick orange curtains, although there were none at the window, so the room was lit sodium yellow by the street lamp on the pavement outside. She was lying on her back, in his arms, on a pile of coats, on a single bed. He held her gingerly, as if she could break, and actually, she was afraid that she might. She felt insubstantial, a tissue-thin girl. Back there, on the dance floor downstairs, she'd felt so complete, so sure of herself, and she'd known Daniel was watching her, and she'd known how good she looked; but now she had no idea what was expected of her: no idea what Daniel expected her to do. She felt foolish, and fragile, and at a loss.

Daniel knew what to do – certainly he knew what he'd like to do – but he felt her tremble with each in-breath, and she was holding her limbs very, very still, like a person waiting for news and expecting the worst. She closed her eyes and gave a shivering sigh and he said, 'Are you OK?' and when she opened them, she didn't answer, but her eyes looked directly into his, because he was hanging over her now, studying her face, propping himself up on one elbow while his other arm formed a loose circle around her body. She nodded, and he lowered himself to kiss her. This, she could do; this, she'd done before. Her lips were warm and dry against his, and he was careful not to press too hard, or to appear too hungry, too desperate, so he moved away from her mouth and kissed her face, again and again, and when she closed her eyes, he kissed her eyelids. Finally, now, she moved towards him, making a half-turn so that their bodies were pressed alongside each other, and, encouraged by this, he kept her busy with kisses as he ran a hand through her hair, down the side of her face, along her neck, over her shoulder. Her shirt slipped and slid under his palm, and he found the opening, and then skin, and the curve of her breast. Which is when she sat up, and it all stopped.

'What?' he said, dazed with lust, sitting up next to her with some effort.

'Nothing.'

'What's up, though?'

'I don't know. I just . . .' She petered out, and shook her head sharply, as if she was exasperated with herself. She wouldn't look at him, but when he reached out for her shoulder and pushed her gently back down on to the bed, she acquiesced and lay there passively, staring up at him. He stared back, taking her in.

'Alison Connor,' he said.

'Daniel Lawrence.'

'Look at you.'

'What?'

'You're bloody lovely.'

She smiled.

'That's the first time you've smiled all night,' he said.

'Sorry,' she said. She reached up, cupped his neck in her right hand and pulled him towards her, and they kissed again, but when that ended he drew away to remove any sense of pressure, and just lay down next to her, holding her hand, and they both stared up at the ceiling. There was an ugly jagged line in the Artex plasterwork, as if the room was trying to split in two.

'I'm seeing a giant Toblerone,' Daniel said, and Alison said, 'It's too irregular for that, more like, oh, maybe a streak of lightning,' and they solemnly regarded the crack, considering its possibilities. Through the filter of the floorboards and carpet, Blondie was seeping into the room: 'Picture This' again. The party tape must be on its second loop, thought Alison. She sang along, very quietly.

'You can sing,' he said, and she blushed and said, 'Oh, sort of.'

'No, you can, that was nice, sing some more,' but although she laughed, and was pleased, she wouldn't, not on request like that, not a chance. 'OK, let's dance,' he said.

She turned her head to look at him. 'Downstairs?' she asked doubtfully. She didn't want to go back into the melee, where Stu Watson would leer at her and Tracey Clarke's knowing eyes would make assumptions when Alison and Daniel came back into the room.

'No, in here,' Daniel said. 'On our own.'

Alison looked at the room, the floor, the discarded junk. 'Is there space?'

'Course there is. Come on, you like this one.'

'How would you know?' She narrowed her eyes, and he winked at her.

'Educated guess. Come on,' he said again.

He sprang off the bed, vaulting over her on to the floor, then held out a hand with a flourish. She laughed, and took it, and they stood among the detritus, holding on to each other, and danced together: a sweet, incompetent, improvised jive.

Whole swathes of Attercliffe were being demolished around the people who lived there, and when Daniel walked alongside Alison through the streets after the party, they could've been in a war zone, passing rows of bombed-out houses, bricks and mortar turned to rubble, homes reduced to dust. This part of the city was a far cry from Daniel's home in Nether Edge, and when in the past he'd thought about Attercliffe at all, he'd thought: What a shithole, doomed and degraded, the death row of Sheffield. But now it turned out that Attercliffe contained Alison Connor, and she seemed like such a wonderful treasure that all he was fully aware of was the way she couldn't quite match her stride to his, and the slenderness of her shoulders beneath his arm, and the fresh, clean smell of her hair. She hadn't wanted him to get on the bus with her after the party, she'd tried to insist they say goodbye at the bus stop, but he didn't want to send her away into the darkness on her own, and she'd had to concede it was nice being together, more than nice, it was lovely, so yes, it made sense to be together for just a while longer, before Christmas kept them housebound. She'd found her voice now; he could barely get a word in edgeways. She knew her music, knew what she liked: post-punk, mostly, Costello, Blondie, the Buzzcocks, and a new band, with a new sound, the Human League, Sheffield lads. Daniel knew them, he and Kev and Rob had seen them play plenty of times, they were sort of on speaking terms with Martyn

Ware, and he managed to get that in, but now she was talking about Christmas and how much she hated it – the bogus bonhomie and crass commercialism – and he considered how he'd never said 'bonhomie' in his life, or heard anyone else say it either. He wondered if she was too clever for him, and then he wondered if a snog would be out of the question. He really, badly, wanted to stop walking and press her against a wall, and kiss her until the sun came up. Instead he said, 'Well, Christmas is the reason Kev Carter had a party, so there's that to be grateful for.'

She laughed, and it was like music to him, and he thought, Christ Almighty, what's happening to me?

'Stu Watson's such a creep,' she said. 'But he was the only person other than you that I knew there.'

'You should pity him,' Daniel said. 'He fancies you. Everybody does.'

She stopped walking, abruptly. 'What?'

'It's true. You've got a right army of admirers out there.'

'Oh yeah, since when?'

He shrugged. He couldn't quite read her tone; she might be genuinely puzzled, she might be furious, she might be flattered.

'It's just,' she said, 'I've lived here all my life, seen you on the bus maybe four times a week for the past five years, and you never looked twice at me till last week.'

They were still stationary in the street, facing each other, and now she'd folded her arms. OK, he thought. She's pissed off.

'Not true,' he said. 'I've been looking twice at you for a long, long time. I was just too much of a half-wit to do anything about it.'

She opened her mouth to say something, then changed her mind, stepped towards him and put both her hands around his neck, and kissed him, for a long time. Daniel thought: She's so fucking beautiful. It was all he could think, the only thought in his head. She'd flooded his mind.

When she stopped, she stepped away and smiled, all sunshine again.

'I'll walk myself home from here,' she said.

Now he was totally thrown. 'What?' He just couldn't keep up with this girl; she was like quicksilver.

'Seriously, that was a goodnight kiss. I'm not far from here. This is where we part company – I'm only round the corner.'

He had no idea where she lived, and felt panic at the thought of her striking out, alone, in these black streets. 'But I want to see you walk into the house,' he said.

'No need.'

She started to move away from him, backwards, so that he could still see her face.

'Alison!'

'It's all right,' she said. 'It's fine.'

'It's not fine with me,' Daniel said, and started to follow her, and she held out a flat palm.

'Please,' she said in a low voice. 'Please don't,' and something in her manner compelled him to stand still; then she turned away from him, and ran.

Peter opened the door before she knocked, and Alison smiled at him with relief. She was out of breath from running home, and it was much further than she'd told Daniel, but she was here now.

'Is she still up?' she said.

He nodded and rolled his eyes. 'She's got him round.' Her brother was wearing his steel-toecapped boots and a donkey jacket.

'Are you just in, or just off?' Alison asked.

'Just off.'

Her heart sank. 'Funny time to be going to work.'

'They sent a lad to get me. Two fellas injured or summat.'
He saw her face and said, 'It's extra money.'

'No, I know.'

'Sorry. Just go straight up, she dunt even know you're in.
Was it good?'

'Oh, yeah, y'know . . .'

'I do know. Pissed dickheads doing "Tiger Feet".'

She laughed, then clapped her hand over her mouth. Down
the narrow hallway, her mother's voice, unsteady, reedy, called
out, 'That you, Alison?' and Peter grimaced at her.

'Got to go, kid,' he said, and he left the house. She listened
to the sound of his boots on the pavement, listened to them
until they faded entirely, then she walked down the hall and
pushed open the door to the living room, where Catherine Connor was sitting at a tilt on the settee, leaning into a bulky,
bull-headed man with a can of Tetley's Bitter in one hand and a
cigarette in the other. Martin Baxter. Martin Bastard, Peter
called him. There were empty cans on the floor, a greasy newspaper bundle from the chippy, and Catherine's face had that
sour, pugnacious look she got when she'd had too much to
drink and she knew it. Her lips were pursed and thin, and Alison knew she was having to concentrate to speak; when she did,
she did so slowly, and with a slur.

'Where were you, were you at work?'

'No, I was at that party.'

'Oh, with that lad. Where is he? I wanted a look at him.'

Martin grinned, teeth stained a delicate brown, and said,
'Oh aye? Who is it, then?'

'Nobody you'd know,' Alison said.

'Try me.'

Alison ignored him. She was still at the door, poised for flight, but her mother patted the sofa cushion on the other side of her.

'Sit,' she said. 'What you stood there for?'

The room stank: a miasma of smoke from the fags and the fire, beer, chip fat, fish. Alison longed to be upstairs, alone, with her books and her records and her thoughts, but she sat down to avoid a scene, and Catherine immediately – although not without effort – leaned away from Martin and into Alison instead. Her shoulder was sharp; she was skin and bone these days. She looked down at Alison's Wranglers and tutted.

'Always in trousers.'

'Jeans,' Alison said.

'Same difference. Put a skirt on, show the boys your legs.'

Martin belched, then said, 'Lads like a lass in a skirt.'

For a few minutes, no one spoke. Martin swilled the beer in its can and stared at the fire. Catherine's eyes were closed and her breathing was slow, as if she might be falling asleep. Alison bided her time then said, 'Right, well, it's late, I'm going up to bed.'

Her mother's eyes snapped open. 'Where's Peter gone?' she asked in a plaintive voice, looking about her as if he'd been there until a moment ago, as if his absence was hurtful, and surprising.

'Work, y'silly cow,' Martin said, and Catherine laughed and flapped a hand.

'Oh yeah,' she said.

Her face was pinched with alcohol and fatigue. There were spoiled traces of the make-up she'd applied before Martin arrived: a smudge of blue on her eyelids, a spot of pink on her cheekbones. Alison eased herself away from the place where her mother's shoulder had her pinned, and as she did, Catherine fell sideways, in slow motion, into the arm of the settee, and started to laugh helplessly. Alison stood and walked to the door, and Martin said, 'Ey, get back, who said you could go?' but the challenge was half-hearted, and she didn't even turn around as she left the room.

5

Dan and Katelin, Duncan and Rose-Ann: on Thursday nights, they were Show of Strength, top of the league at Gordon Fuller's weekly pub quiz. It was Duncan who'd got them all into it. Duncan Lomax with his collector's habits and magpie mind, filing away facts just as he filed LPs in his record shop; there was nothing he liked better than the opportunity to showcase his quizzing prowess. He absolutely needed the other three, though; he could be wrong when he was certain he was right, and Rose-Ann never let him hold the pencil, because he wouldn't consult. He wasn't collaborative, she said; he was a quiz autocrat.

The two couples arrived at the same time from their different directions, rushing to get through the door to beat the incipient rain. Katelin and Rose-Ann hugged as if they hadn't just seen each other yesterday for lunch at a Victoria Street café. They'd met, originally, through the men, but had a friendship now that had a life of its own. Sisters under the skin, Rose-Ann said, but she hailed from Santa Monica so was always coming out with stuff like that. The women took their usual seats – back of the room, tucked into an alcove, a small wooden settle, just room for the two of them – and chatted while they waited for their drinks to arrive. At the bar, Dan and Duncan ordered two pints of bitter and two glasses of red. *Astral Weeks* was playing through the sound system, and this was one of the reasons they came to Gordon's place; the guy had impeccable taste. Gordon didn't care about upbeat, unless upbeat was what he wanted. He'd play only what he wished to hear, and if it was Van Morrison's anguish, then so be it. If anyone complained at his choice, he only turned it up louder.

'This album should be compulsory,' Duncan said as they waited.

'Yeah, too right, they should hand it out with the polio jab.'

'Great idea! The government taking responsibility for every child's musical judgement.'

Dan laughed. 'I think we're on to something. *Astral Weeks* and *Abbey Road*, just to be on the safe side.'

'Look,' Duncan said, glancing over his shoulder at the women, as if he thought Rose-Ann might overhear and shut him up, 'I got an idea,' and, like a man with only one shot at the big time, he rapidly pitched a scheme to start a record label, an indie-folk/rock outfit, under which he could gather his rapidly growing collection of brilliant misfit introverts. He wanted Dan on board.

'An investment opportunity,' he said. 'Ten grand should do it.'

'Do what?' Dan asked.

'Get us up and running.'

'So, five grand apiece, you mean?'

Duncan winced. 'Och, man, you know how skint I am, and I can't spend Rose-Ann's dosh on something like this.'

'Right. So, ten grand from me, nothing from you.'

'Nothing but my bottomless talent and energy and remarkable ear,' Duncan said. 'And that's gold bullion, my friend.'

Dan laughed. 'My ten grand would be wasted,' he said. 'Money down the drain. What you could do is cherry-pick from your East Neuk artists, then get them gigs, create a buzz. That's what you could do.'

'And you, too.'

'You don't need me to do that.'

'Ahh, but Dan, to start a label . . .'

'. . . would be a one-way ticket to being screwed over by somebody bigger and richer than we are.'

'OK,' Duncan said. 'OK. Let's do the other thing then.'

Gordon's daughter Meredith plonked two pints on the bar in front of them, sloshing beer on to the polished wood, then swivelled away to find the red.

'That's fifty-pence-worth she just spilled,' Duncan said.

'She's got a face on,' Dan said. 'She wants to be somewhere else.'

'So, shall we do it?' Duncan said.

Dan shrugged, deeply sceptical, but Duncan said, 'Good man, good man,' anyway, as if a deal had been struck. When Meredith approached with two glasses of wine he picked up the pints and said, 'Get those off of her before she chucks half of it away,' and he made his way through the packed tables to Katelin and Rose-Ann. Dan followed, and handed over the wine, and the two women took their glasses, clinked them, and Katelin said, 'To the road trip.'

'The road trip,' said Rose-Ann.

'Eh?' Duncan said.

'We're going on a road trip?' Dan asked.

'You're not,' Katelin said.

'But we are,' said Rose-Ann.

They did this sometimes: an irritating little double-act, finishing each other's sentences, grinning at private jokes.

'Very nice,' Dan said, nodding approval, provokingly and deliberately relaxed.

Duncan, less gifted in the feigning arts, said, 'What? Where to? Cambridge, you mean? To see Alex?'

'Men,' said Rose-Ann to Katelin. 'They just can't see the bigger picture.'

'But hang on,' Duncan said, 'whose car will you take?'

'We'll hire a car, Duncan,' said Katelin patiently, and then to Dan she said, 'Have a guess where we're going.'

He smiled at her, picked up his pint, took a mouthful, then put it down.

'Go on,' she said. 'You'll never guess.'

'Santa Monica,' he said. 'You're going to fly in to JFK, then drive all the way across the States to the West Coast.'

The women gawped at him.

'God, Dan Lawrence, you're an annoying bastard sometimes,' Katelin said, but she was laughing.

'You're never doing that?' said Duncan.

'We are, we just decided, while you boys were at the bar,' Rose-Ann said. 'It's been a long time coming, but we're breaking the chains.'

'What chains?' Duncan said.

'Ah, dearest Duncan,' Katelin said. 'There are no chains, it's a playful metaphor.'

'But it's going to take weeks!'

'Five or six,' Rose-Ann said.

'You're kidding me!' He looked at Dan to share his outrage, but Dan was seeing only the upside: a potential six weeks of unscrutinised, unjudged, unmonitored living. And Katelin would benefit from cutting loose for a while, because he knew how good it felt, he'd done it himself in the past, jetting off after bands and staying away – sometimes, perhaps, longer than was strictly necessary.

So, privately, Dan applauded Katelin's impulse, but when she said, 'It's going to be great!' he only said, 'Yeah, three thousand miles at sixty miles an hour in a hire car, what's not to love about that?'

'You're jealous,' Katelin said. 'Patently jealous.'

'Not at all. Well, OK, maybe a bit. I'll make you a few mixes, help pass the time.'

'Thanks,' Katelin said, 'but that'd be like having you on the back seat. We're going to talk to each other, and sometimes listen to the country stations, aren't we, Rose-Ann?'

'WJLS, the Big Dawg,' Rose-Ann said in a southern drawl, and they both fell about laughing.

At the bar, Gordon cleared his throat into the microphone. He was looking as inscrutable as ever: unsmiling, commanding, scanning the crowded pub with his eyes of steel, looking for lightweights and lawbreakers.

'OK, people,' he said. 'So-called smartphones off and out of reach; anyone found googling will be ejected immediately and banned on a Tuesday night for ever after. Write your team name on the answer sheets, legibly please, and same goes for your answers. Any answer I cannae read will be marked as erroneous, no arguments, quizmaster's word is final. Pencils at the ready for quiz number two hundred and eleven. Meredith' – he paused here to indicate his surly daughter, who stood behind the bar inspecting her fingernails – 'will bring the table questions to you all in due course, for you to complete during the interval. First round, happening just now, is literature.'

'Over to you then, Rose-Ann,' Dan said, and he pulled his iPhone from his jacket pocket to switch it off. On the screen, it said: *@AliConnorWriter followed you.* He paused, raised his eyebrows, smiled. Took your time, girl, he thought. Three weeks since he'd followed her.

'Switch it off,' Katelin said. 'Or Gordon'll have your guts for garters.'

'Which winner of the Nobel Prize for Literature,' said Gordon, 'was also a first-class cricketer?'

'That's sport, not literature,' Katelin said loudly, hoping Gordon would hear. Rose-Ann pushed the sheet, and the pencil, across the table to Dan.

'I think Golding was a cricketer,' Duncan said in his quiz whisper.

Dan was thinking only about Alison Connor, whose sixteen-year-old ghost had turned his head towards her own. Dark brown hair and the smell of fresh air and her impenetrable, infuriating secrecy.

'Dan?' Rose-Ann said.

'What?' he said, remembering where he was. His phone was still in his hand.

'Turn your goddamn phone off,' she hissed.

'And answer the bloody question,' Katelin said, tapping the answer sheet in front of him with an index finger.

'It's William Golding.' This was Duncan, leaning in and whispering urgently again. 'I'm almost certain.'

'What question?' Dan said. He pushed the off button on his phone and slid it away, back into the dark warmth of his pocket. There you go, Alison Connor, he thought, you'll be safe in there for a while.

Katelin heaved a sigh. 'Nobel Prize for Literature, first-class cricketer, who is he?'

'Oh, right,' Dan said. He picked up the pencil and wrote Samuel Beckett. Duncan peered at the answer.

'You sure?' he said. 'I'd swear it was Golding.'

When Dan was still Daniel, he'd shared a bedroom with his older brother Joe, who had a job in the sports centre by day, but by night was a snake-hipped, Oxford-bagged Northern

Soul disciple who hitched to Wigan Casino whenever he could, carrying talc to keep the slide on the soles of his shoes. Their sister Claire – four years older than Dan, two years younger than Joe – loved the Osmonds, and only the Osmonds, as if extending her listening habits would have been a betrayal of her Mormon vows. There was just one record player in the Lawrence household, and it was Joe's, so whenever he was home Dan listened in on the Vel-Vets, the Pearls and the Dells, and watched his brother spin and drop on the plywood square he'd taped on to their bedroom carpet, then when Joe was at work or on a Wigan odyssey, Claire would claim the turntable, and it was wall-to-wall schmaltz and groove with Donny and the boys. Up to the age of thirteen, Daniel tolerated this state of affairs, but then he heard Genesis at a friend's house, and he was up, up and away on his own musical journey: the one that had brought him to where he was now; the one he was still on.

At first, Genesis gave him everything he needed, but then he found Pink Floyd, King Crimson, Cream. For an ardent few months he made himself publisher, editor and staff writer of his own handwritten prog-rock fanzine called *Us and Them*. He got his mother to make photocopies in the offices of Hadfield's steelworks, where she was PA to the managing director, and he sold them at school, two pence an issue. The magazine business went under when he started a different company, making party mix tapes for people to rent and return. The tapes had titles such as *Air Guitar, Guilty Pleasures, Heat Wave*, and – thinking himself canny – he organised them so that, if you wanted to please everyone at a party, you had to rent more than one tape. Nobody coughed up the money, so he jacked that in, but by then he had the mix-tape habit and he carried it on, making real mixes, properly mixed up, just for himself, or for friends, or for girls he fancied, speaking to people through music. He believed himself a cipher, for a while, through which the right music reached the consciousness of the uninitiated, the misguided or the uneducated, and he felt, at sixteen, seventeen, even eighteen, that there was no one he cared about whose life couldn't be immeasurably improved by a Daniel Lawrence mix tape.

Then Alison Connor had come along and he'd thought he was *born* to make mix tapes for this girl, but she'd told him thanks, but in fact she preferred to listen to music differently to this; she liked only to play albums, beginning to end, because that's what the artist intended. Dan was thinking about this now as he hurried home with Katelin from the pub, on this foul, wet night: thinking about how, all those years ago, he'd felt simultaneously crushed, impressed, aggravated, flabbergasted. 'I know that's what the artist intended,' he'd said. 'Obviously, I know that. But mix tapes are something else, aren't they?'

'It's just, if I heard, say, "Alison", I'd want to hear "Sneaky Feelings" straight afterwards. It's the way I am. It throws me when Fleetwood Mac comes on, or Thin Lizzy.' She'd nudged him, trying to gauge how he'd taken her rejection. 'Sorry,' she'd said, although he'd known she wasn't, not really.

Dan's hand, in his pocket, was wrapped around the phone on which *@AliConnorWriter followed you* was still showing on the screen. She'd been the first girl he'd met who knew as much about music as he did, and had the ammunition to shoot him down when she took issue with his hard and fast truths. First girl? Only girl, to be honest, apart from the ones at *NME* of course, where music was akin to religious faith. But of the regular, real-life, ordinary-world females Dan had known, Alison Connor was still the one to beat.

'You were off form back there,' Katelin said, and her voice startled him back into the present: Stockbridge, St Stephen Street, rain like glancing arrows coming at them from the night sky.

'Well, it was tough,' Dan said, slipping easily back to where he should be. 'And there were no football questions.'

'That's not what I mean.'

'What then? Christ, this rain!'

'Not sure, you just seemed to need reminding where we were, now and again.'

'Oh, I knew where I was all right,' Dan said. 'Carrying the reputation of Show of Strength on my shoulders while you and Rose-Ann got pissed. That's a great idea, a trip to Santa Monica.'

'I know. I'm going to ask for a short sabbatical in the next semester,' Katelin said. She hooked her arm through his for warmth. 'I don't want to just use up my summer break. We were thinking end of January, through February, back first week of March.'

'Pretty soon, then. They won't like that, will they?'

'They might have to lump it. Teaching staff are always off on sabbaticals.'

'Right.'

'Well, you went often enough, and when Alex was still only little, running me ragged.'

'Hey! Do you hear me objecting?'

'No, because I'm pre-empting your objections.'

He laughed. 'No need, I have none. Do it.'

'Yeah, well, obviously Alex doesn't need me at all now, and you'll manage fine without me, and McCulloch only loves you anyway, he won't notice I'm gone.'

Dan laughed. 'They'll notice at work though.'

'I bloody well hope they do.'

She worked at the university, in student support, fielding first-year crises of every possible shape and size. All she knew about freshers were their difficulties, and when Alex first went off to

Cambridge two years ago, she'd told him he might experience depression, loneliness, sexual anxiety or panic attacks. 'All perfectly normal,' she'd said. Alex and Dan had roared, and Katelin, only ever half able to laugh at herself, had said, 'Yeah, yeah, I forgot you two know it all.'

'Six weeks in the States,' Dan said now. They were inside the house, shedding their wet jackets, shaking out the rain. Katelin stared at herself in the hall mirror and said, 'Can you see any grey in my hair? I think I can see grey.'

'No,' Dan said, glancing at her reflection. 'I can't see any grey. You could do a gig tour, y'know, east to west. I can check that out for you if you like?'

She looked at him, and sighed. 'Why would I suddenly want to do a gig tour?'

'I dunno, I suppose because you suddenly want to do an American road trip and you could listen to bluegrass in the Bluegrass State, which would be my idea of heaven on earth.'

'Dan, if I said butt out, would you be offended?'

'Nope,' Dan said.

'Good, so butt out.' She yawned, suddenly and violently, Katelin-style; this was way past her ideal bedtime. 'God, I'm knackered,' she said. 'I'm for my bed.' She started up the stairs and said, without looking back, 'Keep it down, won't you?'

'I'll use headphones,' Dan said. 'You'll not hear a peep.'

'Oh, and let the dog out for a pee.'

'On my way.'

'And don't leave the lights on.'

'Oi,' Dan said, 'this is me, not Alex,' but she didn't hear, she was away upstairs, closing the bedroom door, so he just jogged down to the kitchen and let McCulloch out of the back door to sniff the wet night air. He switched on the radio, retuned it from Katelin's Radio 4 to his own 6 Music, and there was Richard

Hawley, crying a tear for the man on the moon, but too far away, in this basement, for Katelin to hear. Then Dan turned on his phone to find Alison, and saw she was almost lost among a fever of notifications, none of which held any interest for him tonight. *@AliConnorWriter followed you*; that's all he was after, and there she was, awaiting his attention. He pushed aside a pile of magazines on the sofa and sat down, and he wondered, was this juvenile? This avid interest in a woman he'd only ever known as a girl? But then: Fuck it, he thought, life is a weird and wonderful thing, and this isn't any old girl, it's Alison Connor. He tapped on her profile to have a look at what she'd said since he last checked: not much, just something he didn't understand, intended for a woman called Cass Delaney, whom Dan now knew – after a spot of judicious stalking – was a journalist in Sydney, on the *Australian Financial Review*. He considered the fact that Alison Connor was fully aware Daniel Lawrence still existed and that, having discovered this, she'd decided to be nice and let him know she knew. He checked the time in Adelaide. He looked at her profile picture again. He thought he really should read her book, although he hadn't read anything other than music biographies for about ten years and he hated the distinct possibility that he wouldn't like it. He heard McCulloch scratch at the door so he let him back into the kitchen and, for a while, the two of them sat side by side on the sofa, the dog watching Dan as he tried to compose a message to Alison. He'd decided, over the past few weeks, that if she ever followed him back, a short, friendly, direct message – privately sent, obviously, not there for all the world to see – would be the thing. But Jesus, everything he tried sounded inane. *Hey, Alison, fancy meeting you here!* Or *Hi, Alison, how's life?* Or *Good to hear from you, Alison.* Jaunty, inquisitive, sober; every approach sounded like somebody other than Dan: somebody dull, somebody desiccated, someone to whom @AliConnorWriter might very well never reply. He sat there in the cold kitchen until even McCulloch gave up on him and went to sleep, and it wasn't until Dan was calling it a day himself and heading upstairs, mission unaccomplished, that he had an idea of such simple brilliance that he wished he was still downstairs with the dog, because at least then he could've shared it. He carried on past the bedroom door and went up to his office. There, on his laptop, he did a quick search for Elvis Costello and the Attractions, 1978, 'Pump It Up', and there they were. A pure white studio set, Pete Thomas's perfect drums, Steve Nieve spinning magic with organ riffs, chic geek Elvis, sneering through the vocals, dipping and staggering on rubber ankles. Dan watched it through a few times. Total bloody genius. And this is what this video would say to Alison Connor: 'Remember this? Because to me, it's totally unforgettable.'

He copied the link, and sent it to Adelaide.

No words, no message. Only the song, speaking for itself.

6

Beatriz Cardoza lived in with the McCormacks, had done for fifty years, and this made her a curiosity in Adelaide, even here, in this lush and leafy North Adelaide avenue, where everyone had money. In the early days of her residency, under Margaret McCormack's exacting regime, she'd been required to slip noise-lessly through the house in a traditional uniform of black dress and white apron, but Margaret was long gone, and for years now Beatriz had reigned supreme in anything she fancied: rainbow-coloured floral housecoats, vibrant turbans. She had three rooms upstairs that were hers alone: a small, perfectly plain bathroom, a bedroom with an iron bed, a rocking chair and Portuguese lace at the windows, and a sort of treasure trove of a sitting room, filled with porcelain knick-knacks and inlaid trinket boxes, mir-rors with heavy gilt frames and a triptych in gaudy oils of saints Peter, Anthony and John. The walls, in each of her rooms, were painted the same inky blue as the River Douro on a summer's evening.

Beatriz still helped clean the house and still cooked for the family. She'd been a godsend to Ali when the babies came, soothing them to sleep with Portuguese lullabies, teaching them the words when they were older, baking *pães de ló* and *pastéis de nata* for their birthday teas, just as she had for Michael and his two brothers, a generation earlier. She would answer the phone – if no one managed to beat her to it – by saying, grandly, 'McCormack residence, who is calling?' which filled Ali with mortified horror every time she heard it. She was, no one could really deny it, a living relic of Margaret McCormack's pretentions and grandiosity, but Beatriz was wholly cherished, she belonged here, and, in a thousand different ways, despite her left-leaning soul and working-class roots that ran all the way through the globe back to Attercliffe, Ali depended on her. She didn't know that Beatriz had intended this – that she'd looked at Ali when Michael first brought her here, an uncertain girl in a new country, and thought: Now there's a child who needs a mother. She'd also understood, with equal certainty, that Margaret McCormack wasn't the woman to fill those shoes, so she'd stepped into them herself, and begun to look after Ali from the day she arrived, so that before long, Ali loved Beatriz unreservedly, and Beatriz loved Ali, not as much as she loved Michael and his brothers, but still with a stern, protective passion. She'd watched over her, even when Ali was unaware of it; watched to be sure she always had what she needed. Beatriz understood the McCormacks: knew them far better than she knew her own distant family, those cousins and nephews and nieces in Porto, who wouldn't recognise her now if she sat next to them on a bus. She knew that James, the late, great McCormack patriarch, had had a string of mistresses, at least three of whom had attended his funeral, and that Margaret's tyranny had often been a disguise for her insecurity, her shattered self-esteem. Beatriz knew, too, that Michael, the eldest of three boys, the great success of the family, the paediatrician with healing hands and wholesome good looks, could be far too set on getting his own way. Ali had still been Alison when she first arrived here with him in North Adelaide, but Michael, with that Australian compulsion to abbreviate, simply kept calling her Ali until everyone else did; until that's what she called herself. Beatriz once asked her, 'Do you prefer Ali to Alison?' and she'd said, 'I think so. I know Michael does.' And yet, Beatriz had thought, Michael is always Michael – never Mike, never Mick.

So Beatriz had quietly cared for Ali and made her pots of tea the way she liked it (brown and strong) and rubbed oils into her bare feet and ankles when she was pregnant with Thea, then Stella, and sewn cool linen dresses the shape of small tepees to accommodate the growing bumps. She'd made her miraculous *canja de galinha* when Ali was sick, or sad, or just plain hungry, and in return Ali made Beatriz delicately lacy English pancakes on Sunday mornings, watched Ealing comedies with her, and old episodes of *Coronation Street*, and taught her to sing 'On Ilkley Moor Baht 'at', which Beatriz liked to perform at the sink, or at the sewing machine, with all the mournful fire of fado, in a passable Yorkshire accent.

Today, Beatriz was sitting in her usual spot in the kitchen, directly below the whirring wooden paddles of the old ceiling fan, where the stirred air cooled her face and head. The sleeves of her pink and purple housecoat were rolled up, her bony elbows resting on the counter, a cup of strong, black Portuguese coffee between her hands. She was listening hard, to the silence. Nothing wrong with silence; nothing at all. In fact, Beatriz enjoyed silence if it was the right kind, the quiet, restful, easy kind: the holy silence of an empty church, say. But the silence now, in the McCormack house, was heavy and potent, and Beatriz knew that Ali was right at the centre of it. The girl – Beatriz always thought of Ali as a girl: as *her* girl – was in the room above the kitchen, the room the family had always called the study, although until Michael brought Ali here, it had been largely unused – at least since James McCormack's death in 1983 – by any of them. Now it was filled with Ali's reference books and novels – the novels she liked to read, not the novels she'd written, which Beatriz had seen were of no interest at all to Ali after they were published, even this latest one, the one that had started this fuss and fandango with the newspapers, the television, the radio.

Beatriz cocked her head, wondering what it was that had brought the girl to this standstill. When Ali was working in that room above there was always music, and until perhaps fifteen minutes ago, there *had* been: the 'boom-boom' beat of the kind of songs Beatriz only tolerated and Ali dearly loved, thrumming down through the floor, just as usual; then, abruptly, nothing. Quarter of an hour of silence. Not so very long, really, but Beatriz remembered this phenomenon from other times over the years, when the onset of deep quiet from the study had proved to be a portent of sorrow, an unwelcome nudge from Ali's clouded, untold past, appearing like a fault line in the perfect surface of her everyday happiness. She was a storyteller, thought Beatriz, but Ali Connor kept her own tales to herself.

'Ali, my girl,' Beatriz called, cupping a hand to her mouth to send her voice up through the ceiling.

Nothing.

'Ali?'

Nothing.

This, undoubtedly, was a cause for concern. Beatriz hauled herself off the stool and rubbed her left hip – a reflex action as much as a remedy – as she walked carefully to the foot of the staircase, where she saw that Ali was in fact at the top, on her way down, popping her earphones in, her iPod tucked into the band on her arm. She was wearing shorts and a vest, and had a faded Crows cap jammed on her head and trainers in her hand.

Beatriz tutted, immediately reassured, immediately displeased. The girl needed more meat on her bones, not less.

Ali smiled and said, 'Oh hey, Beatriz,' pulling the buds from her ears, 'you OK?' and Beatriz just folded her arms, her habitual outward sign of disapproval.

'I'm word blind,' Ali said. 'Stuck in a rut. Thought I'd jog it out.'

'Running, running, running,' Beatriz said, rolling her eyes, 'all that toil for nothing at all,' but Ali just shrugged and said, as she always did, 'I like it, it helps me think. I won't be long.' Ali sat down on the bottom step to put her trainers on. 'How's that hip?' she said.

Beatriz rubbed her bones and heaved a sigh. 'Can't complain,' she said mournfully. 'Not at the great age I am.'

'Michael says with a new hip you could come running with me.'

Beatriz blew a short, sceptical puff of breath. 'You'd never find me chasing my own shadow in the parklands.'

Ali stood up and gave Beatriz a kiss on the cheek. 'See you later then,' she said.

'You be careful,' Beatriz said. 'It's hot enough to cook eggs in that sun.'

Ali patted her hat. 'Precautions taken,' she said.

'And mind those horses,' Beatriz said. 'Kick from a horse, you'll know about it.'

'Honestly, Beatriz, give it a rest,' Ali said, but she blew a kiss at the old lady as she closed the door on her, and Beatriz, reassured that one of her favourite people was in good spirits, took herself back to the kitchen, where her coffee was still warm but she herself would be cool, on her comfortable stool, sitting under the fan.

*

Outside, Ali sat for a while on a wall and took a few moments to collect herself. She'd done a sterling job of foxing Beatriz, but man, she was in a spin. The cause of this turmoil? Daniel Lawrence – Dan Lawrence, @DanLawrenceMusic – had landed boldly and with perfect pitch into her peaceful day, delivering to her a beautifully judged slice of 1978, a song – no, not just a song, *the* song, the very one – that had sent her spiralling back in time. She'd been dealing with a crowded inbox – so many emails, so few of import – when she'd seen the Twitter notification, seen his name, opened the link (with a lurching, pitching sensation of the heart) and had immediately fetched up back in the past, at Kev Carter's party, for God's sake; the party where she'd dropped into a sort of Costello-inspired trance, then opened her eyes at the closing chords and realised everyone in the room had been watching her dance. She'd looked immediately for Daniel, and there he'd been: dark-eyed, intense, his gaze locked on her face, and then he'd crossed the room, taken her hand, and led her upstairs. 'Pump It Up': a track of tracks. She'd played it, in a mesmerised state, perhaps five or six times. Such a familiar song to her, but this morning, strangely and acutely new because – and she couldn't explain this either; couldn't understand why it should make a difference – it had been sent to her by Daniel Lawrence, from across the world. Daniel, who'd been everything to her for a short while, but whose place in her life had long been relegated to a part of her past she was careful not to visit. But this morning, from out of the clear blue sky, there he'd been, and he'd felled her with his good taste and judgement, and the pared-down genius of sending only the song, with all its new-wave attitude, its post-punk resonance.

She hadn't dithered, this time, or panicked or prevaricated, as she had for a few weeks when she'd first seen his name. This time she'd replied in kind, very decisively, without a moment's pause: sent a link back to him, Blondie – of course – 'Picture This'.

She'd propelled it through cyberspace to Dan in Edinburgh, to show him she understood, she remembered too, she believed their shared past was worthy of homage and what better than another nostalgic high point in Kev Carter's mix tape? For a while she became as obsessed with this as she'd been with 'Pump It Up': pressed play each time the song ended, entirely drawn in by Debbie Harry's fallen-angel face and unmatched magnetism, her astonishing allure in a demure yellow frock. She played it four times, then played it once again, just for Clem Burke's drumming, and then, mid-listen, she'd suddenly been poleaxed by a seismic shift in mood, a violent landslide into a melee of regret and sorrow and dry-mouthed anxiety. Ghosts and shadows filled her head: a mother, a brother, a household loaded with shame.

She'd stopped the music at once, snapped shut the lid of her laptop, and sat for a while, steeling herself against the ancient grief, and then, because she knew Beatriz could sniff out sadness like a bloodhound after quarry, she'd got herself into her running gear and made it to the top of the stairs – just in time, as luck would have it – to head her off with a display of cheerful nonchalance, pulling out her earphones and smiling, batting away Beatriz's doomy warnings in the way she always did, the way Beatriz expected.

A run was a good idea though, a great idea, her go-to antidote. Pounding it out through the parklands, it was a kind of meditation that stopped her thoughts from running amok; it tamed and contained them if all she could hear was music in her ears and her own steady breathing. She put the earphones in and the iPod on shuffle, and first up, there was Lynyrd Skynyrd with 'Free Bird', and her heart lifted at once because here was her all-time favourite running track, not for the glory of the build-up or the epic guitar solo – although there were those things, too – but for Ronnie Van Zant's voice, which Ali loved beyond all reason. She sang as she ran, and she didn't care who heard her, because this was all the therapy she needed, and it didn't cost 250 dollars an hour. She was already two minutes into the ripping solo, picking up her pace to match the guitars, when, in her peripheral vision, she saw there was someone steaming up at a right angle to her on her left-hand side, bearing down on her fast, so she flinched, braked, and then processed the fact that this sweaty stranger chasing her down through the gums was her husband, Michael.

'God,' he said. 'You're hard to catch.' He wore a button-down Oxford shirt, blue chinos, shiny tan loafers, and beads of sweat bloomed on his brow. He bent over, hands on his knees, to recover his breathing.

'Bloody hell.' Ali held a calming hand to her pounding heart. She pulled the music from her ears with a stab of regret. 'I thought you were a mugger. What're you doing here?'

'I rang your mobile,' he said, as if this was an answer.

'Well, I didn't bring it with me,' Ali said. 'So, what's up? Are you running away from work?'

'I rang you, two or three times, about an hour ago,' Michael said with a distinct hint of reproach. 'I kept getting voicemail, so I came home and Beatriz sent me after you.'

'Right,' Ali said, thinking: Jesus, an hour ago – did the phone ring? All she'd heard was Elvis Costello; all she'd seen was Daniel Lawrence. 'Well,' she said, 'go on then – what's the urgency?'

Then Michael said, 'Ali, listen,' in a grave voice that instantly flooded her guts with fear.

'What?' she said.

'It's Stella, she rang me at work.'

'Hang on – what? Stella rang you?'

'Yes.'

'But I saw her before she left for school.'

'Well, anyway,' Michael said.

'To say what?' Ali thought about Stella this morning. Moody and uncommunicative. She hadn't eaten anything, Ali remembered. She'd said she wasn't hungry, and Beatriz had thrown her hands to the heavens and asked why nobody ate in this household, and Ali had laughed, because she herself was eating a bowl of porridge, right there and then, in front of Beatriz. But Stella hadn't laughed. Instead she'd drunk a glass of water, slung her schoolbag over her shoulder and left the house. Had she said goodbye? Possibly not.

'Right, don't freak out,' Michael said, and Ali felt a flash of irritation at his momentary advantage: of knowing already what she should know herself, if Stella would only talk to her as she'd apparently talked to Michael.

'Michael, just tell me!' A string of scenarios rushed through her mind. Stella was being bullied. She wanted to leave school. She'd lost her mobile again. She'd got a tattoo; pierced her navel; pierced a nipple.

He exhaled, a long outward breath, as if he was steeling himself. Then, 'She's pregnant,' he said.

Ali stared at him. She felt stupid; stupid, naïve, devastated – all these things, all at once. She sat down heavily on the scrubby grass and put her head in her hands. Stella. Her beautiful girl.

Michael dropped down next to Ali and said, 'Hey, it's a shock, isn't it?'

Ali looked at him, stricken. 'I didn't even know she was having sex,' she said. 'I had no idea. How could I not know?'

'It's Stella, Ali. The family clam.'

'She told you. Why didn't she tell me?'

'Who knows? She rang me in the office and maybe that felt . . . I dunno . . . neutral.'

'I *knew* there was something she wanted to say. I knew weeks ago.' Ali suddenly grabbed Michael's arm. 'How pregnant is she?'

'Six weeks, she thinks.'

'Shit. Shit!' Ali lay down now, and moaned into her hands. 'That weekend with a crowd at Victor Harbor in September? She was weird when she came home from that, wasn't she? Ran upstairs, laid low for the rest of the evening. Ah, God. Why didn't I make her talk to me?' She lay still for a while, seeing Stella in her mind, the girl's expression this morning as she left the house, a kind of resigned sullenness, and herself, Ali, dealing with emails, organising her diary to fit in a flight to Sydney, barely looking up from the screen of her phone as her daughter left the house. She sat up. Michael waited, watching her.

'OK, I'm putting all work on hold,' she said. 'This book, it's taking up too much headspace, and the publisher's always on at me to do this or that, and meanwhile there was Stella, getting pregnant, and I didn't even know she had a boyfriend.'

'Um . . . she doesn't,' Michael said.

'What?'

'It was a one-off,' Michael said. 'She wouldn't tell me the boy's name, said it didn't matter.'

'Oh, good God. I need to talk to her.' Ali got to her feet. 'Where was she when she rang?'

'No,' Michael said, patting the air between them as if this way he could quell her urgency. 'I've told her we'll see her later, at home, sort it all out then. There's no point rushing headlong into it, Ali. I'm going back to the hospital now, you do whatever you'd planned to do today, and we'll deal with it later.'

He smiled at her with a kind of studied empathy, and she saw he was using his bedside manner on her, calming her ragged nerves with professional kindness. She felt a sudden wild impulse to push him over, dirty his chinos, but instead she said, 'No, I reckon I'll go find her now,' and before he could object again she set off at a clip, cutting a diagonal line towards home across the sun-baked parklands, and Michael could only stand and watch her go.

7

Peter said it was a waking nightmare at Brown Bayley's, said the open furnaces were like staring into the mouth of hell, and that it was a miracle men didn't die every day, given that the only protection most of them had against harm were the hard hats on their heads and steel caps on their boots. Catherine Connor's boyfriend Martin worked there too – well, who didn't? Attercliffe seemed to breed menfolk purely to feed the steel industry – and that was another reason why Peter hated it, knowing he might turn a corner and see Martin's beefy mug leering at him, poking fun, raising a laugh from the other men who thought you were a killjoy if you couldn't take a joke. Peter went to the steelworks at sixteen, because somebody had to bring money into the household and Catherine was drinking too much by then to hold down a job. He went as an apprentice and was put to work burning off twisted metal misshapes from ingots as they came off the rolling mills, or welding and repairing those parts of the furnaces no one else wanted to go near. When he came home from his shift in those days he smelled of burning metal and his overalls were black where they'd caught fire. Now though, he worked a crane, shifting steel around the factory, and his main complaint was the cold, up there in the gods, where his donkey jacket suddenly didn't seem so thick and his hands could freeze on the levers if he forgot his gloves.

But it was Saturday morning, he had the weekend off, and he was letting Alison look after him, watching her make him beans on toast, six slices of white bread, margarine, and a pile of baked beans sliding about the plate like molten lava. Dave Lee Travis was on in the kitchen, Catherine was in her bed, dead to the world, and Martin was gone, back to his own house more than likely, where he periodically retreated to feed the miserable whippet he kept on a long chain in the back yard. This was as good as it got in the Connor household.

'So anyway,' Alison said, sitting opposite Peter to watch him eat. 'Don't be mad, but I'm not just going out this afternoon, I'm going to Hillsborough.'

He looked at her over the top of a forkful of beans.

'He's a Wednesday fan?' he said.

'Die-hard,' Alison says. 'It's in his blood, apparently.'

'Thought you were a Blade.'

'No, Peter, I'm the sister of a Blade, as you well know. My interest in football is about as keen as your interest in, oh, I don't know, origami.'

'Well then,' he said, 'why go at all?'

'It's life experience,' Alison said. 'And it's an FA Cup tie, against Arsenal.'

He rolled his eyes. 'I know who they're bloody playing,' he said. 'Toddy's talked about nowt else all week.'

'He'll be there then?' She hadn't met Toddy, but liked the sound of him. He was Peter's slinger, he loaded the crane with steel for Peter to shift, and they shared their snap and talked about films, which was the sort of topic that would normally earn a man a reputation for being soft, so Peter and Toddy kept themselves to themselves. 'What's he look like?' Alison said. 'I'll say hello.'

'Very funny,' Peter said.

'Daniel says there'll be twenty thousand fans on the Kop.'

Peter grunted. 'You be careful. They're a rough lot.'

'He said not to wear my red coat.'

Peter laughed. 'You'd be lynched on the Kop.'

'Can I wear your donkey jacket?'

'Aye, if you promise not to come home an Owls fan.'

'Promise,' she said.

'It's a good idea that anyway, Alison, nobody messes with a lass in a donkey jacket. You'll need it today, chuffing freezing.'

She nodded and then said, 'You got anything on today?'

He shook his head. 'I'll see what state she's in when she crawls out of bed.'

'Yeah,' Alison said. 'I'll do next Saturday, Pete.' This was the second weekend in a row that Peter had been on Catherine duty: assessing her suitability to be left at home alone before making any plans for himself. Meanwhile *Superman* was showing at the Gaumont. That was what he'd do, if he could get away later.

Alison met Daniel at Pond Street in the city centre, at the number 53 stop, and she was startled at the crush of supporters waiting for the bus. Hard to find him in the crowds, and everyone had blue and white hats on, and blue and white scarves, so they all looked the same. He spotted her first, swamped in her brother's jacket, the collar turned up like a frame for her lovely face, which was pink with the cold.

'Here,' he said, and wrapped his own scarf twice round her throat. 'Now you're one of us.'

'Don't say that to our Peter,' she said. 'I've had to promise not to turn. All these people! They'll never get on the bus.'

'Just as long as we do, that's the main thing.'

And they did, Daniel sheltering her with one arm and fending off queue-jumpers with the other until they were standing toe-to-toe on the number 53, hanging on to the overhead rail, and she was grinning at him, loving it, even though the inside of the bus was swampy with wet boots, foetid with sweat and beer. They piled out at Hillsborough and, outside the ground, they moved slowly forwards with the teeming throng under a lowering sky that threatened more snow. He told her this crowd was huge, bigger than usual, biggest of the season, the biggest he'd seen since he was six and his dad brought him to see the Owls play Man United, and Alison laughed at him, at his earnest, ardent enthusiasm. These FA Cup fixtures were special, he told her. Arsenal was top-tier, Division One royalty, did she know that?

'So, you mean they're better?'

'No,' he said. 'I mean they're jammy,' and he wagged a warning finger at her. 'Behave yourself, you're in church now.'

It did feel that way as they clicked through the turnstiles and climbed the steps to the top of the towering Spion Kop. Alison was an agnostic among a crowd of true believers in an extraordinary cathedral of sound. She thought she might weep with awe at the noise, then write a poem when she got home, because it was so stirring, all those voices rising in unison to make great waves that swelled and rolled around the terraces as if the noise itself had a mass and momentum of its own. She was stunned by it, but Daniel was completely unmoved and hell-bent on a spot behind the goal, and there was no time to stand still being spellbound. They moved gingerly, trying to keep their footing on their way down the Kop, where the snow had turned to ice, pushing their way from one small space to another until they were close enough to the pitch to see the breath from the players' mouths, hear the impact of their boots on the ball. Alison was all rapt attention: the effort, the noble struggle, the punishing impact of a fall on the cold, unyielding ground. The snow had been shovelled off the pitch, cleared away to the sides, and it was heaped up in a mucky drift at the bottom of the Kop. It was cruelly cold but the donkey jacket and the crush all around kept Alison warm, and so did the battlefield glory of the occasion – she felt like a spectator at a gladiatorial fight; she felt part of something ancient and tribal, and not entirely safe, as if she might be called upon to pitch in. When Arsenal scored and the Kop started up the call to arms, abusing the jubilant away fans, the jammy Gunners who deserved nothing but a good kicking, Alison joined in, and there was something so inspiring, she thought, about the group endeavour, their perfect timing. Daniel shoved her with his shoulder. 'Hooligan,' he said. 'Bloody yob.' She laughed at him, and then for a while she just watched him, watching the match, and he was so fixated on Wednesday's performance, so intent on the ball, that he didn't even notice. She found this endearing, and mysterious, and she wished she had something of her own, something just as powerful, just as important, that she could share with him, and that he wouldn't understand.

The afternoon got better and better. They had Bovril at half-time – for the warmth, Daniel said, not the taste, but Alison liked it: only vaguely beefy, very intensely salty; she'd certainly been given worse at home. Then, just before the start of the second half, when the Arsenal goalie Pat Jennings was making his way to the Kop end, he was pelted with a hail of snowballs from the terraces, and everyone could see the big Irishman just wanted to give the Wednesday fans hell and hammer them back with balls of ice. The referee got involved, wanted to stop the match, then Wednesday's manager Jack Charlton left the dug-out and stood in front of the Kop, and he was snow-balled too, but he stood his ground and the missiles petered out, and then less than a minute after the ref blew the whistle for play, Wednesday equalised and the Kop went wild, Daniel went wild, Alison went wild. A burly man on her other side squeezed her tight against his beer gut and together they danced a jig.

It ended one–all, a bit of an anticlimax, a rematch in three days at Highbury in unreachable North London, but they left the ground in high spirits and bought two bags of chips from a van, and set off walking for Nether Edge because there was a crush for the buses, and a posse of pissed-up Wednesday fans were roaming the crowds looking for men in red. It was bitterly cold and thick sleet fell like pins from the leaden sky, but when they landed on Peter's donkey jacket they glinted and sparkled like gems against the black wool.

Daniel took her to his house; he wanted to show her off, although he didn't say as much. Kept it casual, offered a cup of tea and said he had something for her, a present. Alison had no wish to go home yet, although she knew she probably should, so they headed for Daniel's, and everybody was there, Mr and Mrs Lawrence, Claire, even Joe, who didn't live there any more. It was the first time they'd met her and they were all smiling, fuss-ing over her; it was 'Hello, love' and 'Give me your coat' and 'Ooh, your hands are red raw' and 'Now then, what did you make o' that match?' Claire, who was twenty-two but seemed much younger, stared at Alison with a sort of guileless admir-ation, then said, 'I really like your hair,' and Joe said, 'Ey, Daniel, struck lucky this time,' and it was all so chatty and friendly, there was barely time to answer one question before another one got asked. Daniel's mum said it was Bill and Marion, not Mr and Mrs Lawrence, so Alison called them nothing at all.

Claire offered to paint her nails at the kitchen table, and

Alison sat next to her and spread out her fingers while Claire chatted in an effortless stream of inconsequence and applied a rose-coloured gloss with a steady hand. She had a job in cosmetics at Cole Brothers, which was a proper career, she said, not just shop work. She was still wearing the navy skirt and the white and navy polka-dot blouse she wore behind the counter, and she smelled of cologne, something musky and adult, but honestly, thought Alison, you'd think she was a fourteen-year-old, play-acting, dressing up in her mum's clothes. She was lovely though, Claire: totally unthreatening. Alison liked the sensation of being the focus of her careful attention, and of only having to listen as she prattled on, although she told her about her own job, Thursday evenings after school, and some Saturdays, stacking shelves in a supermarket. 'What do you have to wear?' Claire asked, and Alison said just a horrible nylon overall, green and white checked, and Claire looked devastated for her. Meanwhile Daniel talked to his dad and Joe about the match, Jeff Johnson's perfectly placed header less than a minute into the second half, Pat Jennings fending off snowballs and Alison chanting menaces at the away fans. Everybody laughed at that; nobody believed him.

Mrs Lawrence put a huge brown teapot on the table and a packet of chocolate digestives. 'That's a pretty colour,' she said, looking at Alison's nails. 'Claire, you're in the way there, love.'

'Finished,' Claire said. 'Waggle your hands, Alison, dry them off.'

Alison did as she was told. Daniel was trying hard to ignore the fact that she was there, or at least trying hard not to keep staring at her and grinning like a fool, but when he did glance over, she was looking right at him, and they both smiled. Mrs Lawrence poured the tea and sat down at the table, asked

Alison questions about school and if she liked it, and did she have any brothers or sisters, so Alison talked about Peter, her big brother. He was the same age as Claire, but they'd never met. Different schools, said Mrs Lawrence, just like you and Daniel. Hmmm, thought Alison, different lives too. Alison told her he was at Brown Bayley's, on the cranes; Daniel's mum said that was a job she'd choose if they let women do it and she wasn't stuck with office work; she said she'd love to spend her day looking down on everybody, and then she laughed at her own joke, and pushed the packet of biscuits at Alison, told her to take one because tea was too wet without a digestive.

Mr Lawrence, who was much quieter than his wife and had so far hardly said a word, suddenly asked Alison if she liked pigeons, and the rest of the family shouted him down, but Alison said, 'Homing pigeons?' and he said, 'Aye, I've some beauties in my loft, I can show you if you want?' So Alison said she'd love to see them, and Mr Lawrence took her out the back door into the yard, Daniel following to make sure she was all right, and that his dad didn't mistake politeness for avid interest.

But the birds were beautiful. Their loft was a converted shed where the pigeons – six of them – sat glossy and plump like little Prince Regents, gazing at Alison from their boxes, with eyes as dark as currants. Mr Lawrence fetched out a bird, cupped closely in two hands. Its feathers were the softest grey, with a glamorous shimmering band of mauve and emerald green at its neck.

'This one's a champ,' he said. 'Clover.'

'Clover?' Alison said.

'Yep,' said Daniel, from the door. 'Great name – for a cow.'

Mr Lawrence ignored him. 'Aye, Clover. She's a beauty, a pure Janssen, bred her myself from a cock and a hen I bought in

Elsecar. Feller who owned 'em were winning everything, then he dropped dead and his wife had a clearance sale.' He was talking to the bird as much as to Alison, and the pigeon seemed to be listening closely, watching his face with her steady black eyes. 'She didn't know what she were selling, did she? Underpriced every bird.' He offered her to Alison, but she shook her head; she was wary of that beak, those clawed feet.

'I might drop her,' she said. 'You keep hold.' She looked round at Daniel, who was leaning on the frame of the open doorway with his arms folded. He didn't speak, but raised his eyebrows at her, as if to say, 'Had enough yet?'

Alison turned away. 'What if she flies out?' she said, pointing at the open door, the evening sky, and Mr Lawrence laughed.

'She'll not leave my side, this 'un, unless she's racing, then all she does is sprint back, fast as an arrow.'

'Aren't you worried, y'know, that she won't find you?'

'Never, she's a champ.'

'You said that already, Dad,' Daniel said, from the door.

'She flew six hundred miles from Lerwick once,' Mr Lawrence said, ignoring his son. 'See her coming in, tail fanned, wings back, it's like nowt else, nowt else. She's a champ.'

Daniel tutted, and Alison said, 'Clever girl,' to the pigeon, then smiled at Daniel's dad, who looked pleased as punch. 'Thanks for showing me,' she said.

'Nay, lass, any time,' he said, and Alison and Daniel left him in the loft, where he was settling Clover back in her box, talking to her all the while.

'Got a fan for life there,' Daniel said. He stopped her before they reached the house, and turned her around so that she was leaning against the wall, and he kissed her, holding her face between his two hands, and she closed her eyes, felt a liquid heat low down in her belly and thought, Oh God, oh God, oh God.

She had no idea what to do with the desire she felt for him: no idea at all. But anyway, they were in the back yard, his dad was in the shed, his mum was in the kitchen, so all that happened was he drew away from her and said, with his mouth still very close to hers, 'So, I've got a present for you, remember?'

She nodded. 'Go on then, what is it?'

'A mix tape,' he said, and she sighed, smiled, shrugged, but he said, 'No, no, a mix tape with a difference. Tailor-made for a tricky customer such as yourself.'

She laughed. 'Oh, is that so?'

He led her back into the house and on a shelf in the kitchen there was a cassette in its box. *The Best Last Two*, it said, *For Alison*. There was no track list.

'The best last two?'

'Yep. You'll get it when you play it.'

He gave her her coat, and when she put it on he slipped the cassette into one of the pockets and sent her away with a chaste kiss on the cheek. She left the house in a hail of goodbyes, caught the bus and rode back to Attercliffe in a hazy glow of good spirits, wondering how she could capture today in words and wishing her current idol Sylvia Plath had watched Sheffield Wednesday play at home and then written about it in her journal. This reverie took her all the way home, where she stepped into a house so devoid of light and life that she was for a few seconds derailed. She stood, forlorn and still, and listened for the sound of Catherine, or for Peter's footsteps on the landing, or for Martin, blundering to the kitchen for another can from the fridge. But there was only a ticking, abandoned silence and a fried-egg smell, and a broken glass on the lino by the cooker. She shed her coat, picked up the fragments of glass and binned them, then tried to wash the plates and the frying pan in the sink, but there was no hot water so all she was doing was swilling grease across the surface of the crockery, and there was something so futile, so wholly depressing, about this that she gave up. There was no note from Peter, which was unusual; she hoped he was out doing something nice, something that he'd chosen to do. She dried her hands on a grubby tea towel in the cold kitchen; thought about Daniel's house, his mum, the fire blazing orange and blue in the grate, a bottomless teapot, Clover the pigeon, Daniel's kiss. And then she remembered the mix tape, fished it out of her coat pocket, and went upstairs to her room.

8

EDINBURGH,

15 NOVEMBER 2012

The girl doing Journalism Studies at Stirling University – Sky?
Star? Something celestial – scribbled frantic notes as Dan spoke,
as if his own haphazard career was some kind of blueprint for
success. He always said yes to these young people when they
asked to talk to him, because, after all, any one of them could
be Alex, and they were only trying to make their way in the
world. But this girl was taking it all down word-for-word, while
totally missing the point. When Dan talked about his own
break, the piece he wrote for *NME* after that gig in Minne-
apolis in 1983 where Prince showcased his new backing band
and Dan chanced upon a ten-minute interview with the young
Wendy Melvoin, Sky-or-Star only wrote steadily for a few
moments, then looked up and said, 'Could you spell Melvoin
for me?'

She was very young, though. She'd asked for a hot chocolate
when he bought her a drink, and said yes to whipped cream.
He'd had a double espresso, and really hadn't expected their
chat to last much longer than his coffee, but here they still were.
Dan glanced at his watch. He had to be at Waverley Station in
twenty minutes, for the London train.

'So, anything else you'd like to know?' he said.

For a few moments the girl continued writing her conscientious notes, and then she looked up. She had wild green eye make-up and her hair was dyed a gothic bluebottle black. She wore it in a sort of choppy, spikey mullet, some sort of homage to a past that wasn't really her own.

'Erm . . .' she said. 'Just, I suppose, what do you think makes you a great music writer?'

'Oh, blimey, don't ask me that, there's plenty wouldn't agree with the thesis.'

She flushed at once, and he felt bad. 'Look, music writers come in all varieties,' he said. 'But most of us have an obsessive streak, and that helps.'

'Obsessive about music?'

'Well, yeah, I mean, not *all* music, but definitely at the very least I bet every music writer would have an unreasonable attachment to one band they'll love for all time, a band they'd defend to the death.' He was trying to make her smile, but she just said, 'Right,' and chewed her pen reflectively, as if she was considering her options. He wondered what she listened to, and decided not to ask. He had a bit more advice for her though, so he said, 'The thing is, Sky – it is Sky, right?' She nodded, thank God. 'The thing is, if you like listening to music, then just get on with it. It's not a divine calling; it's a job. I'm just a hack, with a job to do. So as soon as you start *writing* about music, you're a music writer – even if it's a blog that nobody but your mum and your granny reads. Just get cracking, OK? Don't wait for the music press – what's left of it – to beat a path to your door, because it won't. Now, I've got a train to catch, so . . .'

'Oh!' Sky said, jumping up, reddening furiously. She held out a hand. Each slender finger was adorned with a bulky metal ring in the shape of skulls and snakes, and her fingernails were painted black, but her manners were those of a 1930s debutante. 'I'm so sorry,' she said. 'Thank you so much for your time.'

'Pleasure,' he said. 'Best of luck with it.' He shook her heavy little hand, then walked to the door.

'Dan,' she said urgently. He turned.

'Limp Bizkit,' she said. He looked at her, thinking: What the fuck?

'My obsession,' she said.

He laughed. 'Ah, right, yeah, good one. So, you have five seconds to defend them.'

She took a deep breath. 'Well, the way they mix musicianship with aggression, I think that's unique, and they . . . they define the scope of what metal can do when it's fused with hip-hop and pop.'

'Ha!' Dan said, nodding, pleasantly surprised. 'Excellent. Really, excellent. You'll go far.'

She beamed. 'What's yours?'

'Comsat Angels,' he said. 'Look 'em up.' And he swung out of the café into Cockburn Street and headed down the hill to the station.

So, he was on the London-bound train, his mobile office, a place without distractions where all he could do was listen to music or write. Twice a month these days, sometimes three, he'd make this journey, and years ago, when he was young and hungry for work, he'd disappear down there for days and days, dossing in Kentish Town with Rocco and Kim, who freelanced at the *NME*, Rocco a writer, Kim a photographer, and between them they got the occasional subbing shift for Dan, although writing was what he wanted: a picture byline, a staff job. He'd dropped out of Durham University after only a year there, and he was lost for a while, drinking and smoking with Rocco and Kim and their sketchy friends. There was a big, friendly guy who ran a Jamaican restaurant just off Kentish Town Road, with a sign on the wall that said 'A Friend with Weed is a Friend Indeed', and he kept them in cannabis and fed them rice and peas when the post-high hunger descended. But that was then; these days he had meetings to attend, gigs to see, deadlines to meet. He had a narrowboat home, too: a permanent mooring on the Regent's Canal, a rock 'n' roll solution to the crazy cost of bricks and mortar in the capital. Nothing nicer than sitting on the towpath with a beer, nodding at the neighbours whose boats were nose to tail with his own.

He had three nights ahead of him on this trip. Three meetings, two gigs, one pressing deadline. But as usual he'd managed to build in some loafing time, keeping tomorrow night free to hang out with his friends Frank and Lisa on their boat before bed. So, one gig tonight, another Saturday, then home on the slow Sunday train, King's Cross to Waverley, working all the way; he never took the overnight sleeper, hated those narrow bunks and the sway of the carriage, and arriving in Edinburgh at half past seven, feeling like shit. What he liked was a daytime journey, a table to himself, a seat facing the direction of travel, a power point to charge his laptop, and a – admittedly patchy – stream of free wireless connection to the internet.

He had all these conditions in place now, as the train plunged south through the soft green lowlands of border country, but he'd done nothing yet other than consider Ali Connor, who once was Alison. She'd made him smile with 'Picture This', hit the nail on the head, and he'd realised when it came that he'd have been disappointed if she hadn't picked that very track to reply. Not that he'd been testing her in any way, or at least not consciously, but it was . . . what was it? A validation, perhaps, of a bank of memories so distant they'd almost morphed into myth; one of those glittering pieces of the mosaic that he'd forgotten, but still carried around with him anyway, waiting for the right time to rediscover it. And he found, to his great fascination, that what he meant to do now was send another song, back to Adelaide, and that the choice of song was a matter of utmost importance. Since he sat down on this train he'd been scrolling through the many hundreds of contenders on his iPod, playing some of them, enjoying all of them, but none of them was what he was looking for. He didn't know, of course, what he was looking for. He wouldn't know, until he found it.

'Is anyone sitting here?'

Oh fuck. Dan glanced up, and there was a man smiling at him, sliding sideways into the seat opposite, which was patently free.

'Nope,' Dan said. 'All yours.'

He turned his attention back to the library of music. Stevie Wonder, Patty Griffin, the National. More Blondie? John Martyn? The Killers? Jesus, so much fucking music. And what was it he wanted to say to Ali Connor, after all these years?

'Erm . . . Daniel Lawrence?'

Oh fuck, fuck. He looked up and the man opposite was smiling again – grinning, actually – and staring. He looked about Dan's age. Not Scottish. Slim build, dark hair, short back and sides, blue eyes. He wore a Harrington jacket and a T-shirt that looked as if it might have an image of Bob Marley on it. Dan couldn't stand grown men with T-shirts bearing music legends, or tour dates.

'Sorry?' Dan said.

The man opposite offered a hand, which Dan took, and shook, still mystified, although there was something about this guy that rang a dim bell. Meanwhile the fellow himself was very much enjoying himself.

'Bloody hell,' he said. 'Bloody hell.'

Dan said, 'Look, I'm sorry . . .' and the man laughed and said, 'You don't recognise me, do you?'

'I don't.'

'Well, it's been thirty-odd years. Dave Marsden. Rob's brother. I once put a tent peg through your thumb?'

'Christ Almighty!'

Dave nodded. 'Insane,' he said.

'Dave Marsden!'

'That's me. I knew you straight away. Mind you, I see your mug in the music pages.'

'Dave Marsden,' Dan said again. 'Oh my God. How are you?'

'Yeah, all right, you?'

'Yeah,' Dan said. He raised his right thumb to show a short, jagged white scar running from the base of the nail all the way round to the fleshy pad at the back. 'Apart from this disfigurement, obviously,' and they both laughed. Reighton Gap, 1974, and Rob and Daniel had only been allowed to go camping there if Dave went with them. Dave, sixteen to their fourteen, and all he'd done by way of supervision was put up the tent, which was when he'd driven a metal peg through Dan's thumb. It'd needed stitches really, but there was a woman in a caravan with a first-aid kit. She'd swabbed the wound and poured Dettol over it, then bound it in a series of pink Elastoplasts, one on top of another, until the blood stopped seeping through.

'I blame you for my failure to make it as a lead guitarist,' Dan said. 'Couldn't use my strumming thumb for months.'

'Reighton Gap,' Dave said. 'What a fucking dump. I lost my virginity there though.'

Dan laughed. 'Easily done, I should think.'

'Wendy, her name was. I think it was anyway. Might have

been Wanda. I was clueless, but she seemed to know what she was doing.'

'No wonder we never saw you.'

'She opened my eyes, that girl.'

'Is Rob doing OK?'

Dave's smile faded. 'No. No, he's not. He's a drinker.'

Dan said, 'Ah, right.'

'We all drink, us Marsdens, but our Rob doesn't stop. He started when he got made redundant.'

'What did he do?'

'Steel. Darnall Works.'

'Oh, but Rob was . . .' Dan hesitated, not wanting to offend.

'Brainy? Yep, he was. Is. Cleverest lad in our family anyway. He went in on a management scheme, but brains didn't save you from the chop in the steel industry.' Dave sniffed, and gazed for a moment out of the window, then turned back to Dan. 'You did all right though.'

'That's tough, about Rob,' Dan said, and he thought about the passing of time and the lad he'd known, a steady kind of individual, thoughtful and quiet. At Reighton Gap, Rob had searched for fossils on the beach – ammonites, belemnites, crinoids – while Dan had stared at the girls in the sea and imagined them naked. He sat back in his seat and regarded Dave. 'This is crazy,' he said. 'You, on this train. It's like back to the bloody future.'

'I know, right? You look the same, sort of. Good-looking bastard.'

'Why were you in Edinburgh?'

'Checking out a new site for a bar. This company I work for, they take over derelict buildings and turn 'em into artisan gin palaces.' He put speech marks around 'artisan' with his index fingers.

Dan raised his eyebrows. 'In Edinburgh?'

'Leith, believe it or not. By the waterfront.'

'Is that Bob Marley on your T-shirt, by the way?'

'One of the Wailers, I think,' Dave said. 'Got it in Oxfam. Do you see anybody? Y'know, anybody from Sheffield?'

Ali's face formed in Dan's mind like a portrait in smoke, there and gone, too ephemeral to trust. Dave Marsden was real; Alison Connor was a memory. *Ali* Connor could be a figment.

'No,' Dan said. 'Well, I saw Kev Carter about four years ago. We talk online, now and again. D'you still live in Sheffield?' he asked.

'No bloody chance,' Dave said. 'I married a posh lass, we live in Guildford.' He laughed. 'Mind you, everybody seemed posh when I went down south.'

'I went further north,' Dan said. 'Not south. Followed an Irish girl, settled in Scotland.'

'Oh, I know all about you,' Dave said. 'Read your column, read your reviews, read that book about the Bunnymen an' all.'

'Right,' Dan said. 'You always did like your music.'

'Do you remember that gig in Donny?'

'Which gig?'

'Comsat Angels. Chuffing hell, you were like a bloody groupie.'

Astonishing, thought Dan. He stared at Dave. 'Astonishing,' he said.

'What is?'

'Comsat Angels. Second time they've come up in the past half-hour. Were you there, then? I know Rob was.'

Dave nodded. 'Me and Rob were nearer the bar than the stage, but you were stood up front about two feet from that lead singer, staring at him like it was the second coming.'

Dan shook his head, smiling; he'd told that girl, Sky, all

about Prince and the Revolution at the First Avenue Club, but for truly pivotal moments – those times in his life when destiny showed up and made him consider his future – he couldn't top Doncaster Sports Club, 1979, a Monday night in June. Dan and his crew of mates had come in somebody's Ford Transit, and there were about fifty people in the club to see the band, but only Dan was up front, transfixed in front of a smoke-filled stage. He could still hear in his head now exactly what he'd heard then, all the layers of sound that kept him rooted to the floor, made him feel stunned and lucky and clever to have come here. The wailing guitar, an aching, suspended, searing chord; drums coming in with the relentless momentum of a train on the tracks; a hypnotic bass, then soaring keyboards; and a frontman, Stephen Fellows, dark-haired, chisel-featured, sharp-suited, delivering tense, sparse lyrics like a disillusioned urban poet. Daniel had thought: That could be me. That *should* be me. What he is, up there: that is what I am.

'You followed 'em about after that,' Dave said, bringing him back to the here and now.

'I went to their gigs, you mean,' Dan said. 'You make me sound like a sodding stalker.' He had, in fact, *almost* stalked them – the Fusion Club in Chesterfield, a hotel in Sheffield two days later, Rotherham a week after that. He'd even watched them rehearse, in a room above a café in Division Street. But hey, he'd been nurturing a fledgling obsession, and at the time it seemed like these boys were gilded: glittering with nascent success. The future pulsed with fame and glory for them, for Dan, and for anyone who wanted to come with him for the ride. Alison saw them with him at the Rotherham gig. But by then, she was slipping through his fingers, not that he'd known it.

Dave nodded at Dan's iPod, lying abandoned on the table in front of them. 'What you listening to these days then?'

'Everything,' Dan said. 'As usual.'

'But what're you liking?'

'Oh, I spend a lot of time in the past,' Dan said. 'In my own time, I mean.'

'What's the last thing you reviewed?'

Jesus, thought Dan; it was great to see Dave but this could be tiresome, all the way to London. 'BadBadNotGood,' Dan said. 'That's their name, not my review. Canadian boys, jazzy-bluesy.'

Dave sniffed and pulled a face. 'Sounds lame to me.'

'It's good. Probably even better if you're stoned. Look, do you want a coffee? I'm off to the buffet car, shall I bring you something back?'

'Oh yeah, thanks, mate. White, one sugar. And a KitKat? Split one with you.'

'Is it your birthday?'

'Feels like it,' Dave said. 'Bumping into the legendary Dan Lawrence.'

'Yeah, right,' Dan said, 'don't push your luck.' He left his seat, and as he walked down the carriage he pulled his phone from his jacket pocket and opened Safari, then typed Comsat Angels into the search box, and there was the band, young men captured in black and white in a series of moody shots from the early days. At the buffet counter, he joined a small queue, and tapped on 'Songs', which led him to a long string of Comsat tracks. Any of them would do, but he scrolled on down, taking his time. Hovered over 'Missing In Action', which had opened the set, back in Doncaster in 1979, but then he hesitated, and continued. Down, down, down. There. This one. Twenty-five songs into the list. 'Waiting For A Miracle'. He didn't play it: didn't need to. Instead he copied the link, sprinted with his thumb on to Twitter, on to messages, on to @AliConnorWriter and the short thread of two songs that they'd already shared, then he pasted the link and pressed send.

Done. A seminal piece of post-punk genius on its way to Adelaide. And a seminal piece of Daniel Lawrence too.

'Aye-aye, what you up to, texting an old flame?'

Dan looked up, startled, and the woman behind the counter laughed at him.

'Och, only teasing, my love, what can I get for you?'

Dan smiled and put his phone away, to prove how very trivial his business with it was, compared to the matter in hand – coffee, KitKat, a bottle of water. He ordered in a steady voice, and engaged in mild banter as his heart rate slowed to normal. But God almighty, he thought when the woman turned her back to deal with his order, what would Katelin think? And what's the game here? And why was it so fucking important, so *paramount*, that Alison Connor didn't slip away from him for a second time?

9

It was all wrong, really: Ali, Michael, Thea and Beatriz downstairs, Stella upstairs in her room. But she wasn't speaking to any of them, so this unhappy domestic apartheid was difficult to avoid. Thea had flown home from med school in Melbourne, adding to the atmosphere of extreme crisis. Ali wouldn't have told her – at least, not yet, not so soon, not if it implied she was somehow needed at home – but Michael had made the call, clued her in, and sent her airfare when she insisted, in spite of looming exams, on joining them for a weekend of unhappiness. Thea was her father's daughter, a McCormack through and through: possessed of an inherited, unshakable belief in her own indispensability. The pair of them had yet to face a problem that couldn't be solved by the application of good sense, hard cash or sheer strength of will. But here was Stella, not quite eighteen, furious with everyone, fiercely defensive, and eight weeks pregnant by a boy she wouldn't name. She was determined, she said, to keep the baby.

'Well, she's not in her right mind,' Thea said now. 'Or she's just being provocative.'

They were in the kitchen, gathered around Beatriz, who was peeling potatoes with steady hands and a peaceful expression.

She was the calm, still centre of their lives, thought Ali. She gave the impression that nothing in the world was more urgent right now than this simple task of preparing dinner. It was an illusion; they all knew that. Still, the smell of onions caramelising over a low heat was comforting, in its way.

'You need to book a termination, and tell her it's a done deal.'

'Thea, be quiet,' Ali said.

'Mum, get real. Dad agrees, don't you, Dad?'

'I certainly don't want her to continue with this pregnancy,' Michael said, and looked at Ali, who looked away.

'Well then.' Thea held out her palms, as if the issue was resolved, easy as pie. She was brisk and bright and organised; never in a million years would she have got herself in this pickle, thought Ali.

'It's not a question of whether Dad agrees with you,' she said, trying to be patient, trying not to snap. 'It's a question of listening to Stella and respecting her views.'

Thea made a small sound, almost a laugh, but not quite. 'She won't thank you, a year down the line, when she's stuck here with a kid and her friends have all gone off to uni.'

'Oh good God, give me strength.' This was Michael, his voice raised in a sort of frustrated anguish. He brought a fist down hard on the worktop and a potato rolled over the edge and on to the tiled floor. Beatriz stopped peeling and looked at him.

'God *is* good,' she said.

Michael groaned. 'Beatriz . . .'

'No,' she said, pointing the sharp end of the peeler at him. 'You should remember that God is good, Michael. You all should.'

There was silence, because no one was much in the mood to

tackle Beatriz on the subject of her faith. Upstairs, there were footsteps on the landing and everyone looked at the ceiling. The bathroom door slammed shut.

'Listen,' Ali said. 'If Stella says no, what can we do? We can't drag her to the clinic by the hair, can we?'

'No,' Michael said. 'But we can talk sense into her, instead of pussyfooting around and "respecting her views".'

'Exactly.' Thea nodded in approval. 'Well said, Dad.'

Ali glared at her hands. This was a familiar scenario: the combined force of Michael and Thea, wearing her down with logic and mutual self-belief.

'Suppose she has this baby,' Michael said, attempting a conciliatory tone. 'Do we look after it for her while she completes her studies? Do you give up writing, Ali, to play grandma?'

'Oh, give me a break, Michael. Is that meant to shock me into agreeing with your point of view?'

'Another baby in this household could only be a gift,' Beatriz said. 'A gift from God.'

'No, actually, it would be a gift from some unnamed and oversexed teenage boy,' Thea said.

'Thea McCormack!' Beatriz, so rarely rattled, used the voice that might once have made the girl hang her head in shame. No longer.

'Facts of life, I'm afraid. It's not the Immaculate Conception, Beatriz.'

'That's enough,' Ali said.

Thea flicked her hair away from her face and sighed. 'This is ridiculous,' she said. She looked at Michael, who met her gaze and smiled. 'Dad,' she said. 'You're going to have to sort this out. Mum's too flaky.'

Michael opened his mouth to speak, but Ali beat him to it. 'Thea, button it, you're being objectionable.'

'You are, sweetheart,' Michael said. 'A bit.'

'Fine.' Thea's face took on a chilly, shuttered look. She picked up her phone and began to scroll idly through her messages. A sleek curtain of blonde hair fell over one eye.

'Dinner will be at seven,' Beatriz said, fighting for normality.

Ali looked at her. 'Actually, Beatriz,' she said, 'I think I'm going to be out.'

Michael, startled, said, 'Are you? Since when?'

'Just decided. I'm going to see Sheila.'

'Sheila?'

'Yep, Sheila Baillie.' She slid off her stool and gave Beatriz a kiss on her soft cheek. 'Sorry, Beatriz, needs must,' she said.

'Sheila?' Michael said again. 'That's a four-hour drive. Why?'

Ali shrugged. 'Feels right. I think she might be able to help.'

'Oh, sure, just go, Mum,' said Thea without looking up from her phone. 'We'll sort all this out in your absence.'

Ali looked at her older daughter, so assured of her place in the world, so convinced of her own excellence, and she could admit to a sort of pride and pleasure that Thea was strong and sure and a world away from the 22-year-old self that she, Ali, had been. Good grief though, this girl could be arrogant.

'You'll do no such thing, love,' Ali said. 'I'm taking Stella with me.'

So now they were in the car, well on their way on the main road north, which the city planners had named Main North Road, as if they were all out of ideas. It surged through and beyond Adelaide, crowded at first by suburbs, then discount stores, truck stops, car yards and petrol stations, before carving a trajectory through wide, scorched fields as the city, on its astonishing flat plain, fell further and further away. Stella was the happiest

Ali had seen her for weeks. When she'd gone upstairs, knocked on the bathroom door and said, 'Stell, will you come with me to see Sheila and Dora?' she hadn't expected the door to fly wide open and Stella to say, with something like hope, something like relief, 'When? Now?' Ali had almost begun to believe she would never again say anything that pleased Stella, but her daughter's stony face had in an instant lost its sullen defences, and she'd smiled and said, 'I'll pack some things.'

They hardly ever saw Sheila, because she was rarely at home. When she was, she lived these days in Quorn, an endearing little outback town on the edge of the Flinders Ranges in a tiny cottage she rented from an artist. She'd based herself there many years ago after she'd shocked all of Elizabeth by walking out on her engineer husband Kalvin and taking up with a woman, Dora Langford, a volunteer driver on the Pichi Richi Railway, who wore a boiler suit and a peaked cap, and shovelled coal with strong, callused hands. So when Stella, aged two and a half, had been introduced to Sheila for the first time, it was on a dear little steam train, barrelling along past gum-lined creeks and bluebush-studded hills, and Dora had put her in charge of the whistle. Such experiences leave a legacy in young hearts: ever after, when Stella thought of Sheila and Dora, she'd experienced a flush of pure joy.

Stella was sitting, now, in the passenger seat of Ali's car, her bare feet up on the dashboard, gazing left, out of the window. The city limits were far behind them and the evening sky was unstable; clouds in shades of charcoal shifted and rolled towards them from a lowering horizon, but the car felt snug and solid, a sanctuary. They'd called Michael on speakerphone with a progress report. He sounded lighter, thought Ali; he sounded relieved. She'd literally taken away the problem and, for the time being at least, he could legitimately think about something else.

So could Stella, for that matter, and so could Ali – this journey, this trip: it was an act of escapism, an exercise in being happy. Thus far, Stella's pregnancy hadn't been mentioned, and if Stella didn't bring it up, Ali certainly wouldn't. Now and again she stole glances at her daughter, and could see from the way she inhabited the seat – her limbs loose, legs up, arms slack across her bent knees – that she was contented, relaxed. She was like a different girl, heading north to Quorn, running out on reality. Plenty of time for home truths, Ali thought, but first, a dose of Sheila.

'So, can we have some songs?' Stella said eventually, when the landscape became too relentlessly unchanging to watch. 'Did you bring your music?'

'Don't be daft,' Ali said. She handed over her iPod and Stella plugged in the aux cable. She spun the control, watching the screen options change, and the cursor clicked like semaphore, dot-dot-dashing its way down the list.

'You should ditch this old thing,' she said. 'Put it all on your phone. It's much handier.'

'I love that iPod like I love you,' Ali said.

Stella laughed. 'What shall I put on?'

'Whatever you fancy. No, wait, go on playlists, there's a new one I made. Should be first up.'

'Called?'

'*Best Last Two*,' Ali said.

Stella said, 'Your playlists have weird names.'

'The songs are great though. Oh God, I love this track.' She whacked up the volume on the stereo and the swaggering beat of 'Suffragette City' swung into action like an instant party.

'Ahh, Mum, this is the best,' Stella shouted. 'Who is it?'

Ali grinned at her. 'Bowie,' she shouted back.

They let it roll. Ali sang the words, Stella tried to pick them up. At 'Wham bam, thank you, ma'am' she hooted with joy and played it back again until she had the timing just right and could belt it out with Bowie and her mum, and when the song slammed to its halt, she heaved a sigh and said, 'Loved that, what next?'

Ali said, 'One more Bowie, then the Byrds – two of those as well – then Talking Heads, two, the Kinks, same, the Police, T. Rex, the Animals, Jimi Hendrix, the Buzzcocks and, finally, the Beatles. Two of each, every time. The best last two.'

Stella stared. 'You're *such* a music nerd,' she said.

'Thanks.'

'Hmm, not sure about this one though,' Stella said.

' "Rock 'n' Roll Suicide",' Ali said. 'The last track on *The Rise And Fall Of Ziggy Stardust And The Spiders From Mars.*'

'That's the weirdest name for an album,' Stella said. 'So "Suffragette City" is second last?'

'You got it.'

'Why?'

'Why what?'

'The "best last two" thing?'

'Oh,' Ali said. 'It wasn't my idea. A friend gave it to me, years ago, when I was even younger than you are.' Daniel's image formed in her mind. She recalled a lingering kiss against the wall of his house, the feel of the cassette in her coat pocket, and the very first time she heard the playlist, alone in her bedroom, in an empty house, before she'd discovered where her brother had gone that night, and where her mother was, and what Martin had done, or what he was yet to do. Like light before dark, she'd listened to this tape in her cold bedroom, and loved it, and loved Daniel for thinking of it. 'I didn't listen to mix tapes in those days,' she said to Stella. 'He made this for me, so each pair of songs was in their proper order, from the album they came off.'

'He sounds like a nerd too,' Stella said. 'A bit of a try-hard. Did he fancy you?'

'Ah, it was a lifetime ago,' Ali said, dismissive, evasive. But still, she thought, here he was, with them in the car, with his meticulously curated *Best Last Two*. She'd remembered the cassette yesterday evening, gone up into the roof space to look for it after he'd plunged her back in time with the Comsat Angels. Two hours later, and somewhat to her astonishment, she'd found it in a cardboard box of sundry items, safe and sound in its plastic case. There was no track list, he hadn't written one, so Ali had to dig out an old cassette player to remind herself what he'd chosen all those years ago. She'd listened to the songs in the permanent twilight of the loft, feeling melancholy, nostalgic, and entirely lost for a while in Daniel's musical obsessions of 1979. Then she'd corralled those of the songs she already had, bought the ones she hadn't, and organised all twenty of them into *The Best Last Two* on her iPod.

'This one's good,' Stella said.

' "The Girl With No Name",' Ali said. 'The Byrds. Second to last track on *Younger Than Yesterday*.'

'Is it old? Doesn't sound it.'

'Good music never gets old.'

'He did a nice thing,' Stella said.

'Who?'

'That boy. What was his name?'

'Daniel.'

'He did a nice thing,' she said again.

'Yes,' Ali said. 'He did a very nice thing.'

'Hey,' Stella said. 'Remember "California Dreaming"?'

'Always,' Ali said. 'Always and for ever.' It was their duet on any long journey, their party piece at any family gathering, when Stella was still at primary school and would rather be with Ali than anyone else in the world.

'You be the girls,' Stella said. 'I'll be the boys.'

They switched off the music and sang their parts lustily, and outside the car evening turned into night and there was no longer anything to be seen in the darkness, until ahead, eventually, the warm, scattered lights of Quorn revealed themselves, winking at them, beckoning them in.

Sheila and Dora were waiting for them, so the door was flung open even before they knocked. The little house was suffused with the cinnamon scent of a lamb tagine, and when Sheila wrapped Ali in her arms, she smelled sweetly exotic, orange blossom and rosewater, a Turkish delight of a hug. Stella hung back, suddenly shy, but Sheila drew her in.

'Beautiful, beautiful child,' she said, holding Stella's face. 'Look at her, Dora. The image of Alison.'

Dora was square-shaped, sturdy, and her face was creased with smiles.

'How I loved your book!' she said to Ali. 'So moving, and so real. I cried when it ended, because I couldn't bear to lose my new friends, all those wonderful people you invented. Clearly, you're blessed with creativity, like my Sheila. Now, how long can you stay, dear? Can you stay until Saturday? Sheila has a private view at one of the galleries in town, we'd love it if you could be there.'

'A private view?' Ali said. 'Sheila, are you painting?'

'Oh, she's a hit,' Dora said. 'She's a sensation.'

'Alison, it's so good to see you, it's been too long,' Sheila said. She had hold of Ali again, one arm tight across her shoulder now, keeping her close.

'It has,' Ali said. 'Way too long. You smell lovely, Sheila.'

'Thank you, darling. We're not long back from Marrakesh, and we found a woman at a stall in the medina with her own fragrances. You can keep your Dior and your Chanel, can't you, Dora?'

'You bet,' Dora said.

Ali smiled at them, two beaming old ladies with a glow and sparkle about them, an air of youthful energy. 'You look marvellous, both of you.'

'We're trying to forget we're the wrong side of seventy-five,' Sheila said.

'Well, you look marvellous,' Ali said again. 'I'm really sorry it's been so long. We should come and see you more often.'

'That you should,' Sheila said. 'But catching us at home is the challenge.'

'What do you paint?' Stella asked. She'd taken a seat on an expansive green leather sofa which was cracked with age and spilled stuffing from its arms. Stella plucked at it unconsciously as she took in her surroundings, so eccentrically furnished with unmatching pieces, as if this was a small sale room and they were all here for the auction. As well as the sofa, there was a chintz-covered armchair and a footstool upholstered with palomino hide. Also, there was an oversized, rough-hewn red-gum carver, and a coffee table – knotty burl top on a white mallee base – which stood like a rare fungus in the centre of the room.

'What do I paint . . . ?' Sheila said in reply, pondering the question. 'Well, it's hard to say, darling. My work's very . . .'

'Organic,' said Dora. 'Their content and meaning is in constant flux.'

'Wow,' said Stella.

'And they're large canvasses,' Dora said. 'Aren't they, dear?'

'Too big for this little doll's house,' Sheila said. 'I paint them outdoors, so that I can have full freedom of movement.'

'Sounds fascinating,' Ali said. 'Do you sell them?'

'Certainly,' said Sheila. She paused, then added, 'In principle.' Then she tipped back her head in a full-throttle laugh that was impossible to resist, so the others joined in, laughing at Sheila laughing at herself.

Later, after lamb tagine and couscous and a bottle of hearty Malbec, the household settled down to sleep. Dora made Stella a nest out of cushions and blankets on the floor of the lounge, while Sheila showed Ali to a room upstairs which had a ceiling bedecked with Tibetan prayer flags and a wide but extremely thin sleeping mat on the floor.

'Dora used to meditate in here,' Sheila said. 'Om, mani, padme, hum, all that rigmarole. Total hogwash, if you ask me, and she's given it up now, but the flags are pretty. There's a guest kimono on the back of the door.'

'You think of everything,' Ali said. 'By the way, does Dora still drive the steam train?'

Sheila grinned, winking at her. 'Oh, that,' she said. 'Not likely. We please ourselves now.'

Ali laughed, and said, 'Well, good for you,' and Sheila left her after another hug, another kiss, and a promise of a real talk the next day. With Sheila gone, Ali stripped down to T-shirt and knickers, lay down on the sleeping mat under the canopy of ragged flags and – feeling slightly guilty in this room once devoted to spiritualism – delved in her bag for her phone. A trapping of soulless commercialism, she thought; and yet, wasn't it something that because of it, Daniel Lawrence had been able to take her back to the Rotherham Arts Centre, 1979? And that here in Quorn, ten thousand miles away from Edinburgh, she could listen again to the Comsat Angels, and consider her reply. Simple Minds, perhaps: the big-time, stadium version of the Comsats.

Or, no, maybe a contemporary choice might be more the go; haul them out of the musical past and into the twenty-first century. No encrypted message from the 1970s, just: This is what I sometimes like to listen to, and I'm sharing it with you. Something light and lovely and melodic.

Belle and Sebastian, maybe. Yeah, Belle and Sebastian.

She opened Twitter on her phone, and did a quick search through their albums for the perfect track to strike a different tone in their fledgling playlist, and there it was, jumping straight out at her. 'I Didn't See It Coming'. Nice, because, well, why not state the obvious? She'd not heard from Daniel Lawrence for over half a lifetime; she'd severed their bond all those years ago, and made herself forget him by loving elsewhere, and yet now, thinking of him thinking of her . . . so yes, she thought; this would be her return gift, a sweet and whimsical song, with those perfect opening lines: classic Stuart Murdoch, the poet king of indie rock.

Make me dance, I want to surrender,
Your familiar arms I remember.

Daniel's familiar arms. She played it through, for herself, and lay back down on the mat, remembering, then she swiftly copied the link, and sent it to @DanLawrenceMusic.

'Hey, Mum?'

Stella was in the room. Ali slipped her phone away and smiled at her daughter. How often had Stella done this, through the years; appeared silently at Ali's bedside like a spirit child in the night?

'Can I sleep with you?' she asked, as Ali had known she would.

Ali patted the mat. 'It's a bit hard,' she said. 'But the flags above are pretty.'

Stella lay down beside her, looking up. 'Is it bunting?'

'Tibetan prayer flags.'

'Oh, right.'

'Here.' Ali passed Stella one bud of her earphones, which she'd now plugged back into her iPod. 'Let's fall asleep together to something mellow.'

Beside her, Stella snuggled into her, sighed, and closed her eyes.

IO

Peter was six years old when baby Alison was brought home from the hospital and, though no one expected him to, he'd loved her as soon as he laid eyes on her, a squalling bundle, red-faced, furious, unsafe in their mother's arms. He'd been afraid Catherine would drop her, because she'd already – famously – dropped him; everyone talked about it, the time she lost her footing on the stairs and tumbled to the kitchen floor, break-ing baby Peter's fall with her own body, as if she was heroic, as if it wasn't her fault in the first place. Young as he was, Peter couldn't understand why other grown-ups laughed at this story. He watched his sister, this baby, as Catherine carried her into the house for the first time, plonked her down on the settee like a parcel and reached for the drink that someone handed to her. All the adults in the room said, 'Cheers!' and Catherine said, 'Make the most of it, Geoff, because there won't be another one.'

This was Peter's earliest memory; Alison roaring with new-born rage and nobody but him seeming to care, and the hot fire warming the room beyond comfort, the perilous, clumsy clink of glasses, his mother's laughter.

In Alison's first memory she was perhaps three years old,

and sitting, in shorts, T-shirt and sandals, on the kerb of the pavement in the street, the same Attercliffe street where they still lived. She had no concept of time, but it was dusk, approaching dark, and all the children from the neighbouring houses had gone, called inside from the street by their mothers, one or two at a time, until Alison was alone. The chalk lines of hopscotch were on the pavement, there was a ball in the gutter which she could just reach with her left foot, and Alison's bare legs were very cold. She waited and waited, until Peter came, swinging a kit bag and whistling. They waved, and she was very glad to see him. He gave her a cuddle and then let her into the house with the key he wore on a string around his neck.

This, then, was her earliest memory, but there were many, many subsequent times when Alison waited to be found, and she remembered them all: if not the specifics, then the cycle of sensations. She remembered, for example, the uniquely lonely feeling of extreme hunger; a wariness of encroaching night; an inarticulate infant desire for Peter to never go anywhere without her. Every time she waited for him, Alison would close her eyes and try to conjure up different places she might like to be. In a basket, with a pile of warm puppies. In a feathered nest, curled among the baby birds. In a field of corn, like a mouse, very small and hidden, very secret, very safe. Then Peter would seek her out, or come home from wherever he'd been, and he'd try to gather her up in his skinny arms, and all his warmth flowed into her, and he could always make her smile. At three, she loved him so dearly there was no space in her heart for anyone else, and still, at sixteen, she was devoted to her brother: her safe harbour, her trusted ally. When he was at work, or out with Toddy, she still listened for the sound of his key in the lock, breathed more easily when it came.

Last night, after the football, when Alison had come home

from Daniel's house and gone immediately upstairs to listen to his mix tape, Peter didn't come home at all, but Martin Baxter did, letting himself in and raging about downstairs, looking for Catherine, shouting her name. His feet were heavy on the stairs, thundering up, pushing open Catherine's bedroom door with so much furious force that Alison immediately got up from where she was sitting on the bed and crossed the room to open her own door before he could get to it – a small, defiant gesture, denying him his power to startle and intimidate. The Byrds were singing 'The Girl With No Name', and Alison was facing Martin, who stood on the landing, all sweat and grimace. She thought of Mr Lawrence in his pigeon loft, and imagined herself still there with him, imagined him placing a sleepy, placid bird into her cupped hands, imagined herself not being afraid to cradle its soft weight and feel its plump breast rising and falling against her fingers.

'Your mother's a slag,' Martin said. 'A fucking slag.'

Alison watched him. There was nothing to say.

'Where is she?' he demanded, his voice loose and slewed by beer. 'Who's she wi'?'

Alison had no idea, and said so. She recognised this bluster in Martin; she'd seen it before. There was spittle on his lips, which were incongruously, revoltingly feminine in his brutish face, plump and red and soft. In his right eye a burst blood vessel had filled in half of the white, which gave him a ravaged look, disorderly, off balance. He had reddish hair cut close to the skull and a tattoo on his neck, a blank-eyed snake curling around the flat blade of a dagger. The Byrds ended their song and started another, 'Why', the final track on *Younger Than Yesterday*, and Alison, steady as a rock, registered this although only on the margins, because she was imagining, from the distance of her mind, the horror of being Martin, pitying him his useless bulk, his foolish, clumsy torment, all his responses slowed down by beer, humiliated by Catherine who – he was probably right about this – was more than likely in another man's bed, trading her body for the promise of more booze, postponing her shame and remorse until the next time she was sober.

Martin stepped closer to Alison, who stood her ground. 'If you dunt tell me where she is, I'll fucking beat it out o' you,' he said, and he let his fingers roam over the buckle of his belt.

'I've been out all day,' Alison said steadily. 'How would I know?' Contempt made her calm. She felt certain she'd kill him before she'd let him lay a finger on her. Martin breathed like a bull through flared nostrils and Alison half expected him to start pawing at the floor with one of his black boots. She wanted Daniel, suddenly, urgently. Daniel, his family, his house; she wanted it all with a shocking, desperate longing, but most especially, she wanted *him*, his arms around her. Not here though. Never here.

'Anyway,' she said, 'wasn't she out with you?'

Beer, the effects of it, made him suddenly stagger backwards and then plunge recklessly forward, as if the landing was tilting like a boat in a storm. He cursed, righted himself, and slowly but deliberately focused his gaze on Alison's breasts, and this was meant to intimidate her, but she wasn't afraid of Martin Baxter, not at all.

'She's at the Carlton,' Alison said, realising suddenly that any old lie would get Martin out of the house. 'Yeah, that's what she said. The Carlton.'

He raised his head and regarded her with his bloodshot, swimming eyes.

'You said you dint know,' he said, pointing a fat forefinger at her face.

'The Carlton,' Alison said again, to imprint it on his mind, and he made a careful forty-five-degree turn, swayed for a moment at the top of the stairs, and then lumbered down them, recklessly, two at a time. She waited to hear the door shut behind him, and then she closed her bedroom door again. Now, on the mix tape, it was that band Dan went on about, the band she'd never heard of, Talking Heads, 'Take Me To The River'. Alison sat down on the edge of the bed and listened, to see if she could hear what Daniel heard in them: to see if they'd speak to her as they seemed to speak to him. She turned up the volume and lay down.

In the morning, Peter was back and when Alison came downstairs he was sitting at the kitchen table in his donkey jacket. He looked sheepish, Alison thought, so she nudged him and said, 'Got lucky, did you?' It was so rare for Peter to stay out all night. In fact, she couldn't remember when he last did. He shrugged and didn't answer, so she didn't push it, only pulled up a chair opposite him and sat down.

'Is there tea?' she said.

He nodded, and pushed the brown teapot across to her, followed by a cleanish mug.

'Good time?' she said.

'Saw *Superman*, at the Gaumont.'

'And?'

'And what?' He sounded defensive, and she laughed.

'And what did you think of it?'

'Oh. Yeah, fantastic.'

'With Toddy?'

Peter nodded. 'So, you a Wednesday fan now then?'

Alison laughed. 'No, but oh, I had such a laugh, Peter. We threw snowballs at Arsenal's goalie.'

'I know,' Peter said. 'It were ont radio.'

'We walked back, took us ages, eating chips and talking. Went to Daniel's house. His dad keeps racing pigeons. His sister painted my nails.' She spread them out on the table, perfectly pink, and considered them for a while, then she looked up at Peter. 'It was nice.'

Peter smiled at her. 'It sounds it. I still wish he were a Blade.'

There was the sudden muted clatter of a key in the door and then it burst open and Catherine could be heard in the small front hall, kicking off her high heels and dropping her bag and coat on the floor. She came into the kitchen and brought a smell of fags and stale alcohol, but the look on her face wasn't blank or hostile, only weary. She dropped heavily into the remaining empty chair at the table, then she tilted her head to look first at Peter, and then at Alison.

'So,' she said, and laughed. 'Just we three.' They smiled, uncertainly. She was thin, as a woman who smokes instead of eats must be thin, and pallid, and her left cheek bore the yellow traces of an old bruise. She once was a beauty – a long, long time ago now. The blue seersucker blouse she was wearing was inside out, and the labels showed on the side seam and at the collar. She shivered in the cold room, and Peter poured her a mug of tea, which she took from him silently and held in two hands against her chest but didn't drink.

'Did Martin find you?' Alison asked. 'He came here, looking.'

Catherine rolled her eyes, put down the mug and pulled a squashed packet of Benson & Hedges out of the waistband of her skirt.

'I wish he didn't have a key,' Alison said.

Peter shook his head. 'No, he shouldn't have a key, Catherine. He comes here, mouthing off, shouting the odds.'

'Oh, he's harmless,' Catherine said, flapping a hand. 'All mouth, no trousers. Find me a match, love.'

She said this to Alison, who stood up at once to get the matchbox from the back of the stove. She clutched at moments such as these, when her mother was lucid and sober. If she could keep her talking, light her cigarette, make her smile . . . She struck a match and held the flame to the end of Catherine's cigarette.

'Ta,' her mother said. She took a long, shuddering drag and released the smoke through her nostrils. 'Christ Almighty,' she said. 'Where would I be without my ciggies?'

'So, did he find you?' Alison asked again.

'In a manner of speaking,' Catherine said. She looked at Peter. 'He found you as well, he said.'

Peter looked at her. 'What?'

'You and Toddy, walking down Darnall Road.'

He held her gaze, but shifted in his seat and swallowed. She regarded him narrowly, her cigarette poised at her lips. 'You walked right past him, and never saw him.'

'He could've said summat,' Peter said. 'Why dint he say summat?'

Catherine shrugged. 'Who knows?' she said.

'I hate the bastard.'

'Yes,' Catherine said. 'I know you do. He knows it, an' all.'

Alison watched her brother's face. If only he'd look at her. But he didn't look. He wouldn't.

Catherine smoked for a while, wordless, then she said, 'If I were you, Peter, I'd be civil to Martin. Makes life less difficult.'

A silence hovered between the two of them that Alison couldn't interpret, then Catherine stood up. 'God, I need a drink,' she said, and she started flinging open the cupboard doors then banging them shut, searching for a bottle. Alison shot Peter a look of despair and Catherine, catching her, said, 'Oi, Goody Two Shoes, where'd you hide my vodka?'

'It was me,' Peter said, at once. 'I hid it.'

'Oh, right, well, you can fetch it then.'

Just for a while he seemed about to defy her, and Alison held her breath. Then he said, 'It's there, behind that cereal box.'

Catherine smiled. 'Good lad,' she said.

They watched her pour vodka into a plastic tumbler with an unsteady hand, then she said, 'Cheers,' into the silence.

Alison glanced at the wall clock. It was ten minutes to nine.

Alison spent more time at Daniel's house as the weeks went by. She kept schoolbooks there, sometimes did her homework at the kitchen table, peeled carrots and potatoes for Mrs Lawrence, leaving them on the worktop in saucepans of cold water, ready for later. She loved the kitchen here, its order, its sparkling stainless-steel sink, the bountiful fridge, and the toaster with its picture of wheatsheaves on the sides and a wider slot for teacakes. All Daniel's family were good to her, but sometimes she wondered what they really made of her, especially Mrs Lawrence, whose smile didn't always correspond with the watchful worry in her eyes. And of course, Alison knew her own shortcomings: her reticence in company, her wariness and her reserve, which could come across as indifference. But then, Mr Lawrence was reserved too, so she felt he perhaps understood her, and of Daniel's parents, she certainly liked his father best. His kindness to her seemed infinite and, she thought, a sort of organic, natural thing, part of his being, a function of living which came to him as breathing did, or sleeping. He'd been a mining engineer, Daniel had told her, highly skilled, highly regarded. But he hadn't ever gone back to work after being trapped underground for two days and one night, behind a rockfall. This was years ago, Daniel said, and he'd got the pigeons soon afterwards, and now they were his life; he poured all his time and a great deal of his love into them, and in his pigeon loft Alison believed she knew how his birds felt: suffused with a cosy sensation of belonging. He treated them, and her, with the same gentle respect, and she basked in it, as if in sunshine. Daniel, whose school was further away from his home and who got back later than Alison, knew she was there by her coat on the peg and her satchel on the chair, but almost always he had to fetch her from the pigeon loft, and then they ate toast in the kitchen and larked about, and he always managed to get his hands up her blouse before his mum got home from work, or his dad wandered in through the back door. Sometimes, but only rarely, they had the house to themselves and then, if Alison allowed it – which she didn't always – they had sex on his single bed. And somehow, somewhere in her mind, Alison felt it was strictly forbidden. This development in their relationship – so private, so adult, all skin and heat, limbs entwined and damp desire – was still so new to them both that afterwards, they didn't know what to say to each other, and they reassembled their clothing swiftly, silently, so that they could be themselves again. But there was the secret knowledge of each other in their eyes now, and Alison felt like part of the sisterhood, happy to have shed the enormous burden of her virginity, and happy that it was Daniel who'd taken it, not some loud-mouthed Attercliffe lad with bragging rights over her for evermore.

What she liked best, though, was simply to lounge against his bed on the floor next to him, in a nest of pillows and cushions, and listen to the music they played on his brother's old record player, or on the JVC Boombox, Daniel's pride and joy. She sang to him. He played his guitar for her. They put on . . . oh, anything, everything, sharing their favourites, enduring the stuff they thought they *should* like, replaying time and again the music they could lose themselves in: Jimi Hendrix, T. Rex, Pink Floyd, Blondie, the Beatles, John Martyn, Elvis Costello and, over and over, Rory Gallagher – obsessively, religiously, with proper reverence. He handed on his old love for prog rock, persuaded her to lie down and close her eyes for the duration of *Wish You Were Here*. And she revived his brother's old Northern Soul records, rare finds, his Motown sounds, and Daniel, who grew up watching Joe dance on his plywood square, showed her the moves and together they re-created Wigan Casino in his bedroom with Jimmy Radcliffe and Dean Parrish, the volume whacked up loud enough to make them feel the music in their blood and their bones.

This evening, she stayed for tea. It was Wednesday, quarter to six in the evening. Shepherd's pie, boiled carrots, peas. Mrs Lawrence told a story about her office, about the man in charge of them all, Mr Whitely, who put on airs and graces, considered himself a cut above. Claire said she knew a woman like that at Cole Brothers, who put on a posh voice to customers, but got all her aitches in the wrong places. Mr Lawrence never said much at the table; neither did Daniel. They each looked at their plates and shovelled in the food, and only spoke if they were spoken to directly. Alison, listening, smiling, occasionally eating, wished Peter was here, with a plateful of hot shepherd's pie, and wondered what there was for him to eat at home.

'What was it you said your mum does?'

Alison started as if bitten. Claire had asked the question in all innocence, and her mum looked up from her forkful of mash, knowing – because she'd asked Daniel about this – that Alison wouldn't talk about her family, apart from the brother. A deep blush suffused Alison's neck and cheeks and she swallowed and said, 'She doesn't work,' then looked down to escape Claire's expression of polite bafflement at the evident discomfort she'd caused with a harmless question.

'I wish I didn't have to work,' Claire said, meaning to lighten the tone but making things worse. Daniel glowered at her from across the table and she looked at him, puzzled.

'That were grand,' Mr Lawrence said, breaking his habitual teatime silence, but only to rescue Alison, whose distress was palpable. 'Right tasty, and if there's any more, Marion, I'll take another spoonful.' Suddenly there was movement and busyness, Mrs Lawrence fetching the pie dish from the stove and offering seconds. Alison looked up for Daniel, and found him gazing at her, trying to convey without the help of words that it was all right, there was no harm done.

'There's nothing wrong with not working,' Claire blundered on. 'Dad doesn't work either, do you, Dad?'

'Claire,' Bill said quietly, and Claire said, 'What?' and then Alison stood up, her food only half eaten. She excused herself, blaming homework and a headache, brushing off all the inevitable concern and kindness, and left the kitchen in a rush. In the hallway, by the front door, she struggled into her coat, grabbed her bag, burst out into the cold February evening, but Daniel was right behind her so she turned and clung on to him for a few moments, her face wet in the warmth of his neck. He held her while she steadied herself.

'Alison,' he said, after a while.

'I'm sorry.' She drew away. 'I'm really sorry. Tell your mum I'm sorry.'

'But what's happened?' Her distress caused him pain, actual pain. He wanted to take her sorrow and own it, deal with it, annihilate it. 'What's wrong?'

'Nothing, now,' Alison said, although this was patently not

the case. She tried to recover, sniffing like a small child and wiping her eyes with the backs of her hands. Daniel reached for his coat from the peg inside the doorway, because obviously she was in no state to go anywhere alone, but Alison shook her head at him, furious in her distress. 'No!' she said, much louder than she'd intended, and she saw the alarm in Daniel's face. For a few seconds she breathed slowly and deliberately, facing down the rising panic. 'I'm sorry,' she said again. 'I'll be fine, I just need to get going.'

Daniel said, 'You know what, Alison, I'm getting on your bus with you tonight. I'm seeing you home. I'm worried about you.'

'No!' she said, backing away towards the gate. 'No, please,' but he had his coat on now, and he'd closed the front door behind him and followed her down the path, so she started to run, and he jogged after her, saying her name, trying not to shout. When she ran straight past her own bus stop as if she meant to flee on foot all the way to Attercliffe, he slowed to a walk, ended the chase, and called out to her.

'OK, Alison, I'm not coming with you,' he shouted. She ignored him, though, flying down the pavement with her coat sailing open and her school bag thumping against her hip.

'Alison, please stop!'

There was a catch of distress in his voice, and it was this that she couldn't ignore, so she stopped and turned, and looked at him from the distance between them, her chest heaving.

'Please,' Daniel said. 'Come back, wait for your bus. I'm going home.'

She came back towards him and together they walked in silence the short distance back to her bus stop; then she said, 'I'm really sorry, Daniel. I can't really explain how I feel.'

He was silent, head down, hands thrust into his pockets.

'I don't have a house like yours or a family like yours,' she said.

'Right, well, I don't care a toss about that,' he said.

'No, I know, but, oh, I do care, and I . . . Daniel, please, just leave things be, will you?'

He looked at her and nodded. 'You bet,' he said; then he kissed her dryly on the cheek, and walked away without looking back, towards home, where he knew his mother would be at the window, waiting for him with her questioning, sympathetic face.

'I'll see you tomorrow though?' Alison called with a rising note of insecurity in her voice, so he raised a hand to show her he'd heard, and that yes, she'd see him tomorrow, but he didn't turn and smile, because he was hurt, and bewildered, and if she was going to hide her feelings, then so was he.

His mother was standing in the hallway when he got in.

'Well?' she said.

He shrugged.

'Whatever's the matter with her?'

'Mum, I don't know.' He felt a failure for not knowing, and she could see this so she didn't push. He started to climb the stairs.

'There's crumble,' she said, but without conviction. If she could, if he'd listen, she'd tell him to go carefully with Alison, she'd tell him not to lose his heart to a girl who fled at the mention of her own mother. But when he went into his bedroom and closed the door, she only sighed and let him be.

The bus lumbered towards Attercliffe, and when it finally stopped for her, Alison walked briskly through the short network of streets to her house. She knew she could mend things with Daniel tomorrow, but there was a cold knot of anxiety in her belly now, as she opened the door and braced herself for whatever lay in wait. All was quiet. No chaos, no mess, no Martin. There was a smell of stale urine, but that wasn't a mystery because there was a pile of Catherine's underwear on the floor by the sink, waiting to be washed.

'Peter?' she called.

'Upstairs,' he shouted back.

She was flooded with gratitude that he was in, he was here, when she'd been at Daniel's for all those hours, pleasing herself. She shed her coat, put her mother's tights and knickers in a bucket of cold water to soak, then trudged up to Peter's room, to be with him.

11

Dan's immediate neighbours on the canal were Lisa and Frank at the stern end, capable Jim at the bow. Lisa and Frank were old hippies, summer-of-love originals who claimed to have stayed on an ashram with the Beatles, but it was probably just the pot talking. Jim was lonely, a retired merchant seaman who couldn't live in a house, needed the gentle wash of water to rock him to sleep at night, missed his crew and the force-nine gales round the Bay of Biscay and the sardine sandwiches on the ten o'clock watch. He was also a first-rate handyman, always in a boiler suit, tinkering with his pristine narrowboat, *Veronica Ann*, rubbing down her paintwork, greasing her innards. Lisa and Frank's *Ophelia* was going to rack and ruin. She peeled and rusted with quiet grace while they cooked aloo gobi in the galley and ate it cross-legged on the flat roof, then lay on their backs and shared a joint. Jim battened down his hatch on this nefarious activity but many a time Dan joined them, although never if Katelin was with him. Student counsellors couldn't smoke pot, she said, and she wouldn't bend, even for Frank's home-grown cannabis, which – as Lisa said, without irony – was full of goodness, organically grown. But Katelin rarely came to London anyway; this was Dan's orbit, Dan's world. This city, these streets, this boat; her name was *Crazy Diamond*, the choice of a previous owner, but what a choice! Shine on, he'd thought when he saw her for the first time, a for-sale notice taped to her side, a phone number and 'Call Paddy' scrawled underneath in biro, like an instruction for Dan alone. So he'd called Paddy, and within two weeks he'd had a key to the boat and another to the towpath gate, and a licence from the Canal & River Trust to say, yes, *Crazy Diamond* was his. This was ten years ago, and Katelin had liked the idea very much at first, but then discovered she felt too confined to relax here, and the whole cassette-toilet thing freaked her out, so the boat had shifted, over time, from the notion of joint ownership to being only Dan's, his lair in London, and here, among this canal-dwelling crowd, he felt off-grid, cut loose. His stuff was all over the cabin and the place was a tip, a comfortable tip, on his own terms, and smoking pot with Frank and Lisa was just part of the same scene. They weren't reckless about it, or irresponsible; sometimes they burned bushy sprigs of rosemary on a barbecue on the towpath to mask the smell.

Tonight, the conversation meandered with the smoke from the fat joint, spiralling aimlessly into the sky. Frank and Lisa often spoke in riddles. Their minds had been expanded, back in 1967 on the ashram in Rishikesh, and now they couldn't think straight. Instead, they scattered observations or ideas into the beautiful chaos of the universe, without responsibility or ownership.

'Lisa, baby,' Frank said in his Haight-Ashbury hippy drawl. 'Awesome weed.'

Dan nodded. 'Compliments to the chef,' he said.

'We're a long way from finished,' Lisa said.

'The weed?' It was Dan's function, on nights like this, to weave something real from the loose threads.

'The journey,' Lisa said.

'Right,' said Dan. She held out the joint and he shook his head, so she passed it to Frank. Dan was done: already high, already happy. A couple or three drags were generally enough to loosen him up to a level where Frank and Lisa's conversation seemed half-cogent. He had his phone in his pocket, with Belle and Sebastian on it, from Ali. He felt warm, warm thoughts about Alison Connor as he lay here on the forgiving bulk of *Ophelia*. He'd smiled at her choice; he didn't mind a bit of Belle and Sebastian. He'd written enough about them in the late nineties, when they were taking off, a savvy bunch of students, just signed up with Jeepster. He wondered, did Ali know they were Scottish? She would, yeah, course she would. She wouldn't know that their drummer used to sell pies on match days out-side Celtic Park, though.

'Hey,' he said now. 'You want to listen to a song?'

'Sweet, sweet music,' Lisa said.

'Yep,' Dan said. 'So let's give it a listen.'

He fished his phone out of the pocket of his jacket, and clicked on to Ali's link, so that the weightless beauty of Sarah Martin's voice drifted around them in the night. Frank, stoned, thinking any song was his song, started to sing 'Waterloo Sunset' over the top of it and Lisa spluttered with merriment in that crazy way she had: unhinged, machine-gun laughter. But then, by some mir-acle, they both fell silent and let the song play out, and when it ended Lisa sighed feelingly and said, 'It's a bummer, getting old, being old.'

Dan smiled at her. No point denying it, she *was* getting on; the lines on her face and the backs of her hands told that story. But she'd dip-dyed her long grey hair into every shade of pink and she was still thin and loose-limbed, still wore her denim flares and cheesecloth shirts with panache. 'You're fucking amazing,' he said. 'Look at you.' She dipped her head modestly, and Frank raised the joint, what was left of it, in a sort of vague salute to Lisa's lasting beauty. Frank was older than her; he was *really* old, pushing eighty, not that he cared, the incorrigible old goat; he still watched women with a connoisseur's eye, as if he was a player, as if he stood a chance.

'So,' Frank said now, after a few beats of silence. 'What was that ephemeral shit we just heard?'

Dan laughed.

'It was the very young,' said Lisa. 'Singing a song.'

Dan said, 'Sweet song, sent to me by a sweet girl.'

He hadn't meant to say this, hadn't meant to say anything about Ali to anyone, ever, but there were no questions from Frank and Lisa. Sometimes, they were perfect company, thought Dan. With this pair, you could say anything at all, and still be safe.

'Familiar arms,' Lisa said. 'Make me dance.'

Frank turned his head towards her and studied her face, as if he was trying to remember who she was. 'Ell oh ell ay, Lola,' he said. 'You really got me. Give me the Kinks, every time.'

Lisa looked up at the stars, doing their thing as best they could in the over-lit London sky. 'Sometimes,' she said, 'I think I could just die of happiness.'

'Don't do that, baby,' Frank said. 'Don't do that.'

The pub in Camden Town was decorated with Día de los Muertos skulls and a big neon crucifix, and was rammed with rockers by the time Dan got there for the gig the following night. The venue was upstairs: 150 capacity, and a high-end PA system that allowed the rock, punk and metal bands that played here to go all the way. It was heaving tonight and Dan found his spot at the back of the room, leaned against the wall, and listened to the set. He had a lot of time for Lionize, their energy, their personality, the nod to Led Zep and Deep Purple, dusty vocals, great guitars, gorgeous melodies, some soaring psychedelia, a crazy dose of Hammond organ. It took him back to boyhood, but still ducked and weaved in the here-and-now. Clever guys. After the gig he switched on his phone, and found three missed calls from Katelin and two from Duncan. Shit. Duncan probably wanted to borrow some money, but Katelin only ever rang when there really was something to say. He stood in the late-night squalor of Greenland Place and called her back, and she picked up at once.

'Tell me that Duncan's not having an affair,' she said. Her voice was brittle.

Dan gave a small, surprised laugh. 'Gladly,' he said. 'Duncan's not having an affair.'

'You're lying.'

'What? What the hell, Katelin?'

'Duncan's having an affair, and you're covering for him.'

'Hey, Katelin, steady on, what is this?'

The violent siren wail of a speeding police car suddenly cut through the conversation and drowned her reply, and then another followed hard on the wheels of the first, so that Dan had to wait for a full thirty seconds before he spoke again.

'Sorry,' he said finally. 'Couldn't hear for the sirens. Look, just tell me what you think's happening.'

'Don't you take his side,' Katelin said.

'Katelin! I'm not taking his side. I don't know what you're on about.'

She started to speak but stopped immediately, as if suddenly struck by a new thought. Then, 'Hang on,' she said. 'He tells you everything, it's just not possible that you don't already know what he's been up to.'

He felt a pulse of anger now; this was Katelin with a few glasses of wine inside her, ready to take him on. She'd have spent the evening with Rose-Ann, and turned against him on the grounds of his gender, his friendship with the accused, his socks on the bedroom floor. He lowered the phone from his ear and allowed himself a couple of seconds to fume silently while Camden life teemed all around him; the pubs were kicking people out and a drunkard took a piss against the wall not two feet from where he was standing. He moved away, towards the entrance of the tube station, and when he spoke to Katelin again, he kept his voice level, steady, reasonable.

'Look, just tell me what's happened,' he said.

'Lindsay Miller, that's what's happened. She's a singer in a band, but you probably already know that.'

'Right, fuck this,' Dan said. 'I'm ringing Duncan,' and he hung up, filled with righteous indignation at the rank unfairness, her us-against-them affectation. He found Duncan's number and hit it, then waited, backed against a wall on Camden High Street, the phone pressed to his ear. There was the usual mayhem all around him. Cars in gridlock on the roads, cyclists jumping lights, too many people on pavements too narrow to contain them. Also there was a sickly smell: popcorn or candied peanuts, the wares of a street vendor somewhere nearby. Meanwhile, in Scotland, Duncan took his time, but he answered in the end.

'The universe as we know it,' he said with a sort of doleful humour, 'is officially over. It's life, Jim, but not as we know it.'

'Right,' Dan said. 'So I gather. A singer in a band?'

'Yeah, lovely Lindsay.'

'Fuck, man,' Dan said. 'Rose-Ann!'

'Yeah,' Duncan said. 'It's shite. She's mad as a sack of snakes, and fair enough.'

'Tell me she's not twenty.'

'She's not twenty.'

'Is she twenty?'

Duncan sighed. 'Thirty-two.'

'Christ, Duncan, I thought you'd finally become the original Steady Eddie.'

'Turns out there's life in the old dog yet.'

'Where are you now?'

'In the fucking doghouse, where else would the old dog be?'

Dan laughed, glad – oh, beyond glad – that Katelin wasn't party to this conversation.

'Go on then,' he said.

'She played a gig in Dundee a year or so ago, and I watched her and we got chatting afterwards, and it was like: Oh hello, here you are at last.'

'Fucking hell, a *year* ago?'

'No, no, nothing happened, and I never would've chased her. But then I saw her again in a bar in Glasgow three weeks ago, and she recognised me, grabbed my arse and kissed me hard.'

'Bloody hell, she came on to *you*?'

'Cheers, pal.'

'So you can't be that involved if it was only three weeks ago.'

'It doesn't feel that way to me right now.'

'Oh God, Duncan, I hope you know what you're doing.'

'Course I fucking don't,' Duncan said. 'Course I don't.' His voice cracked, and for one appalling moment Dan thought his friend was going to cry. But when he spoke again, he sounded almost cheerful. 'Hey, but look,' he said, 'she's someone you should meet.'

'Who is?'

'Lindsay.'

'Christ, Duncan, Katelin thinks I colluded in all this as it is.'

'She's magic,' Duncan said.

'You said that to me ten years ago, when you met Rose-Ann.'

'Shit, did I?'

'Where are you now?'

'Sat on the steps of Mick's building.'

'Christ, what you doing there? Look, come down to London tomorrow, you can have the boat for a while if you need some space.'

'Ah no,' Duncan said. 'I need to be up here.'

'Mick's a tosser, Duncan. Why'd you go there?'

'Lindsay's here.'

'Where, at Mick's?'

'In Glasgow. She's in Laurieston.'

Dan sighed, already nostalgic for the simple life. 'When I saw your missed calls,' he said, 'I thought it was just about money, or your singers.'

'Yeah,' Duncan said. 'I'd like to talk about that. Could do with clawing back some normality.'

'Yeah.'

'When you back?'

'Tomorrow,' Dan said.

'Who've you seen?'

'Lionize.'

'Oh yeah, any good?'

'Sure, very.'

There was a pause, a kind of short, respectful silence to honour the old days, then Duncan said, 'Come and see me, Dan. Mick's a cretin, and when I ring Rose-Ann, she either cries or spits venom. I need some sanity.' He sounded sad now, as sad as Dan had ever heard him.

'You bet, I'll come on the way home, tomorrow. Meet me on Gordon Street though, I'm not coming to Mick's. I'll be there by two.'

'Thanks, pal.' The line went dead. Dan stood for a while, picturing Duncan, out in the cold, in the stairwell of Mick Hastie's tenement building. He considered calling Katelin back, but decided against it; too late and anyway, it could wait; let her wait. He patted his pockets to make sure he hadn't been robbed as he'd stood talking on the phone, then descended into the rank warmth of the tube station.

Half past midnight at Warwick Avenue, and Dan was the only person to step off an almost-empty train. He loped up the towering escalator, and again up the steps to the exit, then walked quickly up and along to the Blomfield Road moorings, where he let himself through the gate on to the towpath and negotiated his way through the folded wooden chairs, coiled ropes, dead and dying potted plants and other detritus of towpath life. *Crazy Diamond* was waiting steadfastly for him on the black water. All was quiet. At either end, *Ophelia* and *Veronica Ann* were both dark and still. Frank and Lisa would be solid gone, curled on their bunks, sleeping the sleep of the seriously stoned, but Jim had the vigilant soul of a nightwatchman, he could be up and out of the cabin at the creak of a board, sweeping the vicinity with a flashlight, so Dan stepped gingerly on to the foredeck of his own vessel and turned the key carefully, silently, in the lock.

Inside, he flicked a switch and the lamps poured warm yellow light over the panelled interior: floor, ceiling, walls, all the same honeyed wood. He had a few books here, a box of CDs for the tidy little inbuilt sound system, and his old acoustic guitar, which always lived on the boat because nowadays he only ever played for himself, company on a quiet night, a workout for his fingers. There was a small armchair – a legacy from Paddy all those years before – a built-in day bed, a cooker, sink, fridge. A tiny bathroom – shower, sink, the compromised lavatory that kept Katelin in Edinburgh – and an only-just-double bed, built on a raised platform, with a porthole which by daylight framed a ritzy stuccoed villa facing him on the opposite side of the canal.

Dan took a beer from the fridge, flipped the lid, then sprawled across the sofa and – as he often did, these days – permitted himself the luxury of thinking a while about Alison Connor: the girl he used to know, not the woman she'd become. Alison sprang so easily to mind now, after all those years of absence, and when he closed his eyes he could see her clearly in 3D, a perfectly formed hologram girl in his Sheffield bedroom, where most of their hours together had been spent. God, she'd meant all the world to him when he was eighteen. He'd thought they'd break out of Sheffield together, grow up together, live their lives together, raise funky children with a proper appreciation of music together. When she went – bleak, bleak day, the day he realised she'd gone – she put him into a state of pain so dark, so deep, that he didn't properly start to heal until he found Katelin four years later in Bogotá. Alison Connor. The smell of her hair, what was it? Just shampoo and Sheffield, probably, but Christ, it was good. And her laugh! Making Alison laugh was the best, it was payday, because she was such a grave and serious girl, as if all her life she'd been wary of fun. She'd fitted into his family life like a hand into a fucking glove; then she'd left them high and dry. There'd been some competition back then for whose heart was in worse shape, his own or his dad's. Bill had retreated to the pigeon loft for days, and nobody'd believed Alison wasn't coming back.

Dan drained his beer and sat up. He needed a song for Ali and he knew now what it was going to be. Frank Ocean, 'Thinkin Bout You', a slow-burn, beautiful, intimate torch song from R&B's new wunderkind. Dan copied the link, and pasted it on the growing thread he shared with Ali.

There you are, Alison, he thought. See what you make of that, all the way across the globe, down under in your Adelaide bedroom. He binned his empty bottle and thought about going to bed, then at the door there was a tap-tap-tap, a looming shadow, a hesitant voice. 'Ahem, Dan? All well in there?'

Jim.

Dan sighed and hung his head. 'Yes, Jim, fine. You OK?'

'Oh, tickety-boo, but since you're still up, I've some Lamb's Navy Rum, fancy a tot?'

Dan unlocked the door and opened it, intending to say no thanks, early start, train to catch. But there stood Jim, hope like a light in his eyes, a bottle in one hand and two enamel mugs in the other.

'Haven't seen much of you,' Jim said. 'Haven't seen a soul all day, in fact.'

So Dan smiled and held open the door. 'Can't be having that, Jim,' he said. 'Come on in.'

12

QUORN,
17 NOVEMBER 2012

Sheila put two strong flat whites down on the table in the tiny courtyard garden of the Quorn Café.

'Right,' she said, sitting down opposite Ali. 'Time to spill.'

Ali added sugar to her coffee and stirred – her habitual delaying tactic in such situations – then she looked at Sheila.

'You can't share this,' she said. 'You mustn't. Even with Dora. At least, not until we leave.'

Sheila nodded. 'Understood.'

Ali sighed. 'Stella's pregnant,' she said.

Sheila, to her credit, didn't wince or grimace or miss a beat. 'Ah, right, so that's it. I see.'

'We're not discussing it, unless Stella wants to,' Ali said. 'This trip's a temporary escape.'

'Yes, well, this town's perfect for that,' Sheila said.

It was, thought Ali: a perfectly preserved little frontier town in the back of beyond. Right now, Stella was off with Ali's Nikon, taking arty shots of the disused rolling stock on the train tracks, and the faded, filigree grandeur of the Victorian shop fronts. The sky here seemed bigger and emptier than in Adelaide; the sun blazed, unhindered by cloud, on to the tin roofs of the houses, and the heat shimmered and danced above the surface of the roads. It was shady right here, though, under a plane tree in the café courtyard; and a bubbling water feature, a beatific cross-legged stone Shiva, supplied the sound – if not the sensation – of liquid coolness. Now and again, a resident pair of sulphur-crested cockatoos left their leafy perch to dip their beaks into the pool of water in Shiva's cupped hands.

'Does she want to be pregnant?' Sheila asked now.

'She says so,' Ali said. 'But that might only be because Thea's loudly insisting she has an abortion.'

'Do you know the boy?'

Ali shook her head. 'Nope, Stella won't tell us. It was just the once, apparently.' Tears sprang to her eyes, and she groped blindly in her bag for a tissue. 'God, Sheila, I feel such a failure.'

Sheila pulled a handkerchief from her sleeve and passed it across the table. 'Alison,' she said.

Ali took the hankie, wiped her eyes, blew her nose, sniffed disconsolately. 'What?'

'Your success as a mother isn't in doubt here.' She pointed at Ali's cup, still full, untouched. 'Drink some coffee,' she said. 'It's excellent. And don't heap blame on yourself.'

'Hard not to,' Ali said. 'I feel I took my eye off the ball. I've been so distracted lately, I do feel I've let her down.'

'Stella's going to be just fine,' Sheila said. 'She has the same beautiful determination as you, and Lord knows you had a far worse start.'

Ali looked hard at her coffee and Sheila said, 'Oh, sweetheart, we never talk about your life in Sheffield, do we?'

'No need,' Ali said, glancing up, then down again.

'Catherine gave you such a difficult—'

'Sheila, why are we talking about this?'

'Because we never have, and there's something on my mind. When you came to see me all those years ago in Elizabeth, and

I didn't know that you didn't know Catherine had died, and I just blurted it out like a fool – well, you were like stone, you didn't even cry, and I wish I'd—'

'Sheila, please. We were talking about Stella.'

'There must still be a lot of unshed grief there . . .'

'No,' Ali said with a firm authority that brought the older woman to a sharp halt. Sheila knew nothing, nothing, about Ali's life in Attercliffe, the fear and the shame, the dread of scandal, the horror that she might be pitied, the endless efforts at damage limitation that were part of the daily routine. 'No, there isn't a lot of unshed grief, and we're going to fall out, Sheila, if you keep pushing me on this. I'm sorry to snap, but you know nothing about it. Catherine was an extremely sick woman who held life very cheap.'

Sheila, not in the least offended, gazed at Ali with a most unwelcome empathy; then, in a portentous tone that made her heart sink further, she said, 'Well, anyway, I'd like to say one thing more, and it's this. I let you down very badly when you first came to Australia.'

'No, I'm not having that,' Ali said, thinking: This is all so long ago, so far away. 'I had Michael by then, we came to see you together, remember?'

But Sheila wasn't listening. 'I was poor Catherine's oldest friend,' she said. 'And that gave me a kind of responsibility towards you, but I was nearly crazy with my own unhappiness at the time.'

'Listen, Sheila,' Ali said. 'If there's one thing Catherine taught me, it was to take care of myself. I didn't come to you looking for help, we were just visiting.' She had no wish to be dragged backwards into the distant turmoil of Sheila's unhappy marriage, or the whys and wherefores of Catherine's death, the details of which had travelled to Sheila via her own mother, back in Liverpool. And no, Ali thought, she hadn't cried when Sheila broke the news, she'd only thought thank God that's over, because Peter would be free.

Ali knew she was right: Michael had been with her; he'd driven her up there. But he hadn't been party to that conversation, and she hadn't told him afterwards either, because this was her Year Zero, the very start of their marriage, the sparkling, clear-cut early days when she'd reinvented her life so completely it was sometimes hard to recognise herself. And oh, how Michael had hated that visit – Sheila and Kalvin's little house, the smallness of everything, the cheek-by-jowl ordinariness. He'd spent most of the time in the garden pretending to study the herbaceous border. When Ali came outside to find him he'd said, 'Thank God, now let's get the hell out of Dodge.'

Now, Sheila reached for Ali's hands and clasped them tight, and for a few moments Ali submitted to the searching intensity of her gaze, until a young woman in a denim apron approached their table from inside the café and saved her.

'Hey,' said the waitress. 'How you goin'?'

'Great, thanks,' Ali said, tugging her fingers free from the emotional urgency of Sheila's grip.

'Good to hear. Can I get you ladies anything to eat?'

'Ah, no thanks,' Ali said.

'Yes, we'll have some raisin toast, Megan,' Sheila said. 'We've had a heart-to-heart here, and we need the sustenance.'

'Raisin toast for two?'

'Oh no, none for me,' said Ali.

Sheila said, 'Raisin toast for *two*, Megan darling,' and she winked at the waitress, who smiled and raised her eyebrows at Ali in a sort of helpless apology before turning from them and going back inside. Ali looked at Sheila and said, 'Sustenance? We already had Dora's special honey granola today.'

'I know, but there's something about you makes me want to feed you up,' Sheila said. 'Also, I'm terribly greedy.' She laughed and slapped the top of the table, making the coffee cups bounce in their saucers and scaring the cockatoos; they flung themselves upwards, and their beating white wings were huge and quite startlingly beautiful against the hard blue sky.

Over dinner that night, Dora proposed a trip north, two hours' drive, maybe a little less, up the outback roads to Wilpena Pound. It turned out Dora could fly a plane as well as drive a train, and there was a Cessna she could borrow; she could take them up for a bird's eye view from the little airfield out there.

'It's not my plane, it belongs to Clancy,' she said, as if this information clarified everything.

'Nephew,' Sheila explained, and Dora nodded.

'That's right, so will I give him a call?'

Ali wasn't sure: she thought it all sounded irregular, if not actually illegal, but Stella just said, 'Awesome,' and Sheila was already dragging the Esky from the cupboard under the stairs to give it a wipe down inside. So Dora rang Clancy, and very early the next morning they set off in Ali's car, the Esky packed with bottled water in case, Sheila said, the car blew a gasket in the Never Never. The town was still sleeping as they left it behind, and the sun hung tremulously low on the horizon.

'Whack up the heat, sweetheart,' Sheila said. She was wrapped in a voluminous alpaca wool poncho but still she complained about the chill, and it was true there was no heat in the day yet. But the new morning sky promised much; pale and clear, it seemed freshly rinsed. A perfect day, Dora said, for flying.

'You wait,' she kept saying to Ali and Stella. 'You wait. It's just the most incredible sight.'

She was in the front with Ali, and Sheila was with Stella on the back seat. The atmosphere was jolly, no mistaking it; like a school trip, Stella said – like the Year 6 surf day at Aldinga Beach. Their road north was straight and true, an unwavering ribbon of asphalt unfurling through the ancient landscape, and the miles rolled easily by as the golden farmlands of the southern Flinders began to change into something else entirely, a dry and dramatic vista of red desert scrub: saltbush, bluebush, mallee. Stella snapped pictures of incurious kangaroos through the open window of the car, and once they had to stop as a ragged line of dusty emus jogged across the road ahead.

'This,' Stella said, 'is *so* cool.'

'Outback colours,' Sheila said. 'A palette of rust and ochre.'

'Well, I meant the emus,' Stella said. 'And the roos.'

Ali looked for Stella in the rear-view mirror, and winked. Stella's amusement sparkled, like sunshine on water.

They reached the airfield soon after eight, and Clancy was waiting for them there, leaning against his Cessna, a middle-aged ocker, a Victoria Bitter kind of guy: early-morning stubble, bit of a beer gut, weathered bush hat, khaki combats, faded denim shirt. He grinned and waved when Ali's old Holden estate pulled up in front of the wire fence.

'G'day, ladies,' he said when they got out. He tipped his hat and cast a bold, appreciative eye over Ali and Stella and said, 'Well, the scenery just got heaps better,' so Ali folded her arms and held his gaze, as if to say, I've got your number, mate.

'And it's bonzer timing,' Clancy said. 'You're getting up there early before the easterlies blow you to buggery.' He opened the door of the little plane and then watched them clamber up. 'Barge arses up front, for ballast,' he said, slapping Sheila on the rump. 'Sexy arses in the back, and, Dora, I need it back this arvo so don't get lost.'

Dora rolled her eyes and said, 'Rough as bags,' but she blew him a kiss as he slammed the door; then he gave them a thumbs-up and stepped away from the plane, holding on to his hat as Dora, unlikely though it seemed to Ali, took the plane down the runway and lifted it competently up, up and away. Now they had to yell to make themselves heard, but almost immediately they fell silent, giving up on conversation to stare down in a sort of wondering humility at the receding earth, as the little plane banked effortlessly up and over towards the extraordinary serrated crown of Wilpena Pound. It rose from the earth, a primeval amphitheatre of proportions so majestic that the landscape it stood in seemed dwarfed by comparison. The sun, higher now in the cloudless sky, drenched the jagged mountain ridges with a preternatural glow, and as the Cessna followed the jagged ellipsis of the pound, tracking its monumental outline, Stella snapped picture after picture; then she spun round to Ali and tugged at her sleeve and said something completely inaudible into the roar and racket of the labouring engine.

'What?' Ali shouted. Then again, louder, 'What?'

Stella leaned in closer. 'I said: bonzer views,' she shouted, and perhaps it was the altitude that made them light-headed, or the alien beauty of planet Earth, or the coruscating blue of the sky, but they started to laugh and couldn't stop, and Sheila, twisting round to look fondly at them, smiled in recognition of that feeling: the ecstasy of mirth.

Afterwards they drove back as far as Hawker, then stopped for an early lunch in the bar of a small hotel, where Dora seemed to know almost everyone they encountered. Sheila said this was how it always was with Dora; it was as if she'd lived a dozen lives so that she need never be lonely. She'd had husbands too, so had garnered networks of extended families who'd loved and lost her. She was Dora Langford now, having reverted to her own surname when she met Sheila, but once, way, way back, she'd been – albeit briefly – Dora Franklin, one of *the* Franklins, the Franklins who'd established a sheep station in the 1840s and made a mint out of merino wool. For a couple of years Dora had had pots of money and all the conferred cachet of an early settler's surname. Then she'd ditched her Franklin boy and married William Tremblath, the ruddy-cheeked descendant of a Penzance tin miner.

'Wow,' Stella said, enthralled. 'Dora Tremblath!'

'That's me,' Dora said, coming back to the table from the bar with a bottle of good white wine in an ice bucket, and a Coke for Stella. 'I mean, it *was* me.'

'Two husbands and a wife, Dora,' Ali said. 'Good going.'

'Three husbands, actually, sweetheart,' Sheila said. 'There was that opal miner in Andamooka.'

'Oh, shivers, so there was,' Dora said. 'Crikey, I forgot about him.'

She sloshed wine into three glasses and pushed one across the table to Ali and another to Sheila, who raised hers and said, 'Girls on tour,' and they all four lifted their drinks and clinked. Around them, the bar was filling up: tradies, truckers, tourists. The barman appeared with their food order, burgers and fries, and Stella clapped, eyes alight with glee. 'Coke and a burger,' she said. 'Beatriz would chuck a berko.'

'She would,' Ali said. 'And so would your dad, if he could hear you talking like that.'

'Speaking of the mighty McCormack,' Dora said to Ali, 'weren't his family wool barons from Burra way?'

'Copper, then wool,' Ali said. 'But, obviously, way before my time.'

'Is there a lovely big sheep station somewhere up there, then?'

'Oh, you bet,' Stella said, jumping in. 'With a *huge* house and its own chapel, where all the McCormacks got married, until Dad and Mum broke the rules.'

Dora looked at Ali. 'Do tell,' she said.

'Oh, well, we married quickly and very young,' Ali said, stripping her words of all possible drama.

'They married overseas,' Stella said. 'Mum was only eighteen, weren't you, Mum? They met and married while they were travelling. God, this burger is *so* good.'

'Oh, Michael's mother was so angry.' Ali picked up her glass and took a cautious sip of Riesling, and it was so cold and clean, she wanted to knock it straight back, the way Sheila and Dora were doing. But she had to drive in a straight line to Quorn, and even if either of them were offering to drive – and they weren't – she couldn't let them now. Dora had already drained her own glass, topped it up, then topped up Sheila's. They were each going at it as if the wine were water.

'Well, sure,' Sheila said. 'I mean, she would've been cross as a frog in a sock. Those Adelaide matriarchs are something else.'

'What was the rush?' Dora said.

Ali shrugged. 'No rush at all. But he liked the big romantic gesture, and I guess I was up for a new start.' She smiled at Stella and said, 'Grandma McCormack thought I was after the family fortune.'

Stella said, 'Well, big shame she's not still alive because you're way richer than Dad now.'

'Oh, Stella!' Ali said. 'What a load of nonsense.'

'And your book's going to be a film.'

'Yes!' Sheila said. 'I read about that. All that music brought to life. I love Baz Luhrmann. Has he cast it yet?'

'I heard there was to be open casting for the indigenous kids,' Dora said.

Ali said, 'Look, for all we know, it might never get made. Can we talk about something else?'

'But, Alison,' Sheila said, 'you're a raging success, darling. A working-class lass with the world at her feet.'

'Hardly. I'm a cog in the machine.'

'What will you do with all your riches?' This was Dora, half-cut now, and oblivious to Ali's discomfort. 'Will you buy a racehorse? A Maserati? A huge place by the sea at Port Willunga?'

'Ooh yes, Mum, do that,' Stella said.

'No,' Ali said slowly, allowing an idea to take shape. 'I'm going to give the money away.'

Sheila laughed heartily, certain this was only a line to silence them all. 'Don't do that, sweetheart. Just look at Stella's face, look how much she wants the beach house.'

'No, I'm serious,' Ali said. 'I'm having a eureka moment here.'

The McCormack coffers needed no help from Ali Connor. But if she was making a fortune from the musicians she'd invented, why not use it to fund some real ones? She remembered a night, a long time ago now, out with Cass at a gig in Port Adelaide: a Pitjantjatjara girl on stage, intense, absorbed, a singer-songwriter with lyrics, some in her own language, that pulsed with a kind of poetic fury, a performer evidently blessed with such astounding musicality that Cass, when the girl ended her set, had started a standing ovation, whipping the small crowd into communal rapture. Ali had seen her perform many times since then, but it was that first night, that girl, her music: they had planted the seeds, perhaps ten years before Ali wrote it, of *Tell the Story, Sing the Song.* And now, here she was, with the power to bring about a perfect ending in the real world. She felt a sudden and wonderful lightness of spirit, a sort of resolute optimism, as if nothing was beyond her. She smiled at her daughter, lovely Stella, who wouldn't smile back, not yet, not while her mother was being so *weird*.

'It's all going to be fine, darling,' Ali said. 'It's all going to be great.'

Later, as they began to gather themselves for the journey home, Ali switched her phone on for the first time that day, and saw at once, among the notifications, the only one she was looking for. *Dan Lawrence sent you a link*. She slipped out from behind the table and headed for the ladies', where she shut herself in a cubicle and stood with her back to the locked door, and for a while simply closed her eyes and conjured his image and tried – though failed – to hear his voice. She set her mind loose, let it roam where it wanted to go, and she found (and this was extra-ordinary to her) that she wanted to tell him about her big idea: talk it all through with him, hear his thoughts on her thoughts, make him real.

But she didn't have his number and it was pre-dawn in the UK, and anyway, whatever would he think if she should call him out of the blue, a long-lost girlfriend with an Aussie accent? *Hey, Dan, this is Alison, how you going?*

No. No. She must just look at the link, that's all: listen to the song as he'd intended. So she opened her eyes and found her way there, and saw 'Thinkin Bout You' by Frank Ocean – a song and a singer she didn't know, and this not knowing made her shiver with anticipated pleasure of the new, the undiscovered.

Her earphones were in her bag, which was still at the table, so she just pressed play and immediately something brilliant and beguiling filled the space around her, and she leaned on the door and let it happen, hearing lyrics that made her remember how much she'd allowed herself to forget. They spoke of first love, uncertainty, a relationship that lay just out of reach, and beneath the words ran a gorgeous, ethereal backing track, meltingly, achingly beautiful. Daniel Lawrence, she thought, you were, and are, my perfect music match. Then she felt the door rattling behind her, an insistent knocking, and Stella's voice, on a rising note of bewilderment.

'Mum? Is that you?'

At once, Ali stopped the song. 'Hi, darling,' she said. 'You OK?'

'Mum? What are you doing?'

Ali unlocked the door and came out. 'Listening to a song,' she said.

Stella looked at her, her face stern with uncertainty. 'Why?' she said.

'Why not?' Ali smiled, and ruffled Stella's hair. 'Is everything OK out there?'

'They're so drunk,' Stella said. 'They're holding hands across the table and they didn't even notice me leave.'

'Uh-oh,' Ali said. 'Better get 'em home.' She slipped the phone into the pocket of her jeans, then ran her hands under the hot tap, flapping them about to dry them off. 'You need the loo?' she said.

'No. I just came to find you.'

'Right then, let's get those old reprobates out of here.'

'Mum?'

'Yep?'

Stella, about to speak, hesitated instead.

'Nothing,' she said.

Back in Quorn, in the silence left behind when Dora and Sheila crashed out in bed to sleep off the booze and Stella went out with the camera again, to catch the golden early-evening light, Ali selected a song for Dan, taking him back in time to Carole King. 'So Far Away'. Love, loss, longing, regret, and a compelling connection, crossing continents.

Yeah. His face, at her door. That *would* be fine. Really, very fine indeed. She lay down on the old sofa and listened to *Tapestry*, the whole album, beginning to end. They hadn't ever listened to this together when they were kids, it wasn't their thing then, but hey, she thought, if Dan Lawrence didn't love it now, it was all off. Whatever 'it' was.

Stella came back as the day was losing its light.

'Mum,' she said, and Ali sat up, alert to the seriousness in her daughter's voice.

'What is it, sweetheart?'

'I really, badly, don't want to have a baby,' Stella said, and then she started to cry.

13

SHEFFIELD,
27 JULY 1979

There was a local band Daniel sometimes roadied for, three lads
from Sheffield and another from Rotherham. Steve Levitt, Mark
Vernon, John Spencer and a guy they all called Dooley. They
used to be called the National Union; now they were just the
Union. A talented, moody, post-punk outfit, with a part-time
manager and their eyes on a glimmer of light that might just be a
rock-and-roll future. Steve, older than the others by a good eight
years, was founder of the band, unchallenged boss, architect of
their immediate future. Charismatic, confident, ambitious, a bit
of a bad lot: petty larceny, minor assault – a few years ago now,
but that was only to be expected round here, and anyway such a
reputation didn't hurt, to be honest, in a band like theirs. John
Spencer did pot, or speed, he was never without one or the other,
and their manager – a sponsor, really; a local businessman with
a Malcolm McLaren delusion – had considered shopping him to
the police, just for the publicity.

Anyway, the Union were better than most of the bands currently jostling for attention in Sheffield, and they were getting
gigs in cities other than their own – small venues, thin crowds,
but the buzz was growing by the week, and then they were
offered a slot in Manchester at the Mayflower Club, way down

the pecking order, but with serious punk and new wave bands that were making it: Joy Division, the Fall, the Distractions, the Frantic Elevators. It was billed as a 'Stuff the Superstars Special' and it felt like a big break, but two days before the gig, Mark Vernon was killed in a hit-and-run on Arundel Gate in the city centre, and Steve told Daniel he'd have to step in. There was no emotion, no question of bailing on the gig and Steve brooked no objections; he said Daniel knew the set list, knew the sound, he'd got the look. But his guitar was crap, Daniel told Steve; and he'd never played it anywhere except his own fucking bedroom.

'Vernon's dead, but his guitar int,' Steve said. 'Have it.'

So Daniel took Mark's sleek black Gibson from the back of the van and had one night to rehearse with the band, an emergency session in a back room at the miners' welfare in High Green, where John Spencer's dad was barman. Daniel felt like an imposter, stepping into a dead man's shoes, but the guitar felt good, looked great, sounded better than he dared hope.

Alison came along to listen. She put herself way back from the mighty amps, standing in the lee of a hundred stacked metal chairs, and watched the band with a sort of fierce, assessing concentration. They were good together. Steve was better than good. He was brilliant, a proper frontman: hypnotic vocals, and a look all his own, a sort of blue-collar dandy. Daniel was talented enough to appear more talented than he was. Dooley, on bass, was solid, dependable, and John played the drums like a maestro when necessary, like a maniac when he could.

Steve sang every number looking directly, intently, at Alison. Afterwards he stalked across the dusty wooden floor to where she was standing and asked her if she could sing. Steve was tall – well over six feet – and he wore a pristine pair of steelworker's boots, desert camouflage combat trousers, a canary-yellow

T-shirt and a brown twill overcoat. Daniel watched from a distance, Mark Vernon's classic Gibson still slung across his body. He felt about twelve years old.

'Y'what?' Alison said. She screwed up her face, looked sceptical. She hadn't fallen under Steve's spell, but he didn't know it.

'You look good enough to eat,' Steve said. 'Who are you?'

'Alison Connor,' she said, and she pointed at Daniel, across the room. 'I'm with him.'

Steve cast a look over his shoulder at Daniel and widened his eyes, as if recalibrating his opinion of him, then he looked back at Alison. 'I might want a female vocalist, and I definitely want her to look like you,' he said. 'Backing singer, two or three songs. Can you sing?'

'Which songs?' Alison said.

He gave a small laugh and said – patiently, as if he was humouring her – ' "Juliet". "No Safe Place". Maybe "Evermore".'

She nodded. 'Right.'

He stared at her for a moment. Cocked his head. Weighed her up. 'You're fuckin' gorgeous, Alison Connor. But can you sing?'

Alison met Steve's calculating eyes with cool control. 'Yeah, I can sing,' she said. 'But you'll have to say please.'

Daniel thought, Jesus, she's fearless. It was news to him that Steve wanted a female vocalist; news to Dooley and John too, by the looks on their faces. They'd already got their sodding roadie on lead guitar – why would they shove in an untried new vocalist too? Only Daniel had heard Alison sing, in his bedroom, unselfconsciously accompanying Debbie Harry and Marc Bolan and Elvis Costello and Bowie. He knew how good she was. He wondered, should he go over? Wander across the room, nonchalantly, just to emphasise her unavailability? But he didn't, and instead hung back with the band, watching his girlfriend give the local legend a mildly hard time.

'Alison Connor,' Steve said, 'will you have a go at singing backing vocals for me, please?'

'OK,' she said. She was familiar with the songs; she'd heard the band play their full set tonight, and on previous nights too, and lyrics that she liked tended to penetrate her mind like a kind of gospel: the way, the truth, the life. She walked around Steve, across the room to the rest of the band, and stood in front of Daniel. With her back to Steve she rolled her eyes, and Daniel grinned at her.

'You were good,' she said.

He nodded, accepting the compliment. 'But you'll be better,' he said.

'Right,' Steve said, back at the mic. '"Juliet". Dooley, get Alison a mic. Alison, I want you to come in on the back of me, at the last line of the first verse, just, like, repeat it, twice maybe, see what works, we'll muck about with it. Then chime in at the middle eight, whatever sounds right. We'll suck it and see.'

Dooley passed her a mic, plugged her in.

'Thanks,' she said to him. Then, to Steve, 'I'll give it a go.'

'Ah shit, you'll need the words. Dooley, find some fuckin' words, fuck's sake.'

Dooley, hunched once again over his guitar waiting for the off, looked injured. 'Wha'?' he said.

'The fuckin' words!' Steve said, like he was talking to a moron. 'Get 'em, for Alison.'

'No, it's all right, Dooley,' Alison said. 'I know them already.'

Steve looked upwards, to where the gods of rock were watching and waiting. 'She knows them already,' he said. 'Halle-fuckin'-lujah.'

Three or four run-throughs and Alison nailed it, her voice honey to Steve's sulky gravel. She knew his lyrics like he knew them himself and she had all the right instincts: sang without ego, heard the spaces that waited for her in the music, used her voice to complement Steve's with another layer of sound, light and lovely. Only in 'Juliet' did she play about with the words, adding a kind of sweet, insolent comeback to his macho, half-hearted apology to a girl he left behind. Dooley looked at Daniel and mugged an expression of awed astonishment, and Daniel, equally impressed, only shrugged.

Afterwards, Steve was intent on pinning her down to dates and times – gigs, rehearsals – and he hovered about, badgering her with questions, as she came and went from the welfare hall into the muggy summer night, helping pack the equipment back into the van. John's dad watched at the open door, his arms folded across his beer belly, a bunch of keys bristling from his fat fist.

'I said till ten,' he kept saying when anyone passed him. 'Ten o'clock, I said. Not twenty past eleven. Ten.'

Alison stopped and smiled regretfully at him. 'I'm really sorry, Mr Spencer,' she said. 'It's because they wanted me to sing.'

He looked at her askance, noticing her properly for the first time. 'You're never involved with this shower, are you?' he said. He had a florid face, a swollen nose, the curse of a landlord too keen on beer and too free with the optics. 'What a bloody racket.'

She laughed. 'I suppose if you liked it, we'd be doing it wrong,' she said, but so reasonably, and with such a friendly smile, that he took it as a compliment to his own good taste.

'Aye, right enough, lass,' he said. 'Right enough.' And he whistled and waited almost good-naturedly as they hauled their trappings into Steve's Transit. Then they clambered in themselves, Dooley and John slammed behind the doors of the windowless back like hostages, Alison and Daniel up front on the seats with Steve. When he turned the key in the ignition the Buzzcocks bounced violently out of the speakers, and Steve turned them up further still, loud enough that people on the pavements turned to look, and shook their heads. He lit a cigarette, took a hungry drag, then held it in a pinch between right thumb and forefinger and drove left-handed with a sort of reckless, casual skill, letting go of the wheel altogether to change gear. He was going to drop Alison last – it made perfect sense – but she hopped out with Daniel at Nether Edge and wouldn't get back in.

'C'mon,' Steve said, leaning right across the passenger seats to talk to her through the open window. 'Dunt be daft, I'll keep me hands to meself.'

Daniel said, 'Bloody right, you will,' but Alison ignored them both and walked away, so he jogged after her. 'Do you want a lift home?' he said. 'Because I can ride with you to Attercliffe, sit between you and him. It'd save you waiting for a bus?' She shook her head. It was late, but she didn't want to go back home yet, and most certainly didn't want to be driven all the way to her door. Anyway, Steve was already swinging the Transit in a U-turn in the street and screaming away towards the main road, so they went to Daniel's house and found Claire there, and Joe, Daniel's brother, who only turned up once in a blue moon. Both were in the front room, which was softly lit by a single standard lamp and the glow of the television. There was something so peaceful, even beautiful, in the mundane scene, and Alison reached for Daniel's hand, laced her fingers through his, the better to belong here.

'Evening, you two,' Joe said, without taking his eyes off the screen. 'It's the late film, only just starting.'

'Hiya, Alison,' Claire sang, and her voice and smile registered sheer delight. She patted the sofa. 'Sit down next to me while our Daniel puts the kettle on.' She had her bare feet planted in a washing-up bowl of soapy water. 'Foot bath,' she said before

Alison asked. 'It's right good when you've been on your feet all day.' She wiggled her toes, and splashed, and Alison laughed. Claire, softly pink and pampered, was wrapped in a pale blue quilted dressing gown; she looked cherished. Her hands, folded demurely in her lap, were creamy white, tipped with raspberry-red oval nails. Alison sat down beside her. Daniel had gone into the kitchen.

'You smell nice,' Alison said.

'I had a bath earlier, and put some Radox in,' Claire said. She bared a tender forearm and offered it for Alison to sniff, which she did.

'Lovely.'

'Sea minerals, or something,' Claire said. 'Feel how soft it makes my skin.'

Joe glanced across. 'Claire, shut up,' he said. 'I'm watching this.'

Claire smiled amiably. Alison looked at the screen, where some sort of psychedelic dream sequence was unfolding. 'What is it?' Alison asked.

'*The Underground Man*,' Joe said. 'Book's good.'

'I'm not bothered about watching it, myself,' Claire said. 'But there's nothing else on this time of night.'

Joe turned up the volume.

'Where've you been then?' Claire asked, speaking a little louder. 'Somewhere nice?'

'High Green, miners' welfare,' Alison said, and Claire pulled a doubtful face, and when Daniel came in with four mugs of tea, she said, 'High Green, Daniel? Funny place to take your girlfriend.'

He stood in front of Alison and she reached up, took a mug, and smiled at him. His hair had fallen across his eyes again and he blew upwards out of the corner of his mouth so he could see her properly, an unconscious habit, so familiar to her now. They held each other's gaze for a moment; then Alison stood up.

'Shall we take this upstairs?' she said.

She woke with a jolt, as if she'd been prodded. Daylight. She was in Daniel's single bed and he was sleeping beside her, on his back, with one arm flung above his head. His other arm cradled her to him so that to move, she had to carefully peel him away and ease herself from his warmth. She'd never stayed the night here, and told herself now that she really hadn't meant to, although the last bus to Attercliffe was already long gone by the time they'd shrugged off their clothes and tumbled together on to the bed. Each time they had sex, Alison felt a little less self-conscious about it, Daniel a little more competent, each of them a little more at home. Last night, when the sex was over but their bodies were still pressed close, Alison had held her mouth against his ear and told Daniel she loved him, but he was on the very edge of sleep by then, and he didn't really hear, he only murmured something incoherent in reply, hardly words at all. Then they'd both slept, deeply, until that slice of sunlight sidling in through a gap in the curtains had fallen across Alison's face, making her acknowledge the day.

Now, she slipped from the bed and dressed swiftly, watching Daniel, wondering if she should wake him. She hovered over him for a moment, studied the contours of his mouth, considered a kiss, but decided against it. Daniel awake would only delay her departure and she'd see him again in just a few hours anyway; Steve was picking them all up from the bus station at one o'clock, then they were crossing the Pennines to the May-flower Club. So instead, she tiptoed out of his bedroom, holding her shoes in one hand and their two mugs of last night's tea, stone cold, undrunk, in the other. Down the stairs, cautious and light as a cat. At the foot of the stairs she placed her shoes carefully on the floor and went barefoot into the kitchen with the mugs; there was Daniel's dad reading yesterday's *Star* and, in front of him, a freshly brewed pot of tea waiting under a knitted cosy. He looked up and said, 'All right, love?' as if nothing was more natural than that Alison Connor should materialise before him at half past five on a Saturday morning. She blushed, feeling caught in the act, and ashamed, but he just said, 'Sit down, lass, you need summat warm in your belly before you go. Any road, there's no buses yet.' So she tipped the cold tea into the sink and washed the mugs, while behind her Bill Lawrence poured two fresh ones.

She loved Mr Lawrence. She liked Mrs Lawrence too, and Mrs Lawrence liked Alison, on the whole; it was just she had a weather eye out for her younger son and this caused her to hold back, and wonder if this girl was too young, and too unsteady, to be trusted with Daniel's heart. But Bill – he was smitten. Daniel said it was because Alison asked his dad questions about the pigeons, when nobody else was interested. This might have been true, but Alison didn't need to know why she and Bill Lawrence had clicked; she only needed to know she could rely on his smile.

'I'm really sorry, Mr Lawrence,' she said now, taking a seat opposite him. 'I should've left last night.'

'Not likely,' he said. 'Not after dark, not after closing time. You did right, staying put.'

'Well, thank you,' she said. She knew he would never ask if she'd be missed, at home. He seemed to understand Alison's taboos without being told.

She sipped her tea, he slurped his.

'Do you always get up this early?' Alison asked.

'Aye. This time o' year, any road.'

'Because it's light?'

'Aye, and I like the quiet.'

'And the pigeons wake early too, I expect?'

'Aye, love, they do.'

There was a comfortable pause, then Alison said, 'Could we have our tea in the loft?'

He bestowed a beam of pure sunshine upon her. 'Come on,' he said, standing up. He unbolted the back door and held it open for her. 'After you, twinkletoes,' he said.

She laughed and, still bare-footed, picked her way gingerly down the garden path to the shed. Mr Lawrence followed her. He was training a youngster, called Bess, and he told Alison how she was doing – grand – and asked her if she'd like to come out with him in a week or so, on Bess's first five-mile flight.

'Oh, yes please!' she said.

'Right you are,' he said, and they settled down with their tea in the warm, feathered fug of the converted shed. The birds perked up at the company, they danced and swaggered, and dipped their perfect little heads. Mr Lawrence and Alison chatted about A Levels, and the band, and the pigeons. Next January the two of them were going together to the Blackpool Winter Gardens, the Royal Pigeon Racing Association show, staying in two rooms of a boarding house near South Beach Promenade. Daniel thought she was mad, but it was all booked, and Alison said she couldn't wait.

Back home, she paused at the threshold to try to gauge the lie of the land, but the house yielded no information; it was quiet, but this didn't always signify peace. For a while this year, back in the spring, Catherine had come off the booze. It wasn't the first time, but she did better than she ever had before. Early March through to mid-April. Six weeks with no wine or vodka in the house. No

bed-wetting or soiled clothes. No futile rages or tearful atonement. No Martin, either, and no other strange, unwholesome
men tagging along home with her after closing time, for a night-
cap and a no-strings fuck on the sofa with a semi-comatose
drunkard. But on 15 April – the date stuck in Alison's mind,
being her seventeenth birthday – her mother fell off the wagon
again in grand style and embarked on an almighty bender, an
extraordinary, destructive, desperate binge, a twenty-four-hour
festival of annihilation. Since then, she'd been impossible to control or predict, and Martin Baxter was back, with his own key
and a new, disturbing air of ownership, as if, having survived the
brief exile, he'd returned triumphant, and stronger, to his private
fiefdom.

She went in and shut the door, and Peter must've been listening for her because immediately she could hear his tread on the
stairs, and by the time she'd shed her coat, there he was. He
looked shocking, strained and whey-faced, and his eyes were
red with fatigue or sorrow, she didn't know which. She held her
arms out to him and he stepped into them, and she hugged him
for a while, without speaking. He stood in the circle of her
embrace, half a foot taller than her but passive as a sad, sad
child. Then he said, 'There's summat I need to tell you,' and she
let him go.

'What?' she asked, but he just walked away, through the kitchen and into the living room, so she followed him, her heart
hammering. He didn't sit, but paced about, back and forth.

'Peter, please,' she said. 'What's wrong?'

He stood still then, and looked at her. 'There's trouble coming,' he said.

'What kind of trouble?' It seemed to Alison that there was
nothing *but* trouble in the Connor household. There could be
little else to come that hadn't already been visited upon them.

Peter sniffed and sighed – a long exhalation, as if bracing himself for what he had to say.

'Peter,' Alison said. 'Just tell me.'

'OK, I will,' he said. 'I will. I'm queer.' There was a sort of challenge in his eyes now as he waited for a response. She was silent, but she stepped towards him and took his hand. He was trembling, as if he was very cold, and he said, 'Me and Toddy, we're . . .' He stopped, shook his head furiously, then said, 'And Martin fucking bastard Baxter knows.' In his eyes, there were the beginnings of tears.

Alison tried to process what he was saying as swiftly as she could. He needed her, when, for as long as she could remember, it'd always been she who'd needed him. But now, for Peter, for him, she had to be steady and strong, and, after all, this wasn't a disaster, this wasn't something to fear. She hadn't known though, she hadn't known this about him, and she felt stupid and slow and thoughtless, as if all her life she'd looked only to herself and her own concerns, and had altogether missed the truth at the centre of her lovely, tender, patient, dependable brother's being.

'It doesn't matter,' she said. 'You and Toddy . . . it doesn't matter, Peter, does it?'

'He's been following us.' His voice cracked with angry distress. 'The bastard. He's taken pictures, Alison. He's shown me.'

She was horrified, appalled, confused. She wasn't sure what Peter meant. Pictures? Why? Of what? She felt too young and too ignorant to deal with her brother's obvious agony.

'Pictures?' she asked. 'What do you mean?'

He stared at her in abject misery. He really didn't want to tell his little sister that Martin Baxter had Polaroid shots – in bad light, from far off, but nevertheless unmistakably Peter Connor and Dave Todd – from an alley behind the Gaumont, catching the two of them in a desperately compromising act.

Indecent. Illegal. Oh Christ Almighty, Alison couldn't know. He held his hands to his face and bellowed in a kind of private pain, and Alison stepped away from him and started to cry too, she couldn't stop, and she couldn't help it, because fear had her in its powerful clutches; she was cold with it, frozen. Outside in the street, a boy kicked a ball against a wall and the milkman shouted at him, 'Watch them bottles! You break one, you'll know about it.' He swapped empties on the doorsteps for pints on the float, gold top, silver top; they clanked in their crates, and he whistled cheerfully, on this ordinary Saturday, at the end of July.

14

Duncan was sleeping in Dan and Katelin's spare bedroom, but Katelin couldn't bring herself to speak to him. She told Dan to tell his friend that if Lindsay Miller set foot in the house, Duncan could sod off and sleep on the street, for all she cared.

'I mean it, Dan,' she said. 'If I get so much as a whiff of her bloody cologne, he's out.'

Dan didn't say that Lindsay Miller wasn't the cologne-wearing type; that instead she smelled of cigarettes and late nights at live gigs in dingy clubs. But he did tell Katelin she might try to be slightly less judgemental. He understood her feelings of loyalty to Rose-Ann; of course he did. But she'd known Duncan for a lot longer, he was a dear friend, and the guy was in turmoil. And this really was just a flash in the pan, he wasn't *with* Lindsay at all, she'd just added him to her collection, and now his world had blown up.

'Don't make things worse for him than they already are,' Dan said. 'He's suffering, but to her it's a meaningless fling. Lindsay doesn't need Duncan, and he'd probably be back home with Rose-Ann by now if everyone could just calm down.'

Katelin only shrugged at this. 'He knows what to do then,' she said.

'What? Crawl back up to New Town in a hair shirt?'

'Yes,' Katelin said. 'Why not? Those medieval Christians knew how to atone.'

'Have you bothered to consider *why* he may have had his head turned?' Dan asked, but Katelin only shrugged at this too, so he dropped it. He knew she wasn't interested in the case against Rose-Ann, her occasional flint-eyed *froideur*, her tendency to slip into boardroom steeliness. In any case, this situation was as good as over. He'd met Lindsay two weeks ago, the day he travelled from London to Glasgow to see Duncan. She'd been with him in Gordon Street when Dan walked out of the station. Ripped jeans, biker jacket, Levi's T-shirt, black Cuban heels, great cheekbones, bleach-blonde hair and a bold, unapologetic smile. She was lead guitarist, singer and songwriter for an indie-rock band called Many Minds. Together for ten years but still at the stage where even an ultimately unfulfilled promise of airtime on the radio was almost a cause for celebration. They'd had a drink together in a crowded pub, a shouted conversation over three pints of Tennent's and a bag of cheese and onion crisps, and Lindsay sat opposite Duncan on a chair, not next to him on the bench, which Dan appreciated because it made the situation a little less odd. Duncan looked thinner, although it was only just over a week since Dan had seen him. His naturally pale complexion seemed almost bruised with fatigue, but there was a febrile energy about him, a kind of fervent light in his eyes. Lindsay chatted, laughed, asked Dan some questions, called Duncan Dunc, but didn't really notice his evident desire to commune across the sticky wooden tabletop. She looked young and lithe and sexy, and if it hadn't been totally out of order, Dan would've liked to ask her what she was playing at, hanging out with Duncan. When she'd drained her pint, she stood and made her excuses. They'd be wanting to talk about her and they couldn't do that with her sitting there, she said, and gave a throaty smoker's laugh, pure Glaswegian. So away she went, sashaying around the busy tables and pausing to light a fag before she'd quite made it out through the door.

'Christ,' Duncan said, heaving a sigh, watching until she'd gone.

Dan said nothing; instead he got up and went to the bar. He came back with two more pints, and sat down. 'Right, Duncan, my lad. Is it all up with Rose-Ann?'

Duncan stared. 'What kind of question's that? I'm in love with Lindsay!'

'I can see that, pal. I just wondered if she feels the same? Lindsay, I mean.'

Duncan didn't answer, although he seemed to ponder the question, but then all he said was, 'So, what do you think of her?'

'I like her,' Dan said without hesitation. 'But how's it going to pan out?'

'Pan out?'

'Yeah.'

'As in . . . ?'

'As in, pan out.'

They regarded each other solemnly for a while, then Duncan said, 'How the fuck would I know?' and they both laughed, although a little grimly.

Dan shook his head. 'Ah, Duncan.'

Duncan nodded. 'Yeah,' he said. 'I know.'

He'd been here before, standing stage right in the rubble and ruin of a relationship, with a new woman waiting stage left. Rose-Ann had once been the new woman, a wealthy American – a lawyer turned venture capitalist from Santa Monica with Scottish lineage, a house in New Town and a weakness for men such as Duncan, as unlike her as it was possible to be: engagingly down at heel, unmaterialistic, driven by hopelessly impecunious artistic ambitions. She got him because he didn't mind being adored, but she perhaps should've been told that Duncan hadn't been without a woman since he was twenty, and in the past fifteen years alone he'd left Alice for Rose-Ann, Sharon for Alice and Monica for Sharon. For a guy who by any conventional criteria was no catch, Duncan seemed to be irresistible. Lindsay, though, she was your archetypal rolling stone; there'd be no pinning her down.

'So,' Dan said, 'has she asked you to move in?'

'No! What, into the flat in Laurieston?'

'Yeah, obviously.'

'Och, well, it's only a temporary thing, rent-free just now, but it's all a bit vague. A tenement flat with, like, six or seven other people.'

'Right, a squat?'

'Och, well,' he said again, wincing a bit. 'She's always on the move anyway, touring, y'know?'

'Right.'

'They do better on the continent than they do here, that's where the work is.'

'Yep, right.' The picture was crystal clear to Dan, and there was nothing more revealing than Duncan's evasiveness. He thought about Rose-Ann's beautiful, comfortable Georgian house, and no, granted, you couldn't stick with someone just because they had a great house . . . but on the other hand, a woman would have to be pretty sodding special to justify following her to a squat in the Gorbals.

Dan sighed. 'You need to come back to Edinburgh, mate.'

'A-ha, I know, I know that.' Duncan nodded sadly.

'You've a business to run, and, I mean, sorry to be brutal,

but it was only Rose-Ann's money that stopped that shop going under a long time ago. Come back, mate. This Lindsay thing, it's a pipe dream. She'd do your head in, in the end.'

Duncan didn't reply, but he didn't deny it, either. They sat in silence for a while, Duncan staring down into his lager, Dan staring up at the old nicotine stains on the ceiling. His mind drifted to other times, and they were many, that he'd been in Glasgow with Duncan, and it was always for a gig; he couldn't ever remember coming to this city for any other reason, apart from today. After a while he said, 'That Comsats gig, the one we saw at King Tut's.'

Duncan looked up and brightened immediately. 'June twenty-sixth, nineteen ninety-three,' he said.

'Great night, great night. Mind you, I didn't love that album.'

'No. I liked it though.'

'Yeah, but it wasn't the real deal, not if you'd heard 'em in seventy-nine, at the beginning.'

'Well,' Duncan said, 'you got me there.'

'King Tut's though,' Dan said.

'Banging, then and now.'

'Best venue I know,' Dan said.

Duncan nodded, took a swig of his lager, then said, 'Oh God though, that other night as well, the Oasis night . . .'

'Yeah, oh man,' Dan said. 'You, me and only about twelve other people in the room, and Alan McGee on his third Jack Daniel's and Coke, stood there saying are they good or am I pissed?'

Old story, but they both laughed anyway, and now it felt comfortable again, and safe to say goodbye. Out on the street, they hugged, briefly. Duncan said he'd be back in Edinburgh soon, the day after tomorrow, or the day after that, and Dan said, 'Good, good, OK, call me if you need to, and stay with us if you can't go home,' then he walked back up Gordon Street to the station, and Duncan dipped his head against the late-evening cold and headed off towards the badlands of Glasgow, to find Lindsay.

And all the time, all the time, all the time.

With Duncan, with Katelin, with anyone, Dan was holding Ali Connor lightly, constantly, in his thoughts, and if this was hypocrisy, it didn't feel that way, and if it was infidelity, it never seemed wrong. She'd found a way to permeate his mind, so that wherever he was, so was she. He never had to summon her; she was simply there. She formed a whole world in his head, which only he knew existed, and most of it was conjecture, and he didn't know what any of it signified, but oh God, it was a source of wonder and delight. Nobody needed to demonstrate to Dan the power and punch of a good song, and when he'd sent 'Pump It Up' he'd imagined her smiling, and remembering, but only that. Certainly, he hadn't imagined this . . . what was it? An intimate dialogue in music, an eloquence beyond the written word. It was genius. He should market it, invent an app or something.

He wouldn't have given Carole King the time of day when he was eighteen. But what a lovely track Ali had sent, what a masterclass in deceptive simplicity; he'd listened to it on the train and been blindsided by the emotional tug of her lyrics on his cynical, heard-it-all heart, because it was Ali Connor, Alison, that long-lost girl, speaking to him through this song, like solace for a pain he hadn't known he had. Jesus, he'd thought; this was crazy. This was bad. In a good, good way. He'd listened three times to the track, wrung out from it every possible shade and nuance, then responded by sending M. Ward's cover of 'Let's Dance', for the mesmerising poetry of those reinvented

Bowie lyrics and – there was no escaping the truth of this – the stripped-back, aching desire. She was ten thousand miles away; where was the harm?

After he'd sent it, he listened to nothing at all, and found he couldn't write either, or read. Katelin had rung, and they talked about Christmas, his family, who would sleep where, what they would eat, an easy conversation about the real world. But he wanted to talk to Alison Connor. He wanted his phone to ring again, and it be her.

He'd stared blindly at the landscape as the train carved a path north, and let his thoughts travel to Sheffield in the bleak, black summer of 1979, and to what happened that night in July, and what he might have done differently. He thought about Duncan, and his misguided fling, unrelated and incomparable in Dan's mind to his own feelings for Alison. He thought about Katelin, her brittle, implacable sense of right and wrong, and he thought about love in its many guises, and about loyalty, and trust. But time and again his thoughts swept back to Alison Connor, and where this was all leading, and whether he could see her again, and if so, how, and how soon. These songs were incredible, each new track the highlight of his day; but he wanted to talk to her, and he wanted to hold her again; that was all.

Late December, two days before Christmas. Alex had colonised the living room, dragged the sofa into a front-and-centre location, reconnected the Xbox to the television and was doggedly taking Sheffield Wednesday through a sensational season in the Championship, towards the play-offs and promotion. FIFA, Career Mode: a taste of power and glory for the bruised and bloodied fans of a team under siege in the real world. This was Alex's antidote to the rigours of Plato, Kant and Nietzsche at Trinity College, Cambridge, and the Owls had never had a

manager as wise, steadfast and inspiring as Alexander Lawrence. There was a well-known game hack, available via a
two-second Google search, to secure an unlimited budget for
the transfer windows, but Alex refused to cheat. Instead, he
slogged away with the funds he was allocated, growing his
squad and bringing talented youth players up through the
ranks. His dad was proud of him. A steady hand on the tiller,
some home-grown talent, a few canny purchases from unlikely
sources, and result after result that proved you couldn't just buy
success in football, you had to nurture it. This is what Dan had
just said to Katelin, after she'd complained that the boy had sat
on his arse and wasted two days in the front room with the
curtains closed.

'That's just pathetic,' she said, now, to Dan. They were out
with McCulloch, hunched against the cold, walking alongside
the Water of Leith.

'Oh, give over,' he said. 'Give the lad a break. It's harmless.'

'I didn't mean Alex is pathetic, I meant you – the way you
talk about a stupid Xbox game, like it's actually happening.
Home-grown talent, canny purchases, all that bollocks.'

Dan said, 'It's not stupid, have you seen those graphics?
Bloody remarkable. That Wednesday squad – identifiable, to a
man.'

Katelin tutted. 'Yeah, but it's not *Match of the Day*, is it?
There's no real justification for you sitting in there and actually
watching, is there?'

Dan laughed, refusing to be rattled. 'Guilty as charged,' he
said. 'But look, it was the derby.'

The aim was to go a couple of miles or so, towards Rose-
burn and Murrayfield, but it was hard to see the point, now
they were out, and even the little dog trotted glumly at Dan's
heels, with no indication of enjoyment. Dan had intended to

run with him, as he did sometimes, to get the lazy little sod moving at something other than walking pace, and he'd been all ready to go, trainers on, earphones in, iPod in the pocket of his shorts, when Katelin said she was feeling stir-crazy, needed some air, and could she come too? But Katelin didn't run, hated running, wouldn't even run for a bus, and so here they were, trudging. Terrible weather for it, a dreich winter's day, damp but not raining, bone cold but not clear.

Katelin was in one of her habitual pre-Christmas funks, when the imminent arrival of his family – or, on alternate years, her own – would periodically colour her thoughts in shades of grey. She always emerged, perfectly pleasant and sociable, in time for the visit, but there was something about the build-up, the expectations, the length of the shopping list, the fridge bulging with the turkey, the veg, the beer, the wine . . . and the *relentlessness* of it all, and the inevitability, and the way it crept up by stealth, one minute October, the very next, Christmas. *So* annoying. Then there were the beds to make, extra mattresses for the cousins, and meanwhile the bathroom and downstairs loo – was this a universal rule? – had to be cleaner than they ever were at any other time of year, and, oh, the whole terrible festive jamboree, like a well-intentioned invasion, a three-day marathon of fairy-lit madness.

'Hey,' Dan said, putting an arm loosely round her shoulders. 'Let's turn back? Go home and pour a drink?'

She turned her face to his and managed a smile. 'I need Alex off that sofa,' she said. 'It's an awful tip in that room,' and Dan said, 'Agreed, Wednesday's glorious rise to eminence must wait until after Christmas.'

'And there's veg to prep.'

'Alex can do it. He'll need something to do with his hands when he puts that controller down.'

Now, finally, she laughed, and they turned around to retrace their steps, the air around them feeling a few degrees warmer, the atmosphere palpably more relaxed. Even McCulloch looked jollier, but that might just have been the welcome change of direction, the unmistakable scent of home.

There were ten of them for Christmas lunch. Dan, Katelin and Alex, Bill and Marion, then Claire and her husband Marcus, and their three, Will, Jack and Molly. Joe was a ski instructor in Courchevel these days. He hadn't been home for Christmas in years, skied all winter and early spring, then ran cycling tours up and down the same mountains in summer and early autumn. Alex loved his Sheffield cousins, was never happier at home than when they came to stay. There were only these three on the English side, because Uncle Joe had never had kids, but in and around Coleraine there were lots of cousins, nineteen in all, although it was only ever five, the same five, who came to stay. Katelin had four sisters and two brothers and among the six of them, their six partners and their nineteen offspring, there were a few folk she simply couldn't abide. The Christmases past that they'd spent in the farmhouse in Northern Ireland! Like landing in a latter-day Greek tragedy: intrigue, sibling rivalry, fights over birthright and land and money, and all of it stoked by Guinness and Jameson's and great-great-granddaddy's poteen, made by Katelin's father in a 200-year-old still from potatoes and the original recipe. Dan loved the whole scene, but Katelin wouldn't go any more. She said she didn't like herself when she was there.

No such problems today among the Lawrence clan, where a Christmas meal of epic proportions had just been merrily destroyed, the turkey a ravaged carcass, the vegetables, stuffing and gravy only memories. It was late afternoon, dark outside, and sleeting in the deserted Stockbridge streets, but the house hummed and glowed with festive cheer, and the youngsters were sorting the presents into piles, for it was that time in the proceedings when gifts were given, and opened, in a flurry of wrapping paper, a confusion of thank-yous. Socks and boxers; chocolate oranges all round from Marion and Bill; make-up for Molly; scarves, gloves, cologne, calendars, all new this year, but also somehow familiar; it was always music that passed between Alex and Dan, always an LP, Kelley Stoltz this year for Alex, Fiona Apple for Dan. In the hubbub around them, they tried to talk about what they'd given, and why, and then Dan heard Katelin say, 'Oh, Marion, great present! I've been meaning to read this,' and Dan looked round to see what his wife was holding, and it was Ali Connor's bestseller, *Tell the Story, Sing the Song*.

'Look,' Katelin said to Dan, waving the book at him while he tried to stay cool. 'I heard her on *Woman's Hour* not so long ago. She's Australian now, but she's from Sheffield. I meant to say at the time, but I forgot.'

Dan opened his mouth to speak but his mum beat him to it.

'Never!' she said. She beamed at Dan, then at Katelin. 'Well, I didn't know that. I had no idea the author was from Sheffield. I just saw the book in Smith's, and the lady said it was flying off the shelves, and I thought, Katelin might like this, because I know you like to read, love.'

'Yeah, it's great, Marion, thanks.' Katelin picked a route through the gifts and the debris to give Dan's mum a kiss on the cheek.

'That there,' Bill said, tipping his head towards the photograph on the back cover. 'That there is Alison.'

It was the first time he'd spoken since they'd all said 'Cheers' at lunch because Bill, through deafness and old age and his tendency towards depression, was the quietest of souls, a recluse in the family throng. So his voice had an impact, drew the attention of everyone in the room, especially Claire, who said, 'What? Give it here,' and took the book from Katelin. She flipped it over, and saw Ali Connor's publicity photograph – the one Dan had seen when he first found her online and that he saw still, whenever she sent him a song. Blue cotton shirt, cropped dark wavy hair, blue-nearly-green eyes, a sensual mouth, and an intelligent, slightly inquiring, slightly amused expression.

'Oh my God, it *is* Alison,' Claire said. 'She looks the same.' She passed the book to her brother. 'Look, Daniel. Alison Connor! Can you credit it?'

He took it, and for the sake of appearance pretended to check out the biography on the inside front page. He didn't read it though. Instead, he tried to formulate a sentence or two to address the look that he knew was waiting for him on Katelin's face. She knew nothing about Alison Connor, nothing at all. By the time he'd met Katelin, he'd spent four years conscientiously forgetting her. There'd been lots of other girls, and Katelin had grilled him about each and every one. But not Alison, no. Not mentioning Alison had become a habit, born of necessity, for all of them, but especially for Dan.

Bill, sounding more animated than he had for years, said, 'She was grand, Alison was. A smashing lass.'

'Well, I never!' Marion said, rather uncertain now whether she'd done a good thing, or a bad thing. She looked at Dan, then Bill, then Claire. 'Can you believe it? What a coincidence! So she's Ali now, not Alison? And fancy her ending up in Australia!'

'Yeah,' Dan said to Katelin, who was staring at him. 'Ex-girlfriend.'

No big deal.

'So,' Katelin said, head cocked, arms folded, 'did you know she'd written a novel, this Ali Connor person?'

'Alison,' Bill said. 'She was Alison then.'

'No,' Dan said, lying easily, without conscience, because to say yes would benefit no one. 'I'd no idea she'd written a novel.'

Will took the book from Dan's hand.

'Ey, she's a bit of all right, Uncle Daniel,' he said, which wasn't helpful at all.

Molly said, 'Awkward,' in that sing-song voice the kids used. And it was, a little, because Katelin was still deciding whether to be amused or peeved about this new old girlfriend. She said, 'Well, I thought I knew of all your exes, but here's yet another one.'

'Long, long time ago,' Dan said. 'We were only kids.'

'She was always dead good at English though, Daniel, wasn't she? Do you remember? She kept all her books at our house, poems and that – she'd practically moved in, hadn't she?'

This was Claire, always so incredibly reliable at digging an even deeper hole, when everyone else had put their spades down. And Marion, trying valiantly now to haul them all out and back to safety, said, 'Anyway, I hope you like it, Katelin love. The lady in Smith's said it's really smashing.'

There was a short silence, into which Katelin said nothing.

Then, 'I'm glad Alison's all right,' Bill said. 'I've been right worried about that lass.'

15

Summer in Adelaide, and day after day the city was slowed and debilitated by bitumen-melting temperatures that soared up past the thirties and into the forties, until the evenings rolled around. Then the water beckoned and people flocked to the beaches of Brighton or Glenelg, where the sinking sun put on a riotous show of colour as it took its leave. Michael McCormack disliked the beach vibe, so most evenings the household simply gathered for an al fresco dinner, where the air smelled of char-grilled prawns, seared steaks, garlic, rosemary, the Mediterranean tang of lemon and, always present, the old-fashioned scent of Margaret McCormack's English roses, the blooms blousy and bloated with sunshine, too heavy on their stems to ever look up at the sky.

Thea was home from Melbourne for the long summer vacation so the family was complete again and Beatriz was content, except, when they gathered to eat, or chat, or read in the garden, under the hibiscus shade of the long wooden pergola, they were often only four because inside, upstairs, lovely Stella was keeping to herself, inert on her bed, her face pale and doll-like against the fresh white pillow. She was no longer pregnant. At Sheila and Dora's house in Quorn, the very day after telling Ali in a flood of tears that, after all, she wasn't ready to be a mother, the girl had miscarried, as if her body had decided to spare her the cycle of tormented indecision and take matters into its own hands. It was extraordinary how efficient the process had been, how swift and thorough. Ninety minutes it had taken, and a whole heap of Sheila and Dora's Turkish hammam towels. The shock to them all had been immense – all that blood, and the brief but searing bouts of pain, and home being so far away, and then, afterwards, the acres and acres of guilt at the terrible, quiet relief. Later the same day, Stella had been checked over by a nurse with a brisk, no-nonsense air and expert hands, which Ali watched closely as they moved over her daughter's abdomen and inside her body, pressing, assessing. And all the while she talked, about nature's ways and the cast-iron reasons behind just about everything that happens in life.

'You've slipped it for a reason, sweetheart,' she said. 'You grow up on a farm, you soon understand that a mare slips a foal, a sheep slips a lamb, there's always a why and a where-fore.' Stella didn't respond. She lay on the gurney, with her eyes closed, but when Ali's hand squeezed hers, she'd squeezed back. 'Right-oh,' said the nurse, gathering her tools. 'A scrape and a polish, and you'll be good to go.'

'That would've been Brianna,' Dora said when Ali recounted the story later. 'Bedside manners of the bush, but she knows what she's at. Stella's going to be fine.'

And she was, but somehow she wasn't. She was less Stella-like, a listless, thoughtful, much quieter version of herself. Beatriz said give her time, but Michael, a solution-finder, a fixer of problems, believed a family trip up to Burra was what was needed – just the four of them, because Beatriz hated going bush; a few weeks at Lismore Creek, just like the old days, when the girls were little and all summer could be spent swinging on the gates in the shearing shed and riding ponies alongside the stockmen and their horses.

'But it's years since we were all there together,' Ali said, now, to her husband.

'Exactly my point.'

'Do we want to be inland, in the heat?'

Michael sighed. 'Well, I do,' he said. 'C'mon, I want to take some time to be with my girls. Life's slower up there, Ali, remember?'

'Yes, of course I remember – and anyway Stella and I were in Quorn not so long ago, to be fair.'

Michael waved his hand, as if Quorn was nothing. His childhood memories of the family sheep station were gilded and rosy, frame after frame of picture-perfect scenes. The elegant homestead itself, built for his ancestors in 1866: an expansive 'English' country house, coach house and stables, all of them heritage-listed now; the grounds, landscaped and tamed into lawns, knot garden, herbaceous borders and a sunken bower of roses, all of this maintained and manicured by four full-time gardeners; Michael and his two younger brothers, Rory and Robert, running wild, damming the creek, driving the ute from the age of nine, racing ducks and spitting cherry stones at the country fair, trapping rabbits and shooting roos. So Ali, sitting on the porch swing next to Michael, knew this discussion was purely cosmetic. A one-way street. His heart was set, the decision made.

'Rob'll be there by now, netting the vines,' he said. 'You like Rob.'

'I know I like Rob.'

A pause, then: 'Apart from anything else,' Michael said, 'I'm thinking of Gil and Alma. These past few weeks must've been a slog. It must've been hell, even with all the help. Fires up there've been terrible. You know what Gil's like; he's seen too many to ever relax . . .'

'Yeah,' Ali said, 'I know.' Gil Henderson, the big boss, the main man, and Alma, his wife, queen of the homestead; together they ran Lismore Station as if it were their own. Gil had been hired as a lowly jackeroo by James McCormack back in 1962; Alma had come in '68, to help clean the house. They were in the weft and the weave of the McCormack world.

'So,' Michael said. 'I think we need to go.'

Need to go. There it was, the subtle change of emphasis, from inclination to obligation. Ah, what the hell, thought Ali. They could all go to Lismore Creek, why not? Michael was probably right: Stella might well come back to them there, and Thea needed a change of scene too. She was moping about the place like she was under house arrest.

'Fine,' Ali said. 'Give me a few days here. I need to square things up with the publishers, see to a few things.'

Michael was pleased. He reached out and brought her closer, his arm across her shoulders, and Ali knew that if she'd resisted the Lismore plan he wouldn't have done this; but she had learned the habit of compliance. She closed her eyes and retreated into her own mind, switching realities from this life in Adelaide to her other life, where Daniel was always waiting, thinking about her thinking about him. She knew he did, knew he never really stopped, because neither did she; she was in touch with his presence, and he with hers.

She considered the utterly beautiful song he'd sent, and how unexpected tears had coursed down her face as she listened. Then she thought about the track she'd sent back, Bowie's version of 'Wild Is The Wind', with all its emotion and intent and conviction, and she imagined herself lying beside Dan as he listened to it.

She looked at her watch. In Scotland, it would be half past nine in the morning. She thought about Edinburgh, and wondered why life had taken him there. She knew he had Katelin, and together they had Alex, because it was all there to be seen on the web, and it had triggered curious feelings of regret and uncertainty, but also of a kind of relief that he was living a good life. She would never have searched for him on the internet before the first song came: never. He would have remained in 1979, just as all of her Sheffield life had, shadowy and distant, the clocks stopped, a vault of memories sealed against the passing of time. But here Daniel was now, front and centre in her private mind, and because of him, inevitably, other ghosts were moving towards the light too, other memories of her youth, among them her brother, whose remembered smile caused her to bow her head in shame that for far too long she'd – stubbornly, stoically, selfishly – turned her face away from her past, believing it to be the cure.

Michael was talking about work, staff issues, an incompetent registrar. She half listened to him, and to the cockatoos bickering their way towards bedtime, to the sprinkler hiss on the parched summer lawn, to the thrum and chirrup of grasshoppers in the shrubs. This was certainly a kind of heaven, but she wondered now if in fact she'd always belonged elsewhere? Another life, that other world, where January meant not sultry heat but rain and sleet, and the Attercliffe bus throwing arcs of icy brown water at unwary pedestrians, and her mother, who always plunged into a hating mood after Christmas, doing anything, anything, for another drink. In Sheffield, in 1979, heaven had been Daniel's bedroom, Daniel's music, and the urgent, consuming heat of his body alongside her own. But her sanctuary then, her place of complete safety, had been the cloistered quiet of Bill Lawrence's pigeon loft, where he'd one day placed a quivering bird into her careful, cupped hands and the anxious little heartbeat in its breast had made Alison feel – just for that short while – invincible.

Cass said it was time she was invited to Lismore Creek, and since Michael would never ask her, she thought Ali should. Ali spluttered with laughter and spilled some of her wine.

'What!' Cass said. 'What's funny?'

'You.' Ali wiped the table ineffectually with a beer mat. 'You, proposing a visit to the land of *Hoofs and Horns*. You can't get a skinny latte at Lismore, you know.'

'Hey, I was a girl guide, y'know, I can rough it, and I still think it's a scandal you haven't taken me,' Cass said.

'Well, I hardly ever go myself. And, well . . .' She hesitated, thinking about it.

'And, well, it's Michael's, not yours?'

'Kind of, yeah.' It was true, and a little awkward, somehow. Lismore Creek was part and parcel of the family legend, a proud outward sign of their history and status, and Ali never felt more like a Connor and less like a McCormack than when she was there. To take Cass up to Lismore, without Michael, at her own invitation? Well, it seemed unlikely.

They were in a bar on Pirie Street. Grungy, crowded, loud. She and Cass hung out here on occasional Fridays – late, live-music nights, where genius and mediocrity rubbed shoulders on an upstairs stage. Tahnee Jackson was on tonight, half past ten, and Ali had come only for her. She was the Aboriginal girl who, twelve or so years ago, had brought them to their feet in a pub in Port Adelaide, and whenever she'd played in the city since, Ali had tried to be there. Tahnee was twenty-eight now; her voice had matured into something even richer, fuller, more knowing. Her gigs had the feel of confessionals, as if there was nothing she wouldn't share, and when Ali heard her she thought of Joni Mitchell, Nina Simone, Carole King. But also, Tahnee was entirely herself: unique, a Northern Territory troubadour, singing to a devoted following of strangers, of her life, her thoughts and the desert land in which she'd grown up. Ali had already talked to a guy at Arts South Australia, a development officer for young indigenous musicians, and they were meeting on Monday, before the McCormack household left for Burra. Cass asked would they still be friends when Ali was a music mogul, with a smoked-glass office and Kanye on speed dial?

They were sharing a bottle of white, biding their time in the bar, waiting for the music to start upstairs, gossiping and larking about. Ali felt light-hearted, almost giddy. The proposed trip to Lismore Creek had gone down well with the girls, and it was so good to see Stella smile. As for herself, she was going to try to do some writing when they got there, she said; or rather, think about doing some writing, in the hope that writing would follow. The fact was, *Tell the Story, Sing the Song* didn't really lend itself to a sequel, and she felt dragooned by what Cass called her 'people' in Sydney – agent, editor, publicist – who always wanted to talk timescales and titles.

'Don't sweat it,' Cass said, 'you can call the shots now you've hit payola. Or do a Harper Lee and write nothing else, ever.'

'No, I will write another book.'

'So what'll it be?'

'Dunno. A love story, maybe.'

Cass raised her eyebrows.

Ali grinned. 'Why not?' she said. 'Who doesn't love a love story?' She pushed her glass forwards for a refill. 'This is a very fine Riesling,' she said.

'Yeah,' Cass said, 'especially considering the state of the bar we're in.' She tolerated these dingy, cramped venues that Ali dragged her to, but would always favour space and light and exclusivity, a rooftop cocktail bar or some new restaurant with a waiting list for tables.

Ali held up her glass and they clinked. 'Here's mud in yer eye,' she said; then she sighed contentedly, and looked around at all the other people milling about in the bar, all the strangers who'd chosen to do as she and Cass had done, and come and listen to Tahnee Jackson tonight, and she felt a great warmth towards everyone; whoever they all were, she belonged among them, these disciples of live music.

'Y'know,' she said, 'it might be the wine talking, but I have a really good feeling about the future.'

Cass scrutinised her for a moment and then said, 'I can tell you do.'

Ali laughed. 'Oh yeah?'

'Yeah, you look different. Why do you look different?'

'Different how?'

'You look really happy.'

She drew back and looked at Cass, askance. 'Well, that's because I am, by and large.'

'Happi*er*, I mean. Brighter, lighter. You've been a bit of a misery guts.'

'Well, there's been Stella and—'

'No, before that, way before. You were flat, but now you've got your bounce back.'

Ali picked up the bottle for something to do, and topped up their glasses. Cass stared.

'What're you looking at?' Ali said.

'You have a kind of . . . a kind of glow.'

'Well, it's hot in here.'

'A loved-up glow.'

Ali was startled now, and felt a kind of thudding anxiety

that her body, her face, might so easily give away the secrets of her heart and mind.

'And you said you might write a love story.'

'So what if I do?' Ali said. 'I'm a novelist; I make stuff up.'

'Hey,' Cass said. 'Are you having an affair?'

Ali managed an incredulous laugh, but she couldn't help the blush that bloomed in her cheeks and on her throat. 'No, Cass,' she said. 'I'm not.'

'You wouldn't have an affair and not tell me, would you?'

'I'm not having an affair.'

'Oh, c'mon, spill. We tell each other everything, remember? You've got all the dirt on me, every crumb.'

Ali managed to hold her friend's gaze, and it crossed her mind to tell her: tell her that it wasn't an affair, but it was certainly something, something absorbing and enveloping, between her and Dan Lawrence. But she didn't. She kept him hidden, kept their connection to herself; it was too precious to expose to scrutiny, even here, with Cass, her best friend, who might be able to read her mind, Ali couldn't be sure.

'You can't kid a kidder,' Cass said. 'I've been where you're at now. What's going down? Who is he?'

Ali was resolute. 'Absolutely nothing,' she said. 'Absolutely no one.'

'Right, well, you tell me when you're ready.' Cass had searching eyes, but still Ali said nothing, only looked at her watch.

'Nearly ten past,' Ali said. 'Come on, let's go upstairs.'

When Ali first went to Lismore Creek, it was for Rob's eighteenth birthday party, a black-tie affair thrown in fine style by Margaret, along the time-honoured lines of the Bachelor and Spinster Balls of her own youth. It was March, two years after

Michael had brought Ali back to Adelaide. Prior to that, the only farm she'd ever visited had belonged to the uncle of a primary school friend. It had clung to the ragged fringes of Rotherham, a drab patchwork of fields, its limits marked by tumbledown dry-stone walls and thin hedgerows. But at Lismore Creek she saw a world without end, and all of it belonged to the McCormacks.

Michael drove her up from Adelaide to the Clare Valley, and when he said, 'Here we are,' and turned off the road on to a white stone track, she assumed they'd arrived. But he continued, on and on, then onwards still, through an undulating landscape rendered in greens, gold and brown: pastures, coppices and vines unfolding around them with infinite grace. Finally, they reached the house, standing stately and gravely beautiful, flanked by mighty oaks, Alma waving from the shade of the porch, a jug of cold lemonade, a plate of cucumber and dill sandwiches, and Gil appearing from the stable block, clapping his hands at the sight of Michael, and taking Ali by the waist to waltz her through the dust of the yard.

She'd been spellbound by this free pass to an apparently enchanted land, where the McCormacks had shifted within their privileged ranks to make room for Ali, a lost girl without a pedigree or much of a past. Rob's party had been a blast, the shearing shed mellow with fairy lights, decked out with bunting and flowers. There was a band, then a DJ, and the Country Women's Association did the catering, with Margaret in command. Ali and Michael drank and danced and skylarked, then finally retired to a swag by the creek and made love under the benign eye of the Southern Cross. In the morning, they all played cricket in their crushed and crumpled finery, and ate pancakes and bacon. And then Ali – who had never ridden a horse, was terrified of them, truth be told – sat on the wooden steps of a small pavilion and watched her husband play polo, deft and fearless, golden in the sunlight, born to this life, like a prince, the heir to his father's kingdom.

Now, of course, Michael *was* king. Never mind that he had little to do with the merinos – it was Rory, the middle brother, who was always there for shearing, always at the sales. And Rob, the youngest, managed the vines, lived up here from January through to harvest, netting, checking, watering, singing to the little bunches of Shiraz and Riesling grapes. But no, never mind all that. When Michael arrived at the homestead with Ali, Thea and Stella, Alma cried with happiness and Gil's walnut face cracked into a wide, warm smile, and he held open his arms for the girls, who ran at him like puppies. They were old people now, Alma and Gil, but sprightly and lean, full of old-fashioned vim and vigour. They believed they'd led a blessed life, and the absence of children of their own only made them cherish the McCormacks more. Neither of them saw any neglect in Michael's long absences from Lismore; after all, he was a doctor, a *kiddies'* doctor, no less. Pride and joy flowed from them to him, but it always had, so he didn't really notice it now.

The next morning Ali slept late. When she came downstairs, Michael was gone, making a dutiful tour of the estate with Thea in the old ute. Alma was cleaning out drawers and cupboards, piling linens and crockery and cutlery on the kitchen table, her traditional hot-weather chore. They chatted about the heat, and how washing on the line dried cardboard-stiff before the next wash was out of the machine. Then Ali wandered outside with a coffee to the porch and saw Gil and Stella hosing the wooden sheds, drenching them against the possibility of destruction. He didn't like the wind coming at them off the desert, and east of Burra there was a fire raging that had already burned through close to a thousand hectares and wasn't yet anything like under control. Most of the Lismore hands were out there today, helping beat it back. Stella, in an old T-shirt, shorts and wellies, waved at Ali and came over to her to tell her one of Gil's stories, about a gum tree that had once burst into flames three months after being struck by lightning, its roots like dormant kindling, quietly burning deep underground until a south-westerly – just like today's, just the same – had fanned the buried flames and destroyed twelve thousand hectares of farmland and every dwelling in its path.

'Fire,' Stella said. She was damp, and filthy, her hair not brushed, untied. She looked beautiful. 'It's awesome, really.'

'Like the ocean,' Ali said. 'Makes you feel small.'

'Yeah,' Stella said, and looked back at Gil, protecting his domain. 'Small, but not completely helpless.'

'No, not completely helpless, not with Gil on our side. Does he really think the fire's going to reach us?'

'Nah, don't think so,' Stella said. 'It's just he's a worrywart.' She sat down, close to Ali. 'I'm glad we came here.'

'Then I'm glad too.'

They sat in silence for a minute or two, then Stella said, 'Mum, there are some people in Adelaide I never want to see again.'

'Oh, sweetheart.' Ali stroked Stella's hair, waiting for more. There was never any point pressing this girl for information. She alone decided what she was prepared to divulge.

'And I don't think I want to go to drama school.'

'Then don't, darling.'

Stella looked at her. 'Is it that simple?'

Ali smiled and kissed her on the cheek. 'Sure is,' she said.

16

Alison didn't show up that Saturday afternoon, on the day of
the Manchester gig. Daniel quartered the bus station, pacing
about, checking his watch, checking the timetables. Dooley,
John and Steve waited in the van on double yellow lines, and
Steve drummed his fingers on the steering wheel while the
engine of the Transit ticked over. He waited longer than he
should've done, longer than he would've done for anyone else,
and when he finally roared off without her, they were cutting it
fine and he was fuming, and gutted. Daniel, feeling obscurely
responsible, was first pissed off, then agitated, then anxious,
trapped by obligation to stay with the band when all he wanted
was to jump off the moving van to go and find her. But he still
didn't know exactly where she lived, and he was ashamed of
this now, although she was fierce in her refusal to take him
home, and it'd been weeks now – months even – since he'd
pressed her on the subject. She came to his own house in Nether
Edge with such dependable reliability that he'd stopped even
wondering about her home, and where it might be in the war-
ren of Attercliffe terraces. So while the white van screamed over
Woodhead Pass, Daniel was quiet with concern, and the other
three thought only of their set, and all of them had a strong

sense that something good had gone bad before it really had a chance to get started.

Peter needed help, Alison could see that, but she didn't know what to do. He'd stopped his terrible, jagged crying, but now a dense silence had replaced the sobbing, and his face was stony and withdrawn. If he looked at her at all, it was only glancingly, as if he kept forgetting she was there, then, seeing her again, remembered she was irrelevant. 'Peter,' she kept saying. 'Please, please, Peter,' tugging at his arm, pulling his sleeve, trying to find her brother behind that mask and bring him back, but her own voice sounded wheedling and pleading to her ear, so she stopped, and tried to think instead.

Toddy. She must find Toddy. If he knew about Martin's vile behaviour, creeping about after them, taking photographs in the dark, then he could be here, with Peter, helping him through this pain. If he *didn't* know, then he ought to. She kissed Peter on top of his bowed, beloved head, told him she wouldn't be long, and left the house. She was still in the clothes she'd worn last night, the clothes she woke up in at Daniel's, but she didn't think about this. She didn't think about the gig at the May-flower Club either; it hadn't even crossed her mind.

Dave Todd lived a few streets away from the Connors, practically in the shadow of Brown Bayley's. The streets around here were partially demolished, and in the blasted-out interiors of former homes, Alison passed cowboys and Indians, cops and robbers, and their tag-along siblings, toddlers who squatted unsupervised among the loose bricks, poking about in the dust. Alison knew which street was Toddy's, but had no idea which house number, so she hammered on a few doors, hysteria rising in her chest, until a woman answered, showing only her cautious, tight-lipped face through a narrow gap in the doorway, as if this house might be the next to go and she expected to see a wrecking ball. When she saw only Alison she opened the door properly, and listened with kindly patience to her ragged, breathless explanation. Toddy. Dave Todd. David Todd. Did the Todds live down this street?

'Yes, love,' the woman said. 'Yes, they do, they're over at forty-five. But I saw him leave early doors. Try the works.' She smiled at Alison, who felt reassured at this ordinary, pleasant transaction of words, and then an ice-cream van in a parallel street played a tinny, allegro rendition of 'Greensleeves', and this, too, was comforting. She breathed a little more easily, noticed that this was a lovely day, a cloudless sky, the sun warm on her legs and her bare arms. But still, she trembled a little as she jogged towards the hulking buildings that made up Brown Bayley's, although she had no idea where, in that vast cauldron of industry, she might find Toddy. But she only got as far as the main gates before she was stopped by a big fellow in a donkey jacket and a high-visibility waistcoat.

'Ey,' he said. 'You can't come in 'ere, lass.'

His meaty palms were held out before her. Men were coming and going across the yard in hard hats, and some of them stared at the girl in denim shorts and a thin cotton T-shirt.

'I need to see Dave Todd,' Alison said to the man in front of her.

'Oh aye?' he said. 'And who shall I say wants him?'

'Alison Connor.'

'Oh aye?' he said again. 'You Pete Connor's sister?'

'Yes.' She nodded eagerly, thinking thank God, thank God, but then she saw that he wasn't being helpful, he was stringing her along for his own amusement, because suddenly he was laughing, and shouting, getting the attention of the men in the yard, who gravitated eagerly towards him.

'Ey, look 'ere, this lass's after Toddy,' he called, and some-body shouted back, 'Wasting thi time, love, tha not his type,' and there were hoots and catcalls and more mocking laughter. Tears welled up again and Alison wanted to run, but the thought of Peter held her there. Peter. Head in his hands, his face blank, stony, unreadable.

'Is Toddy here?' she asked. 'Is he here?' Her voice was rising; she was having to shout now to be heard above the racket. One or two of the men, the older ones, saw her distress and tried to shush the rabble, but then the nightmare shifted into darker territory, because Martin Baxter was striding towards Alison, centre stage, seizing his moment of triumph. He'd waited for this, and you could see what he was thinking, just from that twisted sneer: *The little bitch has it coming. I'll bring her down off her fucking high horse.* Alison scanned the collection of men for Toddy, but there was no sign of him, and Martin was looming at her now, shoving something at her. She couldn't shift her limbs: her legs wouldn't move to run; her arms wouldn't move to protect herself. He thrust it at her, this object in his hand. He held it in her face. It was a photograph of a man on his knees in front of another. Alison registered this image, only briefly; then she defied Martin and closed her eyes.

'Yeah,' Martin said, 'go on, shut your eyes, you stuck-up cow, but it makes no difference. Your filthy pervert brother's finished.'

Now Alison opened her eyes, moved as close to him as she could bear, and spat in his face. The group around them was large now; they cheered at Alison's direct hit, and she looked around at them, at their pathetic animation, their flushed excitement, and she despised them all. Martin took a swing at her, but she dodged his fist, made him look a fool.

'Bitch,' Martin said, wiping his face on his sleeve. 'Little bitch.'

Alison snatched at the photograph, grabbed it from his hand, but he just laughed and said, 'Dunt worry, you can keep it. They've all seen 'em anyway, seen what those fucking queers do on a Sat'day night.'

She didn't understand, but followed his eyes across the yard and saw, now, a building, a squat shed with rough wooden walls and, stuck on to them, an ugly, haphazard patchwork of photographs. She turned her gaze back to Martin, who folded his arms and smiled, cold-blooded, gloating. Alison had always loathed this man, but now her loathing fuelled a very pure, intense fury, and gave her strength, and purpose. She surged forwards, pushing through the crowd, running at the men in her path so they seemed to have no choice but to step out of her way, and she threw herself at Martin's photographs in a frenzy, tearing at the pictures, ripping them down. There was some jeering from the men, some shouting, and a sort of scuffle over by the gates, but she didn't look, she was intent on her task, and even Martin's voice above the rest calling her bitch, and whore, didn't matter – it only drove her on. Then an old man – he seemed too old for the steelworks though he had on the gear, the hard hat, the boots, the overalls – appeared at her side, and he didn't say a word, only laid his hand on her shoulder for a few seconds, peacefully, as if he was calming an animal in distress. She paused under his kind gaze, and gathered herself, and he smiled at her and then began to help her, and together they started again, picking up the fallen photographs from the ground, pulling others from the walls, keeping them all face down and unseen, and between them it didn't take long before she had all of them collected in a bunch, in one hand.

'Thank you,' she said to him, and he waited with her while she steadied her breathing. His compassion and kindness in this bear pit seemed nothing short of an act of salvation and, perhaps because of it, the baying crowd had dispersed now. Only Martin Baxter still stood there, glowering; but without an audience, his power seemed diminished.

'Now then,' the old man said. 'You get yersen home.'

'But I came to find Dave Todd. Do you know where he is?'

He shook his head. 'No, I don't, flower,' he said.

'Somebody told me he'd be here.'

'Aye, well, I don't think you should go looking,' he said. 'This is no place for a lass. Go home.'

She looked at him, and felt the balm of his sanity. She nodded, he smiled, and she walked away, passing Martin Baxter without even a glance. As the distance between them grew, he continued to roar and bellow, chucking curses and insults after her, but she'd placed herself beyond his reach; he could see this, and it made him boil with helpless fury.

Her mother was in when Alison got back to the house. She was lying on the sofa with her face turned away from the room.

'Catherine,' Alison said. The photographs were still in her hand, and she didn't immediately know how to destroy them. Peter should have them, she thought; he should take them away and burn them. But Peter was nowhere to be seen.

'Catherine.'

Her mother said, 'What?' without moving or looking round. Her voice was groggy, thick with sleep. In the late-morning sunlight, the room looked hangdog and unloved, a sorry collection of mismatched furniture, a three-bar electric fire unplugged from its socket, a carpet burned black here and there by cigarette ends.

'Have you talked to our Peter?'

No reply.

'Catherine? Have you seen our Peter?'

She rolled over, very carefully and slowly. Her face was a mess of blood and bruising, and an untreated gash at her right temple was a raw and livid red. Alison felt weary beyond words. She put the photographs down on the mantelpiece, fetched a bowl of water and clean cloth from the kitchen, and a tin of plasters from the sideboard, and sat down on the edge of the sofa. She dampened the flannel and then very gently began to clean up her mother's face. Catherine submitted to the attention like a child, sighing and snuggling closer. She smelled bad; she often did these days. Sweat, smoke, secretions.

'I've just seen Martin Baxter,' Alison said. She leaned in to examine the cut. It wasn't too deep, didn't need stitches, just antiseptic, gauze and a strip of Elastoplast. She wet the flannel again, cleaned away blood and streaks of mascara, and the remnants of the sky-blue eyeshadow her mother favoured. She'd been doing this job for as long as she could remember, sharing the task with Peter: cleaning up their mother, dabbing away the results of a night on the tiles. Catherine's eyes were closed. She was relaxed and comfortable, still too numbed by vodka to feel any pain.

'Catherine?'

Her mother opened one eye. 'You're a good girl,' she said.

'Have you seen our Peter?'

Her mother nodded unsteadily. 'Upstairs,' she said.

'He's having a bad time. Martin took pictures of him and Toddy.'

'Help me up, love,' Catherine said. 'I need the lav.'

'In a minute. Just tell me, do you know what Martin's done?'

Catherine pulled a face, a grimace, and said, 'He shouldn't be so nasty.'

'Martin?'

'No, our Peter. He's nasty and it makes Martin go mad.'

'It's not Peter's fault. Martin's a pig, he's a monster, and you just let him do whatever he likes.'

Catherine opened her eyes wide. 'Me?' she said, befuddled, astonished.

Alison looked at her with ineffable sadness, and her mother said, 'What?'

'Do you think we don't need you, me and Peter?'

Catherine tutted. 'Oh, this again,' she said.

'We have to help him, Catherine.' Alison's voice shook. 'I don't think I can do this on my own. I don't know what to do.'

Catherine gave a splutter of laughter and shoved Alison, in a matey way. 'Don't know what to do? Get away with you,' she said. She pointed an unsteady index finger too close to Alison's face. 'You're my clever one. You're my bright spark.' She yawned and drew a hand over her face, and when her fingers grazed the wound she winced. 'Ouch,' she said. 'What the bloody hell's that?'

Alison looked down at the flannel in her hands, the bowl on her knees. The water was filmy now, the flannel smeared with blood and make-up. Her mother was sobering up, which meant she'd soon be hitting the booze again, and Peter was too quiet; she had to find him, face him, but, oh, she didn't want to, all on her own. Nothing was right here. Nothing was good. She'd go to Daniel's. She'd make sure Peter was OK first, then she'd go to Daniel's. She'd take a bag, some clothes. She couldn't be here.

'Ey,' Catherine said, attempting sympathy. 'Don't cry, pet lamb. What you got to cry about?' Then she pushed herself up to a sitting position. 'Right, shift then,' she said. 'I need the lav and you're in my way.'

Alison moved to let her mother stagger off the sofa. 'And don't lock the door, all right?' she said.

'Don't lock the door, all right?' her mother repeated in a simpering echo.

Upstairs.

Catherine was crashing about in the bathroom, Peter was in his room and Alison was standing in front of her dressing-table mirror, analysing her appearance.

She'd gone to Peter first, taken a tentative look around his bedroom door and found him prone on the bed, eyes closed, peaceful. This was heartening, so she went into her own bedroom and stripped off her clothes, put on some fresh ones, brushed her hair and tied it back into a ponytail. A wash would've been good. A bath even better. But the bathroom was full of her mother, and anyway, she felt adequately restored by clean clothes, and she stood in front of her mirror for a while, looking for signs of Catherine in herself. She knew she looked like Catherine used to look; there were old photographs that proved this. Catherine with a gang of girls on the club trip to Blackpool. Catherine in an off-the-shoulder dress, going dancing at the City Hall. Catherine in lace, carrying lily of the valley, standing in the lychgate of the pretty church at Dore, golden with promise and happiness. Peter was the image of their father, that's what everyone used to say, but there was no evidence of it now, because Geoff Connor had been savagely excised from the family archive, hacked away from every picture he'd ever appeared in. Geoff Connor, famous for having sex with his sister-in-law on the morning of his own wedding, and many a time afterwards, and many other women too, oh, legions of them, although it was hard to say where fact ended and fiction began. Where was he now? He'd scarpered soon after Catherine came home from hospital with Alison, but there was no love lost there, because by then there'd been none to lose, not a scrap.

Geoff had slung his hook, and he did at least give Catherine this: a person to blame for every bad thing that had happened since.

Ancient history. Alison stared back at the image of herself in the mirror. Her eyes were red-rimmed – she'd done way too much crying today, she reckoned – but other than that she looked OK, all things considered. Young, good-looking, a girl with a future. One more year, and she'd be out of here. University, perhaps Durham, where Daniel was going if he got the grades. Or perhaps another city, far away, Exeter maybe. Her fresh start, the beginning of another beginning. Solemnly she raised her hand and placed it on the glass, palm to palm with herself, then made a brief and silent pledge to be more resolute in this coming year, less daunted by circumstance. One could decide to be happy, and happiness would surely follow. This is what she'd say to Peter when he woke. Because bad as things were, they surely couldn't now deteriorate further? Martin had done his worst, and if Peter was finished at Brown Bayley's, so what? He hated it there anyway. He could do anything, Peter. He was clever with his hands, practical, skilful; he was wasted on a crane at the steelworks, wasted.

There was a loud clatter of something falling, or something thrown. Alison heaved a sigh at her reflection and went to the bathroom door.

'Catherine?' she said, and she tried the handle. For once, her mother had heeded Alison's words and not locked herself in. She was stripped down to her knickers, sitting on the lavatory seat, trying to cut her toenails.

'You do it,' she said without looking up. 'These damn things are so fiddly.'

'I heard a crash,' Alison said.

'Well, it wasn't me for once.' Catherine glanced across at her with a half-smile and held out the nail clippers.

'Hang on,' Alison said. 'Back in a tick.'

She went to Peter's room and pushed open the door. Peter was facing her, hanging by a noose round his neck from the light flex, staring directly into her face with wide, terrified eyes. There was a chair on its side and now he seemed to be fighting to stay alive, his hands clutching uselessly at the tightening rope, his legs flailing for the chair. His mouth was opening and shutting, but he made no sound. Alison took a second to remember how to breathe, then she entered the room, picked up the chair and put it back under his feet, to take his weight. He felt the solid safety of it beneath him, and then he dropped his hands down towards his sister in a pleading, remorseful gesture, a kind of supplication. She stared at him, and backed away. That Peter could attempt this . . . that he could try to leave her, and in such an ugly, selfish, craven way. She saw his face, wet with sorrow, but just in this moment, her heart seemed frozen.

'Cut it,' he said, his voice a rasping whisper. The chair was at an awkward angle and unsteady, just a plain wooden desk chair, spindle-backed with thin barley-twist legs. It wasn't built to stop a man from killing himself. He moved his feet tentatively, trying to centre them, to keep the chair upright. 'Alison,' he said, then again, 'Alison.'

She saw, suddenly, that she must act, and she turned and ran down the stairs and took a pair of kitchen scissors from the drawer. They had black plastic handles and the blades were blunt and discoloured with age. They could barely cut through paper these days, and certainly they'd never been called upon to save a man. Alison, preternaturally calm, took a second chair with her too, so that she could stand beside her brother without jeopardising his safety. She placed it alongside him, climbed up on to it, then began to press the blades of the scissors against the rope, sawing and pulling, while Peter wobbled and moaned, and reached for her with his hands, clutching at her arm. She ignored him. 'This isn't working,' she said, as if to herself. 'I'll have to cut the flex.' She shrugged off his hands and got down from the chair, went back downstairs to the fuse box by the front door, and switched off the mains. Back upstairs again, back on to the chair.

'Let go of me,' she said to Peter. 'I need to stretch up and I can't if you paw at me like that.' She knew she sounded hostile, but there was work to be done here, and she soldiered on, stretching up above her brother to the light flex, which – though resistant at first – gave way at last to the dull blades of the scissors. The loss of tension from above threw Peter off balance and he fell to the floor, landing badly. Alison stepped down from her chair. They stared at each other, then she bent down and worked at the noose until it was wide and slack enough to pull over his head. He watched her face but, now, she wouldn't meet his eyes.

'There.' She placed the rope and the flex, still with its light bulb attached, on to the floor next to him; then she took a few moments to steady herself and to hide her anger. He'd wanted to die. He'd been prepared to leave her. She felt a wave of loneliness, the cold reality of betrayal.

She had to go to Daniel. She needed him.

'Peter,' she said then. 'I have to leave for a while, as long as you promise me you'll be here when I come back.' He closed his eyes and nodded. Tears coursed down his face, but she had no strength for his unhappiness just now. She stooped to rest her palm on his head though, leaving it there for a few moments in place of all the words she didn't have, then she stood up and left the room, shutting the door and resting her head briefly against it.

'Alison,' Catherine shouted from the bathroom, petulant, demanding. 'Alison, come here!'

But she descended the stairs, put the mains switch back on, picked up her satchel from the floor, and left the house. The clock said two forty-five, although she felt she'd suffered for days and days on Peter's account. There was a bus leaving Shortridge Street in five minutes. In under an hour, she'd be at Daniel's house, where the world was a safer place to inhabit.

17

Katelin had hoped she'd hate the book, but *Tell the Story, Sing the Song* was brilliant: intelligent, accessible, lyrical, colourful, all the things the reviews had said, but more so, annoyingly so, and she hadn't been able to stop herself from loving it. She hadn't been able to stop talking about it, either; it'd sparked a sort of intellectual thirst for Australia and, as a result, a country she'd never given a moment's thought to was suddenly front and centre in her mind. She was reading Bruce Chatwin now, *The Songlines*, and kept on to Dan about the dreamings and the ancient tracks criss-crossing the land; about the songs, the ancestors, the sacred totems. Dan had no idea what she was going on about, and it was true Katelin hadn't totally grasped the essence either, but it was a slippery concept, to be fair, difficult to articulate. Didn't stop her trying. Didn't stop the interrogations either. Her interest in Ali Connor was a natural and unfortunate consequence of all this, and Dan was fed up to the back teeth of pretending he couldn't remember much about her, playing her down, denying her significance. Claire hadn't helped, with the 'practically moved in' line. Dan had had to fudge the issue, and make out Alison was more of a friend than a girlfriend, really. He had no intention of telling the truth; it would benefit Katelin not a jot. She had a jealous heart, and a possessive soul, and if he'd said to her now or at any point in their history that there once was a girl called Alison who almost destroyed him, shattered his faith in love for a few years, and nigh on broke his dad's heart too, it would never, ever have gone away. But by the time he met Katelin, who'd always been thirsty for information about his past, he'd been able to regale her with enough stories – enough cheerful tales of one-night stands and insignificant significant others – to protect himself from having to relive the trauma, while still providing Katelin with the details she seemed to crave. Old girlfriends were like scabbed-over wounds to her, and she couldn't help picking at them to make them bleed. Dan couldn't understand this, couldn't see why she might be needled by his relationships with girls he'd known before he met her. Himself, he couldn't care less which boys she'd snogged behind the bike sheds. It was irrelevant. But Katelin, God! Dog with a bone.

'She must've been clever,' she'd said this morning, standing at the bedroom mirror, dabbing concealing make-up on to the bluish shadows under her eyes. He knew immediately, of course, who was meant by 'she' and he groaned inwardly. He was lying in bed, wishing to be asleep, not answering her questions, rebutting her statements. 'I mean, to write that book?' she said. Yes, this sounded innocuous enough, but oh no. No, no, no. They had wandered into dangerous territory.

'She was good at English,' Dan said, then added a precautionary, 'I think.'

'Yeah, well, Claire said that much at Christmas. But she must've been a cut above, at school?'

'No,' Dan said. 'Well, maybe. We were at different schools, so I can't really say.'

Silence. Then, 'So, how did you meet, again?'

He sighed, and pushed himself up so he could see the back

of Katelin's head. He was dead beat, hadn't come to bed until 2 a.m. because he'd had a rambling, indulgent live chat on air with a New York radio station where an old friend of his from the *NME* years peddled classic British rock on a weekly show. He glanced at the time on his phone. Ten past seven. Jesus! He should've gone to sleep in Alex's empty bed – foolish to crawl in here expecting to be left alone. Katelin eyed him briefly, then looked at herself in the mirror again, waiting.

'Like I said, we got the same bus sometimes,' Dan said. 'We got chatting.'

'About what?'

'Seriously? You do realise how long ago this was, don't you?'

'I mean, did you have much in common? Or was it just that you fancied her?'

'Look,' Dan said, 'don't get fixated.'

She laughed, and turned around to face him. 'I'm interested,' she said brightly, ominously. 'That's all.'

'OK, well, she liked the same music as me.'

Katelin nodded slowly. 'I see, right. Music,' she said, as if he'd just said stamp collecting, and actually expected her to believe it.

'Yeah.' He was not going to lose his cool. 'We talked about music.'

'So the fact that she was clearly bloody gorgeous had absolutely nothing to do with it?'

He closed his eyes. He cursed his mother's guileless purchase. He cursed Katelin's forensic insecurity. Of course she was on to something, this wasn't simply her imagination working overtime, but – he repeated to himself – neither was this a Katelin versus Alison scenario, because . . . well, one of them was here in Edinburgh with him, the other ten thousand miles away. And anyway, what was he supposed to do? Tell Katelin everything? Yeah, right.

'I bet you've googled her,' she said.

He was silent, but she knew he had, and of course he had. Most days now, for over three months.

'Well, I certainly have,' Katelin said. 'There's not a single photograph online in which she looks anything but beautiful.'

Agreed, thought Dan. He'd listened to the *Woman's Hour* interview too, found it online after Katelin told him about it. Ali's voice was altered, she sounded Australian, and of course she would after all these years. But there were traces of Alison Connor in those vowels, and he'd thought: Get that woman back to Sheffield and it'll all come flooding back. Listening to her, hearing her speak: this had caused him pain, as well as pleasure. To this day he had no idea why she'd gone. He knew it was something to do with her fucked-up family, her mother, her brother, but it had been difficult at the time not to feel that he, Daniel, had failed Alison on some fundamental level, and her bailing out on him was his punishment. God, what a punishment. It'd felt like being denied oxygen. For a long time he'd been in purgatory, and it certainly screwed up university for him; he hadn't dealt with that experience at all well, all those privileged boys and girls on his course and in his hall of residence, popping champagne corks and mixing cocktails, partying to Queen and Abba, navigating their way through life with supreme, unchallenged confidence because all the friends they'd had at private school seemed to be here with them, in Durham. Dan had lasted three terms before packing it in. Even now, when he heard 'Bohemian Rhapsody', he was right back in college, alone in his room, the dark, brooding northerner with a mighty chip on his shoulder and a default expression of naked disdain on his face. He'd worked hard, though, at forgetting Alison, chasing away her ghost by playing all the music they'd never shared while having lots of sex with edgy girls from Newcastle Poly who were more his type than the university crowd, and, later, even edgier girls in Camden and Kentish Town. He'd worked hard, too, at pleasing them; made sure he was better at sex than he ever had been with Alison Connor. He was serious about it, he concentrated, and in this way, he elevated the activity from ordinary, mindless shagging to a higher plane. It took a year for the pain to feel less than visceral, and another year before he stopped wanting her, and yet another before she rarely crossed his consciousness. But he was young, and wounds heal, and he did, eventually, rub out the memory, or at least diminish it until it was forgotten. And now here she was, back again in this tantalising distant form, apparently still joined to him by what might only be a gossamer thread, but he wasn't going to let it break, there was to be no forgetting her again. He knew her. She'd helped create him. She was part of his DNA. On the radio, talking to Jenni Murray, she'd been a little spikey at first, a little chippy, and he'd realised then that she hadn't really altered. She'd gone on to claim she was happy as a clam in Adelaide, but he knew, he just knew, that she was protesting too much, she wasn't as happy as she made out. Well, nobody ever was.

'Why didn't I know about her, Dan?' Katelin said.

He lay back down with a heavy sigh and stared at the ceiling. 'Katelin, please, please retreat before we fall out. There's something so fucking undignified about this.'

She regarded him through the mirror. 'I do know that,' she said. 'I do know you think I'm being juvenile. But I've seen that woman's lovely face on the inside cover of the best book I've read in twenty years. Show me a female who wouldn't feel a stab of jealousy at the arrival of an old flame of this calibre.'

He understood her, he entirely took her point, and he felt for her, he really did. She was searching for the truth and being met only by disingenuous, weary patience. Yet Dan knew he had nothing at all to gain by full disclosure, only a landslide of further questions that he wouldn't be able to answer.

'It's a strange coincidence, Katelin,' he said. 'That's all.'

'No, I'm sorry, I don't believe that. It just doesn't ring true.'

'OK. Fine.'

'I think she was important to you.'

'She was a friend! I had other friends I've never mentioned to you either. Do you want a roll call from the class of seventy-nine?'

'Yeah, a friend, and looking the way she did, and bright as a button, it never entered your eighteen-year-old head to have a crack at her?'

'She was too good for me,' Dan said, trying another tack. 'Out of my league.'

'Oh, great!' Katelin's voice rose with indignation. 'Marvellous. So you started looking in the second division instead? How fortunate for me.'

Now he finally gave up on sleep. He threw back the covers and swung out of bed.

'What you doing?' Katelin said.

He came over to her and ran one hand up her thigh to rest firmly on her backside and the other up through her hair to hold the back of her head, then he pulled her close and Katelin said, 'You've got to be joking! Some of us have a job to go to.'

Six thirty, the same day, and Dan had lost an afternoon to beer and music, a pleasant enough pastime for a Thursday in January. He'd been listening to Nick Drake, choosing a reply to send to Ali, but you can't make these decisions lightly, especially not after the fourth beer. One song leads to another, then another, then they all demand to be heard again. He compiled a longlist of ten, then a shortlist of five, then, after a tense three-way play-off, he found he couldn't choose only one, so he sent them all: 'Northern Sky', one of the loveliest songs ever written, loaded with feeling; 'From The Morning', because he thought she'd like it; and 'Road', because it simply blew him away every time he heard it. Three Nick Drake songs, bang, bang, bang. Then he played some Rory Gallagher – genius, genius – and thought about his bedroom in Nether Edge, and how listening to blues guitar with Alison had felt so sophisticated. Man, though, they'd had great taste for a pair of kids, great taste! Daniel and Alison, meant to be. Everybody said so; well, they did after she'd vanished, after she'd evaporated into the July sky without a trace. She'd missed that gig at the Mayflower, the one that was meant to make them all famous. Steve Levitt, fuming all the way to Manchester, then blaming her bitterly after the set for the rest of them being off kilter. Well, there'd been some truth in that. Dan knew he'd screwed up that night because she hadn't shown up, for sure. Watching the back door during their set as if she might walk in at the last minute. Drinking too much because she didn't.

He fetched another beer from the kitchen, then decided to send her some Rory along with the other stuff, in fact he couldn't think why he hadn't done this already. It had to be 'I Fall Apart': perfect, just perfect, spot on. So, four songs. Was that too many? Then, as an afterthought, he sent 'I'm Not Surprised', which was a sort of belated kick up the arse from him to her for deserting him. Five songs. Seriously overdoing it, but anyway, they were gone now, miraculously teleported to her screen. Let her be bombarded. He drank his beer and listened to them again, in order, and he was musing on the possibility of a third Rory

Gallagher track when a blast of cold air and a bang signalled the opening and closing of the front door and suddenly Katelin was in the house, then in the room. She switched on the light. McCulloch, curled into a tight warm ball on Dan's lap, raised his head and cut her a baleful stare.

'God's sake, what're you pair doing in the dark?' she said, shouting over the music, all brisk and professional in her trench coat and suede boots. 'Dan? Good grief, you're worse than Alex. I can't hear myself think!' She shrugged off her coat, sat on the armchair and peeled off her boots. Dan silenced the Bose and switched off his phone. He was on the floor, with his back to the sofa.

'Anyway, what *are* you doing?' Katelin said, looking between him and the bottles lined up like skittles on the hearth. 'You're not drunk, are you? You're never drinking alone, like an old saddo?'

He patted the floor next to him. 'Join me,' he said. 'For old times' sake.'

'Old times' sake? Catch yourself on, cheeky sod.'

He stared into the neck of his beer bottle.

'Ahhh, you're pissed. Are you pissed?'

He thought about it. It was possible. Certainly he was comfortably numb.

'Have you made dinner?'

He hadn't, of course. Instead, he'd feasted on the superlative guitar skills of Nick Drake and Rory Gallagher. Oh shit, he'd just said that out loud.

Katelin stood up and gave him a pitying stare. She told him to pull himself together and join her in the kitchen in twenty minutes, but he knew better than to take her at her word. He shoved McCulloch off his lap, hauled himself to his feet and followed her.

'So,' he said, watching her bustle about, a little dazed by her busyness. 'What's happening in the world?'

She pulled a pan from the drawer and ran cold water into it, looking at him pityingly. 'Have you been holed up here all day?' she said. He nodded. She put the pan on the hob, switched it on high, then set to work on an onion. Dan leaned against the worktop and studied her profile. This was precisely the angle he'd seen when she first caught his eye in the bar in Bogotá. Back then, he'd immediately liked the look of her, although she wasn't exactly pretty. 'Striking' was what his mother said when he introduced her, a few months later. 'She's a *striking* girl,' Marion had said, and she'd managed to swallow the 'but' that seemed to be about to follow. With Katelin, though, it was the package, the whole shebang, that drew you to her. She was a force to be reckoned with, back then. There weren't many girls in the mid-eighties who travelled on their own through Colombia; he'd been most impressed at that, at her independence, her confidence. She was so certain of her place on the planet. That's what made her sexy. She'd been in a drinking contest when he found her, facing six shots of aguardiente, all in a line, some sort of challenge with a gaucho type, and everyone in the bar was shouting for her. Daniel had watched her toss back the liquor and her hair flew out in a wild auburn wave, and her earrings – feathers, if he remembered right: feathers, ribbons and minuscule bells – flashed and twisted and rang.

The onion, peeled and chopped small, was tipped into a pan of hot olive oil, then she smashed a garlic clove under the blade of a knife, and peeled and chopped that too. In it went.

'Can you make yourself useful and grate some Parmesan or something,' she said, shoving the onion and garlic around in the pan.

'What happened to those earrings you wore in Bogotá?' Dan said.

'What?' She looked at him as a teacher might look at a spectacularly dim-witted pupil.

'The feathers and bells.'

'What a question.'

He shrugged. 'Yeah,' he said. 'Never mind.'

'It's the beer. Too much and it makes you gloomy.'

'I'm not gloomy!'

'Good,' she said. 'I should think not. There's not many of us can drink beer and play music all day and call it work.'

He let this pass, got the cheese out of the fridge and the grater from the drawer, and began to make a pile of Parmesan on a board. 'I was just thinking about that bar in Bogotá, and I liked those earrings.'

'I think I threw 'em away about twenty years ago. They started to moult.'

'Do you remember the band?'

'Was there a band?'

'Yes, there was a band! Two guys and a girl, playing Spanish guitar, and one of the guys had a trumpet. Fucking awesome, remember?'

'No, Dan, I don't remember.'

'They were just locals, not professionals, but they were incredible.'

She pulled a 'beats me' face. 'Pass me the spaghetti,' she said, and held out her hand for it.

'Oh, c'mon!' Dan said, handing over the packet. 'We danced to it.'

'Dan, I don't remember it.'

'The dancing?'

'Oh, I remember larking about, pretending to tango or

something, but I honestly couldn't tell you who was playing or what they were playing or how they were playing it. I'd have said they had a radio on, if anything.'

She pressed the pasta into the boiling water, watching it submit and submerge. Then she chopped a red chilli and added it to the onions, did the same to a couple of stray pork sausages, tipped in a packet of pancetta cubes, and whacked up the heat. When Alex was little he'd named this meal Pasta Everything. They had it whenever there was nothing to eat except odds and ends. A half-punnet of cherry tomatoes went in next, and a few spinach leaves, the end of the bag. Salt. Pepper. Then she turned her back on it and left it to sizzle.

'Right,' she said. 'Five minutes or so, and we're on. That's enough cheese, Dan, we're not feeding the street.'

She poured herself a glass of white wine from a bottle already started in the fridge, then sat down opposite him. 'You're in a strange mood,' she said. 'Bogotá, earrings.'

He shrugged and got up to help himself to another beer. These were strange times, he could have said; strange days, indeed. He wondered what time it was in Adelaide.

'God, I'm looking forward to taking off,' Katelin said. She hooked up her left foot and massaged it through her tights. 'I've earned this trip.'

She was leaving in a week for the States. For a while, it had all seemed in jeopardy, when Duncan had briefly left home for his rock chick, and Rose-Ann had fallen apart, swinging between fury and grief. But Duncan had been back before Christmas and Rose-Ann was triumphant. Lindsay hadn't needed him at all, she'd just wanted him from time to time, and while at first she'd made him feel wonderfully young, in the end – and very quickly – she only made him feel terribly old. So Rose-Ann had taken him back, and now he was having his balls cauterised – very, very slowly. It was depressing to see them together, Dan thought. His friend would never get off the back foot now.

'Dan?'

He looked at Katelin. 'Yeah?'

'Don't let everything go to pot while I'm gone, will you?'

'Oh, give over,' Dan said. He poked at the pasta. 'This is ready, by the way.'

'Drain it then, but put a splash of the water in the sauce. To be fair, I did just find you half-cut, in the dark, listening to God only knows what.'

'Rory Gallagher,' Dan said. 'Irish lad. You ought to know that.' He tipped the spaghetti into the colander, then tipped it out of the colander and into the sauce. Back on the heat, it spluttered and hissed.

'Well, anyway,' Katelin said. 'Just don't.'

'Look, while you're away, I'll do what I always do, which is write about music, listen to music, stare at the wall and some-times drink beer in the dark. Oh,' he said, remembering a phone call he'd had much earlier that day, 'I had a call from Tess at Six Music today. They want me on a regular slot, some kind of panel, me and a couple of other hacks.'

She said, 'Good,' in that tone she sometimes used that drove him nuts. He'd by no means decided to do it – it was a Thursday morning gig, and getting to Media City in Salford every Wed-nesday night wasn't the most tempting offer he'd ever had. But there was Katelin with her encouraging, condescending 'good', as if he'd been slogging away fruitlessly for years and had finally had a lucky break.

'Good, why?' he said.

She raised her eyebrows, as if it was obvious. 'Regular work.'

'Katelin, I *do* regular work, but I do it in an irregular fashion, and it's never let us down yet.'

'No, I know, but there's always that feeling it could all dry up.'

He stared at her over the top of his beer bottle. 'No, there isn't,' he said. 'I don't have that feeling.'

'You know what you should do? You should write another book.'

He laughed. 'Oh, should I?'

'It's a while since that last one, the *Made in Sheffield* thing.'

The *Made in Sheffield* thing. A book he'd written that Katelin had never read, about music she'd never listened to. 'Yeah, well,' he said. 'All in good time. Most music books don't sell. They don't dole out advances like they used to.'

'But you have too much time on your hands.'

'Katelin, that's bollocks!'

'Well, you do!' she said, gesturing at him with her free hand as if he was exhibit A, the living embodiment of an underemployed journalist.

'No, I don't, I'm up to my neck in work.'

'Good,' she said again cheerfully, to properly convey her scepticism. 'Great. So let's eat.'

Later, up in his eyrie, he worked late into the night. He wrote a piece about Bon Iver for *Uncut*, another for the *Quietus* about a new Bunnymen album slated for the end of the year. He made a start on the sleeve notes for a remastered album by The Clash, rehashed an interview with Ian McCulloch for the *Guardian*, read his piece on *Pitchfork* about the top 50 indie albums of 2012, replied to nine emails, then took a call from a journalist on *Rolling Stone*, who wanted his thoughts for a piece about Hunter S. Thompson. Katelin, watching television downstairs, then going to bed at half past ten, was unaware of his endeavours. This was how it was. This was the kernel of the problem. Katelin had no real idea what he did. It was his world, not hers, and ne'er the twain would meet. He'd realised many years ago that Katelin had always thought the music writing would give way to . . . oh, something more respectable, she didn't know what exactly, but something less sketchy than his present existence. Nothing Dan had ever done or said had encouraged her in these beliefs, it was just the way of the world in her view, the natural progression of things, and she couldn't understand why all those years of experience didn't amount to a proper job in an office, rather than merely more of the same. He knew what he was doing though, he always had, and hadn't everything worked out? He'd written the books he wanted to write, he'd made some money, and still did, one way or another. Granted, it had its frustrations; he spent at least a day a week chasing up unpaid invoices, and the rate for those online pieces was pitiful, but the money always rolled in from somewhere, and he'd never, in all his working life, had a bad day at the office. Just, now and again, a bad day at home.

He picked up his phone, checked the time. It was half past two. As ever, the screen was a bunfight, a string of people vying for his attention, but only one caught his eye. *Ali Connor sent you a direct message.* He must, he really must, switch off these Twitter notifications, the very last thing he needed was Katelin catching sight of that name on his screen, at this delicate point in their lives together. But she was fast asleep, and for now, he just navigated his way swiftly to Ali's message and saw that she hadn't answered his bombardment of musical artillery with a link to a song, but instead had sent only a line, a lyric he supposed, and one he recognised, yet couldn't quite place: *And I feel your warmth and it feels like home.*

He stared at the row of simple words, processing them, waiting for enlightenment. It didn't take long. Depeche Mode, 'Here Is The House'. Oh, this woman was pure class. He stared at the message she'd typed for him, hoping for more, somehow; trying to wring some intention from the handful of words, but he found he could speak only for himself, and he knew he had no defences. None. She was utterly compelling, she was spinning through time, she was his once more; he could almost feel the softness of her skin again, the softness of her hair. He rested his forehead on the cool steel of his desk and waited for the violent longing to subside. Christ Almighty, he was inhabited by her and it was driving him out of his mind.

Then he sat up. This is what he would do – he'd go to her. He would. He'd just turn up in Adelaide and see if this was real. The ethics of the scheme, the deception and daring – none of this clouded his mind right now. It was perfectly simple, entirely necessary. On his phone, he opened their thread and replied in kind with a lyric, a perfect snippet of Bunnymen genius, from 'All That Jazz'. He watched it go, wondered when she'd see it, and if she knew it.

See you at the barricades, babe.

She probably wouldn't guess, but it was full of intention; he meant what he said. He pushed back the chair and walked across his office to the wall with the world map, and traced a line with his eyes from Scotland all the long way across and down, down, down to South Australia. There's my girl, he thought; there's my girl, with another guy.

The sooner he got himself to the front line, the better.

18

Beatriz wept with relief when the McCormacks came home. She'd convinced herself they were going to burn to death in a bush fire, because all she saw on the evening news was drama and crisis. Seven men had died near Burra two days ago when a fire whipped over the containment line and trapped them in a vortex of heat and smoke, and a little girl and her daddy had only narrowly survived a wall of fire near Koonoona by drenching a woollen blanket in a stock trough, then lying under it, inside their ute, and letting the fire pass over them.

'Hell's fury unleashed,' Michael said that evening, their first night back. 'But we were lucky.' He fetched a perfectly chilled Clare Valley Riesling from the fridge and began to pour it into five glasses.

'Only a small one for me,' Beatriz said. 'And by the way, luck had nothing to do with it. I asked God, every morning and every night, to spare you, and he did.' She sounded stern. Fifty years of service with this family, and still God didn't get credit for his goodness.

'God, Gil and the CFS,' Michael said. 'The holy trinity.' He slid glasses of wine across the table to Ali, Stella and Thea, then handed a half-measure to Beatriz, and clinked glasses with her.

'Cheers, dear Beatriz,' he said. 'Your prayers are a comfort to us all.'

'It came so close, Beatriz,' Stella said. 'Scary how fast it moves. One minute the fire seems miles away; the next minute it's heading for your hayloft.'

The old lady shook her head in horrified wonder; she felt blessed that they'd survived, when disaster had seemed, to her, a nailed-on certainty, and she'd cooked up a *caldeirada* to show how happy she was to have her family safely home. Portuguese fish stew, the celebration meal, the thanksgiving offering. She hauled the dish from the oven and lifted the lid to check the seasoning, and fragrant steam rose like a promise from the trusty, battle-scarred cooking pot.

'Alma won't cook fish,' Thea said. 'She says it makes her kitchen smell.'

Beatriz sniffed and said, 'A cook who won't cook fish is no cook at all.' She rarely, and unfairly, had anything good to say about Alma, whom she'd met only twice, but whose reign at Lismore Creek represented an imagined threat to her own pre-eminence here in Adelaide.

'It is kind of smelly though,' Thea said. 'In the morning, I mean, when you get the bones and heads going in your stock pot, Beatriz. A bit gross.' She wrinkled her pretty nose.

'Ingrate,' Michael said. 'This wine is perfect, Ali. Ali? Taste your wine.' She was lost in thought, and jumped a little at the sound of her name.

'Sorry?' she said. She was thinking of Daniel Lawrence and Nick Drake and Rory Gallagher.

'Try the wine, it's delicious.' He watched her take a sip, nod her approval. Michael liked feedback for his wine choices; really, he'd have preferred more than a nod, a little appreciative analysis perhaps. But Ali was no connoisseur, he'd failed to turn her into one, despite his best efforts; if the wine was cold, white and dry, that was good enough for her.

Beatriz said, 'My street in Porto, when I was small, smelled of boiled fish heads every Friday. The whole street!'

'I might go to Portugal on my travels,' Stella said casually. 'Italy, France, Spain, Portugal.' She gazed into her glass and swirled her wine, watching it lap the sides.

Ali nodded, then remembered Michael didn't know that Stella had changed her mind about drama school in Sydney. She opened her mouth to broach the subject, but Thea, sharp as a tack, said, 'After NIDA, you mean?' and Stella said, 'No, instead of,' and Ali thought, Oh jeez, here we go.

'I beg your pardon?' Michael said. He paused, with his glass en route to his mouth, and looked intently at his younger daughter. Stella looked at Ali. Michael put his glass down and looked at Ali too.

'Stella's decided she doesn't want to take up the place at NIDA,' Ali said. She couldn't think why she hadn't told him. It was a huge oversight, for sure.

'Oh,' Michael said. 'Nice of you to mention it. When was this decided?'

'At Lismore,' Stella said. 'But it wasn't, like, a big moment or anything. You were out in the ute, checking fences or something. We didn't mean not to tell you.'

'Not a big moment?'

'Oh, Stella, you're such a pain in the ass,' Thea said, and she sighed heavily. 'I suppose we're going to have to talk about you all night again now.'

'Who's going to Portugal?' Beatriz asked, beaming widely, bearing her stew to the table, entirely oblivious to the tension that had suddenly filled the room to its corners. She placed the pot in the centre of the table. 'Now we can eat,' she said.

'You flew through that audition in November,' Michael said to Stella. 'They loved you. You were barely out the door before they offered you a place.'

'Well, anyway,' she said. 'I'm not going.'

'Yes, you are.'

'Mum!' Stella said, appealing to Ali.

Michael took the ladle and began to dole out fish stew into the topmost bowl of a stack of five in front of him. Always, when they ate together like this, Michael dished up the food Beatriz had cooked. Why was this? thought Ali. Because his father had, before him. Because Beatriz understood him to be head of the household. Because Michael simply took charge, naturally, easily, without debate.

'Michael,' Ali said. 'Let's have this conversation later.'

'Bad enough that she chooses drama in the first place,' Michael said, shovelling at the shellfish and rattling mussels and clams into the waiting bowls. 'But at least she aimed high with NIDA. Now, apparently, she's not even prepared to do that.'

'Dad!' Stella said. Her eyes filled with angry tears.

Michael looked at her, his face grim. 'Your IB score was phenomenal,' he said. 'Phenomenal. You could do anything, anything. Christ Almighty, it was better than Thea's, and she's a med student.'

'Michael! Do not take the Lord's name in vain,' Beatriz said, and Thea said, 'Cheers, Dad, appreciate that.' She took the bowl he'd filled and passed it to Beatriz, the next to Ali, then Stella, then took one for herself. Michael filled the last bowl, then pushed what remained of the stew back to the centre of the table. Yellow with saffron, red with tomatoes, green with herbs, it looked ambrosial, but even Beatriz realised now that her food was no longer the main event.

'If you think you're loafing around Europe alone, think again,' Michael said. He was deeply aggrieved, with Ali more than with Stella; he was pale with suppressed anger.

'You're going alone?' Beatriz said.

'I won't be on my own, not at first,' Stella said.

The girl was trying to speak levelly, trying not to betray her emotion. She was their rebel, always the one with her own agenda, but even so, thought Ali, she was still affected by her father's disapproval. He had the knack of making her feel very young, very uncertain. But Stella had fought for her right to apply to drama school when he – and all her teachers – thought she was destined for languages at ANU. Now she'd fight for the right not to do drama either. Stella would win; Ali knew this.

'I'm going to volunteer for three months with an NGO, in Italy,' the girl said now.

Ali and Thea, both impressed by this statement, said, 'Are you?' at precisely the same time.

'No,' Michael said. 'No, Stella. You. Are. Not.'

'I don't think you can stop her, Dad,' Thea said, still narked by his reference to her IB score, which had indeed been three points lower than her sister's.

'I'd really prefer to discuss this later,' Ali said. 'Beatriz made this lovely food, we should all just enjoy it and postpone this conversation until after dinner.'

Beatriz dipped her head at Ali, in recognition of a point well made. Stella immediately said, 'Yes, sorry, Beatriz, it's the best, *obrigada*.' Beatriz smiled at Stella, then for a few long seconds no one said anything. The sound of cutlery on china was awkwardly loud. Ali drank her wine, too quickly. Thea picked up a half-opened mussel shell and peered suspiciously at its insides, poked at it with a fork, then held it up to Beatriz, who nodded yes, it's fine, eat it.

'Stella,' Michael said, and everyone looked at him. He wasn't a man for dropping the subject if he hadn't yet got his way. 'You've shown me in the past three months that you're not capable of looking after yourself. You can travel afterwards, do the degree you applied for first, do some growing up.'

Stella carefully put down her fork and spoon. 'When I told Mum I didn't want to go to uni, she just said, "Then don't."'

'Right, well, that's only because Mum doesn't know what you'll be missing.'

'Excuse me?' This was Ali. She reached for the bottle and refilled her wine glass.

'I only mean, you didn't go to university yourself,' Michael said. 'You didn't even finish school. So you're not the best judge.'

Ali laughed, without amusement. 'No, Michael,' she said. 'It's not because I'm ill-informed, it's because I want Stella to make her own choices. She can go to NIDA next year, or the year after. They'll take her – they've never auditioned a girl with her talent, that's what they said.'

'My point is,' Michael said, 'she's too young to travel.'

'I was only eighteen when you met me in Spain.'

Michael looked at his wife with an expression of incredulity that she should raise her own example to support her case. 'Found you, not met you,' he said. 'I found you in Spain. And God alone knows where you'd be now if I hadn't.'

Alison Connor had been sitting cross-legged on the ground, alone, in the shade of a stone archway within the medieval walls of Santo Domingo de la Calzada. She was wearing denim shorts, a plain khaki T-shirt adorned only with the words 'Wild Willy Barrett', and a pair of flat leather sandals. She had a cotton cap, also khaki, which was beside her on the floor, and a canvas bag, a kind of small satchel, which she wore diagonally across her body. Her face and limbs were tanned but those parts of her feet not covered by the worn leather of her sandals were the same pale grey as the dust on the street. Her dark brown hair was chopped to just above her shoulders, but rather haphazardly, as if she might have done it herself, with blunt scissors and no mirror. Her eyes were closed. She appeared to be resting, but she wasn't out of place here; there were lots of footsore pilgrims breaking their journey in this lovely Spanish town, so the world flowed around and about her, as easily and naturally as a brook.

Michael McCormack stared at her until she woke up and looked at him.

'Hi,' he said. 'How you going?'

She showed no surprise or concern at being observed by this stranger, only gazed at him placidly. He'd thought, at first, she might be begging, but he could see there was no cup for loose change, no sign hand-scrawled on cardboard. She was just a sleeping girl, who'd now woken up. He squatted, so that he no longer looked down on her. She had greenish-brown eyes and dark lashes, golden skin, a perfectly symmetrical face. He held out a hand, and said, 'Michael, Michael McCormack,' and, after a brief hesitation, she took it.

'Alison Connor,' she said.

'Are you walking the Camino?' he asked.

'Pardon?' She yawned and ran her hands across her face, then through her hair. He watched.

'The trail, y'know, to Santiago?'

'Oh,' she said. 'Sort of. Are you?'

He laughed. He had a loaded pack, strong boots, wet-weather gear, a tent, a sleeping mat.

'Can I buy you a drink?' he asked. He tried to sound casual, as if it wasn't essential she say yes.

'You're Australian,' she said.

'And you're a Pom.'

She smiled. 'I sort of know a woman in Australia.'

He stood up. 'You don't say? What's her name? I'm sure to know her too.'

Alison found this funny, so she took his proffered hand and allowed him to pull her to her feet. He was a handsome boy, wholesome-looking, with sandy-blond hair, broad shoulders and slim hips, a swimmer's physique. He looked supremely fit and healthy, and wonderfully well organised, Alison thought. She'd met all types since accidentally becoming a pilgrim, and Michael McCormack belonged to the category she'd identified as mountaineer. He'd be perfectly at home at Everest base camp; he had all he needed to make a summit attempt.

They found a tiny bar and he ordered two beers. While they waited, she told him she'd walked here from Logroño with three German nuns, who'd felt good about sharing their loaf with her, and their cheese. Before that, she'd walked to Logroño from Los Arcos, to Los Arcos from Estella, to Estella from Puente la Reina. Sometimes she was alone, she said, but more often she'd walk alongside other people, who fell into step along the way.

'Well, you'll know what I mean. Folk just join you, don't they, or you join them, and chat?'

He thought for a moment, and pictured narrow dusty tracks disappearing into infinity. 'I think I walk too fast for that,' he said.

Oh, Alison thought: a racer, then, a competitive type, not a mountaineer. She'd encountered a spirited Scottish woman a few days ago, bearing down on the dawdlers and amblers, calling out, 'Single file, on the left, single file,' as she forged her own path through.

'Well,' she said. 'If you dawdle like me, you meet all sorts of people.'

'But they don't all speak English.'

Oh dear, she thought.

A waiter slid up to them, balancing their beers on a tin tray. He placed them on the table, along with a plate of tortilla, cut into narrow slices. Alison said, '*Ah, gracias,*' and he winked at her, and grinned. Michael noted this; noted, also, the way she offered the plate to him first, before she took a piece herself.

'So,' he said, 'where's all your gear?'

'Gear?'

'For the trail?'

'This is it,' she said. 'What you see is what I've got.'

'Jeez,' he said. 'What're you thinking of?'

She shrugged. 'The Camino will provide, they say, and I reckon it has. I wasn't planning to walk, I just set off one day. Got talking to a man and his daughter in Pamplona who said they were walking to Santiago de Compostela. They said, "Come with us," so I did.'

Michael considered this statement, the miraculous simplicity of it. He'd been planning this adventure for eighteen months from his home in Adelaide. He'd pored over guidebooks, compared the relative merits of the different routes – distance and terrain, variety and natural beauty, the prevalence of historic landmarks, the best trail for medieval authenticity. Before he left South Australia, he'd had rooms booked at hostels and *refugios* all the way from Le Puy to Santiago. He had a thick wad of traveller's cheques in his money belt, and an emergency private telephone number for the Australian Embassy in Madrid, where an old friend of his father was chargé d'affaires. All these contingencies had seemed not only prudent but also necessary, and it was only now, sitting with this pared-down, beautiful, reckless creature, that he felt foolishly over-prepared.

'Where are they now, your Pamplona buddies?'

Alison shrugged. 'No idea. They stopped in Laredo for two nights, but I just carried on. Are you walking on your own?'

Michael didn't want to talk about himself, or think about himself, or about the hundreds of kilometres he still had to walk before this long, lonely journey came to an end. It hadn't been what he'd hoped or expected. He'd anticipated enlightenment, anticipated learning something about history, or life, or himself. This was what the guidebooks promised, but instead, he seemed to be pitted endlessly against whoever was on the road in front of him. It struck him, forcefully, that he'd been doing the Camino all wrong. So he ignored her question, and asked another of his own.

'Do you even have a map?'

She shook her head and laughed. 'It'd be hard to go wrong, but to be honest, I don't really mind if I get there or not,' she said. 'I'm not after spiritual insight, I'm just enjoying the walk. And people are kind. Incredibly kind. When somebody says, *'Hola, buen camino!'* I just feel, y'know, cheerful, and part of this crazy joint endeavour. Don't you? I hope you do, after all the effort you've gone to, all the kit you packed.'

He stared at her.

'What?' she said.

'Where've you been sleeping?'

'Wherever I can.'

'Outdoors?'

'Once or twice, but it's been warm, hasn't it?'

'And do you have money?'

'Not right now, but I can always get work in a bar, or a café, if I need to. In Pamplona, I ran the ticket office in a little cinema for a few weeks.'

God, he thought, that was seriously cool. He felt such a fool. A pampered fool.

'You speak the lingo, I suppose?'

She nodded. 'French, yep, and I didn't speak Spanish, but I do now, sort of.'

He stared at her for a while, watching her drink, watching her throat as she swallowed, and then his gaze slid lower. 'Who's Wild Willy Barrett?' he said, reading the words on her T-shirt. 'Is he a cowboy?'

She laughed, a proper full-throated laugh, and he smiled to see it, the way she threw her head back, and her hair swung, and her eyes changed shape.

'Not a cowboy then, I'm guessing,' he said.

'Not a cowboy,' Alison said. 'A musician. John Otway and Wild Willy Barrett? No? Anyway, I found this T-shirt at a jumble sale in Paris, and I figured it'd be wasted on the French, so I rescued it.'

Paris, thought Michael: a jumble sale in Paris, a cinema in Pamplona.

'So,' he said. 'I now know who Wild Willy Barrett is, but who are you?'

'Pardon?'

'Who are you?'

She looked at him steadily. 'I told you that already. Alison Connor.'

'No, I mean, who *are* you? Are you for real?'

Daft question, she thought. What did he think? That she was a figment of his imagination? She drained her beer, and put the empty glass down on the table. 'Yep,' she said. 'I'm for real.' She stood up, and he felt a rush of panic. 'Please don't go,' he said. He wanted to say never leave my side, but what kind of weirdo would say that on first acquaintance? As it was she was regarding him with uncertainty, as if she felt a little sorry for him, and couldn't quite decide what to do. He stood up too, and dug into his pocket for some pesetas, which he piled in a heap on the table.

'That'll be about three times too much,' Alison said. 'You'll make his week.'

He couldn't place her English accent; she sounded nothing like any of the Brits he knew in Adelaide, and as they walked away from the bar he asked her where she was from, but she only smiled and shook her head. 'That's a very un-Camino question,' she said. 'Didn't you know it's all about where you're going, not where you've come from?'

'Right,' he said. He was aware that he was following her now, uninvited, but she didn't seem to mind. He adjusted the enormous pack, silently cursing its weight, and the way the camping stove dug into the small of his back.

She glanced at him. 'What exactly have you got in there, pilgrim?' she said. She was laughing at him again, and he couldn't blame her. There was she, unfettered. There was he, with a world of material trappings on his back.

'Where you off to now, Alison?' he asked. 'And wherever it is, can I tag along?'

She stopped walking and gave him a long, considering look. She liked his smile, his straight white teeth, and she liked his pale blue eyes, the way they watched her. She liked his eagerness, his gung-ho demeanour, his good-natured acceptance that she might find him slightly ridiculous. She didn't mind that he didn't know Wild Willy Barrett; she didn't mind that at all.

She'd been on the move now for a year, living on her wits, working here and there, taking favours from strangers, hitching down through France and into Spain, never really settling, never really putting down even the most tender, slender root, and this had been exactly what she'd needed, this all-consuming nomadic life, and yet it was so tiring. So tiring. And here was this young Australian man, a man from across the globe, who knew nothing about her, nothing at all, but he wanted her, she could see that, he might as well have been carrying a banner declaring it, and his expression was so endearingly hopeful.

'Have you seen the cockerel and the hen in the cathedral?' she asked.

'Chooks in church?'

She laughed. 'Yeah. There was a miracle here, involving poultry.'

He smiled and said, 'Lead on,' and she felt a kind of mellow contentment, a kind of settling, as the past retreated further still.

The girls had gone to their rooms, Beatriz too, by the time Michael heard from Ali all of Stella's very sound reasons for not wanting to stay in Adelaide this year, not wanting to hang out with the crowd that included Mystery Boy, with whom she'd had unprotected sex in a beach house at Victor Harbor, just once, and whom she ardently wished never to see again. Michael heard, but he didn't bend. Stella must go to NIDA was his verdict; she'd be in Sydney, well away from the orbit of anyone she didn't wish to see. Next, he did what he considered the right thing, and apologised to Ali for yet again peddling the old family legend, the McCormack Myth, that she, Ali, would be nothing without him. But it was only a half-apology, could only ever be such, because in his heart Michael *did* believe that he'd saved her: saved her from the unknown, unmet catastrophe that must surely have awaited her, travelling through Europe without the protection of family, or contacts, or money. Ali saw the past differently, remembered Michael as the hapless one, with his checklists and safety nets and back-up plans. She was proud of her own resourcefulness in those months abroad, away from home for the first time, although God knows her home life had taught her everything she needed to know, and more, about looking after herself.

But Michael had drawn her in, with his jaunty Aussie ways and stories of the bush. He made his boyhood adventures on the family sheep station sound like the kid's in *Skippy*. Alison had loved that show, because somewhere in the same parched landscape lived Sheila, the lady who'd written the letters to Catherine, and now, in Spain, she had Michael telling her that if Sheila still lived in Elizabeth, he could drive her there from Adelaide in no time, half an hour, forty minutes max, and he'd gladly do it, gladly, then he'd bring her back to the city, to his beautiful North Adelaide home, and they'd drink daiquiris on the verandah, and watch the cockatoos pick plums from the trees. She found this a fantastical proposition, sparkling with allure, but Michael kept saying, 'It's not fantasy, it's not fiction, it's Adelaide life, there for the taking.'

They'd stayed together, of course, in Spain. They'd walked the remaining 540-odd kilometres of the Camino trail, and she'd slept with him in his pre-booked hostels, and – occasionally – talked him into sleeping outside, to be stirred at dawn by the clank of bells as goats on their way to be milked slid down stony paths on a dry and fragrant hillside. In Santiago, Michael had queued with a couple of hundred fellow pilgrims, waiting for the cathedral authorities to issue him with his certificate of completion, while Alison, who felt she didn't qualify and anyway couldn't see the point of paperwork to prove what they'd done, hung back and waited for him, sitting on the edge of a fountain in Platerías Square. The cold water on her hot feet was everything she needed in the world, but anyway an old Spanish lady had blessed her with a torrent of Galician prayer and a dry, papery kiss to the forehead.

Then Alison and Michael had journeyed together, up through southern France and into Italy. For three weeks, they harvested grapes in a vineyard in Umbria, then travelled on down through the length of the boot to Puglia. She acquired a rucksack of her own, and new clothes: a gauzy pink cotton dress, a green silk shirt, a white linen skirt, blue espadrilles. Michael bought these items for her, pleaded – when she resisted – to be allowed to indulge her, and she had to admit it was pleasant to submit, after so many months of scraping by on so little. Michael was besotted. Bewitched. He, who had everything, wanted only Alison Connor. At Gargano he proposed, but it was a whole week later, in the white baroque city of Lecce, that she said yes. In Ostuni, Michael's money having eased their passage through municipal bureaucracy, they were married by the registrar before witnesses who didn't know them, and on the same day they sailed from Brindisi to Kefalonia, from where they island-hopped for another month, before making the long, long way back to Adelaide, Mr and Mrs McCormack, Michael and Alison, Michael and Ali.

She'd had nothing to lose, back then; nothing but her absolute freedom, and she'd placed no great value upon that. Freedom had been born of necessity, in Alison's case, and she'd known she could learn to love this man, because he loved her so much, and such devotion, she'd felt, ought to be rewarded. She had loved him. She *did* love him. Yes, she'd lost something of herself over the years, but perhaps he had too, perhaps it was a condition of a long marriage that part of one's spirit must be sacrificed, in exchange for material comfort, children, companionship. Certainly, at some point soon after her arrival in

Adelaide, she'd found herself conceding that the McCormack way was the only way; as a united front, they were irresistible, and irrefutable. Alison Connor was enveloped by them, she was claimed by the clan, and it was comforting, in so many ways, to succumb.

She glanced up at Michael, now, across the kitchen. He'd said sorry so easily, so glibly, for being high-handed and condescending, and was idly leafing through *The Advertiser*, perfectly satisfied with his behaviour. He didn't know that his world was unsteady, that his word wasn't always law, that Stella was upstairs looking at flights to Rome. He didn't know that Ali, from this very room, had just sent a song to Dan Lawrence: the Arctic Monkeys, 'Do I Wanna Know?', a song Michael wouldn't know, a Sheffield sound, from Sheffield lads.

He didn't know how the lyrics made Ali feel, didn't know, couldn't know, how they spoke to her. He didn't know – when Ali finished her wine, stood up, said goodnight – that by looking up from the newspaper and smiling at her, or by putting down the newspaper and kissing her, something small but significant might have been salvaged. But he did neither of these things, so she turned from him and went upstairs to bed.

19

SHEFFIELD,
28 JULY 1979

When she knocked on the door of Daniel's house, and his mother answered, there was a short, startled hiatus in which each of them realised Alison shouldn't be there on the doorstep, so when Marion Lawrence said, 'Oh! I thought you were in Manchester, with Daniel,' Alison immediately replied, 'No, oh God, yes! I should be,' and started to cry wildly.

You see, this was the problem, thought Marion, even as she clucked with concern and ushered her into the house: Alison Connor was as jumpy as a fawn; look at her sideways and she'd cry, or bolt. Oh, lovely-looking, granted, and good for Daniel, to a point, because he'd been a lot less moody round the house since they started going out, but she was a worry, oh yes, she was that; she was a youngster troubled with too many secrets.

'Did you just forget?' she asked, but Alison couldn't answer because she was crying too hard, crying beyond all proportion to the event in Mrs Lawrence's opinion. She hugged her and made all the right noises, while thanking God for Claire and her uncomplicated, sunny nature. 'Now then,' she said. 'Now then. There's no need for this, it was only a silly concert.'

Alison shook her head and pushed herself away from Mrs Lawrence's embrace. She didn't have the words or the will to explain herself, to explain this excessive outpouring of grief, which was all for Peter and had nothing at all to do with the missed gig.

'I'll put the kettle on,' Mrs Lawrence said. She went through to the kitchen, grateful to be busy, and Alison stood for a while, marooned in the sparkling living room, with its plumped-up cushions and smell of Pledge. She longed to crawl unnoticed up to Daniel's room and change into one of his T-shirts, curl up in his bed, make a nest of his sheets; there'd be comfort in that. She could wait for him there, wait until it grew dark and late, and Daniel came home, and he'd get into bed with her so she could explain everything to him. But then, she thought, could she? After all, he was entirely protected from the shameful reality of her life; she'd been so scrupulous in her efforts to keep her world separate from his, to hide the chaos. How could she now lay all that on him: all the messy, miserable, private details of her life; all the turbulence of Catherine, Martin, Peter – oh God, Peter. She closed her eyes, but when she did that she could see him, terrified, staring at her from the edge of death, so she opened them again, and there was Mr Lawrence, Daniel's dad, looking round the door at her, his gentle face creased with anxious sympathy.

Marion had fetched him, nipping out to the pigeon loft to tell him Alison was here, she was upset, and he was better with her than she was, he had more patience. Mr Lawrence had come gladly, and now he stepped into the room, and Alison began to cry again, she couldn't seem to halt the tears, but he said nothing, nothing at all, just held her until she quietened, and then he said, 'I've a new pair of birds, just settling in, come and see.' He spoke perfectly normally, as if there was not even a sniff of crisis, and he took her hand and led her through the house, out of the back door and down the garden. He sat her down on the bench in the loft and let her be while he did all the talking. The new pigeons were Flash Pied Emperors, he said, a breeding pair, strong birds, both from a fine lineage of race winners. Alison, passive, worn down by events, listened to him and was soothed.

'I've called this one Violet and this one Vincent,' he said. The two birds were tucked together on a wide shelf, and they regarded Mr Lawrence as he spoke, for all the world as if they were in on the conversation. They were pretty, like all his pigeons. Piebald, white with markings of dark and pale grey. 'I've no idea why I chose them names, they just came to me, and I'll tell you what, they suit 'em, because they're a dignified little couple, Mr and Mrs. It's only been two days, but they travelled well, and there's been no bickering. They'll be grand flyers when they're ready. Back here like boomerangs, I expect.'

He lifted Violet carefully from her spot next to Vincent and handed her to Alison, who accepted her in cupped hands. She was used to this now; used to handling his birds, no longer worried about their beaks or the feel on her hands of their startling red feet. She held Violet aloft and looked her in the eyes, and let her fingers sink into the softness and warmth. It's a bird's life, she thought; oh, to be a cossetted pigeon under the care of a man such as Mr Lawrence. She could feel the calm of Violet's heartbeat inside her fragile frame, and felt immensely privileged, and touched, by the bird's quiet trust in her.

'See that brightness in her eyes?' Mr Lawrence said. 'And her upright stance, that beautiful, gradual slope from the top of her head to her tail? That's a winner's stance, that is. See how she's watching you? When I picked her out, it was more like she'd chosen me, she were watching me that intently, and that means she's alert, not flighty. She's grand, she is.'

He lifted Violet from Alison's hands and placed her back,

next to Vincent. 'But you know, don't you, it's what you can't see that'll make her a champion,' he said.

'Her brain, her heart and her lungs,' Alison said.

'Aye, that's it, them's what she'll be relying on when she flies five hundred miles back here.' He smiled at her. 'Folk say, "Oh, why do you bother, they're just birds," and I know I've told you before, Alison, but there's nowt like the feeling when a bird comes back to me, nowt on earth. They use every last scrap of strength and intelligence to get back where they belong. My birds kept me sane when I was invalided out of work. They still do.'

He paused, and looked at Alison with such deep affection she felt she was one of his very own, as dear to him as anyone ever had been. 'I don't know what ails you, love, and I know you'd tell me if you could. I wish I could help, but I can say this, you come here any time you want to. Come and sit in here with these birds, and find some peace.'

'Mr Lawrence,' Alison said, 'you're so good to me.'

'Aye, well, you're a grand lass, and you've a lot on your plate, I can see that.'

There was a tap-tap on the door, and Mrs Lawrence pushed it open with her foot. She had a mug of tea in each hand. 'I've brought you this,' she said, bustling in and handing them over, causing a momentary flutter in the boxes, a kind of communal agitation, a gentle hubbub that lasted only seconds before subsiding.

'Now then,' she said, looking meaningfully between her husband and Alison. 'Now then, what was all that about?' Bill shook his head at her, a subtle warning to go easy, and she understood well enough what he meant, but she said, 'No, Bill, enough pussyfooting about. I need to know what's wrong, because if she's this upset, it might affect our Daniel.'

'Oh,' Alison said, alarmed. She stood, abruptly.

'Nay, lass, sit down,' Mr Lawrence said, but she didn't.

'Alison, tell me what's happened.'

Mrs Lawrence had had enough, Alison could tell this from her voice, from her demeanour, and she tried, she really tried, to respond in kind, to be as open and straightforward as Mrs Lawrence was being, and wanted her to be, but all she managed was, 'It . . . I . . . My brother, he . . .' and then she stopped.

'Well, so, your brother . . .' Mrs Lawrence said. 'What about him, Alison?'

She wasn't being unkind, not at all; she made every effort to keep her voice soft with sympathy. But Marion Lawrence had a limited capacity to wait and see, and whatever troubles this young woman had, Daniel mustn't suffer because of them, and he wouldn't, not if she had anything to do with it. Somebody needed to get to the heart of the matter, and if Bill wouldn't, she would.

Alison put her tea down on the bench she'd been sitting on. She felt hemmed in; three people was one too many in this small shed full of pigeons, and Mrs Lawrence was standing full square, with her arms folded and her chin up, waiting for answers. 'I'm sorry,' Alison said. 'I'm so sorry.' She felt completely unequal to this encounter and desperate to leave. She had no right to be here without Daniel, no claim on their time or their kindness, these good, good people; she should leave, she must go.

Mr Lawrence said, 'Nay, Alison, there's nowt to be sorry about,' but his wife said, 'Sorry for what?'

'Marion,' said Bill. 'Gently.'

'Alison, what exactly are you saying?'

Mrs Lawrence's searching voice. Mr Lawrence's sorrowful face. The watchful black eyes of all those birds.

'I have to go,' Alison said. She darted out of the loft, and Mrs Lawrence, who wasn't anything like as nimble, but was determined to discover at least part of the truth behind this drama, flashed a look of annoyance at Bill – for being useless, for being soft-hearted – then followed her down the garden and back into the house.

'Alison!' she said. 'What am I to tell our Daniel?'

Alison stopped on the threshold of the front door. 'Tell him I'm sorry about the gig,' she said. 'Tell him I'm really, really sorry. But I've got to get back. This isn't right, I shouldn't be here. I'm sorry, Mrs Lawrence.' She stepped out into the street, and began to walk away. She was two buses away from home. What if Peter had suffered some injury she wasn't aware of, a delayed reaction she hadn't considered? What'd she been thinking? She'd thought, she supposed, that she could forget herself, forget everything, with Daniel, but all she'd forgotten was that he wouldn't be here, and now she was in the wrong place altogether. She didn't belong in Nether Edge without Daniel.

'And what shall I tell him happened?'

Mrs Lawrence was having to call to Alison down the quiet Saturday-afternoon street now, standing at the gate to their small front garden. This wasn't very respectable in their tree-lined avenue, but she didn't care if anyone heard, she just wanted answers; but Alison said nothing, only kept walking.

'Alison! Is there something our Daniel needs to know?'

Again, nothing.

'Alison!' Mrs Lawrence said again, raising her voice further still, and now Alison stopped and turned around. She looked wretched, Marion thought: wretched, and sort of defeated, and possibly – because of this – dangerous. This girl was no good for her boy.

'I love him, Mrs Lawrence,' Alison said. 'I love him, that's what your Daniel needs to know. Please don't worry, every-thing's fine.'

She raised a hand, a half-farewell, turned away again, and walked out of sight.

It took over an hour to get back to Attercliffe, and when she did, Alison slid into the house as a mouse might, through the smallest crack in the door, without a sound, hoping not to be noticed. Terror made her heart thud in her chest as if she was walking into a crime scene, but there was nothing untoward to greet her, in the kitchen at any rate. She stood, as she'd been doing since childhood, and listened for clues, but there were none. She was shocked at herself now, shocked that she'd left the house so decisively, immediately after cutting Peter down from that noose, and she was sorry for it, and had no explan-ation, except perhaps that until then her brother had only ever picked her up in life and never, never let her down, and maybe she'd suffered a kind of emotional freeze at the terrible reversal of roles. But she'd known, when she left, that he wouldn't have another go, knew she wasn't going to find him dead upstairs in his room, because she'd looked in his eyes, and she'd known he hadn't meant it, hadn't wanted to die. He just hadn't known that for sure until death was a distinct possibility.

She went upstairs and knocked on his bedroom door.

'Yeah,' he said.

He was sitting on the floor with his back against the bed, and they looked at each other sadly. Alison could see weals, red raw on the soft skin of his throat where the rope had chafed and tightened, but other than that, he appeared quite normal. Jeans, sweatshirt and his Gola trainers. He looked like he had at fif-teen, sixteen, off for a kickabout in the rec with his mates. She sat down next to him, and he put an arm round her shoulders.

'Alison . . .' His voice scratched, a sandpaper sound.

She shuddered and said, 'Shush. Let's not talk about it.'

She didn't want to think about what he'd done, what he'd tried to do. It'd been such a long, terrible day, packed with incident, with horror. Peter didn't know the half of it: the steelworks yard, Martin, the ugly photo gallery. She thought about those prints, and hoped they were still downstairs where she'd left them.

'I only wanted to say sorry,' he said.

She nodded. She gazed around Peter's room, which had never acquired a personality in the way that her own room had. Peter was too self-contained, too private. There were no posters, no pictures, no books or records or cassettes, nothing that might betray his interests, his passions. This room was purely functional: a place to sleep, to dress, to hide. It was a kind of cell.

'I really do regret putting you through that, Alison.'

'I know.'

'Where did you go?'

'Daniel's, but he was out.' She wouldn't mention that she should've been with him now, in Manchester. 'What's Catherine up to?'

He shrugged. 'She got up and went out, an hour ago. Meeting her cronies at the Carlton, I expect.'

'Did you see her? She had a black eye and a cut.'

Peter shook his head. 'She didn't look in on me,' he said. 'She was too interested in opening time, and finding some mug to buy her a drink.'

'Sometimes I think we should just change the lock while she's gone, and not let her back in. Except she'd show us up, banging on the door.'

He turned his face to hers. 'I want you to leave, Alison.'

She said, 'What, right now, this minute?'

She wasn't serious, but he nodded. 'Well, as soon as you can get your stuff together. I want you to leave.' He was speaking in a loud whisper to spare his throat, but it only made everything seem even stranger, and although he was in earnest, Alison wasn't really taking him seriously; she only sighed and rested her head on his shoulder, and closed her eyes. She'd fantasised many a time about another existence: it would be a bluestocking life; she'd have digs and a bicycle, and she'd pedal through leafy streets to an ivy-clad college where she'd talk to a professor about Jane Austen or Shakespeare or Milton. She'd have tea with fellow students, and make toast on a long fork by a real fire.

'So,' Peter said, 'I've got an escape plan for you. Been planning it a while.'

She smiled. 'Oh yeah? A rope ladder from my bedroom window?'

'I mean it, Alison. I'm stuck here, this is my lot, but you're not, you were meant to be somebody, that's what nature intended.'

'I couldn't leave you,' she said. She still hadn't realised that he meant what he said. 'We're a team.'

'I'm a fucking mess, Alison. My life's a mess. Yours isn't, yet. But you stay here, you'll be tainted by it, you'll be dragged down. I can't watch that happen, so clear off, get away, over the Channel, anywhere. Put some water between yourself and Sheffield. Don't look back.'

She shuffled sideways to make some space and get a better look at him, so she could tell from his face if he meant what he said. It was such a strange and outlandish proposal, but Peter said, 'Do it,' and he looked so serious, grim even. The spit of Geoff Connor, people said; the one that got away, the architect – by his spectacular absence – of their misfortune. Apparently,

Peter had the same hair – dark blond, naturally wavy – and the same patrician, aquiline nose. If Peter had worn a suit to work, and black Oxfords, and if he'd shaved more often and had his hair cut, he could pass for a young MP, or a lawyer. But he'd never had the chance to shine; he'd left school at sixteen, kept the family fed and clothed with his wages from the steelworks, a place he'd always loathed, until he met Toddy, when life brightened for him. Alison understood what she owed him, she truly did. She understood, too, that their father's disappearance had been far harder on Peter, who'd been six when he left, old enough to have scattered, fractured memories, and to feel the perpetual chill of abandonment. Geoff had never been back. Never checked on his children, never come to see them, never written to them, never sent a present at Christmas, a card on birthdays, a chocolate egg at Easter. He could be dead, for all they knew, and Alison didn't much care. But Peter did. Peter had had a daddy, then lost a daddy. And then, because he was a thoroughgoing decent person, he'd filled the gap that Geoff Connor had left in their lives, so that even at six, seven, eight years old, Peter could be entirely depended on by Catherine to make sure Alison survived. This was what he was doing again now: trying to do, anyway, but she was having none of it.

'I'm hungry,' she said to him. She hadn't eaten all day. 'Come on, keep me company.'

She stood up and offered a hand, but he pushed himself to his feet without her help. The marks on his neck were violently red, and Alison could see bruising too, a purplish, bluish hue high on his neck where the rope had been tightest. This was the day that Peter had tried to kill himself and then changed his mind; this was the day he could've died. But there'd be tomorrow, and tomorrow, and tomorrow, and together, they'd cope.

*

She heated up some tomato soup and made sardines on toast too, and Peter watched her, but didn't eat anything. He was quite calm and considered, though, and he told her he'd been planning her escape for a good while now, setting money aside every week, and he'd made her apply for a passport three years ago, did she remember? She'd been awkward about it at the time, asked what was the point, but in the end, she'd signed the form that he'd completed for her, and had gone and had her photo taken in the booth at Woolworths. Alison said, 'Oh God, you're right. I forgot about that. Did you send it off then?'

He nodded. 'I did, and it came here, and now it's in an old Oxo tin with the savings I've put by. Nigh on a hundred and forty pounds.'

She gawped at him. A hundred and forty pounds! Her own savings from her job at the supermarket were nil. Occasionally she paid the gas or the electric with her wages, but more often they were spent on music, or – less often – clothes.

'It's so you can take off, if you have to,' he said. 'And I'd like you to do that, now.'

'But, Peter, I've only got a year left at school,' Alison said. 'What about my A Levels?'

'Do 'em another time. Or do wi'out 'em.'

She looked at him askance. There was no logic to what he said. This was just a panicked reaction to the events of the past forty-eight hours. English, French, History: these were her A Levels, and she planned to take them and get herself to university.

'It's in my top drawer,' he said.

'What is?'

'Your tin. In my bedroom, top drawer, underneath everything. I should've told you before.'

She looked down at her soup. Before he tried to hang

himself, he meant. As if she'd have been able to go anywhere, with him dead. As if she'd have been able to function at all. She continued eating, mechanically feeding her empty stomach, like shovelling coal into an engine or filling up a car, and she listened to him speaking to her in his temporarily strangled voice, on and on in a kind of rasping whisper, and she wished he'd stop.

He told her again she had to go, he told her he had a feeling worse was to come, with Catherine beyond help and Martin Baxter, the fucking psychopath, with his access-all-areas pass to their house. He told her she needed to steer clear of Martin, he was deranged, and if she was set on taking her exams, she should move in with Daniel Lawrence and try to stay safe that way.

She listened, and she didn't reply. She thought he'd gone mad. There was a time when Alison acted upon every piece of advice that her brother gave her, because he was generally right. But now he was being irrational, he'd see that himself in a day or two, and whatever he said, she was going nowhere for the next twelve months. He could give her the escape fund this time next year, if he wished, or he could spend it on himself. Either way, come September next year, she'd be gone.

Peter went out, just for an hour or so, he said, but he didn't say where and Alison didn't ask. Toddy's probably. She hoped so anyway, she hoped Peter could count on him to help him through the next few weeks and months. She washed up, then fetched the heap of photographs from the living-room mantelpiece, and burned them one at a time, dropping them into a metal bucket where they bucked and curled and shrank to harmless black remnants. Martin had the negatives, of course, but unless he planned to try and sell them to the *Sheffield Telegraph* there wasn't much more damage he could do with them.

The kitchen stank of acrid smoke so she went upstairs to her room, and lay down on the bed. She felt better for having eaten, but she was exhausted, bone-weary. She thought about Daniel at the Mayflower Club, opening the gig, warming up the crowd, sharing a bill with Joy Division and the Fall, and she wished she was there, the girl in the band, harmonising with bad boy Steve Levitt. Oh well, she thought, there'd be a next time; she'd make sure of it: she'd make them forgive her.

She reached for the radio and turned it on, and if she hadn't done that, she might have heard the door as Martin let himself into the house. Donna Summer filled the room, 'Bad Girls', toot toot, beep beep, not quite what Alison was in the mood for, but you took your chances on Radio 1 on a Saturday night. She was on her bed, eyes closed, dropping like a stone into sleep, when he entered her bedroom, and even then she didn't hear him immediately because he was sober and had taken the precaution of removing his boots at the bottom of the stairs. Then she sensed a presence, a malevolence in the room, and she opened her eyes, but it was too late and everything that happened next did so in a fearful, uncontrollable rush, a worst nightmare, a horror story. He was at her and on her, monstrous and full of hatred, dragging her off the bed by the hair, gagging her with a scarf he'd brought for the purpose, ripping at her dress, her pants, her bra, tearing into her with silent determination. He said nothing at all but she screamed fit to fetch all the street in until the gag silenced her fury, then she fought like a lynx, scratched and kicked, but she was slight and he was a heavy brute, and he pinned her body to the floor, crushed her into submission, one hand round her throat, the other clutching her hair, and like this he was able to thrust into her, over and over, calling her bitch, cunt, bitch, cunt, to the steady rhythm of his violence. He took his time, so she could fully understand the depths of his loathing, the extent of her helplessness. When it was over, he laughed. Then he stood, zipped himself up, and prodded one foot experimentally into her side and then again into her abdomen, as if she'd just been washed up on a beach and he wasn't certain what she was. He stared for a few moments at her nakedness, and the marks he'd made on her skin. Then he hawked and spat in her face, to remind her of her own sin, and then he left. All of this took less than ten minutes, and Peter came back home, as he'd said he would, an hour after leaving, thirty minutes after Martin Baxter had let himself out of the house.

Even so, by then, Alison was gone. She'd allowed herself no time to cry and cringe and wallow; all that was done now. She'd washed, dressed and buried her ripped dress in the bottom of the kitchen bin. Then she'd left a note for Peter, just a scrawl; she hadn't mentioned Martin or what he'd done, because that would start a whole new chain of events and give the foul act more weight and substance, make it harder to forget. She would not, she absolutely would not, take anyone down with her into despair, especially not her brother, so all she wrote was: 'Dear Peter, you were right, I can't stay here, love Alison xx', and then she packed a few possessions into her canvas satchel: the passport and the money, some clothes, and the mix tape, the only one she had, *The Best Last Two*, from Daniel.

For him, she left nothing at all – there wasn't time, and there was too much to say. She'd write to him when she could. She'd write to him, and he'd come to her, and then they'd never have to part again.

20

At Waverley Station, Katelin clung uncharacteristically on to Dan when they hugged goodbye, and told him she suddenly felt shaky about being so long away from home, and he said a large gin and tonic on the train would soon steady her nerves, but she didn't smile.

'Seriously,' she said. 'I think I'm going to be homesick.'

He held her at arm's length and looked into her eyes while she waited for reassurance. 'You won't, Katelin, I guarantee it,' he said. 'You'll be with Rose-Ann for a start, and you'll be seeing and doing way too much to pine for rainy old Stockbridge.'

'Will you miss me?' she asked, and he wished she hadn't, because he could hardly say no, and he really disliked being manipulated. However, 'You bet,' he said, because it was easier, and kinder. 'But,' he added quickly, 'you're not going to miss me, you're going to have a blast.'

Now she did smile, and drew back. A little way down the platform, Duncan and Rose-Ann were in close conversation. Katelin regarded them for a moment; then she said, 'Keep an eye on him for her, won't you?' and Dan's smile immediately faded and he said, 'Ah, don't ask that of me, Katelin.'

'No, but he looks up to you,' she said.

'I'm not his keeper.'

'No, I know, but he listens to you, you know he does.'

'Rose-Ann has no cause for concern,' Dan said. 'Duncan hasn't seen or spoken to Lindsay since before Christmas, she doesn't want him, and he doesn't need her.'

'Yeah, OK,' Katelin said.

'Get on that train and don't look back,' he said. 'Seize the next few weeks, and really make them count,' and he meant it, he truly wanted only the best experience for her, he wanted this trip to be a high point in her life, but he also knew he was hiding his own profound unease, because he wasn't immune to the crashing irony of being asked to keep Duncan on the straight and narrow.

God knows, he was *not* the man for that job. In the weeks and then days in the run-up to Katelin's departure, he'd begun to feel perpetually disorientated, as feelings and events of another lifetime gained ground on him, while Katelin – blameless, entirely blameless – continued blithely on in their present. He longed, now, for her to leave. Yesterday the house had been mayhem, a vortex of paraphernalia and low-level panic, all the various stages of her packing, the details and documents relating to her imminent departure, the choosing of suitcase and cabin bag, the piles of clothes for sunshine, for cooler nights, for rain. He'd done his best, tried to help, dug out some adaptors for US sockets, then Alison had sent him an Arctic Monkeys track, 'Do I Wanna Know?', and off he went, spinning down the time tunnel, back to Nether Edge 1979 – although, actually, his first thought had been damn, because he obviously should have sent that song to her – he could hear his own thoughts coming back at him through Alex Turner's lyrics, and in a Sheffield accent, too. After that he'd had to drag himself back to Stockbridge and the matter in hand, and Katelin had given him that look, the one that told him she knew he was somehow absent, until he'd shaken himself out of the past and given her 100 per cent of his attention, on this big day, the day before she left.

So he felt like a heel, but all he really understood was that he needed a resolution, he had it in his sights, and for his own sanity, and for all the unanswered, tormented questions of the past, he was going to use Katelin's extended absence to find Alison Connor, and stand in front of her, and then see what happened next. He kissed Katelin goodbye, his dear partner, for whom he really did wish nothing but happiness. Then, as the train moved away from the station, his wayward, ungovernable thoughts went straight back to Alison, and the way her face had always nestled hotly against his neck when they embraced, and she'd breathed him in as though she needed him to stay alive. And the sense he had of Alison's remembered physical presence was stronger, somehow, than the sense he had of Katelin, who only moments ago had been right here, beside him. Alison Connor was intangible yet concrete, unreal yet hyper-real at one and the same time. A head rush, a total fucking head rush; it was like nothing else he'd ever felt.

The train was gone, and the two men bounded up the steps to Waverley Bridge, and it crossed Dan's mind to talk to his friend, as he knew he should, about his lost and found love in Adelaide. But in all honesty, he really didn't want to, and anyway it was easy enough to postpone that conversation, since Duncan was talking nineteen to the dozen about the artists he had in mind for the industry-dominating music-promotion company he believed he and Dan were founding together. Dan was right off the idea – he was too busy, Duncan was too idealistic, and the market was already too tightly sewn up – but he hadn't told Duncan yet, because his friend was so full of energy and verve that he hadn't the heart. Duncan had a list of three contenders: the Anstruther fisherman Willie Dundas; a band called Truth Bites Back, a solid enough outfit comprising four guys from Leith who owed everything – the look, lyrics, riffs, rhythms – to Aztec Camera; and an interesting pair of twin sisters from Largs, Katriona and Jeanie McBride, who sang in eerie harmony about drugs, sex and urban decay, with a palpably disdainful attitude that made them oddly compelling. They were far and away the most bankable proposition on Duncan's notional books, Dan had known that the night he first heard them, dragged along by his pal to a small, underpopulated room at the Paisley Union. They had a thin, wasted look, big eyes in pale faces, scruffy plaits, studs in their noses, eyebrows, lips – anywhere but the earlobes. Both wore their guitars slung low so they had to hunch their skinny shoulders to play. Katriona yawned into the mic at one point, but the yawn melted into the words of the song, so it might have been intentional. They were languid, laconic and clever and in the right hands the McBrides could be everywhere. They called themselves Jeanie and the Kat, another little stroke of genius.

Still, though, there were some mightily effective publishers and promoters out there already, with everything in place to propel a savvy, talented, edgy pair of musicians straight into global recognition, so it was a bit of a leap to imagine Duncan somehow emerging overnight as a contender, even if he could already lay claim to having discovered this pair. After all, this was dear, clueless Duncan Lomax, who spent his days playing music in a record shop, blowing dust off the stylus in the listening booth, drinking coffee with customers who might, or more often might not, buy a record. In all the years he'd owned this shop he'd never bothered to have a website built, never bothered to put his stock online, so that a person who was looking for, say, some early Status Quo, or a white vinyl special edition of *Sound and Vision*, had to get to Edinburgh, talk to Duncan, and wait in hope while he fished through all the likely boxes. So, it was evident to Dan that not only were they too late to this party, but also, they were ill-equipped to join it, and the very best advice they could give the McBride sisters was to sign up with an existing company, get a buzz going, build a digital presence, and hope it translated to the big time.

Duncan's shop was at the top end of Jeffrey Street and although that's where he should've been headed, and despite being way too early in the day for a drink, he'd argued a strong case in favour of stopping for a beer in a new craft-ale bar, all industrial chic, with bare brick and scaffolding on the inside and benches made from stacked railway sleepers. They'd bought a couple of German wheat beers from a serious, bearded young man in a long brewer's apron, then Dan decided the time was now and said, 'Look, I have to say, buddy, it's a complete non-starter,' and Duncan's smile faded to dismay.

'Wha'?' he said, his glass of beer halted on its way to his mouth.

'We don't have the skills, man,' Dan said. 'Or the time. Well, I don't.'

Duncan stared with hurt eyes, as if this was the biggest let-down of his life.

'Have you looked online?' Dan said. 'Have you seen what's out there already, for new artists? They don't need a label to pick them up any more, there's stacks of companies they can go to, get a publishing deal, royalties tracked, money for YouTube views, live performances administered, no strings or tie-ins, wham-bam, hello success.'

'So?' Duncan said. 'We could do that, you and me.'

'No, we couldn't.'

'Aw c'mon, dude, we're the real deal, we live and breathe this world.'

'It's not enough to love music, Dunc, you got to do the admin too, and be clued up on tech skills.'

'But my guys aren't signed up with anybody.'

'No, I know.'

'So we create a company to represent 'em, and get cracking.'

Dan sighed. Katelin was right about Duncan looking up to him and, certainly, it was like talking to a kid sometimes; he should never have encouraged him in the first place. Well, he wasn't sure he *had* encouraged him, it was rather that he hadn't discouraged him, which amounted to the same thing with Duncan.

'I'm just not able to commit to this right now,' Dan said. 'It'd need a hundred per cent effort.'

'What you so flat out with?'

'Usual stuff, plus a potential book contract – I'm seeing a publisher next week – and I said yes to this offer from Six Music, the new music panel – I told you about it? Jesus, Duncan. Don't make me account for myself.'

'Look,' Duncan said. 'Let's just give it a year, see how we go? Those wee lassies, they're awesome.'

Dan nodded. 'They are, they really are. They need some representation, for sure.'

'So?'

Dan shook his head. 'You do it,' he said. 'I'll watch.'

'You might end up famous for being the man who said no to Jeanie and the Kat.'

'A risk I'm going to have to take,' Dan said. He knew what Duncan would be thinking though: that if he, Dan, didn't want in, it probably wasn't as good an idea as he'd thought. Duncan believed Dan knew what he was doing, never put a foot wrong, made only good decisions that didn't land him in the soup.

He really should tell him all about Ali Connor, Dan thought.

He almost did, drew in his breath ready to speak, got right to the very edge of it. But then he didn't.

Back at home McCulloch staggered at him with demented happiness, as if he'd believed he was to be forever alone. He whined and threaded himself in a frantic figure of eight, in and out of Dan's feet, and Dan stooped to briefly scratch the little dog's ears, then he stood up again and said, 'That's your lot,' and McCulloch, who fully understood the rules, immediately composed himself and settled for simply shadowing Dan's every move.

'Just you and me now,' Dan said to the dog. He put the coffee pot on in the kitchen and switched on the radio, retuning it with some satisfaction to 6 Music from the wall-to-wall dialogue of Katelin's preferred Radio 4. Huey Morgan immediately joined him in the room, his Lower East Side drawl taking Dan straight back in time to a basement club in St Mark's Place, mid-nineties, tiny stage, banging music, sticky floor, dim red lights, a long night of revelry with the Fun Lovin' Criminals. God, they'd tied one on that night. Every time he heard Huey on the radio he could smell fresh fried donuts, yet he couldn't recall eating any at the time. The theory of Proust's madeleines gone awry.

He poured himself a coffee and climbed the stairs to his office, McCulloch panting along valiantly behind him, in a house that was filled with a new and very welcome silence. Upstairs, the dog flung himself on to his blanket and Dan switched on the Mac and pulled Twitter on to his screen, to check out @AliConnorWriter, see what she'd been saying, which turned out to be nothing, as, to be honest, was often the case. He got the distinct impression she was part of this particular social media circus at the insistence of a publicist, or her publisher, because her heart clearly wasn't in it. The last tweet from her had been a couple of weeks ago, raving about a young singer in Adelaide, and Dan had googled her – Tahnee Jackson, he loved that name, that name alone could earn her a record deal, but she was a songbird too, and beautiful, exotic, different.

He tapped the direct message icon, and scooted quickly through their thread of songs, fourteen so far, very few in the scheme of things, yet look where it had led him: right back to her, so that she was now his daily waking thought. Where she was, how she was, who she was – these were his obsessions. He'd lined up a track for her by Richard Hawley, a Sheffield bloke with a great line in nostalgic yearning, which seemed to fit the bill. He sent 'Open Up Your Door', and hoped she'd get the connection, because every album this guy made honoured their city, and his music was gorgeous, you could dissolve at the sound of his voice. Then he thought: Right, OK, flights to Adelaide, but still somehow dragged his feet, because, well, it was a mighty leap from brilliant concept to hard reality, and although he knew for sure he was going to go – and without telling her, so she didn't have a chance to scarper – he just needed to think it through: the distance, the deceit, his chances of success, the vast, yawning, unknowable abyss of the future.

Then his phone rang, the screen filling with the name of the caller, Terri Nichols, an industry publicist, and by startling coincidence the very woman who once sent Dan to the East Village to get hammered with Huey.

'Extraordinary,' Dan said when he answered.

'Why, thank you, darling,' Terri said with a laugh in her voice.

'I was just listening to the Huey show on the radio, remembering that trip.'

'Hey, like they say, if you remember it, you probably weren't there.'

'Do you remember it?'

'I remember random snatches of surreal happenings. But look, I didn't ring you to reminisce. How's your diary?'

'Depends,' Dan said.

'Hmm, cagey.'

'I'm just saying I'm pretty committed, but what you got?'

'Well it's a long shot, and it's very last minute, and you'll tell me it's not your thing . . .'

'If you think it's not my thing, Terri, it won't be.'

'Dan! Hear me out at least!'

'Go on then.'

'So we've signed a few DJs, right, and they're part of an all-night linked set at—'

'No, I'm not covering a rave for you, all that bloody zoned-out trance stuff.'

'No, Dan, this isn't a nineties rave, it's an electronic dance music festival, and these guys are album-selling career artists.'

Dan sighed, and idly opened his emails on the laptop. 'No, Terri,' he said. 'C'mon, ask a twenty-one-year-old.'

But she was good, Terri Nichols. 'See, that's just what I don't want,' she said now. 'I don't want some kid with no memories of music before the Spice Girls. I want you, with everything you know about music, everything you've heard, to listen to them and explain their creative genius to everyone else.'

Dan groaned. 'Oh, give over.'

'Honestly, there's a great piece in this, Dan. These artists work just as hard as an old-fashioned rock band. They tour, just the same, they put in the graft and the grind. Plus, the location's knockout, in Kowloon's cultural district.'

'What? Where is it? I thought you meant here, in the UK?'

She laughed. 'No, no, it's in Hong Kong.'

'Hong Kong?'

'Yep, Hong Kong. Kowloon.'

He was quiet for a moment.

'Dan, you still there?'

He said, 'Yeah, yeah, go on, I'm listening,' and while she talked, he let his mind race along another track entirely. Hong Kong to Adelaide, he thought: what would it be, eight hours, nine tops? A hop and a skip in global terms. So here was Terri Nichols offering a free long-haul flight in the right direction, for a nailed-on legitimate reason, thereby providing the salve for his conscience of an almost-perfect alibi. It was fate, he thought. An early birthday present from his own personal deity. In-fucking-credible.

'Yes,' he said, cutting right through her words. 'Yes, I'm in.'

Terri's voice skidded to a halt and she laughed. 'Well, great,' she said. 'But you don't know when it is yet.'

'When is it?'

'Next weekend. You'd fly Wednesday the thirtieth.'

His thoughts spun rapidly to the meeting with the publisher, to lunch with his agent, to the Thursday morning 6 Music gig with Lauren Laverne, to the writing commitments he had, yet none of these things held his full attention in the face of this barely believable turn of events. That this should happen, that Terri should call with this offer, on this very day, was insane. It was perfect. It was meant to be.

'Great,' he said. 'No problem. Thanks, Terri, email me the details,' and he hung up, and gave a great shout of laughter that woke the dog, who stared at Dan with reproachful eyes.

'Sorry, buddy,' he said to McCulloch. 'You're not going to like this.'

*

Of course, the dog was an issue. Dan would be gone for ten days, and old Bridie next door who opened the back door for McCulloch if he was stuck in the house all day couldn't be asked to feed him, walk him and keep him company for this length of time. Or rather, she could be asked, but she would never agree, not with her four cats and a houseful of demanding orchids. His parents might once have taken him, but not now, not with Bill the way he was. He couldn't ask Duncan, because McCulloch would certainly die from neglect. He almost asked Terri Nichols, because she was so grateful to him for accepting the gig, and she had no idea, none at all, that she'd articulated and facilitated his greatest desire before he'd even had the idea himself. It was so outrageous, so bold, and yet utterly legitimate. She didn't bat an eyelid at extending the trip for him – shame to go all that way and not have a mooch around, she said – and this timescale gave Dan the freedom to fly from Hong Kong to Adelaide, before coming back to pick up his return flight. If Alison turned out not to be there, well . . . No, he thought; she had to be there. She *would* be there.

Anyway, he didn't have to ask Terri to take the dog in the end, because he suddenly remembered dear old Jim on *Veronica Ann*: dear, lonely old Jim. He'd met McCulloch once before, must be ten years ago now, when Dan and Alex had had a weekend in London to watch Wednesday *v.* Crystal Palace, but Katelin had made them take the dog. They'd left him all day with Jim, and by the time they got back from Selhurst Park, McCulloch was sitting on the prow of the boat with a navy-blue bandana round his throat. 'Ship's mascot,' Jim had said. 'Splendid little chap. Bring him to me any time you like, Dan, any time you like.'

So, all this time later, Dan had taken him at his word, and had evidently made Jim's week. 'Smashing,' he kept saying.

'Smashing. A nice bit of company for me. We'll get on splendidly.' He stood with the dog on a lead the next day to wave Dan off, and McCulloch watched him go with a committed stare, which he kept up until the very last glimpse of his beloved owner was gone. Dan could feel the dog's eyes on his back; he could sense them, all the way down the towpath to Warwick Avenue.

At Heathrow, he left a voicemail for Alex, to let him know he'd be away, although the chances of Alex caring were close to nil, given the pace of his life in Cambridge: the work, the girls, the gigs. Nice to hear his recorded voice though; it called him very much to mind, so that Dan could see his son's intelligent brown eyes, his charming smile, his dark, unkempt hair. They were so alike: the boy's colouring, height, sense of humour, hopeless passion for Wednesday – all his father's. If there'd been another baby, it would've looked like Katelin, Dan was sure of this, a little Celt, pale skin and reddish hair. But she'd only wanted one child, and it had to be her call in the end, although as the years had passed Dan had sometimes found himself missing the other one, missing perhaps the other two, wondering who they might have been.

He had no bag to check in, he travelled light and always with the same canvas holdall; it'd been everywhere with him, seen it all. His business-class ticket gained him a seat in a chic, capacious lounge, free newspapers, food, wine, beer, but he found himself in a contemplative mood and so he just sat in a leather armchair looking out over the tarmac, where the ground crew loaded suitcases into the belly of the plane he'd soon be on. He reflected on this leap of faith he was about to take, and considered the limits of his own certainties. He had to see Alison Connor and his belief in the feelings she had stirred in him was rock solid, yet beyond this he could not say exactly what he wanted, or how this would end. He knew he was acting self-ishly, chasing her down through the lost years to see her again and discover if such a person, so perfectly constructed in body and mind to suit his own, could possibly exist. But he had to see this through. Yes, it was an act of treachery, but of all the choices, large and small, that had helped construct his life so far, none felt more imperative than his decision to fly to Adel-aide from Hong Kong, to find Alison.

He checked his phone. Details from Terri of the DJs he was seeing. A rescheduled meeting with the publisher. Confirm-ation from 6 Music that his gig with them would start after his return. And a song, from Ali Connor. He opened the link and stared at this gift, this frank and open-hearted gesture, and felt a pulse of pure love for her for sending the Pretenders, and of all their songs, this song. 'I Go To Sleep'. Love and lust and plain-tive regret.

He knew she'd be there when he got to Adelaide, knew it as he'd never known anything before, knew it in his gut. Knew she was there now, too: thinking about him, thinking about her.

21

ADELAIDE,
3 FEBRUARY 2013

Michael had invited a couple of his friends for dinner, people Ali barely knew: Moira Thiemann, a newly appointed consultant paediatrician at the hospital, and her husband Greg Golding, who was something high up in the state's Environment Protection Authority. So that it wouldn't just be the four of them, Ali asked Cass to come along, and, as Cass was currently without a boyfriend, she asked Tahnee Jackson too, so the numbers wouldn't be odd.

'Tahnee Jackson?' Michael said. 'That's a bit passive-aggressive.'

Ali said, 'Why, because your mother will be spinning in her grave?'

'No, because you're pissed off that I don't like your philanthropy scheme, which you're determined to plough ahead with anyway.'

'Michael, I didn't invite her to score a point,' Ali said, trying to keep her voice level. 'I asked her because she's become a friend,' but Michael only laughed and said, 'Sure, right.' Then Ali told him to change his tone because it sounded ugly, and he said well, he couldn't say anything right, so what the hell.

This was how things often were these days with Michael,

and this was why: Ali had gifted a trust fund to an Arts South Australia scheme to support indigenous musicians, and had also, as well as this, begun funding Tahnee's career, while at the same time Stella had officially withdrawn from her place at NIDA and was now planning a year's travel in Europe; and to each of these developments Michael was vehemently opposed. He had passionately, volubly opposed them – but then had to deal with the novelty of failure when his opinion hadn't prevailed, which was tough for him, because he wasn't used to dissent; he'd had very little practice, by and large. Sure, Stella had given him a run for his money these past couple of years, when, on turning fifteen, she'd been inhabited by a rebel version of her own sweet self, but from Ali he'd only ever had agreement, even if sometimes it'd been lukewarm. All their lives together she'd tended to bend softly to his will, give way to his point of view. Now, though, she was standing her ground, defending her own plans and Stella's, and giving their youngest daughter all the support she needed – which wasn't much, in fact, because Stella was resolute.

'Ah, Dad, chill, I'll just apply again,' she said to Michael blithely. 'They'll take me another time if they like me that much. They'll like me even more with some life experience behind me.'

She was leaving for Italy soon, now she'd made her mind up to bail on NIDA, and there was no one in Adelaide she wanted to hang out with any more anyway, no one she even wanted to bump into in a chance encounter in the mall or at the beach. There was a year group party coming up in late February, a lavish formal event at a house in the hills, and it was her ardent wish to be long gone before the photos hit Facebook. This made no sense to Michael, who repeated with futile persistence that drama school in Sydney – surely, surely – would take her far enough away from her demons in Adelaide? But no, Stella said. No. She wanted continents between herself and her mistake; she wanted a hemisphere between them. The boy – the one she still wouldn't name – had bragged about his conquest at Victor Harbor, Stella had told Ali that much at least. Bragged about it and, by so doing, unleashed a scandalfest, a gossip free-for-all, and the peculiar, odious, judgemental piety of a whole bunch of seventeen-year-old girls towards their erstwhile friend. 'I hate them all,' Stella said. 'They're mean and petty, and I want to start all over again, as if none of it had ever happened. I want to erase them all.'

'You can do that in Sydney, darling,' Michael said.

'Dad, no!' she said. 'How many times? I can't do that in Sydney, I need to escape, I need somewhere completely different. Mum understands, don't you, Mum?'

Ali nodded. 'Totally,' she said.

'What a surprise,' Michael said.

Ali and Stella stared at him and Ali opened her mouth to speak, but then the doorbell rang, and it was Moira and Greg, here in the McCormack home for the first time, bearing flowers and wine and wide smiles, so the subject was closed.

Oh, but it all felt wrong, from the start. In the first instance, there was the perennial difficulty of how to explain Beatriz, because it was always so hard to find the right tone when introducing her to new people. Michael tended to say, 'And this is Beatriz, she's the real boss around here,' which somehow always seemed to imply the opposite: that if there was a boss, it was probably him, and it certainly wasn't Beatriz. Ali's favoured introduction was: 'This is Beatriz, she lives with us here,' but this still left unclear the matter of why Beatriz should share their home; was she a lodger? Had she been taken in off the streets? Tonight, the questions hung only briefly in the air between guests and hosts before Beatriz herself made it clear, in a long and convoluted greeting, that she was uniquely useful to this household. When Moira and Greg arrived she'd been heading out to a church social, swathed in purple chiffon, but she stayed on, half in and half outside the house, to offer an expansive explanation of how to make authentic piri-piri chicken and then to give Michael unnecessary instructions for the slow and steady grilling of said chicken, how to apply the sauce to the cooked meat – with a bunch of parsley, never with a brush – and finally to urge and insist that all washing up should be left for her return, this last being the only one of her instructions that would be roundly ignored. There was a brief hiatus after she'd gone, as there might be following a small earth tremor, then Ali said, 'So, congratulations, you've been well and truly Beatriz'd,' and Moira and Greg laughed a little uncertainly. Then Cass showed up, already slightly merry, waving a clanking bag from the bottle shop, and Tahnee appeared just afterwards, straight from the airport, and so Stella – who hadn't realised Tahnee was coming – asked if she could join them for dinner, which of course was fine, except that Greg turned out to be in charge of the radiation protection division of the EPA, and Stella had done her Year 12 research project on the continued contamination at the Maralinga nuclear-testing sites, and Tahnee's grandfather – it transpired, as the conversation blundered on – had been among the scores and scores of indigenous people hounded off their ancestral land in the fifties and sixties by white men in army vehicles, so that the area could be experimentally nuked by the British government.

Michael stood at the barbecue, listening to the steady unravelling of the evening he'd had in mind. He waited for Tahnee to finish what she was saying, then cleared his throat. 'This

chicken's done,' he said. 'Just needs the sauce now. Hope everyone's hungry.'

They were seated outside, under the hibiscus pergola, and
there were tea lights in small tin lanterns, flames dancing like
fireflies down the centre of the table. Tahnee, who was a thoughtful young woman possessed of a quiet, watchful confidence,
said, 'These are difficult subjects for such a lovely gathering,'
and Greg looked fractionally less uncomfortable. Michael began
to anoint the chicken with piri-piri sauce, carefully, meticulously, with his surgeon's concentration and the big bunch of
parsley Beatriz had left for the purpose.

'They were such different times,' Moira said. She'd shown a
tendency this evening to speak in platitudes, but Greg looked at
her now and nodded sagely, as if her remark showed great insight.

'They were,' he said.

'Yeah,' Stella said. 'Very different, if it was OK for Britain to
turn a piece of South Australia into radioactive wasteland.'

'Indeed,' Greg said, ignoring her combative tone. 'Cold War
values.'

'Australia sucking up to the Brits, more like,' Stella said,
'and nobody's ever been held properly accountable for it.'

'It's all been cleaned up, y'know, Stella,' Moira said.

'It has,' Greg said. 'More than once, and, sure, there's still a
low-level risk, but we're well within international guidelines
these days.'

'I spoke to a fella who told me plutonium's considered dangerous for about a quarter of a million years,' Stella said.
'Hashtag, just saying.'

'Stella, will you fetch the salad?' Michael said.

She shot him a look, but stood at once, and went into the
kitchen, and Tahnee said, 'My grandfather seemed to know
that without any understanding of atomic science.'

'How do you mean?' Cass asked. She was having a far better time than she'd expected. She liked a tense dinner table, it made a nice change, and these McCormack occasions clearly benefited from a nuclear-powered rocket up the metaphorical arse. Cass didn't really mind Michael McCormack, he was a bit of a stuffed shirt, a bit pompous and entitled, but the wine he served was always first rate, and he was a big improvement on that old scoundrel, McCormack Senior. But still, she much preferred having Ali to herself. Every time. Any day of the week. Cass waved the Pinot Noir at her friend, and she smiled regretfully and shook her head, because she'd promised Tahnee a lift back to Port Adelaide later, but Greg pushed his glass forwards for a refill, and Moira frowned and said, 'Ah, I see, I'll drive then.'

'I mean, my grandfather totally understood the land was toxic,' Tahnee said. 'They all did, all his family, even years later, after it'd been declared fit for hunting. He used to tell me the kangaroos had yellow insides.'

Ali said, 'Where did your grandfather go?'

Tahnee shrugged. 'They were all moved to a mission. Whole new set of problems there.'

Stella said. 'It's all in my paper, Mum.' She was back with the salad.

'Jeez,' Cass said. 'Yellow roos.'

Greg said, 'Look, I'm not an apologist for what happened out there,' and Michael, coming to the table with the platter of burnished grilled chicken, said, 'Of course you aren't, Greg, and anyway it was nineteen fifty-six, way before your time, mate,' and Tahnee cleared her throat and said, 'Well, our way of life was destroyed long before nineteen fifty-six, Michael,' and he said, 'Sure, yeah, yeah, of course. Well, dig in, help yourselves.'

'Michael, this looks just wonderful,' Moira said. She was

stick-thin though, her chest almost concave beneath her flimsy dress, and she only looked at the chicken, then didn't take any. Instead, Greg helped himself to double, and sent the platter on its way round the table.

The scent of garlic and chilli rose provocatively into the night, and Cass said, 'What's not to like about Nando's?' but only Ali and Stella laughed.

'Beatriz always says we should eat it with our fingers,' Stella said. 'But Dad draws the line at that, don't you, Dad?'

'Hey, suit yourself, Stella, that's how you go now, isn't it?' Michael smiled as he spoke, but they all heard the edge in his voice.

Ali glanced at her husband and saw his mouth was set in that hard, thin line indicating dissatisfaction. She felt a pulse of guilty responsibility at having asked Tahnee and Cass to dinner when Michael had intended it as a getting-to-know-Moira-and-Greg event, but then, almost at once, her guilt was replaced by defiance. She'd had every right, and if Greg was getting a hard time, well, he was an adult doing a grown-up job, and more than capable of defending himself. He looked perfectly content anyway, tucking into the chicken a little too soon, before everyone was served. Moira had placed only salad on her plate, but she looked happy enough too. No, it was really only Michael who was suffering tonight, and Tahnee wasn't the cause, nor was Cass; it was Stella.

'You see, I've decided not to go to drama school in Sydney,' the girl said now to the assembled diners. 'That's what Dad's referring to there, when he said "suit yourself" like that.'

Moira said, 'Ah, really?' and looked politely between Stella and Michael, but received no further clarification from either one.

'Travelling in Europe,' Ali said into the void. 'It's a change of plan.'

'It's folly, is what it is,' Michael said.

'Italy, France, Spain, Portugal,' Stella said, ticking the countries off on her fingers, which were sticky with piri-piri sauce. 'Maybe the Greek islands. Maybe Morocco, actually.'

'Morocco?' Michael said. 'Since when?'

'Since just now.'

'Beautiful,' Moira said. 'Fascinating country, isn't it, Greg?'

He nodded, feeling, correctly, that it would be more politic to have no opinion about Morocco just at this moment.

Tahnee said, 'You're right to spread your wings, Stella, see the world, experience different cultures. I've never been outside Australia.'

'Well, that's going to change,' Ali said. She put an arm around Tahnee's shoulders, and said, 'Tahnee Jackson, a rare and special songbird. Watch this space, everyone.'

Moira said waspishly, 'Oh, Greg's watching all right,' which was quite true, and he immediately looked away and grinned sheepishly. But he wasn't the only one; they all saw Tahnee's allure, the hypnotic quality that drew and held the attention.

'Tahnee, are you going to sing for us?' Moira asked.

'She's a guest, Moira, not a turn,' Stella said, and Michael and Ali, united by their daughter's rudeness, both said, 'Stella!' and Stella held up two hands in surrender and said, 'All right, don't drop your bundle. I'm sorry – sorry, Moira.'

'I'd gladly sing for you,' Tahnee said, 'but I'm feeling all sung out from last night's set.' She smiled at Moira, who seemed to relax a little under her soft gaze. 'It was pretty demanding. Another time, though, for sure.'

'Where've you been?' Michael asked, and then felt,

suddenly, that he ought to know this, that Ali must already have told him and he – through lack of any real interest – hadn't listened. Again. But Ali let it pass and Tahnee just said, 'Oh, I played a little festival out beyond Melbourne. I have a few lined up this year.'

'I wish I'd gone,' Ali said. 'Next year, maybe.'

'She won't be playing little festivals next year,' Cass said, 'it'll be the States for Tahnee, or the UK tour,' and Tahnee smiled and said, 'Hasty climbers have nasty falls,' and Ali said, 'You're very wise, my girl.'

Tahnee blew her a kiss and Michael, watching them, wondered at this surging affection between them, a sisterly connection springing tall and strong out of thin air, Tahnee so comfortable at his table and Ali treating her like a lifelong friend.

Moira and Greg left early, just before half past nine, clutching a signed copy of *Tell the Story, Sing the Song*, and promising to look out for Tahnee's debut album, when the time came.

'Well, they're sweet people,' Ali said to Michael, not meaning it at all, because she thought them dull, Moira certainly, nibbling on lettuce and covering her glass with a prohibitive flat hand when the wine came anywhere near.

Michael just poured himself another glass of red and said, 'What a shame, then, that they were given the Exocet treatment,' and Cass, who'd had way too much to drink, said, 'Aw, c'mon, Mike, don't be a mardy arse,' which helped not a jot. Michael picked up his wine and excused himself to make a start on the washing up, and Cass sniffed the air and asked in a stage whisper if anyone else detected a whiff of burning martyr. Ali told her to put a sock in it, then suggested to Stella she should go help her dad and cheer him up while she was at it – it'd be atonement, Ali said, for behaving so badly at the table.

'Not badly exactly,' Stella said, airily, 'just controversially,' but she followed Michael into the kitchen, because all the McCormacks, even the youngest member, were always keen to beat Beatriz to the dirty dishes, and the old lady would be back any time soon.

'Greg,' Cass said. 'What a total dill.'

'He was more fun than Moira,' Ali said. 'At least he recognised a plate of good food when he saw one. I'm sorry, Tahnee, that wasn't my best idea, dragging you along tonight.'

'Hey, I was fine,' Tahnee said. 'It was . . . interesting.'

'Did you see her plate?' Cass said. 'Two lettuce leaves, a semicircle of cucumber, and a slice of tomato, no dressing. Was that anorexia in action at your dinner table?'

Ali shook her head. 'No idea. Looked very much like it.' She'd delved into her pocket for her phone, and she scrolled through the notifications as she spoke. 'Serious self-control, at the very least.' There was nothing from Dan, and by her reckoning four days had gone by since she'd heard from him. It was kind of hard to keep track, given the crazy time difference that made his today her yesterday, but anyway it seemed as if too long had passed without a song, without a reply to the Pretenders, and she was more troubled by this than she dared to acknowledge.

Cass and Tahnee were chatting now, about the festival, and the others Tahnee was playing later in the year in Sydney and Perth. She had a new management team behind her, a professional machine to carry her career forward in a measured way, a tried-and-tested process. It was weird, she said, years of coping on her own and now there was Donal and Darcy, and cheerful roadies to pack up her kit, and Ali, distracted by the absence of Dan, with only half an ear on the conversation, said, 'Hmm? Darcy?' and Tahnee said, 'Donal's assistant,' and Cass said, 'Donal?' and Tahnee laughed: 'My new manager,' she said.

Cass said, 'Girl, you really are the ant's pants these days,' then she looked at Ali and saw the shadow of concern on her face. 'All good?' she asked.

Ali looked up from her phone, then slipped it away again. 'Yeah, sure, sorry,' she said, thinking, Dan Lawrence, speak to me.

Tahnee yawned, and stretched like a cat, spreading her arms, arching her back. 'I'm whacked,' she said.

'Come on, honey,' Ali said, and she stood up. 'You've had a long day, it's home time.'

Cass, in search of further fun and company, begged a lift to Hindley Street, then Ali and Tahnee drove on in easy silence, westward-bound down the Port Road towards a different world, one Ali had loved since she first came here, of ships' chandlers, wharf-side warehouses, the ghosts of the city's maritime past. Ali had always felt at home in Port Adelaide, more so than in the genteel complacency of North Adelaide; something about this place – the industry, the spirit of endeavour – spoke to her urban soul. But Michael had laughed when, many years ago, she'd suggested they buy a place here, something run-down, something with lofty ceilings and tall windows overlooking the water, something they could restore and make their own. This was before his father and mother died, when sharing the parental home had seemed, to Ali, an unnatural thing to do, a strange, co-dependent, vaguely infantilising existence. In the end, he'd seen she was serious, but he still wouldn't countenance Port Adelaide, so they'd settled on Norwood, a very different proposition but good in its way, probably better than the port, full of young families and funky cafés and wide streets where Thea and Stella learned to ride bicycles and played skipping games with the neighbours' children. The house hadn't been majestic or colonial or expansive, just exactly the right size, and Ali had loved it there, but only for a short while, only three years, because in that time James died, and Margaret began the process of dying, and Michael missed the grand bluestone house, he missed the gracious proportions, the sweeping staircase, the gardens, the pool. Someone must live there, he said, and he didn't want his brothers to have it, or – God forbid – a stranger. It was closer to the girls' school, he said, and didn't Thea and Stella prefer it in North Adelaide, with their own swimming pool and the parklands nearby? Put like that, the little girls had to agree, and Ali, out-manoeuvred, had bowed to the inevitable. They'd sold the Norwood single-storey and trooped back to where Michael belonged, and at least Beatriz had been there, waiting for them with the steadfast patience of a woman who'd known they would come home. And look, it'd hardly counted as a sacrifice, going back to the McCormack family seat; Ali knew she couldn't complain. She didn't complain. She would never be so crass, or ungrateful. It was only that sometimes Michael's rock-solid certainties gave her the sense that she'd led someone else's life instead of her own.

Ali dropped Tahnee off at her building, and watched until she was safely inside, then she swept the car round in a U-turn to head back. In the well of the driver's side door, her phone gave its muted buzz, and she knew it'd be Cass saying *Call me right now*, so she didn't rush to check the screen and instead waited until the next red light to pick it up. *Dan Lawrence sent you a message*, she read. Liquid golden relief washed over her and right through her, startling in its purity, and at the same time she knew she shouldn't have doubted him; like Beatriz, she thought, she should trust in a higher power, practise the healing art of steady patience. She pulled over and parked to look at his message, feeling good, feeling light and bright, thinking she'd play the song, whatever he'd sent, and let it accompany her home, but there was no link to a song, only a message. *Hey, Alison, I'm at the bar of the Exeter Hotel in Rundle Street, saving you a seat xxx.*

The world outside – cars, shops, petrol stations, pubs, people – hurtled backwards into infinity, rushing and streaming away from her like falling water, retreating entirely, until she was quite alone on the Port Road, hands shaking, heart banging, staring with disbelief at his words, but they didn't alter, they didn't mutate or melt away to prove themselves a figment of her imagination. They remained exactly as they were and the time beneath the message showed 22.17, and now it was exactly twenty past ten, just three minutes after he'd written them, from a bar stool in a pub on Rundle Street. He was here, in Adelaide, and he was here for her.

Don't freak out, she told herself. Don't freak out, don't mess this up, don't hide, don't run, don't let him down, don't, don't, don't forget to breathe.

There was no decision to make, but she didn't reply to Dan. She sent Michael a text to say she was still with Tahnee, she'd be late, they had stuff to discuss, and this perfectly plausible lie came so easily she knew she should be ashamed, when all she felt was a kind of elated determination. She'd conquered the involuntary shaking, she'd held the steering wheel of the stationary car and made herself take long and steady breaths, she'd checked her appearance in the rear-view mirror, and now she was simply responding to the dictates of her heart and his, filled with resolve, shining with the clarity of her purpose. She was returning home. How Dan came to be here didn't cloud her mind, the risk he'd taken, the folly of turning up unannounced. No: there was no questioning the ins and outs, the whys and wherefores of an inexorable force, and after all, the world could be crossed in the course of a day and a night, and they had to see each other, of course they did; they had to be in the same city, in the same room, they had to talk and to touch, they couldn't simply spend the years they each had left trading songs across cyberspace. This certainty sustained her for the twenty minutes it took to arrive at the East End, and to park and get out of the car, but then, as she approached the familiar tatty splendour of the fine old Exeter Hotel she thought: Hang on, Daniel Lawrence is in there, and for a few moments she simply froze, even though her hand was already reaching for the door. She stood there on the step, paused in time like a woman spellbound, and a young guy behind her said, not unkindly, 'You coming or going?' then stepped round her and pulled open the door, and Ali could see Dan, saw him at once, knew him at once, although he didn't see her because there was live music playing and he was watching the band, not the door: watching the band, holding a pint, waiting for Alison, as if he'd been doing this for ever.

She felt so sure of him. She walked through the open door and up to him where he stood, leaning with his back against the bar, and he turned his head before she spoke as if he'd sensed her there, and he smiled at her. Just that, a smile, but it was so completely familiar to her that she laughed. She was filled with love and wonder. Daniel put his glass down on the bar. They stared at each other, and his eyes roamed her face.

'Look at you,' he said, and he took her face in his hands, tipping it up towards his so that he could kiss her, very softly, on the mouth, a careful, tender placing of lips on lips. 'There,' he said, and drew away to look at her, but she pressed close to him, so close that their bodies connected, and she reached for the back of his head, pulled it towards her until they were kissing again; then, when it ended, she rested her head against his shoulder and inhaled the smell of his warm skin, and he wrapped his arms around her, and there they stood for a while, like survivors, happy just to be alive.

22

There was a table in the corner, away from the crush of drinkers. Ali was well known in this pub, she'd been here many a time, and yet she'd stood at the bar and kissed Dan Lawrence as if they had the place to themselves. She scanned the crowd while the barman fetched her a bottle of Shiraz and two glasses, but there were no familiar faces, no shocked or reproachful stares, only the young barman, who winked at her in a cocky, presumptuous way, but she stared him down, then crossed the room to where Dan was waiting, and he said, 'You look so fucking beautiful, more beautiful than you have any right to look.'

Ali said nothing, just sat down next to him and looked him over for a while, taking him in.

'You're the same,' she said. 'Older, obviously, as am I, but you wear it well. I'd have known you anywhere.'

'But you're an Aussie,' he said. 'Your accent – it's like listening to Kylie.'

She laughed, poured the wine, raised a glass. 'Cheers, Daniel,' she said.

'Cheers, Alison.'

They drank, their eyes locked.

'You came to Adelaide,' she said. 'That's probably the nicest thing anyone's ever done for me.'

He grinned and said, 'Well, look, I was already in Hong Kong for work, so . . .' and Ali laughed.

'What would you have done if I hadn't been here?' she asked.

He reached out to gently tuck a strand of hair behind her ear, a gesture of ordinary intimacy that made her momentarily sad for all those many other moments they hadn't had. 'I knew you would be,' he said. 'Knew it in my bones.'

'It's so good to see you,' she said.

'You too.'

'But this is sheer madness, isn't it?'

'Yeah,' he said. 'And no.'

She was sitting in the Exeter with Daniel Lawrence, her first love, the boy who'd known her when she was Alison Connor, her uptown boy from Nether Edge with the Sheffield Wednesday season ticket, the lovely family and a penchant for mix tapes, and this fact, in all its miraculous simplicity, suddenly hit her like a breaker, left her winded and a little disorientated.

'Alison?' he said. 'You OK?'

'Yeah,' she said, echoing him. 'And no.'

He looked at her with a kind of gentle scrutiny, letting his eyes linger over her features.

'I thought I'd learned to forget all about you,' Ali said.

'I was certain you had.' Dan smiled, put his glass down, folded his arms. 'You did the biggest runner in history. There was a gig to play, y'know. We could've been famous, you would've been the Union's winning ticket, our Chrissie Hynde, our Debbie Harry.' His tone was light as he teased her with the past, but he'd misread her mood, she wasn't being playful, because suddenly it was all too much, she'd been ambushed by the familiarity – his voice, his inflection, the way he dipped his chin to look at her, his half-smile, the line of his jaw, the hollow of his cheek, the shape of his eyes. Here he was, the other part of her, the missing piece. She ached with relief, but also with sorrow, and although she didn't mean to cry, the tears came too fast and too stealthily for her to halt them.

'Alison,' he said, and he took her in his arms. 'I'm sorry. I'm an oaf. I do know this is a big deal, it's bigger than big, and I'm blethering on like an idiot.' He stopped talking and leaned in to kiss the side of her head. 'You still smell the same,' he said into her hair.

She said, 'You do too, and I love hearing you again, I love your voice, and the feel of your arms around me. It's just too good.'

'Alison,' he said again.

She drew back and looked at him, and he wiped away the residual tears from under her eyes with his thumbs.

'What do you want to do?' he said.

'Do?'

'Yeah. I mean now, and tomorrow, and the next day. What do you want to do?'

'Right now, I just want to finish this red wine with you,' she said.

'Fair enough.'

'Then I'll leave the car where it is and get a taxi home.'

'Right.' This didn't sound good.

'Then I'll meet you back here, in Rundle Street, tomorrow morning.'

'OK.' Better, much better, although he desperately wanted to take her back to his hotel room, undress her, and spend all night with her, above her, beside her, beneath her.

'We need to talk,' she said.

'Sure thing. And after that is there any chance I could get my hands on you?'

She tipped back her head and laughed, and he stared at her lovely throat, thought how much he'd always loved to make her laugh, and how rare her laughter had been when he'd known her at sixteen. He said, 'I keep thinking you'll vanish, Alison. I mean now, right here, I'm worried you'll just melt away like an apparition.'

'I won't,' she said, immediately serious. She took his hand.

'I looked for you, y'know,' Dan said. 'When you disappeared from Sheffield. I looked for you. I didn't know where you lived – and that nearly killed me, the shame of not knowing – but anyway I knew it was Attercliffe and your house wasn't that hard to find, once I started asking people about Alison Connor.'

She was very pale now, and silent, watching him, and he didn't want to cause her pain, dragging up an unwelcome past, but God Almighty, he'd suffered as never before or since when she left him, and to this day he had no idea why she'd gone. 'I found your mother,' he said.

Ali withdrew her hand and felt a bloom of cold sweat beneath her shirt, and an old, familiar tightening in her throat and gut, a constriction that made her breathing shallow and difficult. She saw Catherine, mottled bare legs, short skirt, cleavage that guaranteed a few free drinks, and the old stale musk of fag smoke, spilled booze and urine. And she saw Daniel, that beautiful boy, trying to get some sense out of her, trying to piece together a story he'd never really understand.

'She didn't help,' Dan said. 'She couldn't.'

Ali shook her head, only the slightest gesture really, barely discernible, but conveying undiluted misery. 'Can we not do this?' she said. 'Not yet?'

He shrugged and stared into his glass. He felt strongly that the time, in fact, ought to be now; God knows, an explanation was long overdue. But he could see her distress — it was palpable, almost feral — and from what he remembered of Catherine Connor, he could understand she might be a mother to forget. Peter had been more approachable; there was humanity in his eyes. But also, he'd been cagey, on edge, always glancing sidelong at the door, at the window, at Catherine, as if there was nothing here he could trust. Still, though, he'd offered Daniel a glass of water, and sat him down before telling him Alison was gone for good.

'I wrote to you,' Ali said. He was startled, amazed.

'Did you? When?'

'I'd been away about three months. I was in Paris by then, and I wrote to you, three times, as soon as I had a permanent address. I thought you might turn up, or write back at least, but then I decided you probably hated me.'

'Alison, oh my God, Alison, if I'd got a letter from you, nothing would've stopped me coming to you.'

'They didn't arrive, then?'

'Christ knows. I would've been in Durham by then, trying to be a student.' He thought about that abortive first term, the piercing sense of loss that he had carried there with him from Sheffield.

'But my letters . . . did your mum ever forward your post to you at uni?'

'Yeah,' he said. 'She did, occasionally. Official stuff so I could sign on, and the odd dirty postcard from Kev Carter.'

'But nothing from me?'

They stared at each other.

'I think she maybe didn't trust me,' Ali said.

'Oh my God.'

'I think she thought I was trouble.' She remembered that July afternoon, Marion Lawrence shouting down the street after her, *Is there something our Daniel needs to know?*

'She didn't send me your letters.' Dan's mind raced, recalibrating the details of the past. The difference it would have made! The difference, to him, to Alison, to their place in the world. She'd been his technicolour dream, his yellow submarine, his be-all and end-all, and then, for a few years at least, all the colours had drained away and he'd been plunged into black and white. 'I do remember her telling me I'd best forget you,' he said. 'After you went, and I couldn't find you, she said you seemed very troubled and the best thing would be to forget I'd known you. I told her to fuck off, and she went off on one, cried and raged, really unlike her, but I'd never sworn at her before, had to say sorry about a thousand times. My dad hid in his pigeon loft for two days.'

Ali's face softened. 'Bill,' she said. 'I so loved Bill.'

'He loved you too, he probably still does, although he barely speaks these days.'

'Oh, Daniel, I'm sorry, I wouldn't have hurt you for the world, but I had to get away, not from you, obviously not from you, but from everything else.'

'You seemed to be happy enough the night before, at the High Green miners' welfare.'

She was silent. Not a soul on earth knew what she'd endured on that dreadful Saturday, when Martin Baxter had turned up and altered the landscape entirely, so that the night before had seemed to belong to another time, another country, and she'd felt so stained, so ashamed – it had seemed, to her, for a long time afterwards, that all she was, was shame.

'Sorry,' Dan said. 'I don't mean to reproach you.'

'No, it's OK. There's a story to tell, but I don't have the words.'

And you a writer, he thought; he wondered how black her story could be, but he only smiled at her and said, 'Another time then.'

'Did your mum tell you I came to see you?' Ali said suddenly. 'The Saturday you were in Manchester?'

'Nope, my dad did, said you'd turned up all upset then run off. He was agitated, really agitated.'

Ali said, 'I know, I'm sorry, I just really needed to see you.'

'But you knew I wouldn't be there, didn't you?'

She shook her head, trying to cast off the memory. 'I forgot. But oh, look, there's such a lot you don't know, and I don't blame your mum, she thought I had a screw loose.'

'I sodding well blame her!'

She laughed. 'Sodding. Great word. I haven't heard that in decades.'

'Everything changed after that,' Dan said.

Ali nodded, and leaned in to kiss him softly. She was filled with remorse and sympathy and regret, but she allowed herself to marvel at this feeling of belonging. She knew exactly what she'd found in Dan Lawrence; she understood how very much it mattered.

She picked up her glass and took a drink, watching him watching her. 'Y'know,' she said. 'Sending me a song, and that song in particular, all those weeks ago, was unalloyed genius on your part.'

He nodded his head slowly, in full agreement.

'That's why we're here, tonight,' she said.

He nodded again.

'I stalked you, after you sent it,' she said.

'Of course,' he said. 'Who wouldn't?'

'I know what you've done, who you've become, what you've written, where you live, who you're with.'

'Snap,' he said.

'Katelin, Alex and McCulloch,' said Ali.

'Michael, Thea and Stella.'

'Our loved ones.'

'Our *other* loved ones,' Dan said.

She reached out and ran the fingers of one hand slowly through his hair like a comb. She felt besieged by tenderness for him.

'I only told you I loved you once,' she said. 'You were fast asleep, you didn't hear.'

'I'm sorry about that,' he said. 'Did I ever tell you I love you?'

She shook her head: no.

'So, I love you,' he said. 'I love you. Always have, always will.'

They talked until all the lights went on, lights that could wake the dead, so that they realised it was just them and the barman, the one with the knowing look and the arch manner, who said, 'Sleep tight,' as they left, in a voice that suggested he knew there'd be no sleep at all for this pair. He was wrong, though, Ali was going home, and they walked together the short distance to the taxi rank in Pulteney Street, then waited for one to turn up, not touching, standing slightly apart, feeling oddly awkward together for the first time, as if the change in environment from the intimacy of a crowded pub to the midnight quiet of the street had somehow altered the rules of engagement. An old aboriginal man with dusty skin and pale, clouded eyes watched them mildly from his heap of blankets in a shop doorway and a police car split the warm night with its siren. When a cab drew up, she told the driver her address through the open window and then turned back to Dan.

'Be at the Ex at midday, OK?' she said. 'Pack your stuff, bring it along, you'll need it,' and then she got into the car, and Dan closed the door, blew her a kiss and watched her go. He must have had about him an air of abandonment, because the old man in the shop doorway raised his bottle of grog unsteadily and offered Dan a consolatory drink.

'Appreciate it, mate,' Dan said, 'but no, thanks.' He lingered on, though, because he recognised brotherly solidarity when he saw it, and he didn't want to seem ungracious. The old man stared greedily up into his eyes as if he was reading the small print of Dan's soul. He revealed no insight though: showed neither approval nor disapproval, nor did he seem to draw any conclusion. He merely examined Dan intently for a while; then he suddenly lost interest, looked away, took a long, long draught of Bundy, and broke into an odd, disjointed song in a language completely new to Dan's ears. It was so weird, Dan thought, it was all so fucking weird: the heat, still solid as a brick wall at half past midnight; the old man on his bed of blankets, those milky eyes, his oddly mystical presence. Surreal. But no more surreal, on balance, than kissing Alison Connor tonight for the first time in three decades.

It took him ten minutes to get his bearings and find his hotel, and, once there, he stripped off and lay on the bed, and prepared to not sleep – he was physically exhausted but completely alert thanks to the jet lag that had already claimed him in Hong Kong. He didn't switch on his laptop, didn't check his emails – because real life lurked there. Instead, he considered Alison, considered her fine features, the waves in her hair, the jeans she wore so well, and the white linen shirt, her slender hips, the curve of her waist, the dip at the small of her back. He considered, too, the unexpected delight of her response to his message. She'd come directly to him, when she could have panicked, or prevaricated, or cut and run. She'd just stepped into his arms in the spirit of a homecoming, naturally, without inhibition. She was his perfect ten, his Sheffield girl, and God knows how she'd ended up all the way across the globe, with an Australian accent and an Australian husband. Didn't that guy know where she belonged? Dan, suffused with longing, rolled on to his stomach and groaned into the pillow. He wanted her now, needed her, craved her; but tomorrow would do, it would have to, and anyway, how fucking incredible that they had a tomorrow to share.

In the meantime, he decided he'd send her a song, and he reached for his phone. He'd send her John Martyn; he'd send 'Go Down Easy'. It was the only thing he could do, under the circumstances. It was time.

Monday morning, and Ali was busy weaving a web of lies. Michael listened to her in silence as she laid out her plan for the coming week: to go back to Quorn, where the creative block that had descended these past weeks might lift. She must make progress with this new novel, and it wasn't happening here, it just wasn't. In Quorn, she might find a way to make the words flow again, roll the rock from the mouth of the cave, let the light in.

'It's the pressure of a sequel,' she said. He was standing with his back to her, watching the birds at the water bath. 'It's the expectation, I think. I've never had this before. Before, nobody cared what I wrote or when it'd be finished. Now, it's like, "Where's the book? We needed it yesterday!"'

She heard her own voice, a study in guile. There was truth

in what she said – she hadn't written a word for weeks. The lie was in the untold. She watched her husband, who wouldn't look round but remained stubbornly fascinated by the galahs battling it out for a turn at the stone trough. She wondered if this meant he knew already that she hadn't been with Tahnee until after midnight last night, and this idea – plausible enough, given her own reckless behaviour in the pub – sent a wave of anxiety through her gut, which disappeared as swiftly as it had come when he turned around and said in a perfectly normal voice, 'Are Sheila and Dora there at the moment?'

Now she was a little ashamed at the relief, which suddenly seemed to indicate a lack of character, an absence of resolve. 'I haven't called them,' she said. 'I will, soon, but Sheila always leaves a key under the Buddha, she told me it was there, if I ever dropped by and found them gone.'

'Dropped by? Hardly likely, unless you're en route to the desert.' He was pouring coffee now, his second cup, which meant that soon he'd be gone.

'Sorry it all got a bit angsty last night,' she said. 'Cass was pissed when she arrived. I could see it in her face, her eyes were too wide and wild.'

Michael said, 'Cass is a liability the minute she steps through the door. But it was Stella who won the trophy for obnoxious behaviour last night.'

'She's going to stay with Thea in Melbourne tomorrow, she'll be out of your orbit for a while.' Oh, how very hard she was working to keep him sweet! She felt her guilt must surely show, like the scarlet letter, branding her a sinner, forever unworthy.

'I know she is, but she'll be out of sight, not out of mind, and she's driving me crackers.' He drained his coffee cup and put it in the sink, where he stared at it for a few seconds, just stared, as if the dregs at the bottom might hold some answers.

'So,' Ali said, a little uneasy, eager to be alone.

He turned around from the sink and said, 'So?'

They stood either side of the pale oak surface of the kitchen island, and she moved round it now, to the same side as him, so that he could touch her if he wanted to, although he didn't, and she didn't touch him. 'You don't mind, then? If I take off?'

'It's up to you what you do,' he said. He folded his arms and leaned away from her, against the sink. Dressed for work he looked polished and controlled, and it was so difficult to gauge his mood. 'I'm not going to give you permission.'

'I'm not asking for permission,' Ali said. 'I'm asking if you mind.'

'OK,' he said, and he sighed like a man whose patience was being sorely tried. 'Well, cards on the table, I'd rather you didn't go, but I suppose I don't mind, if you feel you must.' He looked at her, and there was a challenge in his expression; she saw it now for sure, and, seeing it, she realised it'd been there all along.

'What's going on, Ali?' he said, and wham, there it was again, that cold liquid fear coursing through her gut, mouth instantly dry, proving her a lightweight once more, even now, at this early stage in the game, when so little actual wrong had been committed. Fight or flight, she thought; how basic we are, how very predictable. She swallowed, and chose to fight.

'What kind of question is that?' she said.

He launched into an attack, bombarding her with evidence. 'You're distant and distracted, you're on your phone at odd times, like last night, at the table – the moment I left for the kitchen, it was in your hands. You lock the bathroom door, you spend hours in your office with the door shut tight, you take off for runs rather than spend time with me, you don't look at me as often as you used to, you don't seem to hear me, and if you do hear me, you don't seem interested. Plus, you hardly smile, unless the girls are with us. I feel – like, really feel – this distance between us, like we're on opposite sides of a chasm, and it's as if it happened overnight, but it gets wider and wider and I can't halt it, because I don't understand it.'

He ceased, and there was a silence. Ali recognised this description of herself at once, but she didn't recognise Michael, the Michael who'd studied her so closely, noticed these differences in her that she couldn't deny. He hadn't ever seemed particularly observant before, had never remarked upon her habits or rituals, but now she realised this was because he'd had no cause to. She hadn't known she'd been so careless, so imprudent in her manner towards him these past few months. She'd forgotten how very well he knew her, forgotten that as she'd allowed herself to slip away from him, towards Dan, he might be watching, and wondering, and worrying. Now, she placed a hand on his arm and caressed it, because the instinct to comfort and reassure ran deep, even as she prepared to betray him.

'I'm sorry,' she said. 'I'm really sorry, Michael. There's nothing to worry about. It's writer's blues. I know I'm retreating inside myself, but it'll pass.'

'Yeah,' he said. 'I knew you'd say that, but I reckon it's something else.' His voice was neutral, but she could see from his expression the effort it cost him to remain steady in the face of this unnamed, intangible threat. 'In all our years of marriage, I've never had cause to doubt our future, but these past few weeks . . .' He tailed off, shaking his head in confusion, but he kept his eyes on her face; his penetrating eyes that suddenly seemed to be searching for more than was visible. 'Something's changed, Ali, and it's not me.'

She steeled herself, chasing away her doubts, clinging on to her right – and it was her right, she felt this most passionately – to go her own way, for once: to explore life's possibilities, to think only of herself. She couldn't tell him the truth, though; she couldn't explode the known universe. If this was cowardice, she was unrepentant now, because Dan Lawrence deserved consideration too, and an explanation, and through him, she thought, she might find the key to herself.

'Well,' she said in a voice that indicated this discussion was ending, 'if I've seemed distant and remote, I'm sorry for it. But look, I'm dealing with it.'

'By running away.'

'To Quorn, not to the moon! And only for a few days.'

'Ali, you're the absolute cornerstone of my happiness.'

'Michael . . .'

'You're all I want, all I need.'

Well, she thought, that's you sorted then; but what about me? She didn't say this, of course, she only raised herself up on her toes and kissed him, a Judas kiss, and said, 'Chill out, honey, I'll be back by Friday.'

The moment she left, she rang Cass from the car, told her everything, because she needed to tell someone the absolute truth, even if that person had fewer scruples than anyone she knew. Still, it was a relief to spill the whole story, and Cass listened intently until Ali said, 'So that's it, and now he's waiting for me in Rundle Street and I just told a whole heap of lies to get a few days clear.'

'Join the club, darling. Or rather, join the waiting list, the club's oversubscribed. Damn, though, I knew it! Didn't I know it?'

'Yeah, you knew it. But nothing's happened yet. I could turn back, right now, with no harm done.'

'Dan's waiting for you at the Ex?'

'He is, yeah.'

'And how does that make you feel?'

'Incredibly happy.'

'Then you have to follow this through. I'm not ill-wishing Michael, but this is about you.'

'It's also about betrayal.'

'Yeah, if you want to get all biblical.'

'Not just Michael, the girls too.'

'Oh, bullshit, Ali, the girls are young adults, with lives of their own.'

'Yeah,' Ali said. 'But they'd never forgive me.'

'They would. Of course they would. You're a captive bird, Ali, you have been ever since I met you, and this guy came over here from Edinburgh and opened the cage door for you.'

'But just pleasing myself . . . I don't know, it's not me, it's not my style, causing pain.'

Cass sighed. 'Y'know, Ali, loss of reputation can be liberating, once you let go of the person you think everyone wants you to be. Trust me, I know what I'm talking about. Follow this through, and see where it takes you.'

'Look, I gotta hang up,' Ali said, and she did, because she was in Rundle Street and could see Dan waiting further down, on the kerb outside the Ex, in faded blue shorts, khaki T-shirt, a grey canvas holdall slung over one shoulder. All that doubt, all those qualms, and yet the sight of him made her heart leap. He reminded her of his younger self, waiting for her at a bus stop, but not watching for her, just standing where he said he'd be, and reading the *NME* until she showed up. He was listening to music, and seemed completely relaxed, didn't even appear to be checking out the drivers of the cars that had passed him already, and when she pulled up in front of him, he jumped slightly, as if he'd forgotten why he was there. He pulled out the buds, opened the passenger door, grinned at her and said, 'Hey,' then slung his bag into the back and got in. Incredible. Daniel Lawrence was in her car, and they were driving north to Sheila's. And yes, she thought, this was betrayal and the world beyond Cass might judge her harshly. But it was also an avowal of the unspoken pact she'd once had with Daniel, so wasn't there some integrity about that? Wasn't there a truth?

He leaned forward and kissed her, once on the lips, again on the cheek, then sat back, strapped in and smiled. 'All good?' he asked.

'A-OK,' she said.

He didn't ask how she'd arranged this trip, what hoops she'd jumped through, what lies she'd told, just as he didn't share the cock-and-bull story he'd told Katelin an hour ago when she wanted to know what he thought of Hong Kong Island because that's where he'd said he was. Perhaps it was because she was happily absorbed by her own adventure, her trans-America drive, but she was helpfully incurious about the full details of his trip, bursting with her own stories about people and places. Dan was happy for her. He'd have to find a way to forgive her for not planning to stop in Nashville on the way through Tennessee, but Austin was on their radar, so that was something. And – as she kept saying – this was her road trip, not his. Too right, darling, Dan had thought, and this is my road trip, not yours.

'So, where you taking me?' he said now to Ali.

'Wait and see,' she said. She pulled out into the traffic and moved smoothly down the street. 'You look after the music, I'll watch the road.'

'Did you like John Martyn last night, by the way?'

'Loved it. Play me some more.'

'You watch the road,' he said, 'and I'll choose the music.'

She laughed and he studied her for a moment, then said, 'Alison Connor, how good it is to see you.'

Her gaze was straight ahead, and she didn't turn to look at him. 'I've been working my way back to you, babe,' she said, speaking in lyrics, as if all of life was a song.

23

There was no one in at Sheila and Dora's little house; in fact all
of Quorn seemed utterly deserted. Wide empty streets, blazing
blue sky, frontier architecture – it all looked strange and wonderful to Dan, and emphatically far from home. He'd switched
off his phone hours ago, to hold back the intrusions of his
world; then he'd slipped willingly through a narrow gap in
space and time to be here in the back of beyond with Alison
Connor. All the way from Adelaide he'd kept glancing across,
checking her profile, and finding excuses to touch her. If someone had told him she wasn't really there, he wouldn't have been
surprised. Devastated, but not surprised.

Sheila's fat stone Buddha looked happy to see them, but Ali
ignored his smile, just tipped him up, and there was the promised key – but they'd have broken in anyway if it hadn't been
there; they'd have smashed a window or battered down the
door, because four hours of proximity in the car had them at a
kind of fever pitch, and they both knew that until they'd had
their fill of each other, they couldn't speak another word. She
unlocked the door and in they went; then she kicked it shut
with her foot, dropped her bag, leaned against the wall and
stared at him. Wordlessly, he came at her, kissing her mouth,

her face, her neck, and she hung on to him, responding with the same furious passion. She moved to the stairs, pulling him with her, and they stumbled up to the prayer-flag room where the window was propped open, though there was no relief from the heat, no breeze at all, and the flags above their heads might have been painted on the walls, they were so still. Dan and Ali fell on to the sleeping mat, half laughing, half crazed, tearing off their inconvenient clothes without ceremony or erotic ritual; they simply flung themselves at each other, and if they should've been solemnly honouring their teenage selves – remembering the first time, remembering the last – they absolutely didn't, not for a second. She'd wondered, in the car – worried, truth be told – if, when this moment came, there might be awkward-ness, or self-consciousness, an awareness of their bodies that in youth were so effortlessly, casually lovely. But then, in the end, all that mattered was here and now: this delirium, the heat and damp, this flood of feeling; they claimed each other with a kind of desperate, selfish urgency, and when at last they fell away, they lay quiet for a while, slightly stunned, face to face, inhal-ing each other's exhaled breath while their heartbeats calmed to an ordinary rhythm.

'Alison,' he said, 'Alison, Alison, Alison,' stroking her hair, her back.

She lay in his arms and felt like lost treasure, found again. It was such a long time, such a long, long time, since sex had felt like anything other than a kindness to a person she cared about, an act of generosity to clear the air, to keep things on an even keel. Desire such as this . . . oh, it belonged to the past, but she remembered it, she did, she remembered the drama of it, the heat and passion, the exquisite longing; it was exhilarating, life-enhancing, empowering. She kissed him and kissed him and he laughed and kissed her back and then, when she'd calmed herself and gathered her wits, she stood up, entirely unselfconscious now under his gaze, and walked to the door, on the back of which hung an old satin kimono, as red as the rising sun. She unhooked it from the peg, and turned around. He was watching her every move; watched her slip into the gown, tie the broad silk sash.

It felt cool against her skin, and light as air.

They stared at each other, stunned by the miracle of being alone together in this room, then he said, 'You look like a very dishevelled and sexy geisha in that. Where you going?'

'Downstairs for a drink of water. Want to come?'

'You bet.' He stood up and pulled on his shorts and T-shirt, and followed her downstairs. 'Where are we, exactly?' he said, looking about him at the peculiar furniture that crowded the living room.

'I told you, it's Sheila's house, she lives here with Dora, who used to be a train driver on the Pichi Richi Railway, but now she's just a nomad, like Sheila.'

'The what?'

'Steam train, named after the Pichi Richi Pass. Long story.'

Dan sat down cross-legged on the wide green sofa and patted the space next to him, so she handed him a glass of water and sat down too. She felt completely comfortable with him, completely at home in every possible way, and then he seemed to read her mind because he said, 'You know that Bill Withers song "Can We Pretend"? That's how I feel. Like there was no yesterday, like all those years away from you never happened.'

She rested her head on his shoulder and didn't reply, because she didn't wish to articulate her thoughts, didn't wish to reflect upon the life she might have had with Daniel, the life she'd felt compelled to let go, and it wasn't exactly that she regretted the years she'd spent being married to Michael – how could she, when they'd made such a life together and Thea and Stella, those glorious girls, were the result of their union? It was more that when she considered Daniel as a flesh-and-blood possibility, she experienced a kind of unease that came from knowing she would be happier still with him, happier than she'd been with Michael, her loving husband, their daughters' loving father. She hadn't fully realised, until she saw Dan again, that there was a different kind of love waiting for her, and that, in some essential, deep-seated way, it completed her. She knew this. She did. He'd turned up in Adelaide and reduced her to a romantic cliché, made her heart race and her spirits soar, and when she looked into his eyes she recognised a kindred soul, her Sheffield boy, and it wasn't just nostalgia, although that was part of it too; but no, it wasn't just nostalgia: it was an absolute certainty that this was meant to be, that the stars were aligned when she and Dan were together. She considered this now, and it made her melancholy, made her face the reality of this life she hadn't lived, which was presented to her now as a possibility for the future, amid all the complications and commitments of her real world, her chosen path, her beloved family. Pain and joy, joy and pain, promised in equal measure, indivisible.

They drank their water, and leaned together, and for a while they were silent, alone with their thoughts, then he said, 'So, talk to me about Sheila,' and Ali told him about Catherine's oldest friend, who had sailed to Australia on an assisted passage and made a new life for herself here just as the sixties tipped over into the seventies. 'Did you miss her, when she left?' Dan asked, and Ali said no, not at all, because she hadn't known her; Sheila used to live in Liverpool, but she'd written to Catherine after she emigrated, brilliant, dazzling letters, full of incident and sunshine.

'Catherine didn't care about Sheila by then, but Sheila kept writing because she didn't know what Catherine was like, and she hoped she would follow her out there, to Elizabeth, because she was all evangelical about it.'

'Elizabeth?'

'It's where she used to live when she first came. It's north of Adelaide. There was industry there, and lots of northerners migrated to work at the car plant.'

Dan said, 'You'd think the last thing they'd want on the other side of the world would be to trade one shithole job for another. You'd think they'd want to try something new.'

'Oh well, it was new all right – the heat and the parrots and the roos: that's what Sheila used to write home about. But people did what they knew for a living. Cornish tin miners came to work the copper mines, Welsh sheep farmers came to run sheep stations, and folk from the industrial north sniffed out the muck and toil and noise.'

'Hey, you're losing your Aussie accent,' he said, and she laughed and gave him a shove; then he said, 'And what about you? You didn't come for the tin or the sheep or the cars. Why did you come here, and stay for ever?'

She turned, and looked at him steadily. 'Honestly? Because I felt completely safe in Adelaide.'

There was a beat of silence; then he said, 'And why didn't you feel safe in Sheffield?' He was shocked. Hadn't he made her feel safe? Hadn't he been enough? Certainly she'd been enough for him. He'd had to rewrite his future when she left him, and that's not easy when you're eighteen and heartsick.

'I wasn't safe in Sheffield,' she said. 'I thought I could stay safe, but I couldn't. I protected you from all the parts of my life I was ashamed of, and they were legion. I was steeped in shame and you didn't know any of it.' She glanced at him, saw his face, and said, 'Oh, don't be thinking you let me down somehow.

Don't think that for a moment. You were my refuge, you and your family, but in the end, I had to go. At least, I felt then that I had to go. I don't know if it was the right thing to do, if the braver choice would've been to stay, but I ran away, and this is where you find me, still here.'

She was looking down now, her head too low for him to see her expression. He could see she was taking long, slow, steadying breaths. He took the half-finished glass of water from her hand and placed it on the floor; then he lifted the curtain of hair that hid her face and said, 'Hey, look at me, darling.'

She shook her head. 'I'm going to tell you everything,' she said, 'but I can't look at you while I speak,' so Dan sat back and waited. He wondered how – and if – he could help her, and decided he should simply be patient, so he let his mind drift as he stared across the small room at the alien world outside the window. In the boughs of a small fruit tree there was a posse of parrots with Day-Glo crests, and they were squawking fit to burst, a terrible cacophony that made him think of Brian Johnson screaming out the lyrics in one of those thundering AC/DC tracks. He thought: This girl grew up with sparrows, and the occasional robin for a splash of colour. Imagine waking each morning to a flag-cracking yellow sun and a heavy metal dawn chorus? He closed his eyes and tried to remember the lyrics to 'Back In Black', something about hitting the sack and being glad to be back, but he couldn't get there, he'd never been much of a headbanger, but then she started to speak, and he listened to a story that was unthinkable, about a world he hadn't known existed. Catherine, Martin Baxter, Peter, and there among them Alison, trying to cope, trying to be strong in the bleak and increasingly messy melee of her domestic life. Dan listened, shattered by this account of a dark and barely manageable life in Attercliffe, bitterly reproaching his younger self for never really pressing her for details, never trying hard enough to overcome her fierce privacy about home, always happy to simply meet her off the bus in Nether Edge, never picking her up, never taking her back to her door, never really questioning her vehemence that he shouldn't do either of these things.

On she went beside him: the drunkenness, the chaos, the role Peter played as her ally and support, until his own shame drove him to attempt suicide. She told him about the scene at Brown Bayley's, the photographs displayed there by Martin Baxter, how she'd torn them down, then gone home and had to cut Peter down from the light flex, and then had fled to his, Daniel's, house, forgetting he'd be long gone to Manchester. Dan groaned, thinking of the hard time he'd given her only yesterday for missing the gig. But she wasn't finished; she continued on in the same low, expressionless voice, as if she was reading a written account of someone else's terrible history. Peter revealing the escape fund, urging her to get the hell out of Sheffield and be free. Her refusal; her confidence in her own ability to tough things out. And then Martin Baxter, fulfilling the menace and violence he'd always threatened, overpowering her, raping her, treating her with bottomless contempt, showing her just how weak and worthless she really was. Dan moaned with a kind of visceral pain, a futile agony that she'd borne this abominable assault and its consequences entirely alone, undefended, unprotected. Lovely, clever, talented, incomparable Alison Connor, thought Dan: his shining light.

'There were two versions of me,' she said. 'Two Alisons, leading two separate lives. Peter and I, we cobbled together a kind of normality for each other, but it turned out to be built on sand. I was ashamed, always, of where I came from, who I came from. Catherine was a liability, an embarrassment, she was no mother, to me or to Peter. It was our job to try and look after her, and we had a father who upped and left us to our fate, probably started again with somebody more functioning, probably never gave me or Peter a thought—' She stopped speaking suddenly, although it'd seemed she was about to go on; then, 'That's it,' she said. 'No more to tell.'

She allowed herself to drop sideways, away from him, until she was lying down, curled on her side like a sleeping child, although her eyes were open, wide and anxious, as if she'd forgotten how to shut them. He placed himself down in the narrow space alongside her and stroked her cheek. She hadn't shed a tear; her face was stone.

'OK,' he said. 'It's OK.' He drew her eyes closed with his fingers and kissed her eyelids softly, and she kept them shut, then reached out and pulled him closer still, so that she could fall asleep, and he stayed with her there and watched her for all the time it took for her to stir and stretch and open her eyes, and then they made love again, but it was very quiet this time, and slow, and healing.

Two hours later, they were both showered, dressed and drinking gin and tonic, a poor version of it with no ice and no lemon – none to be found – but it was better than no drink at all. They were sitting blamelessly and respectably in the living room, chatting about their worlds and the people they'd known, and there was so much to talk about, so much to say, and Dan was now detailing the current state of his Sheffield family with such spin and colour that Ali felt she still knew them. But he hardly saw his parents, he said, and this weighed on his conscience, not that he did anything about that. 'Trouble is I don't like going. It's a time warp, I'm forever a sullen teenager in Nether Edge. Nothing's changed in that house, except Mum talks even more, and Dad talks even less.'

'Does he still have his pigeons?'

Dan shook his head. 'He had a long spell in hospital ten years ago and Mum couldn't cope. She sold them all, without telling him.'

Ali was horror-struck at this. 'Those beautiful birds,' she said. 'Didn't Marion realise how he loved them?'

'She'd wanted rid for years. Hated the smell of 'em, and she got into gardening and wanted the shed for the usual stuff people keep – y'know, spades and shears and whatnot. He was in hospital for the best part of a year, and he wasn't himself, he withdrew, and I think she assumed he'd just not notice, but actually, I think she might have unwittingly destroyed his one chance of rehabilitation. He seems to have been sad for a very long time now, my dad.'

'Poor old Bill,' Ali said. She thought about that pigeon loft. It'd felt a little like sitting in a church, a church with a congregation of birds. It'd had a holy quality to it; at least, that's what she remembered. Perhaps, she thought, the passing of time had elevated it in her mind.

'When were you last in Sheffield?' Dan asked, and immediately he wished he hadn't, because she stared at him with an expression that clearly questioned whether he'd listened to anything at all of what she'd told him.

'OK, right, you've never been back?' he said, trying to keep his voice level, so she couldn't hear the incredulity. Jesus, he thought, that was one hell of a bolt you did there, girl. Ali still didn't answer, just looked at him.

'I didn't realise,' he said. 'I thought perhaps you'd have gone back to see Peter . . . show the girls Sheffield . . .' He petered out. 'I'll shut the fuck up,' he said.

Ali said, 'No, I never went back. I've never even spoken of it, until today. Don't you understand that?'

'Never told Michael? None of it?'

'Dan, no. Like I said, I've never spoken about it until today and I certainly haven't been back for a magical mystery tour.'

Dan exhaled, a long, low breath. 'That's some serious poison you hung on to there.'

'Least said, soonest mended – isn't that what they say in Yorkshire?'

He shook his head slowly. 'But you're not mended.'

She was affronted by this, and she gave a short, bitter laugh. 'What do you know? You know nothing about my life here.'

'I'm not attacking you, Alison, and by the way I know plenty about your life – it looks gilded, from what I've seen online. I'm just saying there's such a thing as—'

'Oh God, please don't say closure,' she said, cutting into his unfinished sentence. 'I can't bear that word.' She brought her knees up to her chest and hugged them, making herself small, and tight, and inviolable.

'I wasn't going to.' He moved a fraction closer to her, although the language of her body made physical contact seem suddenly inappropriate and he knew he'd have to try to navigate her defences with words. 'I was going to talk about justice, a kind of justice, for you, for that girl you were, and I was going to say how going back to Sheffield could be a positive move, if that's what you decide it's going to be.'

'I don't need justice.' She was very pale, and she wouldn't look at him.

'Not justice as in dragging Baxter through the courts, although it's not too late for that if you wanted to report the fucking lowlife weasel bastard. I mean justice in a looser sense, I mean justice as in taking back what's yours, reclaiming the parts of the past you still need.'

'Such as?'

'Well – Peter. I suppose I mean Peter.'

Now her head was resting on her knees, and the very last thing Dan wanted was for her to be miserable; he only wanted to make her happy, and yet, he thought, how had Peter fared? Alison should know the answer to this, and if she didn't, she ought to find out. He placed his hand very tenderly on her back, and she let it stay there, but she was speechless, because hearing her brother's name was an agony; he resided in her conscience, and her neglect of him was a terrible cross to bear. She'd never intended this to happen, this severing of all ties with the person who'd once been her most trusted friend and protector; she hadn't meant to abandon him for ever, but then she hadn't known what she meant to do – there hadn't been any kind of plan at all. In Paris, where she'd first stopped running for a while and found a job as a waitress, she'd felt reinvented, as if after all it was possible to sweep away a past life and begin again. She was just *Al-ees-on* to her Parisian colleagues, a hard-working English girl with decent French, what a find, what an asset when the bistro filled with *les Américains*, who seemed not to realise any language existed other than their own. She'd rented a *chambre de bonne*, a former servant's garret on the sixth floor of an apartment building on the Rue de Courcelles, and from that address she'd written her three letters to Daniel, and one letter to Peter, too, to tell him she was alive, to express her love and gratitude, and to say goodbye. She thought about that letter now, still imprinted on her mind all these many years later. She hadn't told him about the rape – wouldn't share that nightmare with anyone and least of all Peter. So, she'd written:

I saved your life only once, but you saved mine every day, and now I've left, I want you to remember, always, that you are beloved to me. But I think you meant me to go far away, so I shall, and I'll try and live the life you wanted for me. I don't know when I'll see you again, but I'll keep you in my heart, and I know you'll keep me in yours.

Always and for ever,

Your Alison xx

She'd included no address on Peter's letter, and this was because ... well, why was it? She believed now that she'd needed to turn her back on him to survive, and the more time passed, the less she saw a path back to him. Peter had made her escape possible, but he was also an integral part of the horror. While Daniel ... well, he'd inhabited higher ground than the Connors, he lived where the air was pure and clear. She'd stayed on in Paris for far longer than she'd intended, in case he should one day knock on her door.

'I saw Peter,' Dan said. 'When I went looking for you.'

If she hadn't been sitting down, her legs might have given way. Slowly, she turned her head, which still rested on her knees, to look at him.

'He said you weren't coming back, but he said it kindly.'

'You saw Peter.'

'The day after you disappeared, yeah. He didn't say why you'd gone, but he didn't seem to be freaking out, so I figured he knew more than I did.'

She lifted her head. 'Peter was my saving grace, for all of my childhood and adolescence.'

'Wonder where he is now?'

The question was casually asked, and not unreasonable, and Ali knew that not having an answer to it was a disgrace, an abdication of love and duty. She shrugged and looked profoundly unhappy. 'All I can say is none of this seemed quite so abysmally dysfunctional until I said it out loud to you. Michael didn't seem to need to know anything about my past, it was enough for him that I'd pitched up in his life in Spain, and when we went back to Australia together, it felt to me almost like a sort of symbolic flourish, the completion of my disappearing act. I was subsumed by the McCormacks, and I made no protest, put up no resistance. Why would I? It was a relief, on so many levels.'

Daniel heaved a long sigh, leaned back where he sat, and stared at the ceiling.

'What?' Ali reached out a hand and took hold of one of his. 'What is it?'

He looked at her, and considered her question. *What is it?* It was Michael McCormack, Spain, Australia, her disappearing act: it was the series of events that had rolled inexorably onward and kept them apart, when they'd been young enough and full enough of love for each other that they could have conquered anything.

'What?' Ali said again.

'Nothing,' he said. 'I need another drink.'

They slept in the prayer-flag room – deeply, for eight hours, as if anaesthetised – and in the morning Ali woke with a kind of lightness of spirit that puzzled her, given the intensity of the previous day. Catharsis, Dan said, the calm after the storm. She said yeah, maybe, and then said she was ravenous, so he went off into downtown Quorn and bought provisions: eggs, bread, fresh coffee and milk, and when he got back they were no longer alone. First he noticed a little red Renault parked next to Ali's Holden, and then as he pushed open the front door he could hear voices, women's voices. He had an impulse to back away and disappear again until the coast was clear, then realised that if this was Sheila and Dora – and who else was it going to be, realistically? – then they wouldn't be going anywhere. He walked down the small hallway and into the kitchen, and there was Ali with two much older women, both of whom immediately eyed him up and down like farmers at a stock sale.

'Well, hello,' one of them said, the shorter of the two, although the taller one didn't look much over five foot two, and she now approached him with arms stretched wide and said, 'Welcome, Daniel, welcome. I'm Sheila,' and she enveloped him in a powerful embrace. Dan looked at Ali over the top of Sheila's wild grey hair and she grinned at him, and shrugged.

'And I'm Dora,' said Dora when Sheila released him. They shook hands, and Dora moved in a little closer and looked up at him, staring hard into his eyes. 'D'you know, I think we've met?' she said.

Dan said, 'Really? Seems unlikely, but you might be right.'

'In a previous life, I mean,' Dora said. 'You have a very strong aura, and it's familiar to me.'

'Oh, this is exciting,' Sheila said, turning to Ali. 'Dora's got a sixth sense for this. It doesn't happen often, but when it does, hang on to your hat.'

Ali laughed and said, 'Dora, stop staring at Daniel, you're scaring him,' and Dora said, 'Oh shivers, am I?' and let go of his hand, which she'd hung on to while she examined his soul.

'Ah, don't worry, I can cope,' Dan said. 'And look, if you work out who I was last time you met me, I'd love to know.'

'He'll be hoping he was Rory Gallagher,' Ali said.

'I don't know Rory Gallagher from a bar of soap,' Dora said, 'but anyway, darling, it doesn't work like that, it's way more abstract.'

'Well, whoever you think he might once have been,' Sheila said, 'he's certainly a good-looking devil now.'

'Give over,' Dan said, laughing. He was still holding the bag of groceries, and Ali took it off him and began to unpack.

'Like I said before he walked in,' she said, 'he's Daniel Lawrence from Edinburgh, via Sheffield. There's a lot to tell, but I'm not doing it on an empty stomach.'

'Quite right,' Dora said, and she grabbed a whisk from the utensils jar and waved it at Dan. 'Got a treat for you, matey. Eggs my way, coming up. They're the bomb!'

24

Later in the day Sheila said, 'Let's have a natter,' hooked an arm through Dan's and walked him out to the garden, which was small and densely planted, and mercifully part-shaded by the slender arching boughs and foliage of a Chinese tallow.

Dan liked Sheila enormously: a touch loopy, but well meaning, big-hearted. She was generous with her laughter, and she liked to talk but she could listen, too. She was so colourful, her speech seasoned with idiom, her clothes a layered collection of ethnic prints, garments collected on her travels. Like the flora and fauna around them, Sheila seemed too tropical to hail from the north of England; he found it hard to imagine her enduring a slate-grey winter, even in her youth: she'd surely emerged fully formed from the red earth of Australia, rising like a firebird in the sun-scorched bush. She sat herself down on a swing seat built for two, but he didn't fancy squeezing into the small space left beside her, so instead he sat opposite her, on a low stone wall, the perimeter border of a desert rockery where miniature cacti and succulents shared their arid patch with amulets from overseas, an evil eye, a silver shamrock, an alligator tooth; they hung from the tips of the plants like earrings. There was a low table in glittering mosaic, and on it she'd placed two jewel-coloured bowls, one bearing hummus, the other baba ganoush, and she scooped up these dips on fingers of pitta bread and shovelled them in as she listened to Dan answering her questions. She wanted to know all about canal life and *Crazy Diamond*, and then all about his job, and had he been to Australia before? Yes, he said, Sydney, April 1997, when INXS released *Elegantly Wasted*, and Michael Hutchence gave him an interview, but only after nearly killing him on the back of his motorbike. The most beautiful man she'd ever seen, Sheila said wistfully, and then this, by way of contrast, got her on to her German ex-husband Kalvin – the least beautiful man she'd ever seen – and all the details of their disastrous marriage, and the metamorphosis she'd gone through after she'd left him. Then she said, 'Now, tell me this – are you free to love Alison as she deserves to be loved?' and Dan hadn't seen that coming, not at all.

'No,' he said, after only the briefest pause, deciding in that instant to be as direct as the question demanded. 'Not in the sense you mean.'

'And what do you think I mean?'

'You mean, am I single, am I unattached? I'm not. I have a partner at home, and we have a son, just a bit younger than Alison's Thea.'

Sheila shook her head. 'No, I mean, are you emotionally free?'

He hesitated.

'It's very important, Daniel,' Sheila said. 'I never understood how Michael won that girl – I suppose he caught her at a low ebb or something – but I believe they're not connected, except materially.'

Dan looked at her with interest, suddenly warming to her theme. 'Would she leave him, do you think?' he asked.

'Would you ask her to?'

He was silent for a while, not certain how best to answer, then he said, 'Yes, I would, as long as I was sure it was what she really wanted.'

'Don't you already know it's what she really wants?'

He gave a short laugh and said, 'Well, the early indications are good, Sheila, but we haven't had time to have this conversation yet.'

'Oh, come on, what does your heart tell you?' she asked impatiently.

'OK, my heart tells me we belong together,' Dan said. 'But my head tells me it's not that simple.'

'Fiddlesticks. Don't give me that: it's so disappointing.'

He felt a little irritated now: Dora with her sixth sense; Sheila giving him the New Age third degree. 'You barely know me,' he said. 'So I don't see how I could disappoint you.'

'Sometimes I understand very quickly what makes people tick,' she said. 'And I saw right to the heart of you the moment I saw you.'

'OK. So Dora sees an old soul in me, and you saw – what?'

'Well, I could tell you loved her, as soon as you walked into the kitchen.'

'Right. How?' Dan didn't mind the gist of this conversation – he was coming out of it well, after all – but even so he didn't even try to keep the scepticism out of his voice.

'Look,' Sheila said, 'I know this sounds like hokum, but seeing you two in the same room? It's like walking into a warm house on a winter's day. Alison hasn't been within a coo-ee of our place for a long time, but lately I've seen her twice in short order and I'm telling you, she's a different woman with you. There's something inevitable about you and Alison.'

And all this was pure gold, but Dan didn't comment, he

only looked away from Sheila's smile and considered the fact that he and Alison really did need to address exactly where all this was heading. During his solitary sleepless night in Adelaide, he'd contemplated a future without Katelin, and it had been hard, but not impossible; loving Katelin was a habit, but maybe not a necessity – maybe not. She was strong and clever and resourceful, and she'd been a peerless mother to Alex, but he, Dan, had begun to accept, over the past weeks, something that he'd possibly always known: that she wasn't the one he adored. When Alison had appeared in the bar of the Exeter Hotel, he'd feigned a kind of relaxed, easy pleasure at their reunion, but in truth, she'd bowled him over just like the first time. He was no fool, he knew all about the mirage of greener grass, the siren call of lost youth, but he also knew the pure joy he'd felt when he saw her again, and that the world was wonderful simply because it still contained Alison Connor.

Then Sheila started up again, a little impatiently, and decisively, as if she'd waited long enough for him to speak and would wait no longer. 'Two things in life you need to remember,' she said. 'One: follow your heart. Two: if you ever hurt her, I'll have your guts for garters.'

'I never will hurt her,' Dan said.

'And will you follow your heart?'

He gave a small shrug, a rueful smile. 'I'll give it a go.'

'And Katelin, is she the enlightened type? Will she understand?'

'Ah,' Dan said. 'No, Katelin will be fucking furious,' and this made Sheila howl with laughter, and the sound brought Dora and Ali out of the house to join them. Dora wedged herself tightly into the swing seat next to Sheila; Ali sat down on the low wall with Dan. He put an arm around her.

'Sheila rates me,' he said, very quietly, into her ear.

'Dora does too,' Ali said. 'And I do, I rate you very highly, so it looks as if you're all the go.'

They smiled at each other, but then his expression altered and he said, 'Look, we need to talk,' and she understood his tone at once, stood up again and held out her hand. Sheila and Dora looked at them enquiringly, but without offering an explanation the pair walked into the house and went upstairs.

Big subjects: love, trust and loyalty. Big subjects, thorny subjects, although there was a time when Ali thought them unnegotiable; a deal was a deal: she could've had these words engraved around the inside of her wedding ring, or above the door at the McCormack mansion, translated into Latin. Margaret McCormack raised her boys to put loyalty above all other virtues, despite – or perhaps because of – their father's philandering, and Ali, too, in the Italian summer of 1980, had married Michael with solemn promises and a commitment to throw in her lot with this likeable, generous boy from Adelaide. There were no fireworks for her, not even much of a spark, but she recognised in him the kind of dependability she believed she needed. That, plus his patent devotion, and a one-way ticket to Australia, where people went to start all over again. But today, sitting with Dan, talking about the future, she thought, Where are those values now? They were in pieces on the floor, because all she wanted was here in this room. She wanted him. She wanted him, and this wanting was simplicity itself.

They sat facing each other on the sleeping mat under the Tibetan prayer flags, and they clasped hands. I can't let you go, he said. No, she said, don't let me go, I need to be with you. These were their vows. They didn't talk about how this might be managed, the faith they'd have to keep in each other during the coming storm, they only made a statement of mutual intent, knowing the road ahead would be long, and that sorrow as well as joy lay in whatever they chose to do.

'Hey, it's not just about the music, is it?' Ali asked, a little later, and Dan said, 'No, but it might be just about the sex.' They laughed, and Ali thought, I do love this man; I love the very bones of him.

'What happened to the band?' she asked. 'What happened to the Union?'

'Didn't make it,' Dan said. 'Nick Lowe showed an interest, but then he didn't.'

'Were you gutted?'

'I was long gone by then,' he said. In fact, he never went back after she disappeared, never went to another rehearsal, but he didn't mention that now. He pushed her gently backwards until she was lying down, then he hung over her, scanning her face, and said, 'Alison Connor.'

'Daniel Lawrence.'

'Look at you.'

'What?' she said, smiling, knowing where this was going.

'You're bloody lovely,' he said, just as he had in 1978, at Kev Carter's party, on a nest of coats, on a single bed, in a box room lit sodium yellow by a street lamp. They lay side by side, as they had back then, and looked for shapes in the lines on the ceiling – Australian shapes here in Quorn, lizards and snakes – and then Ali talked about her novel, and explained what she understood about the songlines and about the Dreamtime, when spirit ancestors moved across the barren earth and altered its form, created the present-day landscape of mountains and rivers, trees and hills, and made the people and the animals and the elements, then the sun, the moon and the stars, before sinking back into the earth. The sacred places were those features such as rocks, or trees, or mountains created from spirit ancestors themselves, so where the white man would see only geology, an indigenous man saw the mighty coils of an endlessly sleeping serpent.

Dan listened to her and watched the movement of her mouth as she spoke. He said, 'We could only see a Toblerone on Kev Carter's ceiling. D'you think we lacked imagination?' and Ali said, 'I think I said it was a bolt of lightning,' and Dan said, 'There you go, the emergent novelist.'

'Have you read *Tell the Story*?'

'Ah, no, I'm a sport and biography kind of guy, haven't read a novel for years.'

He glanced at her, to see if she minded, but she only smiled and said, 'What about Katelin?'

He looked at her askance now, but her eyes were guileless and she said, 'It's a book written by a woman, and therefore more women than men will read it. Fact.'

'Well, believe it or not, my mother accidentally bought your book for her, for Christmas.'

Ali gasped, and started to laugh.

'Mum didn't know it was you,' Dan said. 'But Dad did. He saw your photo on the back and said, "That there is Alison," and thereby started a right old hoo-ha.'

'What sort of hoo-ha?'

'The "Alison? Alison? You never mentioned an Alison" kind.'

'Did Katelin like it?'

'She did. I think she hoped she wouldn't, but she loved it.'

Ali thought about this: Dan's Katelin, loving her book about South Australia, over there in Edinburgh. Then she said, 'I'd like to see your dad.'

'I'll take you,' Dan said.

'I don't know.'

'Don't know what?'

'If I can go to Sheffield.'

'You could if you went with me.'

She considered this, but didn't speak.

'So forget Sheffield for now,' he said. 'Do you think you could come to the UK?'

'I could,' she said, but then felt the vastness of this small statement, and modified it. 'I think.'

Dan closed his eyes and thought about Alison, fragile, perhaps traumatised, plucked from hearth and home in Adelaide and plonked back down in Blighty, with only him for solace and company. He thought, too, about Katelin and Alex, especially Alex, whom he had never hurt, by word or deed. He imagined their faces as he wilfully dismantled their family life. Could he do this? Demolish beliefs and break hearts? Here, now, he knew he could, if it meant waking up beside Alison Connor day in, day out, being her man, getting to know every atom of her being, body and soul. If this made him a monster, then God, the world was full of monsters, the music industry especially so, a repository of failed relationships; but look, nobody had ever died of grief at being left, everyone moved on in the end, the details of their lives rearranged, often for the better. He could handle this. He could.

'Let's listen to *Crocodiles*.'

'What?'

'I need to make you love Echo and the Bunnymen. I discovered them without you. That was heartbreaking.'

'OK,' she said. He was on his feet, fetching her phone, so she sat up and leaned against the wall, hugging her knees, watching him search online for the album, and said, 'They passed me by, I don't know why, bad timing I suppose.'

He said, 'I saw them in Liverpool in September seventy-nine, blew my fucking mind, the personification of cool, the four of 'em in a straight line – I mean, no riser at the back for the drums. Pete de Freitas was upfront with his kit, so it was de Freitas, Pattinson, Mac, Sergeant, all in a row. They looked awesome, sounded awesome, I was spellbound, then when they started playing I thought I might stop breathing.' He delved into the pocket of his rucksack and pulled out his earphones, then sat down next to her. 'We'll share,' he said, passing her a bud, keeping the other for himself. 'Ah God, this is another box ticked, listening to *Crocodiles* with Alison Connor. If you don't like it, you can sodding well lump it.'

She grinned at him. 'Get on with it,' she said.

They were seven tracks down and just getting started on 'Villiers Terrace' when Sheila's head appeared round the door. Her face was grave.

'Darlings,' she said. 'Michael's downstairs.'

How swift and disappointing was that journey from heartsease to sheer panic, and how undignified. Ali caught what Sheila said, Dan didn't, so he was startled when she leapt up, dragging the bud from his ear, and he said, 'Hey, what's up?' but she didn't answer him, didn't even hear. Michael was downstairs. This fact had an instant physiological effect on her, whipped her heart into a racing overdrive, turned her blood to a kind of poison which coursed through her body spreading fear and self-loathing; it melted her resolve, and shattered her promises, so recently made.

'Alison, what is it?' Dan asked. He was on his feet now, trying to reach her, but she'd gone – not physically, no, she was still in the room, but she wasn't seeing him, wasn't hearing him, she was simply trying to process the fact that her husband was downstairs, waiting to speak to her. Dan grabbed her arm, made her turn. 'What is it?' he asked again, very emphatically.

'Michael's here,' Ali said, and she shook her arm free and ran from the room. She would regret this later, regret not taking time to talk with Dan about how to navigate this first great obstacle on their long road to happiness. She would regret her craven instincts, her childish fear, her inability to react with dignity and calm at the first hurdle. But that would be later. Now, she only wanted to be clear of suspicion and blame, keep everything in its place, preserve the status quo. She did at least register her own shock and disappointment at how weak she'd proved when courage was called for, but she didn't express this out loud, and all Dan witnessed was the flight.

But he wasn't going to hide upstairs; he wasn't going to oblige by playing the role of Ali's guilty secret. Some signal, instinct or information had brought this guy, this Michael, up to Quorn to confront his wife, so, thought Dan, let him confront the lover too, let's ramp up the emotion in this next act of their drama. He clattered down the wooden stairs after her, so when he appeared in the living room it was only seconds after Ali had got there, but she was already standing with Michael, and they stared at Dan together, two against one.

'She's coming back with me,' Michael said. 'I don't know who the fuck you think you are, but you're nobody now.' He was so sure of his rights, so certain of his superiority over this interloper. The McCormacks of Adelaide: social mafia, invincible, entitled. He hadn't yet discovered the details, he'd acted only on a word of concern from Beatriz and a hunch of his own, and he'd yet to decide how he felt about Ali's betrayal, but he already knew he would neither leave her, nor ask her to leave, yet nor would he do what his mother always did and turn a blind eye. He would simply get her home, get to the bottom of this fiasco, and keep a closer eye on her in future.

Dan looked at Ali, who looked back at him with some sort of plea in her eyes, although he couldn't say what. *Help me? Deck him? Don't make my life more difficult than it is already?* Yeah, he thought, probably the last one, probably that.

'OK,' Dan said to Michael. 'Since Alison obviously doesn't feel up to introducing me, I'm Dan Lawrence, a long-lost friend of hers from Sheffield days.' Then he turned to Ali. 'Is this it?' he said. 'Is this how it ends?'

'Yes, mate,' Michael said, 'you can bet your bottom dollar it is.'

Dan ignored him, didn't even blink, just stared at his girl. 'Alison?'

Tears ran down her face, and she took a step towards him. Dan held his ground. He wasn't going to help; it was up to her now: she stood between the past and the future, and only she could choose.

'Her name's Ali,' Michael said. 'And you just spoke your last word to her. You don't get to help yourself to my wife. Ali, grab your things and get in the car.'

Now Sheila, who'd been hovering in the kitchen, agitated, eavesdropping, uncertain how to help, came into the room and said, with a kind of desperation, 'Michael, you should at least give these two some space to talk,' and he turned on her, his face contorted by fury, as if he'd kept a lid on his anger for just this moment, and said, 'Shut your mouth, you wicked old dyke, you've done enough damage already.'

Ali was crying, and through the tears she said, 'Michael, be quiet. Sheila played no part in this. Sheila, I'm so sorry.' Sobbing into her hands, splintered by grief, no comfort to be had from anyone in the room. Dan watched her with a detachment that came from extreme sadness. He hadn't realised she would be so easily overcome.

'Get your stuff and get in the car,' Michael said to Ali.

He shouldn't speak to her that way, Dan thought; I would never speak to her that way, infantilising her, treating her like a wilful child, assuming authority over her fate, as if she had no mind of her own, or couldn't be trusted to use it. But look at her; she *had* no mind of her own. Sheila moved to be beside him, reading heartbreak and loss in his expression, and anger too, and bottomless disappointment. She hooked an arm through his, staking a claim, planting her flag.

Ali, in abject misery, hung her head and thought about Thea and Stella, and about Beatriz, and, finally, Michael. She couldn't leave them all. She hadn't understood this before, but their four hearts mattered more than her one, and if she abandoned them, their united pain would kill her. When she looked up, Dan was staring at her, dry-eyed. 'I'm sorry, Daniel,' she said, choking on sobs, her face a mess of tears. 'We've each made our choices.'

'Don't apologise to him!' Michael said. 'This pathetic soap opera ends here.' He glanced at his watch, and this small action filled Ali with new despair, because she knew he'd be thinking about the traffic, calculating their arrival in Adelaide, hoping to avoid congestion in the city; and the fact that he was capable of such a dull, practical consideration amid the white heat of this crisis was why Ali knew she should take her place next to Daniel, whom she loved like no other, and who had come to find her on the strength of sixteen songs.

'Time to go,' Michael said, not with love, but with finality.

And so that she might spare Dan the pain of watching Ali gather her possessions and follow her husband to the car, Sheila said, 'Come, Daniel, let this settle,' and she walked him to the garden, and kept him there until they heard the roar of Michael's Porsche, driven in anger, screaming away from the kerbside.

He sat for hours in the garden with Sheila and Dora, drinking gin, talking, playing music. They were wise women, and their love for Alison kept them from judging her, or criticising, but they were on his side here, and he felt held by them, comforted, and Sheila wanted him to believe it was a stage in the process, not a conclusion. Dan didn't know, couldn't believe; he just let the combination of the gin and their concern anaesthetise his pain to get him through the night ahead.

Alison was still on his lips, on his hands, and the fragrance of the night-time garden recalled the smell of her hair. She was everywhere, and she was gone. He talked and nodded and smiled, but he was quietly destroyed.

25

She tried to reach him, as she'd reached him before, but her songs weren't enough any more. The first arrived before Dan had left Adelaide; 'You're The Best Thing', Paul Weller, the Modfather in his post-Jam, Style Council guise. At the gate, about to board the plane, Dan saw the link on his phone, but he didn't open it, didn't need to, he knew it well, liked it a lot as a love song, but he wondered, had she listened properly to the words? They made no sense from a woman who'd stepped straight back into the familiar, at the very first challenge. He could've sung it back at her, word for word; he could play the chords and sing the song, standing outside her house in Millionaire's Row or wherever it was she lived, and take another emotional pummelling when she regretfully shut the window, sadly drew the curtains. Or he could close his heart and ignore her. This is what he did.

Then, when he switched on his phone in Hong Kong, Van the Man arrived, with 'Someone Like You', arguably the best love song ever recorded. Christ, she was using these songs like ammunition. And it was bedlam here, a hive of international humanity, queues and chaos through security, and only a two-hour stopover which barely gave him time to find the bar, so he saw the link, and spared himself the agony, taking a kind of strength from not listening and anyway, what was the point of the songs if they led nowhere? A love song sent without any real intent was a hollow gesture. Worse than hollow; it was a mockery of what they could've pulled off back there in the hippy time warp of Sheila's house: the spectacular, life-enhancing coup they'd intended before McCormack arrived, and swiftly left, with his most prized possession safely stowed beside him in his low-slung car.

Landing at Heathrow was like waking up in a familiar bed after a turbulent dream. Here was his world, among people who sounded much like him, in a climate that was as damp and cold as it ought to be in early February. God, he was glad he lived here, he thought; who could bear Australia, who could endure it? Too big, too far away, too damn hot. He was over Australia, done with it.

He strode past passengers milling around the baggage carousels, stalked through customs, and then through arrivals, and was on the Heathrow Express within half an hour of landing, heading for London. Bakerloo line to Warwick Avenue, then down on to the towpath and up the canal to *Veronica Ann* where McCulloch seemed to be standing exactly where he'd left him. By this point Dan was wild-eyed with the strain of staying awake and staying furious, and when Jim stepped ashore to say welcome back, his genial face crumpled with concern. 'Dan, whatever's wrong, are you all right?'

No, Dan thought, no, no, no, and he could easily have wept like a fool, but McCulloch, desperate for attention, suddenly launched himself upwards into his arms, squirming with barely endurable joy at this long-awaited red-letter day, and Dan was able to take refuge in laughter, not tears. He was eighteen the last time he cried, really cried, because that was the last time he'd been slayed by misery, and that had been Alison's fault too.

He stayed the night on *Crazy Diamond*, but might as well have driven through the night for all the rest he got. His internal clock was screwed, and it turned out exhaustion alone wasn't enough to make a man sleep. At 3 a.m. he rang Duncan – God bless Duncan – who answered on the second ring.

'Dan Lawrence, I'm missing you, pal, but is this call costing me?'

Dan laughed, feeling a little better already at the sound of his friend's voice. 'I'm in London, you tight bastard,' he said. 'I'm on the boat sharing a single bed with a dog that snores.'

'You're back?' Duncan was confused. 'That went quick.'

'Not for me, Dunc, it's been a bit torrid.'

'What has? What's gone down?'

'I . . .' He stopped, because he didn't know how to start. 'Look, I'm coming home tomorrow. Let's talk then over a pint, at Gordon's.'

'You OK, Dan? I can come down if you like, travel back with you?'

Sweet guy, a good friend. Once again, Dan thanked the heavens and Cathay Pacific for bringing him home to safety and sanity. 'No, no, I'll get an early train, and I've got McCulloch to talk to.'

'Well, take it easy, travel safe,' Duncan said, not convinced. Phone calls in the wee small hours weren't Dan's style, and despite the quip, he sounded sad, unmistakably sad, and that wasn't Dan's style either. 'Text me when you're back. I'll be right there.'

'Thanks, mate,' Dan said, and he hung up. He closed his eyes, because staring at the ceiling made him think of Alison, but then she filled his head anyway, finding a way in, like light seeping under a door. He knew he couldn't hold on to the anger for much longer, and he dreaded it leaving him, because anger was his only defence.

Back in Stockbridge, it felt like there was no better place on earth. At the pub, Gordon Fuller was his habitual inscrutable self, pulling two pints of heavy for Dan and Duncan without a smile, just a cursory nod as he put them down on the bar, but Dan was seeing comfort and balm in every drab detail of his home town, and Gordon's impassive face was exactly what he'd expected, even hoped for. John Coltrane was on the sound system playing moody blues, and the pub was only sparsely populated, so they had their pick of tables, but they went straight to their quiz-night corner anyway, without discussion, and sat together on the wooden settle where Katelin and Rose-Ann usually put themselves. There was something about it that nurtured confidences – it always worked on the girls – and now Dan found it a blessed relief to tell Duncan his tale, which he recounted in compelling detail, from the Sheffield beginnings to the infinite sadness of their last day. It took a long time, and when Dan finished, Duncan hesitated then said, 'I must say, I wish you'd consulted me, I think you overdid it with three Nick Drakes, and, also, what about "Sunshine Superman"? Did you not think about that? Missed a trick there. All the lassies love Donovan.'

Dan looked at him, aghast. 'Is that all you have to say? My song choices were slightly off?'

'No, no, no,' Duncan said, realising what he'd just done. 'It's not all I have to say, not at all, it's just the songs are the best part of the story, awesome – I mean, God, it's what they were written for.'

'Dunc, it's not just a story, mate. It happened, and it happened to me, and it only just happened, right?'

'Aye, I know,' Duncan said, 'I know.' He took a sip of beer, then he whistled through his teeth and said, 'You kept a lot to yourself, pal, these past few months.'

'I did, I'm sorry.'

'I spilled my guts to you about Lindsay, and all the while you were pining for your first girlfriend and sending love songs to Adelaide?'

'Well, hang on, I never judged you for falling for Lindsay.'

'No, but I still felt like the bad guy, and if you'd said you were looking elsewhere yourself . . . well, it would've made a difference.'

Dan said, 'I wasn't looking. It just happened.'

'Yeah, right, you and me both.'

'Well, OK, but it felt different. Maybe I was in denial for weeks on end, but I didn't think you could have an affair with someone when they're ten thousand miles away, and all you're doing is swapping songs.'

'Aye, well, that was an error for a kick-off, music being the food of love and all that.'

Dan laughed grimly. 'You got that right. I should never have gone over there. I should've kept her as a fantasy, the one that got away, because we went from heaven to hell in no time flat.'

'Aye, it sounds rough.'

'I can't understand why she caved in so spectacularly. She just lost all that . . . oh, all that strength and faith. One minute we were together in Sheila's spare room, the next we were staring at each other like boxers in our fucking corners, from opposite sides of the living room.'

'You were in bed when he showed up?'

Dan shuddered. 'No, we were just sitting there, listening to music.'

'What music?'

'Bunnymen.'

'*Crocodiles?*'

Dan nodded and Duncan said, 'Class.'

'Y'see,' Dan said, pointing at him. 'You're doing it again, getting sidetracked by the sodding music.'

'Sorry.' He took a long drink, emptying his glass, then put it down and said, 'No, I'm not getting sidetracked, though, because the music's central, isn't it? It was the music that took you places, melted your hearts and all that, and I bet that's what she'll be doing now, listening to the songs you sent her, thinking about you, because you started it, and you bloody nailed it, sending her "Pump It Up", and it's not even a love song. I'm jealous. I wish I'd done it.'

He got up to fetch a couple more pints, and Dan thought about Alison, listening to his songs. Was she? He'd had an idea that she might have deleted the lot, cleared their thread of music so that her phone was innocent, the trail gone cold. But then, she was still sending songs. Well, she'd sent two – there'd been none since yesterday – but two stellar choices, the sort of choices that, if he'd allowed himself to listen and reimagine those lyrics as a message from Alison, he'd have had to concede, again, that she was the woman for him, and that this was love of a rare and exceptional kind . . . except there was the unassailable fact, wasn't there, of her hasty retreat?

'She ditched me though,' Dan said, as soon as Duncan approached the table. 'The second her husband was in the picture, she ditched me.'

Duncan pulled a face, shook his head. 'Well, be fair,' he said. 'What would you have done if it'd been Katelin who stormed in?'

Dan answered at once. 'Held my ground. I certainly wouldn't have done what Alison did.'

'Yeah, you would,' Duncan said. 'You'd have done just the

same. You'd have run downstairs and out the door like your arse was on fire. It's human nature.'

Dan stared at his friend, wordless. Duncan had misjudged him, because Dan knew with unqualified certainty that he would never, under any circumstances, have done to Alison what she did to him. If Katelin had turned up instead of Michael, he would've stood at Ali's side and faced the wrath, absolutely and undoubtedly, and more fool him, because twice now she had made him fall in love with her then abandoned him, and he loved her still, and probably always would, and she seemed to be trying to tell him through music that she loved him too, but he had no faith now in her love, or her songs.

'Do not say that,' he said to Duncan. 'Do not say I'd do as she did. Don't even think it.' His friend nodded, uncomfortably. Dan's expression was bleak and dark. 'I wouldn't have bolted, because I love her too much,' he said.

'Right,' Duncan said. 'Well, OK.' He could hear the suffering and the conviction so clearly now, and he regretted his earlier tone, too blokey, too jocular.

'I love her, and she doesn't love me, and it's over.'

Duncan pondered this statement for a moment, and wondered if it might not be best for Dan to hold on to that thought: best for Katelin, best for himself, too, if it kept Dan here in Stockbridge. But then he said, 'You don't know that.'

Dan said, 'I do. I think it's pretty self-evident.'

'Well, I don't,' Duncan said. 'Think about what you've told me. You said Alison has this blighted past, and then McCormack swept her away from it like Sir Galahad, so, who knows, she might feel a lifelong debt of gratitude to him?'

Dan thought about this, and it had a ring of truth about it.

'She might have felt she had no choice,' Duncan went on.

'She might not be as strong as you, but it doesn't necessarily mean she loves you less.'

He sat back in his chair, and looked at Dan with compassion. He believed he'd never suffered for any woman what Dan seemed to be suffering now, and he was gratified when his friend said, 'Yeah, maybe. Thanks, mate.'

It was small comfort, thought Dan, but perhaps Duncan was right. Perhaps, in the terrible heightened stress of that confrontation, Ali had cleaved to her husband from a sense of obligation, not love. Perhaps she was suffering too. Perhaps she was consumed by regret. Perhaps she was listening right now to Rory Gallagher or John Martyn and remembering Dan's mouth all over her body.

Then the screen of his phone lit up on the table and Duncan tilted his head to check it out. 'She's come to join us,' he said.

Dan looked at the screen. *Ali Connor sent you a message.*

'C'mon.' Duncan pushed the phone to Dan. 'Let's see what it is.'

Dan picked it up and opened the link, privately at first, to decide if he felt like sharing. Then, 'Joni Mitchell,' he said. ' "A Case Of You".'

Duncan said, 'What a song,' but Dan only switched the phone off and put it down. They'd listened to *Blue* on that long drive north; she was educating him, she'd said; weaning him off guys with electric guitars. 'You are in my blood, like holy wine.' How could he ever listen to that song again, and not break down from the loss of her? He looked at his friend, and Duncan waited.

'I'm trying to harden my heart,' Dan said. 'I thought I was doing great, but I was fooling myself. It's like trying to shake off my own shadow.'

They were silent for a while, then Duncan said, 'So, you were going to leave Katelin?'

Such a simple question. Appalling in its simplicity. Leave Katelin. Leave his life partner, as if it was no bigger deal than getting off one bus, jumping on to another. Well, yes, in Australia it had seemed that easy. More than that, it'd seemed like the only thing to do, as if his life, his fate, was being adjusted by a higher authority. And there was Sheila, driving him all the way to Adelaide airport, telling him his principal duty was to his own heart. And there was Alison, beautiful, vulnerable, complex, incomparable. She'd sung to him in the car, too; sung 'Chelsea Morning', another Joni song he hadn't known, but God, it was one of the defining moments of his life, South Australia outside the car window, Alison Connor beside him, Joni Mitchell's poetry, Alison's voice. Alison.

Duncan, bringing him back to the present, still waiting for an answer, said, 'So?'

'Yeah,' Dan said. 'I was going to leave Katelin.'

In early March the women flew back to Edinburgh from London, so there was no reunion on the platform of Waverley Station, instead they shared a cab home and it dropped off Rose-Ann in New Town then continued down to Stockbridge with Katelin. Dan hadn't known how he'd feel when he saw her, or if she'd sense a change in him, but it turned out she was too full of her trip to notice that Dan might be more subdued than she'd expect. She was lightly freckled, very talkative, a little plumper than before – Desperate Dan portions, she said – and she wore an LA Lakers baseball cap with her red hair swinging out of the back of it in a ponytail, like a cheerleader on match day. She was golden with sunshine, effervescent; the adventure had done her good, she said. She was ready for a break from Rose-Ann, mind you, but they'd had an amazing time together, amazing. 'She overthinks,' Katelin said when they were in the house. 'That's all I'd say. She overthinks every decision, weighs up the pros and cons until you can hardly remember what it was you're meant to be deciding. And she had a lot to say about Duncan's transgression: we chewed that one over all the way from JFK to Cincinnati.'

'What! That's got to be seven hundred miles,' Dan said. He was making her a pot of tea, which she said would be the first decent cuppa since she'd left home, it was all coffee in the States, disgusting coffee that sat all day on a hotplate, no wonder the refills were free, or Lipton's Yellow Label tea dunked in a mug of lukewarm water. Chat, chat, chat; she was so wired, thought Dan, but jet lag could have that effect, stringing you along with a strange, chemical energy. Or it could sense your own profound unhappiness and drag you down further into a miserable limbo. Perhaps, he thought, jet lag simply adapts itself to match your own state of mind.

'Yeah, no idea how many miles it was,' Katelin said, chatting on. 'But it was twelve hours' driving and I'd say the conversation might have gone on to last longer than his affair did, but I said to her, I said, can we stop talking about Duncan when we cross the Cincinnati line, and she said, "Oh my gosh, Katelin, I am *so* sorry, I'm talking a blue streak here and you've been *so* patient."' This was a perfect impersonation of Rose-Ann's West Coast drawl, and Dan laughed.

They sat down on the kitchen sofa, McCulloch curled between them, and Katelin talked on, about the hillbilly with a rifle who pinged a bullet off their moving car in New Mexico, and the hitchhiker who paid for a lift to Austin by reading their palms. Rose-Ann's money lines were many, deep and clear, he'd told them.

'Sounds about right,' said Dan. 'And what about you?'

'High energy, short temper, ambitious to a degree, apparently. I have fire hands, which basically means my fingers are a bit stubby.'

'I never noticed that,' Dan said, picking up one of her hands. 'But now you mention it . . .'

She laughed, and cuffed him round the ear. 'All the better for hitting you with,' she said. 'Rose-Ann has water hands. They're lovely, her hands, long fingers and oval nails, pianist's hands.'

'But she doesn't play the piano.'

'I know, but she could.'

Dan said, 'I've never wanted to know my future.'

'It's not really about the future, according to Devin.'

'Devon?'

'Dev-IN,' Katelin said. 'The guy we picked up. And the life-line doesn't tell you how long you're going to live, that's a big mistake we all make. Devin said it just indicates what *kind* of life you might lead, your vitality and vigour, y'know? C'mere.' She grabbed his right hand, spreading it out flat before her, and traced the arc of the line that ran from the edge of his palm above the thumb to the base of his wrist. 'Your lifeline,' she said, with a certain amount of triumph, as though she might not have expected him to have one; then, dipping closer for a better look, 'Oooh, see, it's a double line, that's rare, that is. Devin has one, he showed us his.'

'I bet he did,' Dan said. 'I'm not happy about you picking up stray men on the road. Have you never seen *The Hitcher*?'

'It means you either met your soulmate, or you're leading a double life. Which is it?'

'What?' Dan said.

'I reckon it's the soulmate thing,' Katelin said. 'I'd know if you were a bigamist. There'd be less washing in the basket, for a start.'

'Y'know what?' Dan said, pulling his hand away. 'That's enough of your blarney.'

Katelin yawned, very suddenly, and said, 'Jesus, I think I could sleep for a week. I'd love a bath, then I want to fall asleep in front of a film.' The way she said 'film' as if she was trying to squeeze an extra syllable from the word: it was one of the things he'd fallen for, that Irish accent. Katelin Kelly, never, ever Kate – woe betide you if you made that mistake. She had an awkward streak all right, strong-minded and stroppy; what a handful his mother had thought her, so unbiddable and contrary. Katelin hadn't wanted children, then she changed her mind but only wanted one, and from the start she'd scoffed at the idea of marriage and wanted always and for ever to be together only by choice. A major upset, she'd caused, in both families, but Dan had admired her immensely, thought her brave and bold and original. And now, as he kissed her on the cheek and got up to run a bath for her, he wondered, could she honour that freedom to choose, if he told her he loved her still, but loved another woman more, and differently? Not a chance. The guarantee on that arrangement had expired a long time ago.

'Oh!' she called out as he left the room. 'I haven't asked you about Hong Kong.'

'Ah, that was work,' he said, 'it can wait,' and his tread was slow on the stairs, and heavy. He felt oddly disappointed, as if Katelin had let him down, just by being herself.

Two days after she came home, he told her everything. There was no need, she suspected nothing, and almost certainly it was a selfish impulse, a way of making his relationship with

Alison feel real, putting it out there in the world as a fact, so that he knew it wasn't just a fantasy. Oh, he told himself that by telling the truth he was being respectful to Katelin, being open and honest, but it wasn't that, he'd kept many secrets from her over the past thirty years: flirtations, semi-flings, a short dalliance years ago with cocaine, a current pot habit that was more regular than she realised. He hoped she'd kept a few secrets from him too, really he did, everyone was entitled to small bouts of bad behaviour, and if she'd parried with a story about how she'd had sex on the beach in Santa Monica, he'd have felt nothing but relief. But she didn't. She just sat very still on the edge of their bed, and he watched all the newly acquired colour drain from her face as he told her, as gently as he could, that he'd fallen in love with Alison Connor, but it was over now.

'The woman who wrote that book?' Katelin asked, bewildered but at the same time feeling she'd known all along. Dan nodded.

'And that's why you went to Hong Kong? So you could fly on, to see her?'

'Yes,' he said. 'I mean, there was a festival, I was working, but yes, that's why I went.'

He'd expected a storm, but that came later, and instead it remained very, very quiet in the bedroom, although she started to cry, and she cried steadily for a long time, but she barely made a sound. He couldn't comfort her, or reassure her, because she wouldn't let him touch her, wouldn't speak to him, wouldn't meet his eyes. She closed him out entirely from her grief and he had no idea what to do. He had entirely changed the colour and shape of their existence, and he wished beyond wishing that he'd kept her in the dark. The truth was overrated: no benefit to either of them now.

26

In the winter months, this attractive, amenable city could be so damned dreary, thought Ali: cold, wet, windy and oddly inhospitable. In the summer and early autumn there were festivals – books, music, drama – and picnics on the beach, barbecues in back yards. But nobody at all – nobody in the McCormacks' orbit, anyway – seemed to entertain in the long drag of winter weeks; instead they succumbed to a sort of pinch-mouthed reclusiveness, and her spirit rebelled against it, although Michael considered this a new development. This time last year – before Dan, he meant, although he didn't say so – she was perfectly content to sit out the winter like everyone else, by drawing the curtains, watching some television, writing for long hours at her desk, eating Beatriz's rabbit stew, and waiting for the sun to shine.

'I just don't see why everyone needs to bloody well hibernate,' Ali said, hating the world and therefore doing what she could to make it worse. She was outside, on her knees, with her arm down an access pipe, clearing a blockage of rotted leaves from a storm drain. She slapped each new handful down on the flagstones with furious energy. The smell, the slime: they combined to represent her mood, because in the struggle to regain their marital equilibrium, Ali and Michael took turns at being angry. Right now, Ali had picked up the gauntlet. 'God forbid we should have any fun. I suggest getting some friends round, filling the dining table for once, and you react like I just proposed a wife-swapping party. It's so bloody *dull*, Michael.'

He stood watching her, silent and stolid.

'You realise, don't you, that we're living the same life your parents lived, and their parents before them?'

'Well, there's nothing wrong with that, per se,' Michael said, to prove himself as loyal to the memory of his folks as he was to his wife. He was hovering behind her, feeling ineffectual, feeling aggravated, feeling under attack. He'd come home to find her in the garden, in the rapidly descending dusk, hauling stinking clumps of blackened vegetation from the inner recesses of the drains, and if this wasn't passive-aggressive, he didn't know what was. 'C'mon, Ali, you know you could've left all that for Eddie,' he said. 'He'll be here tomorrow. He does this kinda shit, that's why I pay him.'

'*We* pay him,' Ali said. '*We* pay him, Michael.'

'Yeah, OK, we pay him. Jeez.'

She sat back on her heels. 'That's cleared now,' she said, peering into the chasm, then she looked up at the roof. 'The leaves come in through the downpipe with the rainwater. It's that ash, and the tallow, they're a sodding menace.'

He was quiet for a beat then said, 'I'll ask Eddie to clear the gutters more often. Now, shall we go inside?'

She said, 'You go. I'll be in soon, in a few minutes anyway,' and he hesitated a moment as if something was on his mind, then turned and went back into the house. Ali replaced the leaf net and the grate, then sniffed her hand, which smelled foul from the decomposing slime, but she didn't care, and if it hadn't been pitch dark and windy, she'd be dealing with the guttering herself right now, rather than facing another quiet night in on the sofa with Michael. She closed her eyes, and allowed herself five minutes to consider Dan, five minutes to imagine she could turn to him, even now; reach him, wherever he was, and express the contents of her heart with a song.

She ran her hands under the garden tap to get the worst of the muck off before going inside, because Beatriz hated alien odours in the pristine kitchen sink. That is, Beatriz used to hate alien odours in the pristine kitchen sink, before Stella left home and she seemed to stop caring about anything. Back in March, in the days before Stella left, the old lady had suddenly realised the girl was going alone, and this fact had felled her, because she'd immediately seen all the dangers of the mortal world lined up in waiting. Ali, rinsing the slime off her fingers, thought now about Beatriz, up in her rooms, where she spent most of her time these days. Nothing was the same here any more. Stella had been to Italy and was already in Spain, Thea was still in Melbourne, Michael was in torment, Beatriz was in mourning. And herself? Where was she at? Good question, she thought; please don't hold your breath while you wait for the answer.

Eventually her hand began to turn vaguely blue under the running water so she dried it off on her jeans and went into the house through the back door. Michael had found a chicken casserole in the freezer and now it was in the oven, and the smell in the kitchen was comfortable and cosy, a little like it used to be. Then Ali scanned the worktop for her mobile phone and saw at once that it had moved from the place she'd left it; there it was, by the kettle, and there it was not, by her rucksack, and immediately all sense of comfort was dismissed by the low thudding in her chest which was either anxiety or anger, she didn't know, but she picked up her phone and walked out of the kitchen and into the den, where Michael was watching Port Adelaide *v.*

Essendon on the television. He looked up and smiled; then the smile faded.

'You've been looking at my phone,' she said.

It was anger, she decided, not anxiety. She had right on her side this time.

He paused, then held up his hands, unashamedly caught bang to rights. 'It helps keep me sane,' he said.

'You may *not* check my phone,' Ali said. Her voice shook a little. 'I'm entitled to privacy. You can't continue to treat me like a delinquent child.'

The commentary from the TV swelled to a feverish excitement and he coolly silenced it with the mute button. 'Your entitlement to privacy is a moot point,' he said. 'I still don't trust you. I used to trust you, but I don't trust you any more, for obvious reasons.'

How she hated his patrician morality, his bloated sense of disappointment. He was a consultant paediatrician with decades of experience at dealing smoothly with difficulties, and he had this particular way of speaking under duress – calm, considered, rational – that made her want to hit him.

'I think you've been in touch with him,' he said.

She felt sick, slightly faint, and unutterably tired.

'I have not contacted Dan Lawrence,' she said, which was the truth, although not the whole truth. Three songs, she'd sent him, in the first days of their separation. But nothing since then, nothing for five months.

He sat forward on the sofa, his elbows resting on his knees, and he looked at her searchingly for a while; then he spoke. 'You're short-tempered with me. You never show me any affection, never, ever, initiate sex, and did you flinch yesterday when I kissed you? I'd swear you did. You're dissatisfied with our home life. Home life? Why, the whole of Adelaide society's not quite the go for you any more because we're blinkered, limited, narrow-minded, parochial and penny-pinching. You're doing your level best to be as uncomfortable in this house as possible, which is why I came home this evening to find you on your knees in the dark, scooping filth out of the fucking *drains* with your *bare hand*!'

Michael rarely swore, and never shouted, so when he did both, she knew he was provoked. But so was she. So was she.

'What I'm "doing my level best to be" here, Michael, is the person you want me to be,' she said quietly. 'But this relationship isn't tenable if you keep treating me as your subordinate.'

'See, how can you say, "this relationship isn't tenable" with such . . . such equanimity?' he said. 'It's like it's neither here nor there to you, whether we hold it together or not.'

'I won't live under suspicion,' she said. 'I will not forever be this . . . this *lesser* person, the bad one, the weak one.'

'Ali, I admit I checked your phone just now, it was a reflex action, a gut feeling. But it's the first time I've done it in weeks, and I didn't like doing it, I just needed to put my mind at rest.'

'And did you find what you were looking for?'

'No,' he said. 'I didn't know what I was looking for, and anyway my heart wasn't in it.'

He looked a little defeated suddenly, and she felt a beat of true compassion for what she'd put him through – was still putting him through. Neither of them needed this scene. She'd left her phone out; he'd seen it, glanced at it and moved on. No drama.

'How's the game?' she said, nodding at the silent footballers in the corner of the room.

He seemed to soften, letting go of the tension. Maybe Michael wasn't really seeking confrontation, she thought. Maybe all he wanted was his old life back. And after all, the old life had been fine, hadn't it, for both of them? On the whole? She sat down next to him.

'Not pretty,' he said. 'In fact, downright ugly, but they've got Port on the run.'

'Yeah, well, Port's still going better than the sodding Crows.'

He turned his head sharply and looked at her.

'What?' she asked, glancing at him, away from the screen.

'You never, ever used to say sodding,' he said. 'Now you say it a hell of a lot.'

She shrugged, but a blush spread across her cheeks and throat, and he noted this too.

'A Sheffield thing, is it?' he said with acid in his voice. 'Something from the good old days?'

It was the work of mere seconds, but on the turn of his words the atmosphere in the small room curdled, and she knew she could neither explain herself nor stand another scene, so she stood up and left him to stew over the facts; stew over what he knew and what he didn't know, and watch the rest of the game alone.

She'd deleted their shared song list on Twitter months ago, but she knew it by heart because they were all assembled on her iPod, under a playlist she'd named *Mix Tape*. To put on her headphones and play them through without a break was one of her greatest pleasures, from the first throb of 'Pump It Up' to the final fade of 'Go Down Easy'. She'd deleted the final three, the three he hadn't replied to, because she knew she'd lost him by then, but still, she loved this list, loved what it said about her and Dan and the road they'd travelled on to get here. This evening though, it only made her desperately sad, which was something that happened too: sometimes she felt none of the remembered joy, only the distance and the ache of loss. She got as far as 'Let's Dance', then M. Ward got to her with his intimate melancholy and she pulled off the headphones and lay down on the floor of her office with tears streaming sideways from her eyes, down her temples, on to the wooden floor. She was a pulpy mess of self-pity and she hated herself for being her own worst enemy, for wanting what she couldn't have, for not having had the strength or the imagination, when the chance presented itself, to give up one life for another. Cass had been angry with her at first: sympathetic, and angry, at one and the same time. She'd told her that she'd made her bed, so she should lie in it; then she'd said, 'Oh, darling girl,' and held her close when Ali burst into tears of despair. That was months ago, way back in February, when she'd not long been back from Quorn, and oh, there'd been so many tears since then, and now, once more, she covered her face with her hands and gave herself up to misery. Time was not healing this pain. She couldn't think straight any more. She couldn't write. She couldn't make Michael happy – although he refuted this, he trusted in the past, thought happiness lay in how things once were, and could be again, and at first this had been a comfort, but at times such as this, Ali saw that his belief in the perfect order of their previous lives could just be a kind of blindness holding them back. Couldn't they both be freed from constraint? Couldn't they each benefit from the shaking off of all the accumulated layers of habit and expectation? But how to go about freeing a person who didn't consider himself in chains? And anyway, all Michael would say was that what Ali called freedom, he called adultery. He was brutally moral, constitutionally upright. And there was this too: he said he loved her, and he didn't desire any other woman.

But meanwhile they'd both forgotten what harmony felt like, here in their beautiful home. Every day, the emotional temperature seemed to shift, and this kept Ali on her guard, trying to read the nuances in his face, his tone, his body language. She was sick of it, and sick of being a sinner, and she'd told him again and again, but he couldn't comprehend how it might feel to face a life sentence of guilt for being – once, just once in your otherwise unblemished record – so spectacularly disappointing.

She'd tried to love Michael more than she did, better than she had. She had tried, too, to forget how Dan had made her feel, but there were too many memories and you can't unring a bell. There was the music, the recognition of a perfect fit, the certainty that here was her link to a kind of redemption she'd thought impossible, perhaps even a path to her lost brother. And there was also, always and for ever, the bliss, the bliss, the bliss. She never would, never could, talk to Michael about how lovemaking could be elevated, between the right two people, and he steered clear of the subject himself, perhaps from an instinct to protect himself from further harm. He had his theories, and they all came down to this: she'd fallen – briefly – for the lure of her youth, but it was a trick of the light, an illusion; Michael said a true relationship had longevity on its side, proper foundations, heaps of memories. Ali, keeping her counsel, nodding with a kind of ambiguous assent, nevertheless knew that he was wrong. What she'd fallen for was the real thing.

Later, recovered from her descent into the vale of tears, she wandered into Beatriz's room, and there was the old lady in her rocking chair, looking at nothing.

'Hello, Beatriz,' Ali said. She knelt beside her and wrapped one of her frail hands in both of her own. The skin was as thin as a corn husk, and as dry. 'Can I get you something? Coffee, maybe? Some raisin toast?' But Beatriz shook her head sadly, as if those simple pleasures – drinking, eating – were lost to her now. Beatriz, the busy, beatific, beating heart of the McCormack household, had decided enough was enough; there was so much to worry about that, instead, she wouldn't worry about anything at all. She'd just gently rock herself into another dimension and spend time in her head with the people of her distant past, and Ali grieved for her, and knew she was in part responsible for dear Beatriz's decline. She'd been self-absorbed, mired in her own difficulties, and she'd made Beatriz suspicious these past months: she'd made Michael miserable and she'd sent Stella off to Europe with a steady calm that, to Beatriz, was inexplicable. Since Stella left, there'd been no structure to Beatriz's day, no child to nurture, no lovely, growing girl to spoil with sweet pastries and cuddles, and meanwhile, rumbling on like the distant drums of war, there was the ongoing low-level trauma of Ali and Michael's wounded marriage. They'd tried, when they remembered to try, or had sufficient command over their feelings, to protect Beatriz from the zigzag trajectory of their shattered emotions, but look at her now, thought Ali: the old lady had eyes and ears and decades of wisdom; she knew everything, of course she did.

'Listen, Beatriz, I spoke to Stella today.'

'You told me,' Beatriz said flatly.

'I know, but you were sleepy and I didn't say what she'd said. Guess where she's headed next?'

Beatriz sighed and shifted in her chair. She looked down at her hand in Ali's, and then up at the crucifix on the opposite wall. 'Tell me,' she said with no interest.

'Portugal!' Ali said. 'She's going to make her way down through Spain by train. She's going to send you a postcard when she gets to Porto. She'll send you a picture of the Douro twinkling at night.'

'And is she still alone?'

Yes, thought Ali, alone, and perfectly fine. 'No, no, there's a little gang of them,' she told Beatriz. 'Friends she's met along the way.'

Beatriz turned her head to look at Ali. 'Is she still alone?' she said again.

'OK, yes,' Ali said, because she'd told enough lies in this house for a lifetime. 'But, Beatriz, look, she's so happy and well, and she sends her love to you.'

From downstairs, Michael's voice – brightly gung-ho, to show he was no longer in a funk – reached them through the closed door. 'Who's hungry?' he shouted. 'Dinner's ready down here.'

'Beatriz?' Ali asked gently. 'Please will you come and eat with us?'

The old lady shook her head. 'I'm not hungry.'

'But you must be,' Ali said. 'I don't know when you last had a proper meal. Maybe you're hungry without realising it. Maybe if you came downstairs with me and—'

'Ali, I can't eat, I have no wish to eat, and you have matters to talk about with Michael that don't include me.'

'Oh, Beatriz.' She longed for her to say Ali, my girl.

'Go,' Beatriz said. 'Make your husband happy, and leave me be. I'm best left here, on my own.' And she turned her face away so emphatically that Ali released her hand, kissed her cheek, told her she loved her, and left the room. She'd always imagined herself dearly loved by Beatriz, and indeed she had been – until she'd made Michael unhappy. Then Ali had understood with the full force of a revelation that Beatriz's love for her had been conditional, dependent upon the rules of the household, and that this was the cult of the McCormacks in action: this was the closing of the ranks.

*

A little over a week later, Beatriz was dead, and it was as if she'd willed it, walking towards God and the promise of eternal life. Even Michael, who knew there was a solid, biological cause behind every human death, didn't deny that she seemed to have initiated and stage-managed her own exit from a world for which she'd lost all energy. He'd been the one to find her, in the early evening, and the sound of his weeping brought Ali running to find him, her gut churning because she'd assumed she was the cause, but then there he was, on his knees by Beatriz's bed, crying more than he had when either of his parents passed away, because nobody had loved Michael more than Beatriz. He stopped when Ali came into the room, pulled himself together as if he felt unmanned by his grief, but she'd gathered him in her arms, and they'd cried together for the loss of her. If Beatriz could have seen their embrace, it might have brought her some joy.

Later though, downstairs, waiting for the funeral director to come and take Beatriz's body away from the house, Ali said, 'Michael, I have this terrible feeling that this is my doing.' She was unburdening herself of her darkest fear, trusting him to dismiss it as nonsense. 'Her death, I mean. I'm afraid I some-how caused it.'

She longed for him to speak, to contradict her, but he was silent for a while after she spoke and then he said, 'She knew she was deeply loved, that's all that really matters,' and this wasn't a contradiction at all, didn't even address the point, but was merely an assertion of something they already knew. Ali took a deep breath and stepped away from him. A dense quiet descended, circling around and between them, a menacing third presence in the room.

'I'll call Thea,' she said suddenly, moving to the phone on the kitchen wall. 'And we need to tell Stella, and you need to ring Rory and Rob.'

'Thank you, I know what I need to do.'

'Sorry, Michael, I suppose I'm just trying to fill this dreadful silence.'

'I'd be more than grateful if you didn't,' Michael said.

She stared at him. He sounded like his mother, killingly and meaninglessly courteous. 'Michael, do you blame me for this, too?' she asked.

He looked at her. 'Not really,' he said. 'Not entirely. But you're implicated, aren't you?'

'And are you implicated too?'

'Me? I'm innocent, Ali. My conscience is clear, and Beatriz knew that, and probably knows it still, wherever she is now.'

'She's *dead*,' Ali said, wondering if her husband, the esteemed doctor, was quietly having a nervous breakdown. 'Her days of having an opinion are over.'

'Just call Thea,' he said, and he stood up. 'I'll ring my brothers from my office,' and he left her there, where she held the back of a chair for support, feeling momentarily shipwrecked. But she did ring Thea, who took the news gravely but clinically, like the med student she was; then she rang Stella, who cried and cried in her hostel dorm in Seville, and they stayed together on the line until she'd stopped, until she'd promised Ali that she'd be fine and until she'd further reassured her mother by putting another person on the line – Karin, from Dusseldorf – who said yes, she knew Stella, in fact Stella was her friend, although a very recent one, but certainly she'd spend the rest of the day with her, and she'd call Ali at once if it seemed necessary. Then Ali scooped up her car keys, grabbed her bag and drove to Cass's flat, where she cried over Beatriz who had died thinking ill of her, and Cass listened to her woes for a long while then said, 'Enough, enough, I have the antidote to what ails you,' and together they ate salty crackers with Brie, and watched *Terms of Endearment* and

Steel Magnolias; something they could laugh at as well as cry, Cass said, and anyway she believed there was no sadness in this world that couldn't be at least fractionally eased by Shirley MacLaine.

When Cass fell asleep, Ali lay awake for a long time, feeling maudlin, far too unhappy to switch off, but it wasn't Beatriz on her mind, it was that other loss, far greater and more devastating, entirely self-inflicted. When she'd chosen Michael over Dan in that terrible confrontation, she'd told herself afterwards that she'd made a courageous decision, and a selfless, generous one, essentially to preserve the equilibrium of their daughters' lives, and to spare all of them from crisis. But she'd been wrong, she understood that now: badly, epically wrong. She'd been shown a bold, brilliant alternative future for herself, and then rejected it. She lay on the king-sized bed beside a softly snoring Cass, and she wept self-pitying tears for the loss of the life she might have had with Daniel, who, in the melodrama of her grief, she felt was her heart's home, her magnetic north, the darling of her soul. It was only later, when she woke from a fitful few hours' sleep, that she thought, OK, Ali, so quit whingeing and do something.

27

For months after he told her, Katelin's pain raged like fire or flood through every facet of their lives. The house was infected by sadness; it clotted the air they breathed so that sometimes he had to walk outside into the night to fill his lungs with unsullied oxygen. Dan's infidelity had twisted and warped their past and their future as well as their present and briefly, in those first terrible days, Katelin became unrecognisable: savage, vengeful, obsessive. She wanted every single detail of his affair, every single secret, because until she knew exactly – *exactly* – what Ali Connor knew, she couldn't rest. She rang him on the train to ask him what she was wearing when they met in Adelaide, and then again, immediately afterwards, to ask what she wore in bed. What, she demanded, did Ali Connor have that was so irresistible he'd risked everything by fucking her? He couldn't answer truthfully, so he tried saying, 'Nothing, she has nothing irresistible, I was a fool,' and the words were meaningless to them both. She woke him in the night with questions about sex – how often, when, how – and when Dan refused to respond, off they would go on a different tack, new questions coming at him like bullets from a Gatling gun. Other times, Dan would be startled from sleep by the depth of the silence and find her awake beside him, staring at the ceiling with dry wide eyes. At these times, she seemed stronger: resilient, independent, rejecting his offered love in favour of her own inner resources. But they were skin deep, and barely that: her pain was just under the surface, and it stayed there for many weeks, unpredictable, undiminished, unstoppable.

And Dan tried to keep things together, and hear her out, and answer her questions, while still telling her as little as possible, because it felt like a different kind of betrayal to lay bare the facts and his feelings for Alison, to expose her to Katelin's fury with no right of reply. He didn't mention the songs, couldn't expose them to her contempt, so he held them close and treasured what they'd meant to him, although he couldn't listen to them now.

Two months in, Katelin rang Alex and told him everything, and this was hard to excuse. She'd drunk too much one evening, alone in the house, when the damage was still fresh, and after a few hours with only her rage and pain for company, she'd concluded that their son should know the truth about his father. By the time Dan got home, she was a shivering wreck of profound regret, because Alex had been terribly, uncharacteristically quiet, had asked no questions, none at all, just listened for a couple of minutes to her slurred account of the Australian adventure, then said, 'Shit, Mum, sorry, I can't do this,' and hung up.

'I didn't mean to tell him!' she wailed later, pummelling her fists against Dan's chest. 'You made me do it. He hates me now, and I wanted him to hate you.'

'He doesn't hate you,' Dan said. 'He adores you. He just doesn't need to hear about any of this. I'll talk to him. It's going to be fine.'

'Why are you so fucking calm?' she screamed.

'One of us has to be,' he said, and he held her for as long as it took for her to remember the world hadn't ended, it had only changed for ever.

He knew beyond doubt now that he shouldn't have told her, and he couldn't remember why he had, only that perhaps in his wretchedness he'd needed to smash something, and his own life with Katelin had been the first thing to hand. But then she'd pronounced his fate, which was to remain together, building something new from the ashes, and although his heart was bruised and his soul defeated, and although many were the times he wanted to pack his old holdall and walk away, he knew the very least he could do for Katelin now was to let her have her way, dictate her terms. So he took his punishment. He listened to her again (and again and again), and when she asked was it over, were they in touch, did he still have feelings for Ali Connor, Dan said yes, and no, and no, and only this last answer was a lie, but he hoped that as the silence between him and Alison lengthened, the certainty that he would always love her might begin to diminish. The angry disappointment he'd once felt towards her – always a rather manufactured thing – had dissipated entirely a long time ago, to make way for something more dreadful: a kind of bleak acceptance that perfect happiness was now beyond his reach.

'So, you're the walking cliché,' Katelin said in a bistro in New Town in June, on the anniversary of the date they'd first met in Bogotá; her idea, not his. 'And I'm the original one in this partnership, because I've refused to revert to stereotype and make you leave. I'll always think you're a selfish bastard to do as you did, but I'm keeping you, for better or for worse.'

A strange toast with which to affirm their Brave New Partnership, but Dan kept his expression neutral, and wondered if Michael McCormack was as relentless as Katelin at turning acceptance into a cruel and unusual form of punishment. He probably was, if his lone email four months ago was anything to go by, his absurd Victorian posturing at the assault on his property. *Your contemptible and predatory attempt at plundering my life has ended in abject failure, and although my marriage has been wounded, I will never give you the satisfaction of letting it fail. Find another online playmate – my wife has permanently withdrawn from your toxic influence.* Dan had typed *Fuck you, McCormack* but hadn't sent it, just left it there as a draft, gathering cyber dust, while he decided whether no response was more annoying and effective than an offensive one.

'I didn't want to marry you, for exactly this reason,' Katelin went on. 'I never wanted us to be held together only by paperwork and by not being able to face the hassle and expense of divorce.'

'Yes, I know,' Dan said. 'I know you never wanted that. I was there at the start too, remember?' He thought of emails and deadlines, a multitude of professional obligations, which all this time later were still playing second fiddle to Katelin's need to affirm the facts of the case, and declare herself master of them.

'I hate what you did,' she went on, 'and I hate her too, and I'm happy to say my defaced copy of her book's still on the shelf in the charity shop, unwanted by anyone in Stockbridge, but I'm giving you credit, at least, for having told me before I found out, and I would've done, oh, I would have done, in fact I think on one level I already knew. But you told me, and that counts for something.'

Dan regretted every day – deeply regretted – that he'd succumbed to that impulse to tell her; regretted, too, the near-visceral
pain he'd inflicted on Katelin, which she was now recycling into
a bullish, post-feminist power trip; but even so, he felt no remorse
about what he'd done, not a scrap, because he couldn't ever consider the time he'd spent with Ali Connor to be anything other
than essential.

'You love me, I know you do,' Katelin said. She paused
here, and waited for him to respond. It was six months since
he'd told her, and she'd talked so much about what he'd done
and why that it was beginning to feel as though he was the sole
audience member at a dreary stage play, so over-rehearsed that
all life had been leached from the lines, and the words merely
tumbled from Katelin's moving lips like a collection of Scrab-
ble tiles, arranging themselves into flat, dull patterns on the
floor. But he knew his cue, never missed it, and he looked at
Katelin now with a kind of ironic resignation. *Yesss*, he con-
firmed; he loved her.

This was not a lie. He did love her. He did. And yet.

'We're going to stay open with each other,' Katelin said.
'Stay honest, because that's our commitment to each other.'

Ah, honesty, thought Dan: of all the human virtues, the
joker in the pack.

Katelin said let's not tell anyone else, and for a long time Dan
agreed, but then, on a hazy, lazy night in London in July, he
poured out the story and all his woes to Frank and Lisa, in the
onion and turmeric fug of *Ophelia*'s cabin. He knew this was
essentially a self-indulgent confession; they were hardly going
to judge him, these two ageing hippies, relics from the free-love
sixties. But in fact Lisa shook her head sadly as he spoke, and
Frank, looking across at her, said, 'Yeah, bad news, right?'

'What?' Dan said, stopping at once. 'You're not telling me you disapprove?'

Lisa blew smoke from her sensual mouth. She was smoking a Gitanes through a silver holder, sitting opposite him on the floor, and her legs were folded with comfortable ease into a half-lotus. Tin lanterns hanging from the ceiling cast a trellis of light on to the walls. 'You should've told her, Dan,' she said.

'I did tell her! I just said that I did, that's my whole point.'

She shook her head again. 'No, before you went,' she said. 'You should've told her your plans.'

'You're kidding me?'

'Bad news, man,' Frank said. He was ageing by the day, it seemed, and doing it stoned. Lisa had given up weed for a while, because Frank – she said – needed her ration as well as his own. He was stretched out on a narrow bunk in a vest and baggy Y-fronts, his legs – nut-brown and almost fleshless – extending along the length of the mattress, and he looked at the ceiling as he spoke. 'Uncool.'

Dan felt briefly devastated to be chastised by this pair, whose own lives on the very margins of society had been so unconventional, so unfettered.

'Hang on,' he said. 'When did anyone ever ask permission to have an affair?'

Lisa and Frank looked at each other. 'Nineteen seventy-two, nineteen eighty,' Frank said, oddly alert for a moment, using his fingers as counters, and Lisa nodded, and added, 'Nineteen eighty-five, -seven and -nine,' and then they each turned their benign brown eyes on Dan.

'Wow,' he said. He couldn't ever remember them being quite so succinct. 'You're talking about each other, right? Well, look, you guys are very special people, but I know for sure and certain that that wouldn't work for Katelin. She's no good at sharing.'

'But your conscience would be clear. You'd have told her,' Lisa said. 'That's the point.'

'Share your choices, man,' Frank said. 'It'll blow your mind.'

Dan closed his eyes and said, 'I can only imagine,' and resolved, in that moment, to give up on them for anything other than their memories and their marijuana, but Lisa wasn't finished. She reached across the narrow space that divided her from Dan and rested a hand on his knee.

'We love you, Dan,' she said. 'Be happy.'

He opened his eyes and she was looking at him, bathing him in one of her smiles. She was possessed of a warm and generous spirit, and this was part of what made her beautiful still. When Lisa looked in your eyes, when she concentrated on you alone, it was a special feeling, like having essential oils massaged into your temples. If it wasn't for the fact that it meant he'd now be an old man, he wouldn't have minded finding Lisa himself when she was twenty, and hitching his horse to the same wagon. Frank had struck gold, back there in that ashram. He might have strayed, but it couldn't have been very far, or for very long.

'Tell me about Alison,' she said. 'Tell me everything you can about her.'

Oh, this was kind, and unexpected, and for a few moments Dan felt in embarrassing danger of crying with gratitude at her question, which was so simple, yet so bloody welcome. To talk about Alison, who she was, what she looked like, how she'd made him feel, what she'd meant to him, how they'd connected: this was what he needed, because the longer he went without being able to do so, the harder it was to trust his own judgement. He talked a torrent, and Frank didn't even feign interest, just fell asleep, but Lisa listened closely and when Dan stopped she said, 'You really miss her,' and it was a statement of fact not a question, but Dan gave a low groan and said, 'Like I'd miss my limbs.'

'Show me how on earth you send a song to Australia,' she said, and he laughed and reached for his phone, opening Twitter to show her the ropes, and she watched with a vaguely concerned expression as if there might be a test at the end of the demo. Because he knew she'd remember Donovan, he found 'Sunshine Superman', copied the link and pasted it on to the thread he and Ali had made, which was still there, intact, untouched. He hadn't been asked by Katelin to delete anything, and he wouldn't have agreed to it if he had. One thing to be said about shopping himself before discovery, he reckoned, was a continued right to a decent level of privacy. He was no longer in touch with Ali Connor; this was all he'd felt obliged to say to Katelin, who knew nothing about these songs, anyway. Lisa stared at the screen and the links looked like a form of algebra to her, unconnected in any comprehensible way to what she understood a song to be.

'Has she got it now, then?' she asked.

'No, my God, no, I didn't send it. See, there's *send* there, but we're not doing that any more, it's all over, she chose the other guy. Christ knows why, he's a pompous dickhead. But look, I can still play this for you, even though it hasn't been sent,' and he opened the new link and when the string of words and jumbled letters bloomed into music, Lisa gazed around the cabin in awe as if she had no idea where the sound was coming from.

'Oh man, I love this tune,' she said, and she leaned forward and gave Frank's bony foot a shove to bring him back to consciousness, and sang 'when you've made your mind up' along with Donovan and his sweet sixties sound. Frank stirred and blinked and rolled his head as he slowly returned to them.

'Do you remember this, baby?' Lisa said to him. She sang

on, unfurling herself from the floor like a snake charmed out of its basket, swaying from the hips and weaving shapes with her arms.

'Lisa, you're so fucking awesome,' Dan said. She sang like Janis Joplin: soulful, wicked, a smoker's voice, slightly ruined and all the better for that. Frank watched from his supine position and tapped his gnarly toes against the wooden wall in time to the beat.

'Hey, I know what, play *all* the list,' Lisa said when it ended. 'Play *all* your songs, like a total celebration of love,' but Dan shook his head.

'I can't,' he said. 'Half of those songs are hers.'

'No, man,' Frank said. 'Songs belong to the universe.' He'd hauled himself up into a sitting position, and was ferreting about in his stash tin, rubbing it into smaller crumbs for a new spliff. His fingers were too stiff these days to tie a half-hitch or a slip knot, but he was still a craftsman with a heap of weed and a cigarette paper. He seemed to smoke rather than eat. One day, he said, he wanted to wake up dead.

'It's too private,' Dan said, 'like reading her diary out loud.'

'No way, man,' Frank said again, spaced out, still sleepy. 'They're, like, out there, those songs, like fireflies: you can trap 'em and they're yours until you release 'em again.'

'They are, they are,' Lisa said, excited by this idea. 'You just trapped "Sunshine Superman" in a jar for me.'

Frank held out the newly rolled, newly lit spliff and said, 'A gift for you, my friend Dan Lawrence. Join me on cloud nine,' and there was something very appealing about this, because nothing soothed a troubled heart so well as Frank's home-grown. Dan took it. Lisa smiled. The world contracted further still into this enclosed, enchanted space, and he took a long, long drag to pull the mind-altering medication into his lungs, through his bloodstream, up to the agitated, overworked neurons and synapses of his brain. He felt himself soften, lighten, loosen.

'Play us the very last one she sent you,' Lisa said. 'Just that.'

Joni, thought Dan, fondly, as if the singer was a girl he used to know. Well, OK, he thought, why not channel those groovy Laurel Canyon blues? With his free hand, he scrolled up the screen to Ali's final link, and Lisa said, 'See, Frank, look here, the tune's all captured in those blue letters,' but Frank just smiled and said, 'Lay it on me,' so Dan opened the song and Joni Mitchell played her guitar for them, and sang them her lonely love song, and Dan felt incredibly good, incredibly happy, and when the track played itself out to its last plaintive chords, Lisa was very still, very contemplative for a while, listening to the silence left by Joni, then she said, 'No *way* did Ali choose the other guy, no *way*.'

Dan looked at her. He was on the cusp of being heroically high, and this made him slow to process her words.

'She chose you, Dan,' she said, simplifying things. 'She chose you.'

Dan shook his head. 'I saw her walk right out the door with him,' he said. 'Saw her with my own two eyes.'

'Send her "Sunshine Superman",' Lisa said, taking the phone from his hand and making random stabs at the screen with her finger. 'She'll love it, you'll be spreading love and happiness. Come on, release Donovan, let him fly across the world.'

'No. Nope. No way, José,' said Dan. He was dimly aware of regretting the spliff, but only in a stoned, half-hearted way, and only very briefly. 'That horse has bolted,' he said. 'That train has left the station. That toke's been smoked.'

This seemed completely hilarious to Dan and Frank, and they dissolved into a festival of damp-eyed, wheezing, crazy mirth, so Lisa had to wait for quite some time before she was able to say, 'Well, anyway, I'm not totally sure, but I think I might have just sent it.' She held the phone in front of Dan's face to show him.

'Oh,' he said, peering myopically at the screen in the candle-light. 'Yep. It's gone, man, solid gone.'

Frank raised an arm in a kind of slow salute to the magnificent forces of the universe. 'Follow the bliss,' he said. 'Bring it home, daddy-o.'

There was the smallest grain of anxiety somewhere in Dan's melted consciousness, a dim sense that there might be trouble afoot, a storm blowing in; but like a crescent moon in a cloudy sky it slipped out of range and was instantly forgotten. Lisa said, 'She might be listening to that right now,' and because the world was currently suffused in a gorgeous honey glow, Dan only smiled and said, 'I'll pick up her hand and slowly . . . blow her little mind.'

28

The boys were drinking a fancy pale ale, the girls were on pro-
secco. *Sketches of Spain* had ended and had now been replaced
by Simon and Garfunkel's *Greatest Hits*, Katelin's favourite
album, and not a terrible choice as musical wallpaper, although
Dan had never been a fan of Art Garfunkel and he couldn't
stand 'Bridge Over Troubled Water', playing now, bloated and
over-produced. He discreetly turned down the volume, and grimaced at Duncan, who grinned.

They were in the front room, the living room, which was
immaculately tidy for the occasion, all the usual trappings of
their lives – magazines, books, sample albums, remote controls –
stashed away in the cupboard on which the television stood. The
doors were buckling under the strain, and whoever opened them
would start an avalanche. It was only Duncan and Rose-Ann for
Sunday lunch, but Katelin had lately decided she was restyling
their home into a calmer, more neutral space – Rose-Ann's
words, coming out of Katelin's mouth – and as well as tidying
away the clutter, she was also redecorating, by degrees. The
walls in here were Old White now, apparently, which wasn't
white at all, but grey, or greenish, depending where you stood,
and how the light fell. The new curtains seemed to Dan to have

been fashioned out of antique grain sacks, but it was organic hemp, Katelin said, sustainable, biodegradable. Rose-Ann was cooing over the changes, which 'opened up the room' (how?) and 'turned the focus from the general to the specific' (why?). Dan, keeping his counsel, could already picture his mother's face when she next visited. 'It's a bit drab,' she'd say, then: 'I always think yellow's a lovely cheerful colour for a lounge.' Anyway, at least his records were still where they belonged.

In the centre of the room, on the new glass coffee table, were two bowls: one of silvery marinated anchovies, and another of roasted almonds washed in lemon juice. These elegant offerings from the local deli were in lieu of a starter, and Katelin had bought new Turkish-made ceramic dishes for them, from the same shop. Very pretty, turquoise and orange, the colours of the Mediterranean. Duncan dangled an anchovy by the tail and dropped it into his open mouth like a seal.

'Do you remember,' he said, 'when a bag of Golden Wonder cheese and onion was all we had as a snack?'

'All we needed,' Dan said.

'Will I nip out to the corner shop?' said Katelin. 'Get you something more downmarket?'

She was a little tetchy today. She'd been very pleased with the bowls, and Rose-Ann, who had a great influence on Katelin's buying decisions, had noticed them immediately and said, 'Sweet bowls, Katelin, gorgeous colours, they really pop against the neutrals,' and Dan had glanced at them, puzzled, because he could've sworn he'd seen them before, and said, 'Haven't we had these ages?' then remembered Sheila's bowls of baba ganoush and hummus on the mosaic table in her back garden. Probably not identical, but near as damn it, and he'd thought, Jesus, the perils of a parallel life. Katelin had said she didn't know why she bothered, which had a lot less to do with the new crockery than with the fact that he'd been far too quiet for her liking that morning, far too self-absorbed, and when she'd finally asked him what – or rather, who – he was thinking about, he'd said Donovan, and she'd held his gaze as if she had more to say, then tutted and walked away.

She'd been right though. He *had* been too quiet and self-absorbed, because although he really was thinking about Donovan, it was only in the context of Alison, who hadn't responded to the song. Granted, he hadn't in fact sent it; Lisa had done the deed, and then only by accident. But Alison didn't know that; as far as she was concerned this might be him trying to make her turn her head and notice him again. It maddened and depressed him that her lack of response to a song he hadn't meant to send could ambush his mood in this way, so that all his careful defences were suddenly in jeopardy, but anyway it only underlined what he already believed: Ali Connor would never leave Michael McCormack. More than this, he told himself he'd perhaps read her all wrong and she hadn't ever wanted anything more than the frisson but relative safety of a long-distance, phone-based love affair, and that the perfect union of Alison and Daniel had never been any more tangible to her than a fairy tale.

The other thing that had got to him – and this had been needling him pretty much all the time – was that if he *had* meant to send her one last song, it wouldn't have been 'Sunshine Superman', with its jaunty, confident, upbeat refrain. It would've been something dark and brooding, something wounded, something writhing in pain. And he'd sat there in the Sunday-morning calm of the newly neutral living room, thought for a while about this theme, then sent her another song, a definitively final track that best reflected his state of mind: 'I Want You', Elvis Costello's seething anthem to that fine line between love and hate, a dark hymn for the heartbroken, a study in obsessive longing. There was a jagged seam of pure truth in it, and if these songs they'd shared meant anything at all, they had to be honest.

He'd felt better after he watched it go. He hoped it'd send a shiver of regret down her lovely, supple spine. He hoped, too, she'd understand the synchronicity, the Costello full-circle thing, which had started with nostalgia and ended with a demonic ballad about what happens to your head and heart when your favourite girl goes off with another bloke. That's that then, he'd thought. Then he'd gone down the hall to the kitchen, to make batter for the Yorkshire puddings.

Rose-Ann chimed a knife against her glass and said, 'A toast,' and Dan's heart sank a fraction. She raised her Rioja. 'To survivors in choppy waters,' she said, classic Rose-Ann, speaking out loud what she believed everyone thought but no one other than her was brave enough to say.

'Och, Rose-Ann, bugger that,' Duncan said, bold man, probably the pale ale talking. 'To happy days,' he said, and his wife was immediately overruled by the others. 'Happy days,' they said, and clinked glasses, then the conversation round the table fell into its familiar, comfortable groove, roving between those well-trodden subjects that old friends like to revisit, not because there's anything new to add, but only to affirm and reaffirm what they already know. Music was supposed to be out of bounds when they were a foursome – it was tedious (Katelin) and excluding (Rose-Ann) – but you might as well tell the parish priest to quit mentioning God. It was Dan and Duncan's world, it was why they were mates, it was what got them out of bed in the mornings. Plus, Duncan had news. Jeanie and the Kat had four of their original tracks on Spotify, and now they were going gangbusters in Norway and Sweden, like, seriously big. And yesterday he'd heard their music playing in a café in Cockburn Street.

'It's crazy,' he said. 'I was queuing for a coffee, and I said to the guy, "Hang on, what's this that's playing?" and he said, "It's a Spotify playlist, why?" I said, "No, this track, it's Jeanie and the Kat, right?" and the guy just shrugged and passed me the iPhone, and they're on this, like, curated Spotify playlist, Scottish Indie Rock or something, and I said, "I discovered these girls! I launched 'em!" '

'The wonders of the modern world,' Dan said.

'I rang Katriona straight away, she was on a bloody ferry to Stockholm!'

'Who's Katriona?' Rose-Ann asked, newly alert.

'The Kat, in Jeanie and the Kat,' Dan said. 'Duncan's protégées.'

'They're playing a string of gigs – Stockholm, Gothenburg, Oslo, some other places in the frozen north – and it's all being managed from his laptop by a guy called Gavin, some bod from a music company who's looking after the royalties and whatnot.'

'I told you, Dunc,' Dan said. 'It's all there for the taking these days, easy as pie.'

'Sweden and Norway,' Katelin said. 'Why's that good?'

'It hardly matters where you catch your break,' Duncan said. 'These streaming services, they don't recognise international borders, there's this ripple-out effect, it can just spread like a forest fire, and boom, you're a global indie sensation,' and Dan smiled and said, 'Hark at you, Duncan Lomax.'

'Hey, are we going to make some money outta these girls?' Rose-Ann asked, perking up, but Duncan said no, no, *they* were, the two girls. 'They're already picking up royalties, this company collects them, keeps twenty per cent, shoves the rest into Kat's bank account. They're cock-a-hoop.'

'So when you say you launched them,' Rose-Ann said, 'it was more that you *didn't* launch them?'

There was a brief, uncertain silence, then, 'Anyone want more beef?' Katelin asked. She was bored by this conversation, and so, in truth, was Rose-Ann, now she knew they weren't in fact invested in the career of these cat girls, or whatever they were. Rose-Ann looked at Duncan with a flat, dull gaze, and he didn't answer.

'Sorry, mate,' Dan said. 'I wish it could've been. What about the other dude, the fisherman? And Aztec Camera-take-two?'

'More beef, anyone?' Katelin was determined now to wrest the subject away from these tiresome men, who never knew when to stop. 'More carrots? Potatoes?'

'Not for me,' Dan said. 'But more wine, I think.' He topped up everyone's glasses, no one said no to that, then he refilled his own and sat back in his chair surveying the faces around him, none of which looked especially happy. He felt a sudden, unusual detachment and, with it, a disorientating feeling of instability that descended upon him like a short bout of vertigo so that he laid his palms flat on the table to steady himself, and ever after he'd remember this moment as a kind of premonition, his subconscious self one step ahead of the hard facts, because there was the bright 'ting' of an incoming message, and Rose-Ann delved into her handbag on the floor. 'Nope, not me,' she said, slipping her phone back down into the dark interior. Katelin, on her feet now, still offering cold meat and vegetables to her unwilling guests, saw Dan's phone in among the clutter of the Sunday-lunch worktop, tilted her head to read the screen, frowned, looked closer; then in a fluid, furious, extraordinary movement she raised the large oval platter of meat up high and threw it violently down so that it smashed and bled – a terrible sound, a terrible sight, like a grenade attack in their suburban kitchen – on to the tiles of the kitchen floor. Rose-Ann screamed and clutched at her chest and Duncan spun round, thinking Katelin must've fallen or fainted, but she was standing, strung taut like a wire, ready to snap, directing a deep black stare at Dan, who leapt up and seized his phone, then stalked out of the kitchen to read what Katelin had already seen.

Ali was on the move. She'd left Michael as honestly and compassionately as she could, but her honesty and compassion were futile in the face of his implacable disbelief. She told him it was over, and he told her it wasn't. She told him she was leaving and he told her she wasn't. She told him she loved him still, but that she loved Dan differently, and more, and he told her she wasn't thinking straight and didn't know her own mind. Even as he watched her pack a rucksack, find her passport, ring for a taxi to the airport, he'd devoutly believed she wouldn't possess the courage or the cruelty to walk out of the door and away from their life, and when finally he had to accept that she was capable of this, he'd raged at her, dry-eyed and damning.

'You're a fantasist, chasing a bloody teenage dream,' he'd said, maddened and bewildered by the stoicism of her resistance.

'Michael,' Ali said. 'I'm sorry.'

'Is this Cass's idea? Has she talked you into it?'

Ali shook her head and stared at him aghast. 'Do you think I haven't a mind of my own? That I do either what you say, or what Cass says?'

'Yes,' he said. 'Yes, in many ways I do think that about you. You're generally compliant and suggestible, and the way you're behaving now isn't like you, so it's either Cass's idea or you've lost your mind.'

Every word he said worked against him, she thought; every opinion he expressed diminished his case. She felt very calm.

She was beyond his influence now. 'This is me,' she said. 'This is all me, and I'm sane and steady and single-minded.'

'Ali, this is madness. It's beyond my comprehension.' He ran his hands through his hair and over his face in distress and frustration, and she felt a pull of sympathy at his utter confusion, because nothing in his easy path through life had prepared him for failure on a scale such as this.

'Look,' she said as gently as possible. 'There are other things too. I've tried to explain how being with Dan made me feel closer to my past?'

'Yeah, and you use that against me, don't you? My supposed lack of interest in your bad beginnings. What do you think I am, a mind reader? Was I supposed to know your deepest secrets without you telling me about them?'

'No. I know I kept a lot from you because I couldn't deal with it myself. But rediscovering Dan has made me—'

He cut into her words with a bark of laughter. 'Oh, right, "rediscovering" – is that what we're calling it now? Don't try to elevate what you did, Ali, it was only a covert shag.'

She started to shake, and for a moment she looked at her hands, inwardly cursing them for betraying her when she was trying so hard to be calm, and careful, and kind. But she was leaving him, and she knew, in truth, that there wasn't a kind way of doing this, only the usual one, the cruel one. 'I have to go,' she said. 'I'm sorry I've hurt you so much.'

'Then *don't* hurt me,' he said. 'Don't go. Stop thinking of yourself, think of the girls, think of me – how shall I deal with all the pressures at work if I also have to deal with this?'

Ali looked at him then with a mixture of pity and disappointment. 'You'll cope,' she said, and then on the threshold of the door she told him she was going first to see Thea in Melbourne, to explain everything, and from there to Portugal, to see Stella, who she thought should get a different story, an edited one, because Stella was too far away from home to be told the full truth.

'Good God, aren't you the selfish and calculating bitch?'

'No,' she said. 'No, I'm not, I really am not.' She was still shaking, but her resolve was made from pure steel. 'I need to do this, Michael. I'm going to do this,' and Michael, shaking his head, speaking with contempt, said, 'That guy is nobody, he's nothing.'

'No,' Ali said. 'He's not. I think he might be everything.'

In Melbourne, faced with the reality of hurting her beloved eldest daughter, she baulked at first at the truth and said only that she was going away for a while, to the UK. But when Thea said, at once, 'What about Dad?' Ali plunged in and said well, yes, they needed some time apart from each other. Then Thea had flung herself sideways on to her bed, and wailed, 'You're splitting up!' and cried messily, and it was an hour before she'd listen to any kind of reason, and even then she sniffed and glowered at Ali over the top of her balled-up hankie, and sided one hundred per cent with her dad, her poor dad, who shouldn't be left alone in Adelaide now Beatriz was dead. This was Thea being thirteen again, demanding that life remain on her terms and no one else's, but Ali just persisted in treating her as an adult, and told her a few scant details about Dan, and about her own miserable girlhood in Sheffield, her alcoholic mother, long dead, the brother she'd told none of them about, and how she'd left unresolved so many problems from her past that it sometimes felt as if Alison Connor and Ali McCormack were two different people, strangers to each other. Thea listened without interruption, then when Ali finished she said, 'Are you leaving Dad for this other man?'

'All I know for sure right now is that I need to see Dan again, and deal with that part of my life I've always refused to address. But I'm not leaving you, Thea. I'll be back, I promise you that.'

Thea chewed her bottom lip. She looked so young. 'When we were little, you told us you had no family, other than us.'

'I know. I suppose that was me taking the easy road. I'm sorry.'

'Are you telling Stella all this?'

'No,' Ali said. 'Some of it, not all of it, and I'd like you not to tell her either while she's travelling, OK?'

'But you'll tell her you're going away?'

'Yep, seeing her the day after tomorrow, in Lisbon.'

'Then going to England?'

'London, yes. Then, I'm not sure. Sheffield, perhaps.'

'What if your brother's dead, as well as your mother?'

'Well, then at least I'll know.'

'And what about Dad? Is he OK?'

'Well, he's still getting his head round everything,' Ali said, thinking: understatement of the year. She saw in her mind's eye his face when she'd finally left the house, his expression a study in stony dislike as he summoned the healing power of his anger to sublimate the distress, the hurt, the fear. 'You know what I've realised?' he'd said. 'You don't have the first idea what it means to love someone.' Then he'd closed the door before she'd turned away, as if he couldn't wait to get her out of his sight.

She arrived at Heathrow, exhausted and uncertain. Seeing Thea, seeing Stella, the crossing of time zones, the surprising anxiety of travelling alone, the stress of connecting flights and the ordinary mayhem of international airports: all these elements conspired to bring her low, and she felt absurdly tearful in the luggage hall, as if this odyssey across the world hadn't been what she wanted, hadn't been what she intended at all. And then, as she waited for her rucksack to appear on the carousel, she delved into her handbag for her phone, and it wasn't there. Nor was it in the pockets of her jacket, or her jeans. Disbelieving, increasingly frenzied, she patted the same pockets again, emptied the chaotic contents of her bag on to the floor, then sat in the midst of the detritus and let hopelessness claim her. Uppermost in her unravelling mind was a song she'd received in Lisbon from Dan only thirty-six hours ago, a blessed, unexpected song, 'Sunshine Superman', a longed-for miracle. Its arrival had placed healing hands on her anxious, aching heart, but she'd been with Stella so hadn't responded to him, and then, alone at Lisbon airport, she'd seen her phone's battery was perilously low so she hadn't been able to reply at all: had instead switched off the phone, to save its last gasp of life for London. And now the phone was gone, and the loss of it made her feel sick with a kind of exhausted grief: made her remember, too, an encounter on the way to the departure gate, a young woman with vacant eyes, carrying a silent baby on her hip. She'd asked Ali for money, spare euros, small change, anything; and Ali had emptied her pockets, poured a handful of coins into the young woman's outstretched hand, and as they parted she'd felt a light, momentary collision, a hasty apology, too fleeting to seem significant. There was no proof, of course, but she was as sure as she could be that in those moments of distraction and contrived confusion her phone had been taken. So, she thought now, with a feeling of rising despair: how am I ever to find Daniel Lawrence?

'Excuse me, do you need some help?'

This was an elderly Englishman, a fellow traveller, waiting for his luggage. He looked at Ali with a sort of cheerful sympathy.

'Oh, not really,' she said, standing up at once, pulling herself together. She stooped to begin gathering up her possessions, and he did the same, handing her a used tissue, lip balm, an Adelaide metro card, a compact mirror. 'I lost my phone, that's all.' She felt awkward, sharing the contents of her handbag with this gentlemanly stranger.

'Ah, gosh, that's a disconcerting feeling, isn't it?' he said. 'How we all depend upon our phones, even myself, who once swore I'd never use one! Would you like to borrow mine, let someone know you're here?'

She smiled, wanly. 'I'd need to log on to Twitter,' she said. 'But then it'll send a security passcode to my phone, and of course I don't have it.'

'Pardon? Log on to what?'

'Never mind,' Ali said. 'It's complicated.'

'Ah,' said the man, looking crestfallen.

'Don't worry, I'll sort something out – but look, there's my bag, I'd better go.'

'Well, leave a number at lost property,' he said, determined to help one way or another. 'Someone they can call if it's found?'

'Yeah,' Ali said, although there really was no one, because she possessed no phone numbers and not a soul on this island was expecting her. 'Thanks for being kind.' She hauled her rucksack from the belt and waved goodbye to him before making her way through customs, then following signs for taxis, thanking God that she still had her cash and her cards. She had no real sense of where Heathrow was in relation to the rest of London, or, in fact, where Dan's boat was moored, but that's where she hoped to head, because it was a start. She'd heard of the famous wisdom of London cab drivers, so she climbed into the first in line and sat down, and when the driver said, 'Where to, darlin'?' she said, 'I'm kind of hoping you'll tell me.'

'Come again?' he said, looking at her through his mirror.

'Excuse me?'

'What did you say, love?'

'I need to get to the canal, to a narrowboat on the canal.'

All she knew was that Dan's boat was called *Crazy Diamond* and that Lisa and Frank and Jim lived on either side of him, on the canal. In Adelaide, this might've possibly been sufficient information, but she felt a fool now, coming so ill-equipped to this teeming capital city.

'Right,' said the cabbie. 'I might need a bit more info from you, darlin'. Where's it moored, this narrer-boat?'

'On the canal?' As opposed to the River Thames, she meant, but oh God, this was humiliating.

The driver pulled away from the taxi rank to free up the cab behind him, then parked again in a nearby bay. He talked to her through the rear-view mirror and his eyes twinkled with a kind of merry sarcasm when he said, 'See, there's quite a lot of canal in London, love. There's a fair few places to float your boat. Limehouse Basin? Battlebridge Basin at the back o' Kings Cross? Ring any bells?'

'No, I'm so sorry.' She knew she was batting her lashes at him, hoping he wouldn't give up on her and ask her to get out.

'Lisson Grove? Little Venice? Cumberland Basin?'

'Oh!' she said, brightening. 'I think it might be that Little Venice one.'

'That Little Venice one, right-oh, very nice, so let's take a chance that it's on Blomfield Road then,' he said, pulling smoothly away from the parking bay.

'It's *Crazy Diamond*, if that helps,' Ali said. 'The name, I mean,' and he laughed and said, 'Okey-doke, darlin', very rock and roll. It's not Dave Gilmour's boat, is it?'

'No, but good guess,' she said, smiling back at him, feeling that she might have chanced upon London's friendliest cab driver, or were they all this chirpy? And he was so sure of his route! None of the cabbies in little old Adelaide ever knew the way anywhere without recourse to Google Maps, but this guy was off like a rocket, away from the airport and weaving through traffic as if there was someone on his tail.

'Where you from, love?' he asked.

'Adelaide,' Ali said.

'Where's that then?'

'South Australia.'

'Blimey O'Riley, you're a long way from home.'

'Yeah, about ten thousand miles, but they do say home is where the heart is, so.'

'Oh, right!' he said. 'Right! Who've you come to see, then? Who's the lucky feller?'

'A guy called Dan,' she said. 'He's not expecting me.'

The cabbie winked appreciatively at her in the mirror. 'Well, he's got a nice surprise coming then.'

'Hope so,' she said. 'Hard to say.'

She could see a willow tree nodding at its own reflection in the dark water, a pair of regal swans carving a path through vivid green duckweed, and *Crazy Diamond*, a pretty, navy-blue boat with brass-framed porthole windows, her name a flourish of canary yellow on the bow. She could also see that the boat was empty; padlocks on the double doors and a tarpaulin pulled tight over the stern deck, but Ali waved off her new pal in the taxi, because she'd arrived at her destination and the fact that Dan wasn't here was immaterial. She'd sort of known he wouldn't be. It was Sunday, he'd be in Edinburgh, doing weekend things with Katelin, but for the time being, she had nowhere else to go, and no better idea than to stand in Blomfield Road and simply will him to appear, to saunter towards her along the tree-lined street, just as he would in the movies.

She lowered her rucksack on to the pavement so that she could rest against the black metal railings and study this idyllic place, and admire *Crazy Diamond*, and mourn her emptiness, her blank-eyed, dormant state. What had she expected? Of course Dan wasn't here, and anyway, he probably hated her for humiliating him, and she couldn't blame him for that, and she might never see him again, in spite of coming to him as he'd come to her. She was considering this bleak possibility when a languid, disembodied voice broke her desolate reverie. 'Hey, babe? You're Alison, right?' and Ali spun round at the sound, although she didn't really know where to look, and left or right, there wasn't a soul on the towpath.

'Up here, babe.'

And there she was, on the flat roof of the boat next door, partly obscured by the arching willows, a slender old lady with dip-dyed hair and dungarees, kohl-lined eyes, henna hands, bare feet, crossed legs, dozens of silver bangles on each wrist and a rope of azure beads wound around her throat. Lisa, thought Ali. Dan's Lovely Lisa. She smiled, and Lisa smiled too.

'You came,' Lisa said, nodding sagely, as if she'd known all along.

'I did.'

Lisa stood up and raised her arms into the air like a cele-brant, and her multitude of bangles slid against each other with the chimes of tiny bells. 'Welcome,' she said, and she hopped lightly down from her perch on to the path. 'You'll stay with us, until Dan gets here.'

'He doesn't know I'm here,' Ali said. She was mesmerised by Lisa, whose embrace smelled of patchouli oil, and whose bare feet were bejewelled with silver toe rings.

'Then you must tell him,' Lisa said. She took Ali's hand and led her on to the foredeck of *Ophelia*. 'Come, say hello to Frank.'

Dan stared at the text message, which had bloomed on to the screen of his phone, plain as day for Katelin to read. It had Jim's name attached to it, Jim from *Veronica Ann*, and this was simply inexplicable, but hardly more so than the message itself, which read, *Hey Daniel, this is Alison, I'll be at the bar of the Warwick Castle, 8pm tonight, saving you a seat xxx.*

He was in the hallway, just outside the kitchen, and Katelin was raging in there, really raging, while Rose-Ann's voice was another layer of sound, soft and constant, a blanket of soothing platitudes, and meanwhile Duncan had opened the door and was hissing at him: 'What the fuck, what is it, what's happened?' Dan looked at him, without really seeing.

'She's in London,' he said. His head and gut swam with problems and possibilities, and the damage he'd done, and the damage he'd yet to do.

'Then go, pal,' Duncan said at once, reading such agony and conflict in his friend's face that he was compelled to take the decision from him. 'Just go. We'll take care of Katelin.'

For a few seconds the two friends just stared at each other, and Dan imagined the blessed, irresponsible relief of simply walking away, then he said, 'No, I need to try and deal with this,' and he went back into the kitchen, where Katelin lunged at him, bringing her fists down on to his shoulders and chest, raining curses upon him, crying with a ghastly, broken abandon.

'Oh my God, Katelin, please,' Dan said. 'Katelin, please.' He caught hold of her hands and held them tight and still between his. 'Please, come on, can you listen to me, can you?' They were standing on shards of broken porcelain, and scattered roast potatoes, and gruesome pools of bloody juice from the beef, although the remains of the rib itself had been purloined by McCulloch, who was hunched over it in his basket, uncertain if this was legal. Katelin was quieter now, but there was no sense of a crisis passing, only of the briefest pause in violent hostilities. The atmosphere in the room was thick with mistrust and reproach and the terrible, weighty sense of an ending. Rose-Ann had one ineffectual hand in the middle of Katelin's back and Duncan was trying to make no noise at all while moving glasses and plates from the table to the sink, in case she should reach for another missile. Dan released her fists and took her face between his hands, and they stared at each other with a kind of appalled grief. She knew him so well, knew the meaning of every expression she'd ever seen on his beloved, hated face, and she knew now from his eyes exactly what he was about to say.

'Don't speak,' she said. 'Don't apologise. Just go.'

Rose-Ann and Duncan drew back a little, watching and waiting, uncomfortable spectators at a disastrous feast.

'Katelin.'

'Go. I'm sick of not trusting you anyway.'

'I have to do this, and I don't know where it's leading, but first I want to try and explain why.'

'I don't care why, just go, fuck off, go on, go.'

Tears streamed down her face, this woman he'd loved, this woman who'd loved him, and he wanted to tell her that he wouldn't change anything, that she was marvellous and magnificent and he was privileged to have shared his life with her, but that still, he had to go. He had to, *had to*, as if he'd been chipped and programmed, back there in Sheffield in 1979, to be with Alison Connor at any cost, if their paths crossed again, if he found her. It wasn't fate or destiny, it was animal instinct, a primal imperative, as powerful and mysterious as the certainty that gives a swallow the strength for all those weeks on the wing, and leads it home. He didn't speak, though. He hung his head for a moment, collecting himself, and then he picked up his jacket, his keys, his wallet, and he left the house. He was already on the street when he heard Duncan's voice, calling him to hang on, so he waited, and his friend appeared with McCulloch on a lead.

'She says you're to take the dog,' Duncan said.

'Christ Almighty, Dunc, I'm not fit to be in charge of him.'

'Still, though. She says you're to take the dog. "Tell him to take the fucking dog, I'm not keeping it," is what she said, actually. So.' He held out the lead, and Dan took it.

'Right,' he said. McCulloch sniffed the afternoon air and waited for instructions.

'You OK, pal?' Duncan asked.

'Not even slightly.'

'Ring me, y'know, whenever.'

'Thanks, mate. And keep an eye on Katelin, won't you?'

'You bet.'

'Thanks, Duncan. I mean, really, thank you.'

'No worries. Oh.' He plunged a hand into his pocket. 'I brought you these too. They were on the hall table.'

Earphones, oh God, he'd almost left without his earphones.

'You're a lifesaver, buddy, seriously,' Dan said. 'Look, I really should . . .' He indicated the vague direction of Waverley Station with his free hand. He needed to get cracking, and he also needed a cab if he was going to make the three twenty to King's Cross.

'Go, yeah, course, go,' Duncan said, but he still hung about, reluctant to go back into the house, knowing that at best he'd be a spare part in there, and at worst a hapless scapegoat for Katelin's wrath.

Dan was scanning the street without any real hope, but

there, cresting the summit of the sloping road and heading towards them, was the miraculous yellow light of an available cab, so he flagged it down and picked up the dog.

'He looks happy enough, anyway,' Duncan said, nodding at McCulloch. 'So that's something.'

Dan gave a small laugh and climbed into the car, slamming shut the door and saluting Duncan through the window as they drove away. But later, on the train, he thought yeah, actually, yeah. He was only an elderly, arthritic Jack Russell, but there was something very welcome, even helpful, about McCulloch's steady devotion, and his placid acceptance of each new change in circumstances. The little dog's needs were few, and so easily met, thought Dan; we should all be so lucky.

29

Dan and McCulloch walked into the Warwick Castle at ten past eight and there was Alison Connor, sitting at the bar like a mirage.

'Hey,' she said, as if it'd been only yesterday, as if neither of them had crawled over emotional burning coals to get to each other.

'Hey.' He stood for a while and drank her in, so perfectly at home on that bar stool, yet fundamentally out of context. The disconnect between these two facts made him slow to react, as in a dream, when you want to reach out for what you know you need, but your arms are heavy and won't obey the signals from your brain. He stared at her, and didn't move or speak, and she watched him a little uncertainly, then hopped off the stool and hunkered down to scratch the little dog behind his ear. 'So you're McCulloch?' she said. He shuffled closer to her and closed his eyes and gave a small shiver of bliss.

Dan gave a soft laugh, and all the terrible weight of the day eased by a few small degrees. She stood up and moved towards him, then cradled the back of his neck with one hand while she kissed him with gentle care.

'Alison,' he said now, and he was closer to tears than he'd

been all day, way, way closer, keenly moved by her tenderness. He'd believed he would never see her again, he'd begun the process of hardening his heart against her, he'd tried to think her faithless, weak, insincere. But now the sight of her slayed him all over again, and he felt a jolt of fear, because although he might have underestimated her resolve, how was he ever to trust that she would stay? He stepped back, and she let her arms fall to her side.

'Daniel,' she said. 'Please forgive me.'

He'd forgive this woman anything, he thought. That was the problem.

'I was wrong to leave with Michael that day, I was wrong to let him talk to you that way, and wrong to leave with him. I should've listened to my heart and stood by your side. I'm sorry, Daniel. And I'm here now, if you still want me.'

There was a pause, and all she seemed to be able to hear in the crowded bar was her own heartbeat.

'You used Jim's phone,' he said, at last.

'I lost mine,' she said. 'I think it got stolen on the way over.'

'Oh,' he said. 'I sent you a song. Two songs in fact, but the first was an accident, too cheerful by half, so then I sent you another, just this morning, so you'd know for sure that I was certifiably insane.'

'Oh! God, Daniel, sorry, I'm so sorry,' she said, the words tumbling out of her mouth. 'I did get Donovan, but I was with Stella in Lisbon, and I'd have replied, I would, I knew what I wanted to send, but then—'

He placed a hand on her shoulder. 'Hush,' he said. 'Hush. Never mind.'

'Oh, but I'm sorry, Daniel. I'm sorry about so many things, and one of them is not replying at once to "Sunshine Superman".'

His face remained impassive, unsure, but she gave him a

tentative smile, and it tugged at his heart. Seeing her standing there before him with all that anxious love in her eyes – it was golden balm for his soul. He loved her so much. He loved her so much she might never truly know the length, breadth, and depth of his feelings.

'What were you going to send?' he asked.

'The Cure,' she said at once. ' "Lovesong".'

He nodded. 'Whenever I'm alone with you . . .'

'. . . you make me feel like I am home again.'

Now they both smiled. Then she put her head on one side and said, 'Certifiably insane?'

'Psychotic,' he said. 'I never expected to see you again, so you got – or you *didn't* get – "I Want You". Unequivocally deranged.'

'Ah,' she said. 'Yeah, God, *that* song.'

'You put me through hell,' he said. 'You know that, don't you?'

'I do know, I do, but never again. I love you now, and I loved you then, and, if you'll allow me to, I'll love you for ever.' She spoke simply, matter-of-factly stating her case, and Dan couldn't speak, he didn't know why – and yet he did know why.

'I want you,' she said. 'My Sheffield boy.'

She was so much more on top of this situation than he was. She looked at him, mute and helpless before her. 'Let's just go to the boat,' she said.

The thing about *Crazy Diamond* was, you stepped on board and left the real world behind. Perhaps it was being afloat, or being cocooned, or the gauzy, filtered quality of the light inside the cabin. So it was hard to leave it, even knowing – joyous thought – that she could and would come back, but it was Monday morning now, and Dan needed to be in Salford by Thursday, and before then, they had to get to Sheffield.

Sheffield. It squatted in her memory like a toad, one of those

Grimm brothers' toads, the warty, malevolent kind, embodying evil. Dan said she'd only have to step off the train at the city-centre station to realise that the place itself was innocent of all charges, especially as she wouldn't recognise it – he could barely navigate those streets himself since the council started beautifying the place. He kept his tone light, but that didn't mean he didn't understand what an ordeal this was for her, catching up with the ghosts of her past. But look, they were together, she'd come to him of her own free will, and he couldn't help being happy, even if this trip north was, for her, a bit like crossing the Styx to the Underworld. Speaking for himself, he felt renewed, rinsed clean of doubt and bitterness and regret, and shagged out, too, in all honesty: a winning combination of her jet lag and his perpetual ardour had kept them awake most of the night, until they both plunged into spectacular unconsciousness at 5 a.m., when daylight was already seeping through the cracks in the curtains. McCulloch woke them three hours later, demanding – not unreasonably – to be let out, and they'd dragged themselves bodily from the sinking sands of sleep to deal with the dog and make plans. Lisa appeared, a ministering angel bearing a Spanish omelette, and they ate it straight from the little black frying pan she'd cooked it in while she sat with them at the towpath table and smoked her French cigarette. Jim joined them too, proud of the role he'd played in their story, keen to retell it whenever he had the chance, but Ali was mostly under the spell of the hippies, warmed by Lisa's loopy brand of love and entertained by Frank's amiable wickedness. Lisa was possessed of a total lack of curiosity about the practical detail of other people's lives, interested only in the wider picture, the rainbow colours of their souls, the generosity of their hearts. Frank, slowing ever closer to the final halt, generally remained in the shadows of *Ophelia*'s cabin, although yesterday, while

Alison had waited for Daniel, Frank had been briefly reinvigorated by the novelty of her arrival, and had told her a long story about the Beatles at the ashram in Rishikesh, and how one incredible day there'd been John and Paul, Ringo and George, Lisa and Frank, all of them cross-legged on the same flat, hot bungalow roof, practising meditation while being scrutinised by little, grey, sceptical monkeys. Best day of his long life, Frank said, then he'd drifted off to sleep again, worn out by his memories, and Lisa and Alison had talked about, oh, a jumble of subjects, Moroccan spices, stars in the southern hemisphere, the power of music to change the course of a life. Lisa's mind flitted from one big subject to another like a hummingbird at a fuchsia bush, dipping now here, now there, and rarely still. Alison knew this was otherwise known as a lack of concentration, doubtless the legacy of a life on weed, but it was very freeing to listen to her new-age take on life, and comforting too, not least because she'd wrapped Alison in a smoky quilt and given her chai and a bowl of chana dal, because she was frozen, a hothouse flower from Adelaide for whom this so-called summer in London felt no warmer than an early spring dawn in South Australia. By the time Dan hit the scene in Little Venice, Alison and Lisa were forever connected and when they left after breakfast on Monday for the train to Sheffield, Lisa kissed her on her forehead and slipped an engraved silver bangle off her own wrist and on to Ali's, to keep her safe until she returned. Ali liked this, a talisman was exactly what she needed; that, and the warm body of McCulloch sleeping on her feet, and the level gaze and steady confidence of Dan on the opposite side of the table from her on the northbound train.

Dan's phone lay on the table between them. It rang repeatedly, and each time he answered she put on her headphones and listened to music to give him privacy, although she saw the name of each caller bloom on to the screen before he picked it up from the table. Katelin. Katelin. Alex. Katelin. Katelin. Duncan. Katelin. Katelin. Katelin. Not once did he switch it off, and not once did she ask him to. 'Your life's in free fall,' she said at one point, aching with concern. 'I'm so sorry.'

He leaned across and took hold of her hand. 'I love you,' he said, and she said, 'I love you too,' and Dan nodded. 'Then there's nothing I can't deal with,' he said.

So, at last, the fact had to be faced that she was in Sheffield and Dan was right, up to a point: the landscape of the city wasn't familiar at all; but the voices were, those accents that were now all around her, the raw, flat, laconic speech patterns of the northern working classes, her people, hard-working, hard-up, hard-faced, and there was something about them she'd missed, she realised now, and they swept her relentlessly back and back over the past three decades far more effectively than the architecture ever could have done. Dan kept her close, shepherding her through the station concourse, but in fact she felt OK so far, she felt fine, with Dan on one side of her, McCulloch on the other, the sturdy little terrier a surprising and enchanting ally. When he looked up at her, his dark eyes seemed full of intelligent feeling, enough to fill a little space in her heart, although she admitted she was probably reading too much into things; he was more than likely just hungry.

'I always wanted a dog,' she said. She held his lead and he trotted just slightly ahead, as if he was guiding her along the busy pavement. 'As a kid, I mean. I always wanted a collie like Lassie.'

'I wanted a kangaroo like Skippy,' Dan said. 'My mum wouldn't get me one.'

He'd rented a car, thinking cabs and buses might let them down if they needed to make a quick getaway. Also, he'd called Marion, told her to sit down and listen. 'I'm in Sheffield, Mum, with Alison Connor – yes, Alison Connor – and can we come and say hello? No, Katelin's in Edinburgh. No, it's complicated. I'll try and explain later. No, Mum, I told you that, Katelin *isn't* here, Alison is though, so we'll call in, OK? And don't worry, OK?'

Listening to his side of this conversation, Ali's spirits began to sink and she thought, Oh, this is unfeasible, this isn't fair on anyone other than we two, and when he hung up she blurted out her concern and said, 'Daniel, how can we ever be happy when we make so many other people sad?'

'Mum's not sad, she's just a bit perplexed.'

'Well, she doesn't know what there is to be sad about yet. I bet Katelin's sad, isn't she?'

'Katelin's sodding furious, she's already packed half my clothes into bin bags and given them to the British Heart Foundation. Duncan's trying to save my records, but he'll have to look sharp if he's going to save them from being car-booted.'

Ali started to laugh, hard not to, and Dan smiled and said, 'Look, it might get worse before it gets better, but we'll power through, me and you. Does this vehicle have Bluetooth?' He prodded the buttons on the sound system. 'Hallelujah, yes it does, and I'm about to fulfil my teenage fantasy of driving Alison Connor through our city listening to *Reproduction*.'

'Ah, the Human League,' Ali said; then at precisely the same time they both said, 'Before the girls joined,' and laughed.

'Badge of honour, seeing them in nineteen seventy-eight,' she said. 'Private club for the cognoscenti.'

'Kev Carter still tries to lay claim to these guys, because he accidentally saw them at their first gig.'

'Kev Carter, oh my God. This is so crazy.'

'Crazy bad or crazy good?'

'Crazy both. Do you still see him?'

'No, not for years, but we could. He'd love to check you out, I bet.' He glanced sideways at her. 'Not sure I want to let him, mind you.'

She shook her head, rolled her eyes at him, then gazed out of the window at twenty-first-century Sheffield, trying to get her bearings, and then the music came on and it was February 1979 again as the car filled with the tick-tock, synthy start of 'Almost Medieval' and she raised her arms in a kind of ironic reverence and said, 'Marsh, Ware, Oakey, we salute you.'

'And that,' said Dan, whacking up the volume, 'is why you've always been my girl.'

She said, 'Let's bite the bullet and go to Attercliffe,' but of course the street she'd lived in was long gone, demolished years ago, and Brown Bayley's was gone too; nothing looked the same, and none of this bothered her at all, she couldn't mourn the loss of the places where she'd been unhappiest. Still, she thought, putting aside her own feelings, the old neighbourhood had certainly lost a bit of northern heart and soul with the demolition works. Granted, if you grew up with an outside lav and a tin bath, you probably wouldn't have given two hoots for the historical integrity of nineteenth-century back-to-backs, and nobody saw the industrial chic in a Victorian warehouse in the 1970s. But it was all so very changed, an impoverished landscape, somehow, without the sooty brick and corrugated metal of the old terraced houses and the mighty steelworks. On Attercliffe Road, where they parked to talk strategy, massage parlours seemed to be the boom industry: gaudy, seedy, unapologetic.

'Well,' Ali said, surveying the view.

'Yes, indeed,' Dan replied. 'I think sex might be the new steel.'

'If these places had been here in Catherine's heyday . . .'

He'd never known her mother, so he didn't comment, didn't know how to.

'She'd have sex with a bloke for a glass of port and lemon, Catherine would. Sold herself very cheap.'

'Did you always call her Catherine?'

She shrugged. 'I think so. I guess as an infant I might've done the "mummy" thing, but she didn't really put the mothering hours in, so it never stuck, and I think calling her Catherine kind of helped me and Peter to cope. Like, distancing ourselves from her – less disappointing, y'know? It might be called denial now, I suppose. It wasn't her fault, she was an addict, and she'd been abandoned, she got no help from anyone.' She stopped and looked at him. 'You must find this all very dysfunctional?'

'No, no, only very sad.'

She sighed and stared out of the window, lost in her own thoughts. Then she said, 'It's been so wrong, for such a long time.'

'What has?'

'My silence, staying away, my neglect of Peter especially. I mean, it made sense at first, I understood my motives perfectly, but after Thea and Stella were born, that's when I should've come back, made reparations.'

'Alison, you were the victim, not the culprit.'

'I owed my brother such a lot, Daniel. And I left him.'

'You did what he wanted you to do – he packed you off, effectively.'

She gave a fractional shake of her head, refusing to shed the blame. 'The onus was on me to come back, because how could he ever find me? But the longer I was away, the harder it was to go back.' Then she sighed bleakly and looked out of the window again. Without turning to Dan, she said, 'How on earth are we going to find him?' and it was almost as though she was speaking to herself.

Dan had in fact already begun the process, not that she knew this. She'd slept for half an hour on the train, and he'd quickly trawled through the social media sites, knowing this obvious tech-strategy probably wouldn't have crossed Alison's mind, it wasn't her style, and now she'd lost her phone, but he'd saved her the trouble anyway, because unless Peter had changed his name, he wasn't online.

'Well, we can ask around,' he said now. 'Try in the pubs maybe – some old-timer might know where he is. I bet this is still a pretty tight community, and it's not that big really.'

'It hardly seems possible he'd still be in Attercliffe.'

'Why not? My parents are right where I left them. Folk don't move far from round here, as a rule, even when their homes are knocked down.'

There was truth in this, and she acknowledged it with a nod, and said, 'OK, let's go walkabout,' and got out of the car. McCulloch nipped out after her from his chosen place in the footwell, and she clipped on his lead and rubbed his head.

'He suits you, that dog,' Dan said, joining them. 'Right, where shall we start? Pubs?'

'Well, he was never a big drinker,' she said.

'What about that Toddy bloke?'

'His street's gone, same as mine.'

'Well, look,' he said. 'Let's just ask around. There's a pub over the road, it's a start. Wait here.'

He jogged across and she watched him go into an establishment that you'd swear was closed for business if it wasn't for the 'We are open' sign in a mucky downstairs window. Who'd be in there at midday on a crisp, bright Monday? She imagined a miraculous scenario where Dan emerged, followed by Peter, who in her imagination was unaltered, unaged, and whose face would break into shining happiness at seeing her there, waiting for him. But Dan came out and grimaced, and she smiled ruefully, and waited until he was closer before she said, 'Were you not tempted to linger for a pint, then?'

'The landlady looks like an all-in wrestler, and she didn't like the look of me either, I could tell.'

'No joy then.'

'None whatsoever. Two old fellas propping up the bar but no vital signs that I could identify, and bloody Captain and Tennille warbling out of the speakers. Jesus.'

She laughed, and he dipped his head and stole a kiss and saw in her face a kind of glow, an unmistakable golden warmth, and he thought, Well, look at that, isn't this something?

He held her by the shoulders and said, 'Ever since the day I met you, baby, I'll believe I had a hold on you,' and she said, 'Is that a test?'

He smiled and said, 'Might be,' and she said, 'Dr Feelgood, "Because You're Mine". You'll never fox me with lyrics, Daniel Lawrence, I'm weird like that.'

'My favourite kind of weird,' Dan said, and he lifted her chin and kissed her again. 'My all-time favourite weirdo. So, c'mon, let's go find Peter Connor.'

They asked in another pub, then a pharmacy, a tattoo studio, a barber's, a shop selling exotic pets – he might keep snakes, Dan said – the post office, a couple of Indian restaurants, an off-licence and a newsagent's. People were kind, but Peter Connor meant nothing to them. In the old John Banners building they asked at a little café, and their question was passed from one person to another until someone looked up from a steaming meat pie and said, 'Go to Mr Rashid's. Everybody round here goes there,' so away they went, following directions to an Aladdin's cave of household merchandise, where the owner, a venerable Pakistani man with a proud and handsome face, couldn't place the name, but threw himself into their task with surprising energy, blowing the dust off a phone book and making them ring every P. Connor in there from his own landline.

'Facebook? Twitter? Instagram?' he said when the old-fashioned method drew a long string of blanks. 'This is where lost people can be found this day and age.' He had a white, one-hundred-watt smile, and his willingness to help was heroic.

'Tried all those,' Dan said, and Ali looked at him, puzzled, and said, 'Have we? I haven't.'

'Nothing doing?' said Mr Rashid to Dan. 'Then let's put on our thinking caps,' and immediately went on to tell them about his granddaughter and grandson, twins, both studying medicine at Manchester University, clever, clever children, working hard to honour their family. His wife had joined them now, but she stayed in the shadows and didn't speak, only watched.

'My wife is scared of your dog,' Mr Rashid said, and they all looked at McCulloch, who yawned. 'Forty years in Sheffield, and Raiqa is still homesick for Islamabad,' he added. Ali smiled at Raiqa, but the woman only dipped her head modestly in return.

'So shy,' Mr Rashid said. 'And she doesn't speak English, never bothered to learn.' He shook his head as if gravely disappointed, although he clearly relished speaking for them both, and at nineteen to the dozen. They lived above the premises, he told them, and still sent half their income back to Pakistan, where a worrying number of relatives were depending upon it, and if he could go back himself, he would, just for a holiday mind you, because this was home, Attercliffe was home.

Dan, aware of the march of time, said with some finality, 'Well, thanks for everything, Mr Rashid,' and they started to move towards the door, saying their goodbyes, but then an eld-erly man came into the shop, blocking their exit. He was wheezing and thumping his chest, but managed an 'Ey up' to Mr Rashid, who said, 'Ah, right, now this is Mr Higgins, and he knows everybody, don't you, Mr Higgins?'

'Postman,' Mr Higgins said economically, preserving his rationed breath. 'Retired.'

'And a local councillor,' Mr Rashid said, as if this was a matter of personal pride. 'Very esteemed.'

'Aye, well.' Mr Higgins accepted the compliment with a grim smile. 'Darnall ward, for my sins.'

'We're looking for my brother,' Ali said to him, more from politeness than any real hope. 'Peter Connor. He used to work at Brown Bayley's, but that's probably no help.'

'Long gone, that,' Mr Higgins said. 'There's no steelworks here any more.'

'No, we know that. Well, thanks anyway,' Dan said, and he held open the door so Ali and the dog could beat a retreat, but Mr Higgins wasn't finished.

'There's a Pete Connor runs a chippy not far off, over Tins-ley way.' He paused and took a shallow gulp of air. 'Big fat lad wi' a lazy eye, tha can never tell if he's serving thee or t'next bugger.'

Ali said, 'Peter wasn't fat, although I suppose he might be now, but he didn't have a lazy eye.' She wouldn't look at Dan; she didn't want to laugh. She edged towards the open door. Mr Higgins breathed, preparing to speak again.

'And there's a Peter Connor, not Pete, he's always Peter, up at Northern General,' he said. 'Up at hospital, tha knows?'

'No,' Ali said. 'I don't think so. He wasn't a medical man.'

'Porter. Hospital porter.' He thumped his chest again furi-ously, frustrated by the inadequacy of his lungs.

Mr Rashid leaned across his counter to join the conversation without leaving his station. 'Asthma clinic, you see,' he said. 'Respiratory problems. Mr Higgins is a regular,' and Mr Higgins, ready to speak again, said, 'Peter Connor's pushed me on them gurneys more'n once, when I've not been able to breathe enough to walk. Grand lad. No sister though.'

'Oh,' Ali said, her first slim hope dashed. A hospital porter – she could see that; it made sense. Peter's loving, giving, caring nature. His lack of qualifications. His humility.

'Well,' said Dan. 'How do you know he doesn't have a sister?'

'He hasn't got anybody,' Mr Higgins replied. 'He told me he's on his own.'

Ali and Dan exchanged a look. Her heart began to beat a little faster, and she told herself to be calm, be realistic. 'Where does he live?' she asked.

'I can't tell you that.'

'Oh, please, why not?' Ali asked, a little desperate, and too long absent from Sheffield to understand his meaning.

'Because I don't know, lass. I've never asked.'

His chest rose painfully with each laboured breath, and Mr Rashid's quiet wife brought out a chair and offered it, tentatively, giving McCulloch a very wide berth. Mr Higgins dropped heavily on to the seat. 'Thank you, love,' he said. 'I'm right out of puff.' Ali gave him a regretful backward glance as they left. She felt somehow responsible for his discomfort.

'Just suppose he's here?' Ali said.

They were in the unforgiving glare of the hospital's reception area, waiting for a member of staff to find time for their trivial enquiry. Disinfectant masking sickness: the smell of hospitals was the same the world over, she thought, and this made her think of Michael. She shivered imperceptibly, and reached for Dan's hand, and he took hold of hers and squeezed it.

'If Peter's here,' he said, 'then we'll be forever grateful that poor old Mr Higgins has asthma that's bad enough to need hospital treatment.'

He caught the eye of the woman Ali had spoken to when they first arrived. She'd been answering the phone and signing forms and giving directions to patients and visitors, whose labyrinthine course through this vast building was just another ordeal on top of whatever it was that had brought them here in the first place. Now, she looked at Dan and remembered she'd forgotten all about them. She made no apology, however, just said, 'Now then, who was it you were after?'

'Peter Connor,' Ali said. 'He's a porter here, and I just wondered . . .'

'Hang on, love, I'll check.'

She picked up the phone and dialled an internal number. Ali felt her heart going at it again, extraordinary how it pounded, just because this kind stranger was asking a colleague if Peter Connor was on the rota today. In all honesty, at this moment Ali didn't know what outcome she wished for.

'Right you are, Angie. Thanks, love.' She looked at Ali. 'Night shift,' she said. 'Eight while eight.'

'Right,' Ali said, thinking. Dan waited. She looked at him. 'I don't even know if it's him,' she said; then, to the receptionist, 'I don't suppose you have a photo of him I could look at? Or can you tell me his date of birth?'

'No, love, I don't, and I can't,' she said. One of the phones was ringing again, and it was evident she needed to get on. 'You can leave a note if you want, to say you called?'

And this seemed a decent idea. A note saying are you *my* Peter Connor, in which case, I'm your Alison. If it wasn't him, no harm done. If it was, he'd have some warning, time to prepare – or to flee, because that might happen too. But, yes, it would be sensible to give him this breathing space so he wouldn't be floored by the sight of her, unannounced, in his place of work. She took a notepad and pen from her bag, and wrote:

> Dear Peter, forgive the intrusion out of the blue, but my name is Alison Connor and I left Attercliffe in 1979, and now I'm back, looking for my brother, whom I hope – and believe – might be you. I'll be back here, at A & E, by eight o'clock tomorrow morning, when you finish your night shift.

'We could come back this evening, for eight?' Dan said, but she shook her head.

'I'm dead beat, and that's the start of his shift, better to catch him the other end.'

If it was him.

And it might be him.

Let it be him.

She added 'Alison x' to her note, then folded it and wrote 'For Peter Connor' on the blank side. 'Thank you,' she said, to the woman, who placed a finger on the note and slid it towards herself without really looking at Ali, just glancing up and vaguely nodding. She was in conversation again now on the telephone, and Ali saw her note go on to a moderate pile of paperwork, where soon it would doubtless be joined by more. The chance of that slip of paper making it to Peter Connor tonight seemed even slimmer than the chance of him being *the* Peter Connor, her brother, the Peter she knew now that she longed for him to be.

30

So that Dan had some privacy with Marion and Bill, Ali insisted he drop her and McCulloch at a café in Nether Edge, just a short walk from his house. She'd give him half an hour or so to explain their situation, then she'd walk round with the dog and knock on the door. Dan hadn't wanted to agree to this, he wanted her by his side when he went in, but Ali said, 'No, you owe them an explanation without me standing there, the homewrecker.' He wasn't having that, he said; he'd take full responsibility for his own wrecked home, but could he be sure she'd turn up, and not bolt?

'Bolt where?' Ali asked. 'I've already bolted here, there's nowhere else for me to run. Just go,' so he did, and he knew her instinct had been right when he let himself into number forty-two with the key he'd always kept, and Marion had run at him, stricken, saying, 'Daniel, how could you? How could you?' because Katelin had been on the phone, blowing their minds with his treachery. Blowing Marion's mind, anyway – not much reached Bill these days.

Dan didn't go into the emotions of the case, only the hard facts, and he could see from his mother's face, her searching eyes, that she wanted to be reassured, she wanted to know he knew what he was doing. She had always, always, taken her children's side in adversity, and she wanted to now. She'd been the sort of mother who would march along to school and demand to know from the headmaster why Joe had been caned, or why Claire was left out of the hockey team, or why Dan – the youngest, the pet – didn't have a speaking part in the Christmas play. Embarrassing, but they'd known as they grew up that they'd never be alone in their corner, there'd always be Marion, believing they were champions, watching their backs. But this: this was a lot for her to take in, and it carried with it the tinge of disgrace. Already she was imagining saying to her friends the dread words that, oh dear, yes, Daniel and Katelin had separated. Even as she listened to her son, she was dimly aware of – and, now, sorry for – the complacency she'd felt over the passing years when she'd heard similar tales from others in her circle, the underlying smug satisfaction that yes, life together was a challenge, but her own offspring understood loyalty and decency. Well, Joe never married. But Claire and Daniel had made their choices, and hadn't they seen her stick with Bill despite everything? You don't just bin somebody, do you? But now, Daniel had binned Katelin, and Marion didn't know what to think. Granted, she was a prickly girl, so easy to offend, so difficult to please, and why she wouldn't ever marry Daniel, Marion had no earthly clue. But it *had* been a marriage, in the end, hadn't it? As good as, anyway, in all but name. And it was going to be very difficult for Marion to condone and support her dear boy, now that he'd walked away from Katelin, for Alison Connor, of all people. She wondered, had *she* started all this herself, by buying that book for Katelin last Christmas? Oh, how she shuddered and recoiled from this idea. She certainly hadn't meant any harm, and if she'd known who the author was, she'd have put it straight down. Trouble with a capital T, that girl, the upset she'd caused! Daniel sad for months and months, dropping out of university, taking up with any girl who gave him the eye, travelling around after his blessed pop groups like a lost soul. These wounds, inflicted by Alison, ran deep and everlasting in the tender centre of Marion's being. She'd never forgotten, and rarely forgiven, a single slight against any of her children, even the playground spats, so she'd certainly never forgiven Alison Connor. Certainly not.

But, look now, here she was, knocking on the front door, coming into the house with Daniel's dog on a lead, and there was something about this incidental detail – Alison's easy, familiar stewardship of the little terrier – that struck Marion as comfortably intimate, as if everything was now settled between them. She was surprised. She'd expected blushes and awkwardness and averted gazes. But then Alison Connor had been only seventeen last time she laid eyes on her . . . only seventeen, and in considerable distress. She remembered watching her run away down their road. She remembered thinking maybe it'd be for the best if Alison never came back, and then she *hadn't* come back, but it hadn't been for the best, not really; not for Daniel.

'Hello,' Ali said, and gave her such a lovely, full, ingenuous smile that Marion found herself immediately faltering in her resolutions. Ali stepped forward and gave Marion a hug, which she returned, a little hesitantly. 'I'm determined to call you Marion,' Ali said, 'even though I really feel you'll be Mrs Lawrence for ever and a day.'

Australian accent. Slim as a girl. Dark brown hair, brown eyes, pale face, pretty – oh, very pretty. She always was.

'Well, Alison, you've not altered much,' Marion said, stepping back and giving her a full appraisal. 'I can't say this isn't a shock, love, you turning up here, but it's nice to see you. It's like going back in time, looking at you!'

'It's really nice to see you too.' Ali wasn't going to apologise, for either the past or the present. She was here, and that was that. 'Is Mr Lawrence here?' she said, and then she laughed. 'I can't call him Bill, I just can't.'

'Dad's gone upstairs,' Dan said. He tried to communicate with only his eyes that he was *so fucking proud* of her, of everything about her, the way she was, the way she'd handled that arrival, the way she looked. Christ, even the dog was besotted. McCulloch had never had much time for women, but he was all Alison's now.

'May I go up and see him?'

Marion and Dan exchanged a look. He'd been shocked himself at how reduced his dad was, how much he'd deteriorated since he last saw him, which – to his shame – had been last Christmas.

'Sure,' he said now. 'But he's . . . well, he's sort of retreated right into himself. It's hard to know what he's thinking any more.'

'No, I know, but I'd really like to go and sit with him, if that's OK?'

'Of course, love,' Marion said. 'He's in our bedroom. He likes to sit looking out of the window. I'll bring some tea up, when it's mashed.' Anyway, she thought, she'd value a few minutes more on her own with Daniel. She was full of questions she didn't want to ask in front of Alison.

Sometimes, if he waited long enough in front of the glass, pigeons would land on the sill outside and look in at him with black diamond eyes. None of these birds were his. There were house martins too; they'd made a mud nest in the eaves, but they'd be gone soon, off on their travels, and anyway they were never still, and not bold enough to study him like the pigeons did. He saw other things as well, although, oddly, his eyes seemed only able to see what was very close or very distant; the middle ground was grey matter, as if a permanent blanket of low-lying fog had settled on the street. Marion said he couldn't be long- *and* short-sighted, but all he knew was what he saw. Birds at the window, and other things, very far away, such as the weather changing in the sky, way over north-west; he knew what was coming and when it would come, and if Marion said, 'Oh blast, it's raining on my washing,' he always thought, I could've told you that would happen, though he never said it out loud. You could fall out of the habit of speaking, he'd found, and if you did, you had a job to start again. Marion chirruped like a noisy budgie, saying everything, anything. He wanted to say hush, just hush.

So, Daniel was here; that was nice. Marion had somebody to talk to now, other than Claire. Joe didn't come. He hadn't seen Joe since, oh, since all them months in hospital, when nobody knew what was up. Joe came then, sat by his bed, watched him breathe, then after that he stayed away; maybe he saw too much of himself in the silent, sad old man in the hospital bed. Joe liked his own company; he wasn't a family man. Lived in the mountains, in France, a long way from where he started.

There was a low knock on the bedroom door. Bill ignored it, and a woman's voice, unknown to him, said, 'Mr Lawrence, it's Alison.'

He said nothing, because it was always easiest, but she came in anyway; he heard her approach. A nurse, perhaps? Or another one of those cheerful women from the day centre, with an invitation to sit and say nothing there, rather than sit and say nothing here.

A hand on his shoulder, a soft kiss on his cheek, the lightest touch of her hair on his face like the feathers of a prize racer grazing his skin. He looked up and saw at once it was Alison Connor. He watched as she pulled Marion's chair from the dressing table and sat as close to him as she could be.

'I knew you'd come back,' he said, the words rolling like small pebbles off his tongue, heavy and a little misshapen. She lifted his hand and held it, and with her thumb she made small stroking movements, very tender, very loving.

'I'm sorry it took me so long,' she said.

'I knew you'd come back,' he said again, practising the words, the first he'd uttered for six months. The doctor called it selective mutism, but Bill – had he spoken – would've disagreed. It was simpler than that. He just never heard anything that justified the effort of a response. All his life, he'd enjoyed silence, and the less you said, the less you had to listen to. By now, it no longer felt natural to speak, but it felt very natural to sit beside Alison like this. He'd forgotten a lot of the detail of his life, but he remembered as if it were yesterday the first time she'd visited his loft and the first time she'd handled one of his birds without panicking, and, always, that respectful way of listening to him talk about the pigeons, with no mockery in her eyes, only concentration. A kind, quiet, genuine girl. He'd been waiting for her to come back for donkey's years.

'Like one of your homing pigeons,' she said. 'Like Clover.'

His failing eyes brimmed with ready tears, and she said, 'Oh, Mr Lawrence, forgive me, I didn't mean to upset you,' but he shook his head, and although he didn't manage to frame the words, she understood from his expression that he wasn't sad, he was only overcome. Alison talked to him then, in her new voice. She told him every single detail she remembered about his pigeon loft, everything she'd loved about those brave, clever, dignified birds, and all the things he'd taught her about them.

She named them, counting them off on her fingers, and she talked about Clover flying home six hundred miles from Lerwick, about Violet and Vincent, his breeding pair of Flash Pied Emperors, and what made them champions, how he'd known from the light in their eyes and the slope of their shoulders that they were going to be winners. Mr Lawrence tilted his head upwards, closed his eyes, and listened to her in a kind of bliss, the way some people lose themselves in music, or others lift their faces to the warm, repetitive balm of tropical rain.

When Marion came in with tea in her best china mugs, she was stilled and silenced by what she saw. She placed the tea on the nearest surface and walked soundlessly from the room. Outside, on the landing, she allowed herself the release of what she called a good cry, but she did so only for a short while, and very quietly, so as not to disturb the tryst, then she took off her shoes and trod lightly downstairs in her stockinged feet, pausing between steps like she used to do when her children were fractious babies, and mustn't be disturbed from their daytime naps.

'What've you told Alex?' Marion asked Dan.

'An edited version of the truth,' he said. 'Katelin'd already involved him anyway, months ago, when I first told her about Alison.'

She shook her head in a weary, defeated way that irritated him.

'Do you remember throwing Alison's letters away? The ones she sent from Paris?'

'When? I've not thrown away anything of yours!' But she coloured, giving herself away.

'Thirty years ago, I think you did.'

'Oh, thirty years,' Marion said dismissively.

'What? It doesn't count after thirty years?'

'You were only kids. I did what I thought was best.' She hadn't ever erased that memory, though, and there'd been something lasting and terrible about destroying those three unopened airmail letters, addressed to Daniel in Alison's tidy italics. 'You were very upset, Daniel, and I couldn't see how passing on her letters would've helped you.'

'It was wrong of you,' Dan said, and Marion said, 'It seems it now, but it didn't then.'

'Oh, well, anyway,' Dan said, relenting. 'I'm not here to give you a hard time, Mum.'

'I'm worried for you, though,' she said. 'All this hoo-ha, it's upsetting.'

'Try not to think too much about it. Trust me to sort out my own life.' He was making a lasagne, the sort of dish Marion liked to eat but never made. She watched him layering ragu, pasta, béchamel, and marvelled as she always did at a man who could cook, not that she'd ever given Bill a chance to. Not that he'd ever asked.

'How can I not think about it? My grandson's caught up in it all.'

'Alex is pretty mature, Mum, he's living his life, getting on with things, and I speak to him whenever he wants to speak to me. He's going to be fine.'

'Going to be?' Marion said. 'So he's not fine now?'

'Look, no kid ever wants anything to change,' he said. 'No kid ever wants to have to think about their parents' lives at all, let alone their sex lives.'

'Daniel!'

'Sorry, but it's true, right?'

'Well, I wouldn't know,' she said. 'But I never gave you three anything to worry about, I do know that.'

'You didn't.' He smiled at her, but she wasn't quite ready to smile back.

'It hasn't been easy being married to your dad.'

'I'm sure.'

'But I stayed, didn't I? I didn't have to, but I stayed.'

He slid the lasagne into the oven and shut the door quickly on the gust of escaping heat. 'Well, I hope you did that for yourself as well as for me and Claire and Joe?' he said. 'Because none of us would've asked you to be unhappy on our behalf.'

She wagged her head, non-committal, and said, 'I haven't been unhappy. I'm just saying don't assume I haven't been flattered by other offers.'

'God, Mum, I'd never assume that,' he said, grinning. 'But if you're talking about that randy old goat Wilf Barnes, I'd say you've had a lucky escape. He'd still be chasing you round the bedroom at ninety-five.'

She laughed at this, unable to help herself. 'No, you cheeky devil,' she said, flapping her hands at him. 'I do not mean Wilf Barnes.' She didn't know who she meant, really; there'd never been any feasible alternative to what she had, no one to tempt her from the straight and narrow. She just wanted Dan to know that she'd done her very best, for all of them.

'Well, look.' He folded his arms and looked at her with profound affection, and she waited to see what he had to say, full of faith, because he was Daniel, her precious youngest child, the gift she hadn't expected, the late blessing. 'I for one am deeply grateful you stayed with Dad, because I don't know what would've become of him if you hadn't. I do know what you're saying, Mum. I do understand, and I'm not walking away lightly, and I won't let Alex and Katelin down, any more than I already have. But you must be able to see yourself, already, that there's something one hundred per cent right about Alison? Can you not see that? How well she fits?'

Marion considered this for a while before answering. 'I can see that, yes,' she said. 'She's a lovely woman, and she has a way with your dad that nobody else does. But she's left somebody in Australia, I expect?'

'Her husband, Michael.'

'Children?'

'Two daughters, both adults.'

'Well then.'

'Well then, what?'

'Well then, I'm saying yes, I can see how lovely she is, but, Daniel, it doesn't mean I approve.'

'OK,' Dan said. 'Understood.'

Claire came around like a shot when Marion told her about their visitor, and her blithe, non-judgemental, slightly child-like interest in Alison was a relief at dinner, because although Bill looked a good deal happier, he still ate his lasagne as if he had a train to catch, and was as silent as he ever had been, while Marion was wrestling too much with worry to be entirely relaxed. Claire, though: she bounced into the house like Tigger, with indiscriminate scatter-gun enthusiasm and a kind of comfortable, pleasing inanity. Claire had gained a lot of padding over the years, but she was as carefully put together as ever, well groomed and fragrant, and had probably made an extra little effort before turning up tonight to reacquaint herself with Alison. Hair, make-up, nails: all glossy and immaculate. She wore a startling yellow tailored jacket that demanded comment, and when Ali admired it, Claire immediately took it off and said, 'Try it on, it's MaxMara, fifty per cent off at House of Fraser.' She wasn't fazed at all that here was her brother, without Katelin. It was as if all that mattered to her, all that counted, was the here and now. Alison Connor? Great!

'God's sake, Claire,' Dan said, 'you're three sizes bigger than her,' but Ali shot him a look and said, 'Go on then,' to Claire, and put the jacket on, and yes, it was far too big, but Claire couldn't care less, she just bunched in the excess fabric at the back and said, 'Suits you! Aren't you slim though! They've got small ones still, if you want one, they're always the ones left, all them eights and sixes, like the shoes, it's always tiny threes and fours that are left, but I'm a seven in shoes and a fourteen slash sixteen in clothes, and round here those big sizes go first, I have to be quick off the mark.'

This was all very hard to follow, but then off Claire went on another tangent, this time about her neighbour's new book club, and would Ali be in Sheffield long enough to go next month to their first meeting and talk about *Tell the Story, Sing the Song*?

'Claire,' Dan said, before Ali could answer, 'pipe down.'

'Oops, sorry,' she said, all smiles. 'Big gob, me, I do go on, but it's lovely to see you, Alison, I suppose I'm just over-excited, it's a big event, you turning up, famous author, y'know.' Daniel caught her eye. 'Sorry,' she said again, and she applied herself to her lasagne, trying to look contrite.

'No, it's fine, Claire, honestly,' Ali said, 'and it's really lovely to see you too; I don't know how long I'll be here, but I'll come if I can,' and Claire said, 'I can't get over your Australian accent,' and then she blushed in case this sounded stupid, but Ali only laughed. She was remembering the pleasure Claire had given her the first time they'd met; how she'd painted Alison's nails the same shade of pink as her own, how she'd admired her hair, how open she'd been, and affectionate. Claire was entirely without guile, as lovable now as she'd been then. Daniel thought his sister was inexcusably daft, but Ali, miraculously back among the Lawrences, knew for certain that he didn't know how lucky he was to have a family such as this one; a family to get irritated with, to depend upon, to be loved by and to love. He took them for granted – *my parents are right where I left them* – but it was a lifetime's abundance of love that informed this casual complacency, the rock-solid security, the unshakable assumptions about the permanence of familial love and support.

Alison observed them at the table, comfortable in their habitat, and she knew that nothing would ever stop them loving each other, even this present upheaval, about which Marion really wasn't sure. Ali could see from her shifting eyes and uncertain smiles that she was troubled and wary, and fair enough, she was entitled to be, she had Daniel's happiness to worry about, and Alison's track record to date had been lamentable. Oh, to have a mother as vigilant and steadfast as Marion! Ali glanced at her, and saw the concern in her face, and the corresponding irritation in Daniel's, and she wanted to say, 'Be good to her, it's only that she loves you,' and at the same time she wondered if she could ever win Marion Lawrence's trust. She doubted there were enough years left to accomplish such a task, but what a worthy endeavour, what a prize it would be.

The Northern General at 7.45 a.m. was less busy than it'd been the previous afternoon, which was a blessing, because Ali needed to see every single face that emerged from the interior doors and corridors beyond the entrance where she stood, shivering slightly in the morning chill, trying to ignore her churning gut and pattering heartbeat. Seriously, she was almost bored by these symptoms of high anxiety. Marion, knowing what the morning held, had offered her a Valium first thing – a Valium and a cup of tea – and she wished now that she'd accepted it, because a mellow glow of unconcern would be a special kind of state. But she needed to be alert, couldn't risk befuddlement even if it brought with it a sort of comfort. As it was, she felt more than alert, hyper-alert, her senses lean and limber, straining towards their goal, although the truth was that she didn't even know if she'd know him, if this Peter Connor was her brother. She had no photographs of him, only memories, three decades old. But she hoped that if the man she was waiting for was *her* Peter, he might recognise his only sister – he had photographs, after all. He *had* had photographs, anyway; it was possible, Ali admitted to herself, that he had them no longer. But assuming it was him, and assuming he knew her on sight, then his instant look of recognition would reveal his identity to Ali, and she need never let him know that she'd forgotten his dear face, after far too long away. That is, if he hadn't already scarpered to avoid her, through a staff entrance at the back.

It was lonely, standing there waiting. She missed Daniel's courage, and his ease, but he'd dropped her off at the hospital gates and then left her to it, because this was between Alison and Peter. He was coming back at nine.

The big clock on the wall stared at her and took its time. Slowed down. Went backwards.

She scrutinised everyone, men and women alike. Some of them stared back with a challenge in their eyes, and she quickly looked away.

A loud burst of laughter took her by surprise, offended her almost. This seemed no place for hilarity.

Quarter past the hour.

A man ran past her holding a child, and the child was screaming and bleeding from the forehead, and their arrival created a small, contained tornado of efficient activity, sweeping them into privacy, calming the child, calming the father.

Twenty-five past eight, and he wasn't here, and Ali realised that she had no idea how long was too long to stand and wait.

This plan felt flimsy now, and ill-begotten. Too many variables.

Hope was a demon, but hopelessness was worse.

She thought about Peter, aged sixteen, on his first day at work, sent to the workshop by the foreman for a long stand, but it'd just been a trick, a laugh at the rookie's expense. They let him stand for an hour and then sent him packing, and when he told Alison later, she'd cried at the injustice, but he'd laughed and tweaked her ear, and told her to grow a thicker skin, because she'd need it.

There was a man, tall, round-shouldered, grey-haired. He was standing still, searching for someone and, with no real faith, Ali stepped forwards, raising her arm, but his eyes skimmed across her face to settle on another woman, waiting nearby on a plastic chair, flicking through a magazine. 'Maureen,' he said loudly, and the woman looked up, stood up and, without smiling, said, 'Quick, I've only got five minutes left on that ticket.' Ali watched them leave, then turned her face inwards again. Quarter to nine. She'd been here an hour now, and Peter wasn't coming, was he? Disappointment was the only thing keeping her there: a great weight of disappointment, too heavy to drag all the way outside. Five more minutes she waited, and then ten, fifteen, twenty, and at five past nine she decided that at quarter past she would leave, because Dan would already be back, parked somewhere along Herries Road, waiting for her.

She watched the hands of the clock, and at nine fifteen, she turned her back on all her dashed hope, and walked outside down the steps, and it was then that she heard Peter's voice calling her name, although it was more than a call, it was a bellow, a wild and feral roar, as if all of Sheffield needed to know he was looking for her. She turned and saw him before he saw her. He was standing just within the open doors, scanning the faces around and about him with frantic, disorganised haste, and it turned out she'd have known him anywhere, she could have picked him out of a crowd of thousands. She felt a great surge of emotion, a wave of wonder, and relief, and a kind of fear, which caught in her throat because when she tried to shout his name, nothing happened, no words would come. He looked desperately anxious; she could see him losing confidence, and she could hardly bear it, so she just ran at him, and he saw her then – everyone did; everyone turned to watch the woman run up the steps to the man, and they saw the man open his arms and wrap them around her, and lift her off her feet. Then they cried and laughed and clung to each other, so that the people watching them looked away, to give them a kind of privacy on this garishly public stage.

'Peter, I'm sorry, I'm so sorry,' was the first thing Alison said when she found her voice, and he held her face, and looked down at her.

'There's nowt to be sorry for,' he said, and his voice was breaking with joy. 'Nowt at all. *I'm* sorry, I couldn't get away, I thought you'd be gone.'

'I found you,' she said, amazed, incredulous.

'You found me. *Were* you going, just then?'

'Only for a little while. I was coming back. I would've come back every day, to find out if you were the right Peter Connor.'

'How did you . . . ?'

'Mr Higgins, one of your asthma clinic men.'

He nodded at this, unfazed by life's coincidences, and they stared at each other, smiling idiotically, and all the pressing questions they each still had to ask were crowding round them, unanswered. Later, later.

Ali thought: My brother, how I love him, but she didn't say this, because, well, this was Peter, and they didn't talk about love.

'I don't know why I didn't come sooner,' she said. 'I can't explain, but it just got harder and harder to do.'

'Ey, none o' that,' he said. 'You're here, that's what matters.'

'I'm so glad you didn't leave Sheffield.'

'Me? Where would I go?'

She laughed. 'Anywhere.'

'Not me. You've been a long way though, by the sound o' you. What's that accent?'

'Australian,' she said. 'Adelaide. They all think I have an English accent there. Hey, do you remember Sheila, the letters she used to write?'

He nodded. 'Parrots and snakes and kangaroos. Did you go looking for her, then? Did you find her?' No reproach, she thought. Not one hint of reproach.

'Yeah,' she said. 'I can take you to meet her one day, if you want.'

He shook his head. 'Not me,' he said again. 'Unless there's a bus.'

They laughed, and she leaned against his chest again, against the warm, solid reality of him, and he held her and considered all the new feelings that crowded his heart. A nurse, walking briskly towards them, stopped and looked at his damp, dishevelled face and said, 'All right, Peter? Who's this then?'

'My sister,' he said. 'Our Alison.'

'That's nice. I didn't know you had a sister.' She smiled at Ali and said, 'I'm Dawn, nice to meet you, love. Have you been away?'

'You could say that,' Ali said.

'Aye,' Peter said, and his face shone with unalloyed pleasure. 'But she's back now.'

'Right,' Dawn said. 'Smashing. I'll let you get on, then.' She clipped off into the hospital, and somehow her departure seemed a signal to them that they should probably move. When they turned to leave, Alison saw Daniel watching them, standing a respectful distance away, and smiling at her in that way he had that made her feel entirely beloved. They walked towards him, and Peter, who instantly knew who this was, sought no explanation. He'd already witnessed a miracle this morning; that Daniel Lawrence was waiting for them across the car park was almost mundane by comparison.

When Dan went to Salford for his Thursday morning radio gig, Alison and McCulloch stayed in Sheffield and spent the day with Peter, the dog lending some earthy normality to their heightened emotions, their journey into the past. Peter lived in a small flat in a low-rise block near the hospital, a place with an unremitting absence of charm, not helped by the state of disrepair he'd let it get into, and the festering towers of takeaway cartons heaped across the kitchen surfaces like a BritArt installation. He led a solitary life, he said, apart from work and his visits to Bramall Lane to watch every Blades home match he could get to. This was how he liked it. He liked his flat too, just as it was. He wouldn't let her clean it; he'd do it himself when it got just a little bit worse, he said. McCulloch ate a pizza crust under the table, and then whined and scratched at the door to go out, so they clipped on his lead and took a bus to the botanical gardens, where they lost themselves down the winding pathways and then occupied a wrought-iron bench and talked, in a faltering, careful way, about the things they had on their minds. First thing he asked her was did she drink? Yes, she said, but she had rules: never alone, never when she felt sad, and never vodka. He didn't drink at all, he said. Teetotal. He'd drunk himself senseless a few times, after he left Brown Bayley's, and he'd realised he had it in him, the capacity for self-destruction, so he hadn't touched a drop for thirty years.

Alison said his capacity for self-destruction was as much Martin Baxter's legacy as Catherine's; then she told him, without unnecessary detail, what Baxter had done to her before she fled, and Peter's eyes were black with hatred as he listened, and he told her Martin Baxter was killed in a hit-and-run, no more than a year after she left Sheffield. 'Nobody ever got done for it, but he was hit full on by a speeding car, a pimped-up Escort. It knocked him down then reversed over him.'

She listened, and frowned. 'How do you know those details?'

He shrugged.

'Was it you?' Ali said.

'Toddy.' He couldn't look at her at the mention of his former lover's name, just sat stiff-backed and stared ahead at the lawns and late roses.

'I wish I'd done it,' she said. 'I wish I'd killed him.' Then she asked about Catherine, told him that Sheila had told her about their mother's death years ago, and that she hadn't cried, only felt glad that he, Peter, was free of obligation. 'Were you with her when she died?' she asked.

He nodded. 'She didn't know it though, she were in a coma by then. She'd been laid up in hospital for weeks, longest she'd gone for years without a drink.' That's how he ended up as a hospital porter, he said; spent so long at the Northern General, he thought he might as well get paid for it.

'Peter, I'm really sorry I left you alone for so long.'

'No,' he said. 'You did right.'

Such economy of language to express a world of meaning. In three words, Peter absolved her of blame, acknowledged his own role in her trauma, addressed the – far greater – damage

Martin Baxter had done, and granted his full approval of her choice to go as far away as she was able, until she was ready to come home.

She took his hand and squeezed it, and he squeezed back.

'Is Toddy still around?' she asked.

'No, no, long gone, went to work on an oil rig, got married, a Scottish woman. No kids. They breed dogs, them Rhodesian ridgebacks.'

'Did he tell you all that?'

'His mam. I think she wanted me to know he weren't queer any more.'

'Right,' she said. 'A likely story.'

He gave a small laugh. 'Aye.'

'Don't you have anyone, Peter?'

He shook his head, set his mouth in a hard line. She thought about the burdens of his life, the sacrifices he'd made, the fleeting, stolen happiness he'd found with Dave Todd at the back of the Gaumont. His had been a life cauterised by bigotry, ignorance and shame. She'd be forever indebted to Peter, but each time she tried to express this, to thank him, to heap gratitude upon him, he shut her down. All he'd ever wanted was an ordinary life, he said, and to be left alone.

'That's not much of an ambition.'

'Aye, well.' He shifted his gaze from the flowers, to his feet.

'Don't expect me to leave you alone,' she said, 'not again, never again, not likely.' She leaned in and planted a kiss on his cheek, which made him smile. Once upon a time, when she was very young, she'd thought him as handsome and lucky as a prince, tall and fair, funny and brave-hearted. Now he seemed a kind of self-made ruin of a man: his solitary life, his unresolved shame. But still, there was a seam of contentment running through him. She made a silent pledge to help make him as happy as he wished to be, for evermore. 'You're stuck with me,' she said.

They were very happy right now, side by side on a bench in the park, and they stayed there for a long time. He loved listening to her talk about Adelaide, describing her house, her road, the ocean, the parklands. He had no idea she'd written a best-selling book, no idea at all. This pleased her, although she didn't quite know why. He said he'd read it, if she gave one to him, but he hadn't read a novel since *Stig of the Dump*. Ali found this hilarious, and her amusement caught on, so that soon they were both rocking with laughter, defying the miserable ghosts of their past to bring them down.

'I could live in Sheffield,' Alison said to Dan. 'Part of the year, anyway.' It was Monday evening, a week after they'd arrived. He'd brought her to a backstreet dive with an Irish landlord for Guinness and a packet of Walkers cheese and onion. McCulloch sat at her feet, and she reached down to scratch the top of his head. 'We could buy a house by the botanical gardens maybe,' she said.

Dan grimaced. 'God, Sunday lunch with Mum and Dad, and burnt sausage barbecues with Claire and Marcus.'

'But I really think I could write here. I could write a book set in Sheffield, about Sheffield people.'

'It's still a novelty to you, that's all.' If he'd wanted to live in Sheffield, he'd be living here already. He loved his folks, but he loved them most when they were at a distance.

'You could go and watch the Owls.' She liked saying 'the Owls'; it amused her. Crows in Adelaide, Owls in Sheffield.

'That's not much incentive, these days.'

'I could come with you, sing the songs, learn the offside rule.'

'Oh yeah, that's true,' he said. 'That might work.' He smiled at her across the table, loving the sight of her smiling at him. He'd live anywhere with this woman, that was the truth of it. 'But still, if we're going to live in Sheffield, it won't be without a fight from me first.'

She folded her arms, pondered for a while, then said, 'I'll need to go back to Adelaide soon. Face the music, come to some arrangement with Michael.'

'I'll come with you when you go.' No way was he letting McCormack back in. He'd fight to the death if he had to.

'I need to see Tahnee and her crew, too, catch her between gigs somewhere.'

He nodded. He knew all about the prodigious talent that was Tahnee Jackson. 'I'll come with you when you do that too,' he said. 'Wherever you go, there I'll be.'

'Fine by me,' she said.

'We should take Peter along,' Dan said. 'Mind you, he'd need a passport first. And he'd have to be drugged and blindfolded.'

Ali laughed. 'I wonder if he *could* be coaxed on to the aeroplane though? I'd love to show him Adelaide.' It would transform his existence, she thought: jacaranda season, evenings on the beach, the sun warming his bones.

She drained her half of Guinness and thought about how sometimes – and right now – anything and everything seemed possible and happiness buzzed through her like electricity down a wire, then other times her certainties seemed riddled with fault lines. She'd fixed herself up with a new phone, a very necessary move, but the floodgates were open once again to emails, phone calls, texts, and there were days Ali wished she could just fling it into the River Don. Meanwhile Dan's phone rang nine or ten times a day, and it was usually Katelin, and he was always calm and steady when he spoke to her, whatever she accused him of, however much she raged. He knew he was at fault here; he knew he couldn't say, as Alison could to Michael, that in the end Katelin had made him unhappy. It was just he belonged with Alison, and always had.

Dan went to the bar for two more, and while he was gone, Ali's phone chimed with an incoming email, which she opened, then wished she hadn't. Michael, writing to her from the future. It was tomorrow morning in Adelaide, but still pre-dawn, only 3.12 a.m. – a telling fact, which wasn't lost on her.

> Sleeping beside you these past few months, I had no idea how far from me you really were, so by the time you decided to leave, I had no hope at all of reaching you. I know you believe I lack imagination, and perhaps I do, imagination is rarely required in my world. But my feelings for you are as deep as they are true, and I hope you'll look closely into your own heart, and then, if you need to, look closer still, and finally know that what you want, and what you need, is what you already had.

Dan had been gone for less than five minutes, but when he came back with their drinks her face was white with distress. 'What?' he said. She pushed her phone across to him, and he read Michael's words, then looked up at her. She waited for him to speak; she counted on his conviction.

'Yeah,' Dan said slowly. 'I know this is tough to read, and he's really suffering, but look, it's early days, and everything's so raw. The extraordinary will eventually become blessedly ordinary, and this storm will blow itself out.'

She nodded. She could cling to those words; his certainty could keep her afloat. But her breath had caught in her throat as she'd read Michael's message, and she shuddered to think of him, in the small hours of the new day, unable to set his broken world back to rights. He'd written many emails to her since she left but he'd never before expressed his feelings so effectively, although their conversations in the days before she'd left Adelaide had been the most honest and open they'd ever had. He'd wanted to know why, if she'd been so unhappy, she'd waited this long to leave. Because, she said, it was possible to get addicted to a certain kind of sadness. Then he'd said all she was doing by leaving him for Dan Lawrence was exchanging one prop for another, and she hadn't been able to refute this, except to say Dan had given her back a side of herself she'd long ago forgotten, and anyway, she'd said, wasn't it true that Michael's own feelings towards her were altered these days, and born of habit, not emotion? He'd been angry at this, had said she was entitled to decide she didn't love him, but she didn't get to decide he didn't love her. That was just before she left the house, when he told her she didn't know the meaning of love, and slammed the door, and this memory, she knew, would remain like a bad seed, planted deep in her mind.

She did know the meaning of love, she thought now. She did.

And yet, hadn't her heart had a bad start? Certainly, Catherine hadn't known what love meant, and doesn't a child, on some fundamental level, observe the mother for the blueprint?

So.

Dan was watching her, seeing all the shadows of these thoughts pass over her face, and he knew he had strength for them both, and that he'd need it. She looked at him and said, 'It's just, every time I feel totally happy, I remember that soon there'll be a phone call, a text, whatever, to remind me of the price we're paying to be together.'

'Alison,' he said. 'There are going to be more emails from Michael, and more phone calls from Katelin, more demands, more explanations, more apologies, more tears. But there's nothing we can't deal with, and we'll find a path through, and love each other, and show our families the way.'

Then the door of the pub swung open, and a blast of cold air made them both look round. An elderly man walked in, short and stocky, bald, with coarse, florid features, and Dan said, 'Oh shit,' just as the man said, 'Ey, Dan Lawrence, I thought you must be dead.'

'Who's that?' Alison whispered.

Dan was standing up now, and he said, 'Oh, just some geezer who knew somebody who knew Joe Cocker. He got me an interview once, and thinks we're colleagues now. I'd better have a word, but I'll spare you the experience. I'll be right back, OK?' She nodded. He paused and looked at her, and said, 'Keep the faith, right?' as if she might change her mind while his back was turned, then he walked over to where the newcomer stood at the bar, and she could see Dan buying him a drink and giving him the time of day, and from time to time glancing back at Ali, to gauge her state of mind, interpret her expression.

He met her eyes each time he looked, because she kept her steady gaze on him. Oh, she didn't want to cause him a moment's concern! She didn't want him to have to question her belief, not even for a fraction of a second. This was her overriding thought, among all the thoughts she had coursing through her mind: she wanted Daniel to be completely sure of her, to know with cast-iron certainty that he would never, ever again look round and find her gone. She picked up her phone from the table and quickly found a song for him, because that's how their love had first found a voice, and she needed to affirm it now with something beautiful and peerless, soulful and serious; something to articulate this extraordinary welter of emotions, and her faith in him, and her own resolve.

She watched as he felt the buzz of his phone in the pocket of his jeans, watched him pull it out and take a look, and then – as if he was alone at the bar, not with a friend of a friend of Joe Cocker's – watched him click on the link to hear Dusty Spring-field, 'I Close My Eyes': mellow, intimate, perfectly judged. He turned to her, and for a moment they just held each other's eyes across the room. Then he made some hasty excuse, and walked back to her with Dusty still singing, and when he reached Alison, he stooped to kiss her. 'Thank you,' he said.

She looked up at him looking down at her. 'You know, you're everything to me, Daniel,' she said. 'Everything.'

'Good,' he said, and grinned at her grave expression. 'Good, because you're everything to me, too.'

No one should turn their back on happiness such as this, she thought. 'This is our time, Alison,' Dan said. 'We'll just roll with it, right?'

'Right,' she said. 'But look, you might have to keep telling me it's all going to work out, because, for a while, I might have to keep asking.'

The pub was busy, the tables all around them occupied, and although people stared when he pulled her up from her seat into his arms, Daniel and Alison were oblivious, alone together in the crowd. 'Hey,' he said, tilting her face up to his so she could see he meant it. 'Listen to me, Alison Connor. Every little thing . . . gonna be all right.'

She laughed. 'I know what you did there.'

'I know you know. I'll never fox you with a lyric, you're weird like that.'

Then she sat down again, he did too, next to her this time, and close enough that she felt the solid warmth of his body through the sleeve of her shirt. She finished her drink and then scanned the room for a while, taking a snapshot in her mind of this ordinary, over-lit, backstreet pub; all the men and women it contained, the motley collection of drinkers and talkers and thinkers. And some of them stared back into her frank and open gaze, one or two of them even smiled; but all of them, she thought, whether they knew it or not, were witness to her happiness. When she turned at last to Dan, she found he was already looking at her.

'You OK?' he asked.

She smiled. 'Never better.'

'Ah,' he said. 'You know what? That's music to my ears.'

Song credits

Reference on p.33 to 'Big, Blonde And Beautiful' written by Marc Shaiman and Scott Wittman.

Reference on p.53 to 'Cry A Tear For The Man In The Moon' written by Richard Hawley.

Lyrics on p.93 from 'Suffragette City' written by David Bowie.

Lyrics on p.99 from 'I Didn't See It Coming' written by Sarah Martin and Stuart Murdoch.

Reference on p.116 to 'Shine On You Crazy Diamond' written by David Gilmour, Roger Waters and Richard Wright.

Reference on p.118 to 'Lola' and 'You Really Got Me' written by Ray Davies.

Lyrics on p.120 from 'Star Trekkin'' written by John O'Connor, Grahame Lister and Rory Kehoe.

Reference on p.138 to 'So Far Away' written by Carole King.

Reference on p.197 to 'Comfortably Numb' written by David Gilmour and Roger Waters.

Lyrics on p.203 from 'Here Is The House' written by Martin Gore.

Lyrics on p.204 from 'All That Jazz' written by Ian McCulloch, Will Sergeant, Pete de Freitas and Les Pattinson.

Reference on p.268 to 'Yellow Submarine' written by Lennon–McCartney.

Lyrics on p.279 from 'Working My Way Back To You' written by Denny Randell and Sandy Linzer.

Lyrics on p.315 from 'A Case Of You' written by Joni Mitchell.

Lyrics on p.341 and reference on p.344 to 'Sunshine Superman' written by Donovan.

Lyrics on p.366 from 'Lovesong' written by Robert Smith.

Lyrics on p.374 from 'Because You're Mine' written by Nick Lowe, Sparks and Wilko Johnson.

Lyrics on p.404 from 'Three Little Birds' written by Bob Marley.

Acknowledgements

I couldn't have written this book without plundering the experience and expertise of several people: my grateful thanks to Terry Staunton, Derek Owen, Martin Davies, Francesca Best, Darcy Nicholson, Michael Weston King, Andrew Gordon and Chris Couch here in the UK, and to Maggie Dawkins, Louise Rogers, Craig Cook, Sean Williams and Jared Thomas in Adelaide.

The estimable music sites Pitchfork, Uncut and Rock's Backpages were invaluable resources, as was Pat Long's *The History of the NME*, and that stellar radio station BBC Radio 6 Music – long may it reign.

Thanks to Elly, Joe and Jake Viner for continuing to help keep my taste in music current, and to Brian Viner, for so many reasons, but especially for coming up with a magnificent and unbeatable Dusty Springfield track.

JANE SANDERSON is a writer and journalist. She worked as a producer for BBC Radio 4 on *The World at One* and *Woman's Hour* before becoming a novelist. She lives with her husband in Herefordshire, and they also have a houseboat in London.

Jane's previous novels include *This Much Is True*, *Netherwood*, *Ravenscliffe* and *Eden Falls*. *Mix Tape* is her latest.

@SandersonJane